THIGHS WIDE SHUT

BY HAYLEY FLEMING

Thighs Wide Shut

THIGHS WIDE SHUT

HAYLEY FLEMING

QUERCUS

First published in Great Britain in 2026 by

an imprint of Quercus
Part of John Murray Publishing Group

This paperback edition published in 2026

1

A CIP catalogue record for this book is available from the British Library

PB ISBN 978 1 52945 102 3
EBOOK ISBN 978 1 52945 103 0

Typeset by Adobe Garamond Pro

Printed and bound in Great Britain by Clays Ltd, Elcograf S.p.A.

Papers used by Quercus are from well-managed forests and other responsible sources.

Quercus
Carmelite House
50 Victoria Embankment
London EC4Y 0DZ

John Murray Publishing Group
Part of Hodder & Stoughton Limited
An Hachette UK company

The authorised representative in the EEA is Hachette Ireland, 8 Castlecourt Centre, Dublin 15, D15 XTP3, Ireland (email: info@hbgi.ie)

For Campbell, without whom this story wouldn't exist.

THIGHS WIDE SHUT

CHAPTER 1

It feels like an unnecessarily cruel joke that my welcome back to Boston, the city where I fell in love for the first and only time, is the rhythmic pounding of my upstairs neighbor's sexual exploits.

Thump. Thump. Thump.

"I feel like I'm being forced to listen to porn," I whisper, leaning into Jo's ear as we stare at the popcorn ceiling of my brand-new-to-me-but-actually-quite-old basement apartment.

Jo nods seriously. "I've always said, anything can be audio erotica if you imagine hard enough."

Thump. Thump. Thump.

"You've literally never said that. Also, there's no imagination needed."

"Oh! Yes!"

"It's like we're being serenaded," Jo says, matching my whisper.

"It's a Welcome to Boston fanfare. An *un*welcome fanfare, actually."

"A venereal salute." Jo chuckles at herself. Even at this volume, my best friend's laugh echoes through my apartment, bouncing from yellow stucco wall to cardboard box to grimy laminate floor, but doing nothing to block the carnal clamor.

"Well," Jo says, shrugging as she turns back toward me. "Hearing your upstairs neighbor's banging is a rite of passage. Macy and I got a noise complaint once. I consider it one of my greatest personal victories."

"Absolutely did not want to know that," I mumble. "This sucks."

Jo lets out a half laugh, half snort, then winks. "Yeah, it certainly sounds like *someone* sucks."

Thump. Thump. "Oh, god! Yes!"

We tilt our heads toward the ceiling as the thumping increases in tempo and volume. This ceiling is either as soundproof as a piece of linen or the woman above us is moaning with impressive gusto. Probably both, actually.

"We have to do something about it," Jo says, whispering again. She pulls her hair into a ponytail so aggressively that I think the months-old red box dye might rub off on her hands.

"Whatever you're thinking, I'm begging—"

Before I can finish, Jo lets out a horrifyingly inappropriate moan and starts banging her hand against a moving box. A loud *THUMPTHUMP* calls out in response.

At the ripe age of twenty-seven, I should be laughing this off; instead, embarrassment courses through my body. It's hard not to feel self-conscious listening to cries of ecstasy when I myself have the sexual experience of a sacrificial virgin.

Am I trying to change that? Absolutely. Since graduating from college, I've let friends set me up on blind dates (bad idea). I've tried Hinge (worse idea). I've even let my mom connect me with one of her co-workers' sons (The Worst Idea). But when your body makes it difficult to jump into bed with someone, it's tough to get past date two or three. That's when your date starts issuing invitations, and that's when things get complicated.

ThumpthumpBANGthump.

Jo glances upward with raised eyebrows before continuing, her voice raised. "OH GOD, PLEASE! HARDER!"

"I am *begging* you to stop," I hiss, but before Jo can acknowledge me, or, more likely, keep moaning, the thumping pauses.

"Wow, I didn't think that would actually—"

THUMPTHUMPTHUMP.

Jo and I both groan (non-sexually).

"Fine," I mumble. "I'll tune it out."

I rip open a moving box, and I'm greeted by a "Ms. Rogers" nameplate, a gift from a middle school English student. My *former* middle school English student. It has beautiful cursive lettering, and I feel bile and the taste of fast-food breakfast rising in my throat. I toss the nameplate back in the box. It's time to celebrate new adventures, not rehash old failures.

Leaving my hometown of Tampa, Florida, and moving to Boston, the city where I went to college for four brief and painful years, was supposed to be my fresh start. Cross that—it *is* my fresh start. Who cares that this basement apartment is probably going to be one singular degree Fahrenheit in the winter, or that my upstairs neighbor is already making me want to rip my hair out? I'm here, living in the same city as my best friend and working at my best friend's coffee shop. Not that we're codependent or anything.

Jo saunters up to my side and plucks the nameplate out of the moving box. I taste fast-food breakfast again. A honey butter chicken biscuit and bitter coffee from Wendy's. I'm never going to eat there again.

"Keep this out," Jo says. "You can put this on the counter when you're working. That way everyone will know who their barista is."

I reach over and attempt to slap it out of her hand, but she has faster reflexes, so she ends up slapping my hand before I can slap her hand, and then we end up in a catfight that ultimately results in the nameplate being knocked back into the box, thus accomplishing my goal.

Thumpthumpthumpthumpthump.

"Isn't that what name tags are for?" I ask. "I mean, this has apples and yellow pencils on it. How is that relevant to coffee, exactly?"

"Maybe we should start selling branded pencils," Jo says, squinting as she thinks. "Or apples. Or apple-flavored coffee?"

"That's a fall drink."

She points at me, eyes wide. "So true."

"Did your parents never do seasonal specials when they ran the coffee shop?"

Jo nods, shrugging. "Like . . . maybe? But I'm pretty sure they were just putting a pump of peppermint syrup in drinks and calling them seasonal. We can do better. Remind me tomorrow to start brainstorming a list of seasonal specials."

"You're biting off more than you can chew," I say, eyeing her. "Again."

She flips me off, even though we both know I'm right. She has a tendency to jump five steps ahead of where she should be, get excited, and then forget about steps one through four. Case in point: She should be focused on learning the basics of operating her parents' coffee shop—sorry, *her* coffee shop—not daydreaming about seasonal specials for three months from now. Bills have to be paid and paychecks have to be signed before she can move on to taste testing flavored syrups.

I suppose seasonal specials could draw in more money. But what do we know? We both have teaching degrees, not business degrees. Which is perhaps why Jo didn't know how difficult it would be to run her own business.

ThumpthumpTHUMPTHUMP.

"*Ahhhhh,*" Jo moans, thumping her hand against a box.

I stare at her, silently willing her to stop. She stares back.

"I'm putting you in time-out," I say.

"While I'm already in time-out, I have a question."

"You don't get questions during time-out."

"Have you texted him?" she asks, a sneaky grin crossing her face.

I clear my throat, coating my voice with a mask of innocence. "Have I texted who?"

THUMPTHUMP. "Oh! Yes! I'm close!"

"Harri—"

"YOU'RE IN TIME-OUT!" I yelp. There's a loud *thump*, and I lower my voice. "And now you're in double time-out for asking questions you know you shouldn't."

"Fine," she hisses. "I know I swore not to say his name, but I *will* break that pact if you're going to be annoying."

I gasp, and it's only half in jest. "You wouldn't."

"All I'm saying is if you call him, we could go on a double date. You two. Me and Macy, when they move back to Boston," she says, a pang of sadness crossing her face so briefly it's barely visible. She smiles at me reassuringly. "Just like old times."

"Oh, please," I say, rolling my eyes. "That's literally never happened. We have literally never been on a double date."

"That's not true. The four of us used to get dinner at the dining hall all the time."

"That doesn't even remotely count."

"Plus, I heard from a mutual friend that he works near here."

I narrow my eyes. "A mutual friend?"

Jo blinks several times, then has the good sense to look guilty. "Okay, he told me himself. A few months ago."

I freeze, my hands buried in the depths of a box labeled Emma's Random Shit <3. "Wait—you still hang out with him?" Jo opens her mouth, but I cut her off. "Why didn't I know that?"

"I don't *hang out with him.* I just get coffee with him, like, once every three to four months."

"You *get coffee* with him? *I* used to get coffee with him. That was *my* thing."

"Coffee can't be *your thing,* dumbass. That's, like, ninety percent of the adult population's *thing.*"

I stare at her, brows furrowed. "My point stands."

Thumpthump thuthump BANGTHUMP.

"Well?" she asks. "Are you going to ask me how he's doing?"

"No," I say so quickly that I don't even convince myself.

Jo waits for me to change my answer. When I don't, she shrugs it off and lets out another loud moan as she stands up, making her way over to a stack of boxes. I swat her away as she starts to rip off the tape. She carried a bunch of heavy crap inside for me, so she's met her work quota for today. I may have weak arms, but I am *not* an asshole. (Frame that quote and put it on my wall, please.)

"Fine," she says, taking a seat on a particularly large box labeled SHIT <3. "OH, PLEASE! MORE!"

"Anyway," I yell, cutting her off as I throw various winter clothing items from the box onto the floor, "I'm not going to text him. You can't text someone out of the blue after five years."

My stomach flip-flops, and an image of warm brown eyes flickers through my head before I can stop it. Five years may fade some feelings, but it doesn't erase them completely.

"Holy SHIT!" THUMPTHUMPTHUMP.

"What else are you supposed to do? Show up at his door with an 'I'm sorry' cake? He lives in Allston," Jo says, winking.

The image forms in my mind. Me, showing up on his doorstep. I'd wear a sundress—the white one with embroidered sunflowers he used to compliment me on. It wouldn't really fit me anymore, so I'd probably have to wear breath-restricting shapewear. I would spend too long on my makeup, trying to hide the permanent dark circles and tired skin I've developed.

I'd bring a cake, preferably one I'd baked myself, because that seems more thoughtful. He'd open the door. His first reaction would be shock. His forehead would crinkle up, and his mouth would form that small *o* that is so frustratingly endearing. Before he could say anything, I'd apologize, giving him some form of the speech I've practiced in my head (and in the shower, and in my journal, and in therapy) for the last five years. He'd forgive me. I'd smile. His eyes would light up the way they used to. He'd tell me he missed me. We'd make up. We'd be friends again. We'd . . . No, even in my fantasy of our reunion I can't let my mind go there. We'd be friends. Everything would be as it should be.

I tuck the vision away in the Fantasy Corner—the back corner of my mind reserved for dreams that will never come true. It's in good company with extraterrestrial encounters and dragon-slaying knights and successful dates.

"What I'm *not* supposed to do is reach out. It's complicated."

Jo scoffs as I rip the packing tape off another box. "Just because it's complicated doesn't mean it's not worth it."

I ignore that comment, as is best when someone makes a good point you're not willing to admit is a good point.

"And you know that. You're living that right now," she adds.

"What the *hell* are you talking about?"

Jo plops down on an unopened moving box, the cardboard sagging slightly under her weight. "You picked up and moved to Boston. You didn't like your job, so you decided to start over. And that's all I've ever wanted for you—to make a hard decision and follow through with it."

"I did that because you did it first. You quit teaching to do something else, and you proved it was possible to pick up and start over." I also did it because Jo seemed like she was on the verge of a breakdown every time she talked about taking over this coffee shop, especially since her partner is out of the country for work for the next six months. I was unemployed, she was having trouble hiring staff, so: voilà.

"Still," Jo says, shrugging. "Doesn't mean it was an easy decision for you."

"Well. I've made some bad decisions that I've followed through on, too."

I laugh as I say it, but Jo tilts her head, contemplating. "I think what you view as bad decisions are actually just times when you didn't make decisions and had to live with the consequences."

"You're in time-out," I remind her. "*Double* time-out." She *hmph*s in acknowledgment.

"Yes! Yes! Oh god, YES!"

Jo scowls at the ceiling, then lets out one last "OH, YES! PLEASE!" combined with rhythmic pounding against a moving box. Mercifully, the upstairs noises die down with a final *thump*.

"UGH," I yell in the general direction of the ceiling.

"You can't seriously tell me you've never accidentally heard one of your roommates having sex," Jo says. "Didn't you have, like, four roommates at one point?"

I did. That turned into two roommates when roommates three and four married each other and moved out. Roommate two then married her high school sweetheart. The final straw was when roommate one—the last woman standing, other than me—moved in with her college boyfriend.

Roommates three and four are parents now, and both roommates one and two are pregnant.

I'd be lying if I said that didn't make me feel . . . bleh.

"Two of them were definitely banging in the house, but I guess they kept it quiet," I tell her. "The other two roommates mostly went to their respective partners' apartments instead of bringing the partner to our place."

"You scared them off, huh?" Jo asks.

I freeze, eyes widening. "Holy shit. That's never occurred to me. Do I give off No Sex in the House vibes?"

Jo's responding "No" comes too quickly for comfort, but I set it aside for the sake of my sanity.

***

WE SPEND THE NEXT HOUR moving my belongings out of boxes and onto the floor. I'm not sure that's an effective unpacking method, but I don't have cabinets or shelves to properly store anything yet, so neatish piles are the best I can do.

It's perfect anyway. The apartment is tiny, and there's no furniture, and I can hear every noise from above, but it's *my* tiny, empty, acoustically challenged apartment. It's the first place I've ever lived alone, and it's a step in the right direction.

I'm about to take a load of boxes to the recycling bin when I hear the door to the upstairs apartments open. Jo and I switch our attention to my front window, where I have a clear view of the walkway leading to the street. After a moment, a tall, brunette woman dressed in head-to-toe athleisure walks past, a tote bag slung over her shoulder.

"Oh my god, it's her," Jo says. "It's Thumper."

The woman's steps are light and bouncy, and I desperately wish I didn't know why she was in a good mood.

"The landlord told me my upstairs neighbor was one guy. So, is she a girlfriend or a booty call?" I whisper.

"Girlfriend, maybe? If it's a booty call, you don't stick around for an hour afterward, right?"

"Are you seriously asking me? Why would I know?"

Jo ignores me. "Look at the way she's walking. That must've been good sex."

Thumper makes a right turn when she hits the sidewalk, and we move our heads away from the window and back toward my boxes, wary of her peripheral vision. A minute later, her car starts up, and I hear it drive away and count to one-hundred-Mississippi before grabbing my stack of cardboard. The boxes are so large they block my vision, and I stumble forward.

"I'm going to go recycle these, will you grab the door for me?" I ask. Jo obliges, swinging it open, and I slowly maneuver out of the entryway and up the small set of stairs leading to the yard.

Just as I reach the last step, the door to the upstairs apartments opens again, and I try to turn around, but instead, I end up slamming into the handrail. Before I can stop myself, I crumple to the ground, landing on my butt with the cardboard resting on top of my face.

"Oh, gosh!" a man says, footsteps pounding as he rushes down the stairs. The voice rings a bell in my mind, or maybe the odd, old-lady exclamation does, but I'm too stunned to consider why. Instead, I groan as I try to lift myself off the ground, my ass throbbing from the impact on the concrete, my head spinning from the crash landing.

"Here, let me grab the boxes," the voice says, closer now. The boxes are lifted a moment later, and I cover my face with my hands, hiding the blush and protecting myself from the sunlight now streaming directly into my eyes. There's a soft thud as my rescuer sets the boxes down next to me.

"Jesus, sorry about that," I say, my voice winded. "Carrying large items isn't my forte."

There's no response.

Rubbing my face one more time, I finally look up to see if my rescuer has fled the scene.

I'm met with a pair of warm, brown, familiar eyes.

We both freeze.

His forehead crinkles up, and his mouth drops into a small *o*.

I hear a breathless "oh my god" escape me.

A billion seconds pass. An entire history flashes before my eyes. Late-night conversations, early-morning pre-class breakfasts, day trips around Boston, pining, longing, wishing, wishing things were different—

"Emma," he whispers.

There he is, in all his glory. Adult Harrison. *Real* adult Harrison, not twenty-two-year-old almost-college-graduate Harrison. This new Harrison looks almost the same, dressed familiarly in navy pants and a well-cut T-shirt, but his hair is longer than it used to be, long enough that those dark waves are hanging down onto his forehead in a way that begs you to brush them aside. He also has more stubble on his jaw than he ever did in college. And all I will say about *that* is it doesn't look bad, even though it does something to my stomach that makes me feel physically ill.

I am unequivocally fucked.

All thoughts of moving and unpacking and starting over fade away and are replaced with a singular need to reach out, to embrace him, to make up for five years of lost hugs, and before I know what I'm doing, I'm taking a step forward and stretching out my arms and—

He takes a step back.

Harrison's eyes widen as his mouth clamps shut. He looks alarmed by what he did, or at least surprised, but instead of stepping forward and correcting his mistake, he just stands still, staring at me like he's seen a ghost.

Raised eyebrows · Head turn to the right · Mouth clamped shut | *Facial expression* | *Frequency: low*

1. Taken aback.
2. Indicates that the surprise is net negative.

The dictionary entry pops into my head before I can stop it, having been locked away in the Fantasy Corner for the last five years. I used to tally the frequency of Harrison's facial expressions as part of my *Mental Dictionary of Harrison's Emotional Tells*—and while this expression has a preexisting entry, it's the first time it's been used on me. And that's certainly not an indicator that this will be a positive interaction.

"I—"

"You're—"

Our eyes lock in a staring contest.

"You're not supposed to be here," he murmurs, talking more to himself than to me. He blinks rapidly as he speaks, his arms hanging limply at his sides, as if he doesn't know what to do with them now that he's turned down my hug. "You're supposed to be in Tampa. Why aren't you in Tampa?"

I ignore that question, for the time being. "How have you been?"

He ignores me in return. "Why are you here?"

I might be imagining it, but the tone of his second question sounds less *Wow, what a surprise!* and more *What could possibly have inspired you to come here and infringe upon my peace?*

"I live here?"

His eyes widen again. "What does that mean?"

"I—" I pause. "I'm actually not sure how to rephrase that, but yeah, I live here now?"

Harrison's eyes, bronzed in the afternoon sunlight, finally move away from my face and down to the moving boxes now piled at his feet. He stares at them for a moment, then jerks his head back up, his mouth returning to its original *o* shape.

"So, when you said you live *here*—"

"Basement," I say, tilting my head back down the stairs. "As of this morning?" I keep putting statements in question form? I need to stop? I don't know how to act like a normal human being?

"*That* basement?" Harrison looks at my front door like it's a portal to hell.

And then it occurs to me to wonder why Harrison is standing outside of my apartment.

"I . . ." he says, stumbling over his words. "I live upstairs. First-floor apartment."

I stare at him. "No, you don't."

"I . . . yes, I do, actually?"

"No," I say, my breathing growing rapid. "Jo said you live in Allston. This is not Allston."

Harrison studies me like he's studying a patient exhibiting signs of shock. "Yeah, I . . . I moved? Last month. I moved here. To Jamaica Plain." He points to our building. "Specifically, to right there."

Something lodges in my throat, and I'm not sure whether it's my saliva or my sanity. My heartbeat pounds in my ears, but the *thumpthumpthump* is more sobering than comforting, reminding me of a completely different thrill than the blood-pumping evidence of my life force.

Is it possible for my greatest regret in life to be something I had zero control over? If so, my greatest regret in life is unintentionally listening to my former best friend/one and only love of my life have loud sex with his current . . . booty call? Girlfriend? I don't know which option is worse. I don't want to think about it long enough to decide which option is worse. Nor do I want to think about why I care so much.

And is it possible to have a former love of my life, or does "love of my life" suggest the feelings are forever?

No way. It's been five years. Of course I'm not in love with him anymore.

In so many of my memories of him, his eyes are always lit up, his eyebrows always raised in a slightly questioning way. His smile is always soft, and his tone is always gentle and caring.

Now, his brows are furrowed, and his eyes look . . . confused? And hard.*

That's my fault.

I should probably take his stuttering words and his lack of hug to mean he wants me to leave this conversation, and probably also this city, but instead, all I can think is that this is all my fault, and that I would literally do anything to change the expression on his face and erase the tension in his shoulders, and so I add, "Maybe we can get coffee sometime?"

He stares at me blankly. "I don't know about that." He opens his mouth, then closes it, then opens it again. "It's just that, I—"

A pause.

"You—" he continues. "And I, we—"

Another pause.

I clear my throat. "Right. Yeah. Maybe another time."

For the first time during this interaction, his eyes soften the tiniest bit as he tilts his head gently to the left.† Unfortunately, I know this face well, seeing as I was so often the cause of it.

Harrison stares down at the cardboard boxes.

"Right, well, I'm going to bring that to the recycling bin," I say.

Neither of us moves for a full five seconds. When I finally start to bend down to collect my mess, Harrison gives a barely audible sigh and steps forward.

"Stop—just—stop, please. I've got it." He grabs the boxes,

* **Furrowed brows · Parted lips · Bated breath** | *Facial expression* | *Frequency: low*

1. Confused devastation.
2. Unsure of appropriate reaction.

† **Softened eyes · Head tilt to the left · Clenched jaw** | *Facial expression* | *Frequency: medium*

1. Emotionally conflicted.

pulling them gently out of my hands. As he stretches out his arms to hold all the cardboard, his shirt pulls taut against his muscles. I am vaguely aware of my mouth going dry.

I will not objectify him. I will not objectify him. He shakes his head to the side, flinging the waves out of his eyes, and I swear the movement takes place in slow motion. Harrison Carter is the type of man who uses conditioner in addition to shampoo. And I'm not counting 2-in-1 Head & Shoulders. This man goes to CVS and picks out two separate bottles.

Harrison doesn't utter another word as he walks away with my boxes. That's probably (another!) cue that he wants to be left alone, but I speed-walk to catch up.

"Thank you, Harrison," I say, my voice breathy.

Harrison grunts in response, and I do everything in my power not to file that noise away to fill in some gaps in my imagination the next time I hear *thump*ing coming from my ceiling.

Was he this silent in college?

No, definitely not.

No, we definitely used to talk at all hours of the day. I would word-vomit about my homework and my classes and my dorm drama and my hopes and dreams, and he would word-vomit in return. Except "word-vomit" isn't really an appropriate descriptor, because he'd always think before he spoke. I've certainly stunned him into silence before, like when I performed all of "Fergalicious" without looking at the screen during dorm karaoke our freshman year, and also when I told his mom to go to hell (not in those exact words, but in words more similar to that than they should have been) for trying to pressure him into going to law school instead of pursuing a career in nursing during dinner that one time. But those were positive, or at least neutral, or maybe impressed, silences. This silence is weighty and impermeable, less of a fog and more of a brick wall.

We remain silent as we walk to the side of the house, we remain silent as he puts the boxes in the bin, and we remain silent as we return to the front stoop. Harrison starts to walk up the stairs, and—

There's a flash of orange on his socks.

Actually, it's a flash of *oranges,* because he's wearing navy blue socks with tiny Florida oranges embroidered on them.

"Holy shit," I whisper, and he finally turns around to look at me. He seems concerned by my outburst, as if he's looking to see what's threatening me, but I only have half a second to appreciate that before he notices what my eyes are trained on.

He pulls his leg down from the first step, his pants now covering both of his socks. But I know what was there. And I know what that means.

I lock eyes with him. "You still wear those socks."

I bought the first pair for him for Christmas during our freshman year of college, when our dorm's floor did Secret Santa and I, in a lucky turn of events, drew Harrison's name. He wore the socks so much over the next five months that they started to get holes (don't ask me about the quality of these socks), and so I bought him the same pair for his birthday in late May. The following Christmas, I decided I might as well keep it going, and when I noticed they were on final sale clearance, I bought them out.

It was an investment in our friendship. That's what I told him. And that's what I convinced myself.

By the time we graduated, he owned more than a dozen pairs, thanks to a couple of Get Well Soon and Happy St. Paddy's Day gifts thrown in there.

We were dedicated gift-givers, the two of us.

He pulls his lips to the side thoughtfully. Just when I think he's going to deny it, he surprises me. "Yeah, Emma," he says, quietly sighing. "They're still my favorites." I have to stop my brain from automatically translating his sentence into *You're still my favorite,* because I *know* that's not still true.

I'm about to stutter out some incomprehensible string of

words when I see Jo's face pressed against the glass of my window, fog bubbles appearing beneath her nostrils every other second, her eyes wide and a little unhinged as she takes in the scene. Her lips curl into a deranged smile that reminds me of the movie poster for *The Shining*. Here's Johnny!

When I drag my eyes away from the window, I expect Harrison to be laughing at Jo. Instead, he's still looking at me with pained, red-rimmed eyes.

"I guess I'll see you around, then," he murmurs. When I don't respond, he nods his head toward my door. "Neighbors, and all."

"Just like freshman year." I attempt a smile. "Four-twelve and four-thirteen."

The memory crash lands in my brain, and I wish it had stayed locked away in the Fantasy Corner. This memory is best revisited in dark, half-asleep moments, not Saturday afternoons. I don't want to think about the way we met, the way he welcomed me into his life at the one moment I needed a friend more than anything else. I don't want to think about our neighboring freshman dorm rooms or our shared coffees or our late-night study sessions. And I certainly don't want to think about the many, many times he made my heart feel things it never has with anyone else.

Harrison nods silently, takes a deep breath, and walks through the upstairs door. I'm frozen for a moment, but when I finally recover the mental capacity to move, I run back into my apartment and immediately collapse.

"Holy shit," Jo says. She looks like someone surprised her with a new car—wide eyes, unhinged grin, nervous energy.

I shoot her a desperate look. "How hard is it to break a lease?"

CHAPTER 2

Nine years ago

When Hot Boy from Spanish Class sticks a finger up my vagina, three knee-jerk reactions occur in rapid succession:

1. I scream "SHIT" at the top of my lungs as a flash of blinding pain shoots through my reproductive system.
2. I knee Hot Boy from Spanish Class in the balls.
3. I scream "SHIT" again as I realize I've just kneed Hot Boy from Spanish Class in the balls.

On the one hand, the embarrassment that immediately floods my system cleanses the inexplicable pain from my vagina. So that's a huge win.

On the other hand, Hot Boy from Spanish Class is now on the floor, doubled over in pain. And if the force of my knee corresponded to the level of pain I felt, then . . . *oops.* Or rather, *ouch.*

"Shitfuck," I say, kneeling down on the floor of the third-floor single-use bathroom in Hall Hall (Hall Dormitory, but no one calls it that), where we hid about six minutes ago to make out. It's gross, but it's more private than the common room, where there's a herd of drunk freshmen enjoying our first Saturday night of college. The aforementioned crowd wasn't stopping several other pairings from making out right then and there, but that's a level of confidence I haven't reached in my seven days of college. I'm sure it'll come with time and practice.

I don't know his name, but he's hot, and I'm a little drunk (albeit less now), and there's no adult supervision for the first time in my life, and, most important, my roommate Jo and I have an ongoing competition to see who can hook up with someone first. We both went out tonight planning to win. Not a home run, necessarily, but definitely a couple of bases.

So, about eight minutes ago, it was with a competitive spirit that I locked eyes with Hot Boy from Spanish Class and hit him with the Do You Want to Get Out of Here?

Spoiler: He did.

Another spoiler: He's probably regretting that decision.

Oops.

Ouch.

We spent the following eight minutes using our hands and lips with the confidence of people who don't even remotely know each other and will, in all likelihood, never have to talk to each other again. And I probably wasn't going to want to even before the unfortunate kneeing-of-the-balls, because his stubble scratched my face in a really uncomfortable way that's probably going to give me acne, and his lips were kind of dry and crinkly, and his breath smelled faintly of cheap beer. We're talking Natty Light cheap. Also, his hands felt a little sticky, and I'm not sure whether it was from sweat or alcohol or an indeterminate third option, but I'm still trying really hard not to determine the answer to that question.

Maybe that's just what kissing college boys is like. It wasn't the most pleasant experience of my life, although it was perhaps more pleasant than the awkward high school dance kisses that make up the bulk of my experience with boys thus far.

In summary, was it shaping up to be the sexiest hookup in the world? Not even remotely, no. But being desired makes me feel desirable, and I like feeling desirable—and so when he gripped my left thigh and hoisted my leg up to his waist, leaving my dress pooling around my hips and my lacy underwear exposed, I thought, *hell yeah.* And I told him as much.

Because, again, he's hot. And I was trying to get some. (And also, to win this competition.)

And then when his fingers kept moving upward, finally reaching the top of my thighs, a jolt of nervous excitement and pleasure shot through my body and I, once again, thought, *hell yeah.*

But being the overeager eighteen-year-old boy he is, he didn't slow down there. No, teenage boys aren't exactly known for being masters of foreplay. And so, he only allowed me one millisecond of pleasure before he slipped his middle finger inside my vagina.

Cue the kneeing of the balls.

"Shitfuck," I repeat, jolting back to the present as I tentatively reach a clammy hand toward his shoulder. "Shit. Fuck. I'm sorry." My curses come out breathy and weak like I've been punched in the gut.

"What the hell?" he grumbles as he pushes my hand away. He's crouched on the floor, and I'm trying not to think about the amount of piss and puke that's probably coated these pea-green tiles over the years. And, unfortunately, there's a thin sheen of sweat on his face, and he has that pained glint in his eyes that's reserved for people who are about to be physically ill. That *clear the area* look. There's a very real chance he's going to add a fresh coat to the floor's germy varnish if he doesn't pull it together.

"I thought you said that was okay," he huffs, his voice muffled by his forearms. I feel bad for him. Should I be feeling bad for him, since he hurt me? But also, he didn't mean to hurt me. Is it even his fault? I don't know what's happening.

"I did," I assure him, biting my lip so hard my mouth starts to taste metallic. *Inhale. Exhale.* "It was, I mean—I did say that. I'm—I mean—I'm sorry. It was a gut reaction." I can't stop my brain from saying: a crotch reaction, perhaps? *Inhale. Exhale.* "Are you okay?"

He slowly unfurls himself, and his eyes flick over to the toilet, as if my prediction may be about to come true. But thankfully, he looks away and peels himself off the floor limb by limb. With a penetrating glare and no additional words, he limps out of the bathroom.

The door shuts with a deafening *click,* marking the end of my first college hookup.

I drag myself off the floor and manage to find the mental wherewithal to lock the door before stumbling over to the sink. Bile rises in my throat, and it's unclear whether it's from alcohol or from whatever just happened. I swallow it down, but it leaves the taste of Natty Light and stomach juices mingling in my mouth.

Shitfuck is right.

All the blood in my body has seemingly rushed down into my reproductive system, even though his finger only made contact with *maybe* one inch at *most.* My heart beats in my chest and in my uterus, pounding, pounding, pounding, like something's about to burst out of me.

What the hell is wrong with me?

This was supposed to be a casual hookup. This was supposed to be inconsequential. This was supposed to feel *great.* Or at least, like, *good.* I even would've settled for *okay.*

"You *idiot,*" I murmur as I raise my head and peer warily into the mirror. My raspberry lipstick is smeared around my lips, and my mascara hasn't fared much better. Paired with my formerly-sleek-but-now-lifeless dirty-blond hair and the two hickeys forming across my collarbone, I look . . . well, *bad.*

I splash cold water on my face, letting my regrettably non-waterproof mascara streak down my cheeks and mingle with droplets of concealer and lipstick. After wiping it away with one of those brown paper towels that repel water, my face is red and raw, but the color hides the tears.

The muscles in my gut are still so tight that I'm starting to cramp up—something akin to menstrual cramps, but I'm not on my period, and as far as I know, there's no blood down there. I peek to double-check. Yep. No blood.

There's no physical mark to show for my pain.

It's the same kind of discomfort as a clenched jaw or a stiff neck. As if my body is holding the remnants of some past trauma or some severe sexual anxiety I didn't know I had. But is it even possible to have physical symptoms of anxiety without feeling mentally anxious?

That doesn't make any sense.

I rack my brain. Sex is supposed to hurt the first time, but this wasn't anything close to sex. This was something closer to inserting a tampon.

Except I can't wear tampons—I've never been able to get one in.

When you grow up in Florida and spend all your time at the beach or the pool, you start wearing tampons basically as soon as you start bleeding. I was first faced with this dilemma at Katie's thirteenth birthday pool party. My mom gave me a tampon and told me to read the instruction booklet that came with it, but when I got to the bathroom, I could not for the life of me get it inserted. For a few insane moments, I was convinced I didn't have a vagina. But upon closer inspection with a handheld mirror, I was definitely trying to insert the tampon into the right spot. It just wouldn't fit—it was too tight. I discussed this with my middle school best friend, Hannah, the next day, who told me (with all the wisdom of an eighth grader who has a boyfriend with whom she's shared several kisses) that tampons would work better once I'd had sex. Not that I really knew anything about sex, but that sounded about right to me, and Hannah seemed like a trustworthy source of information. Although, as I learned a few months later when I found her crying in the bathroom and had to run to my locker to find a pad for her, she hadn't actually started her period yet. Then there was my friend Marissa, who told me her mom said she wasn't allowed to use tampons until she was older. And then there was also Maya, who didn't know you were supposed to take the plastic part off. She went through an entire swim practice with a piece of plastic shoved inside of her before she realized it wasn't absorbing blood.

All of that said, I've never worn tampons, no one taught me or my friends how to wear tampons, and I've never thought twice about it. We all hate tampons! That was a uniting fact of our girlhood! Maxi pads all day, baby!

Turns out my issue with tampons was more complicated than the tampon itself. It (foolishly, apparently) never occurred to me I'd have the same problem in . . . other situations involving my vagina.

I take a deep breath and throw back my shoulders. I'm a mess, but my boobs still look good in my black spaghetti-strap mini-dress.

At least there's that.

Buzz. My phone vibrates in my bra, sending a surprised jolt through my body. Cursing, I fish it out and open up my messages.

> **Jo (roommate):** remember that cutie we saw in the cafeteria

We'd seen them from a distance while eating lunch this past Monday, the first day of classes. Jo had taken one look at them standing at the self-serve salad station with their beachy, golden waves and corduroys and whispered, "Oh my god, they're like a ray of sunshine!"

Buzz.

Jo (roommate): okay, well, i win our bet. their name is Macy. they're a sophomore and they're from California and i think I'm in love.

Jo (roommate): also i need the room for a while

Jo (roommate): this is my prize for winning. sorry not sorry

Jo (roommate): seriously though, do text me when you need to come home tonight. or even better, go find a hot guy to sleep with. and then text me to let me know ur ok <3

Shit.

Fine. That's fine. My night might suck, but there's no reason Jo's needs to. I'll just hole up in our common room for an hour or two before I kick Macy out.

This was not the plan for tonight. I was supposed to be hooking up (successfully) with a cute boy, preferably someone whose name I actually knew, and preferably in a bedroom instead of a bathroom.

Maybe if I had exercised a single goddamn bit of patience and not seized the opportunity of the first boy who met my questioning smile with a grin, I would still be mingling and enjoying myself, and Hot Boy from Spanish Class wouldn't be hiding somewhere, clutching his groin.

Except the issue doesn't seem to be with the guy. It seems to be with me. Specifically: with my vagina.

I drag myself up the flight of stairs leading to my floor. For the past week, this climb has thrilled me. I finally have a room of my own—not my childhood bedroom, but a bastion of autonomy. But right now, every step sends a cramp shooting through my uterus, and the echo of my unsteady footsteps in the stairwell sounds like a dirge. The thing about growing up and moving out of your parents' house is that suddenly your problems are actually *your* problems. The hand-holding stage of my life is over, and for the first time, I'm not feeling good about it.

Not that I'd be tempted to walk into my parents' bedroom and start crying about how *My vagina clammed up when a boy tried to finger me!* and *No, Mom. I didn't catch his name before I let him suck a purple bruise onto my collarbone!*

But still.

Maybe I would've just cried and told my mom I'd had a bad day, and we would've gone to our favorite coffee shop to get iced chai lattes and gossip about the other teachers at her elementary school. Or maybe my dad and I would've put on a low-budget 1980s horror film, as we've always done on low-key weekend nights.

Now my only company is an empty stairwell and an off-limits bedroom.

As I swing the door to the fourth floor common room open, a blast of cool air hits me. It's mid-September in Boston, and although my Floridian brain associates this time of year with temperatures in the upper eighties, there's fifty-some-degree air seeping into the common room through the windows, which have been thrown wide open by one of the many people in my dorm who grew up in New England and feed off fall weather like it's an addictive drug. For them, it's a mood-boosting high fueled by apple picking and hot cider and weird-looking boots from L.L.Bean, but for me, it's more like a withdrawal, leaving me with full-body chills and a never-ending flow of snot. The chills and snot currently afflicting me may be from the brick-wall-vagina situation, but I'm happy to blame it on the open windows for now.

I collapse into a beanbag in the corner of the common room, the beads making quiet rustling noises underneath my body. I don't sink into it as much as I expect to, and it feels like I'm sitting on top of a rock with a slight indentation in the shape of my butt. Cursing, I let my head fall back and knock against the wall.

"You good there?" a voice says from my right.

"Jesus," I say, whipping my head to the side to find a vaguely familiar and somewhat confused face studying me from another beanbag about ten feet away. My neighbor, I think—room 412. Across the hallway from my room, 413.

"Sorry, didn't mean to startle you." His coffee-colored eyes crinkle as he looks at me, brows pinched with concern even as the rest of his face is soft with calm energy. Dark brown waves frame his face in a disorderly way that is confusingly contradictory to his otherwise buttoned-up appearance.

I scan him from head to toe. "Looks like you're ready to party, huh?" I ask, the combination of anxiety and alcohol in my bloodstream erasing any type of filter I might normally have.

He chuckles, brushing the question aside unselfconsciously as he looks down at his light blue button-down shirt, the sleeves rolled up to just beneath his elbows. At least he's wearing navy blue pants and not khakis.

"Homework," he says, lifting up his book by way of explanation. *The Symposium* by Plato. "This is my only plan for tonight."

"Thrilling." My plans for the night were not supposed to include an anti-social teenage boy reading philosophy, but somehow this is what we've come to.

"Are you okay?" he repeats.

"Huh?" I stare at him blankly.

"You sat down and immediately started cursing."

"Yeah. I hate this beanbag."

"Is that why you were crying?"

"I wasn't crying," I lie. The obviously false nature of this statement makes him raise his eyebrows and smile, which makes me giggle, which makes him chuckle.

And suddenly, we're both laughing, and I don't even know why. My laugh is a hysterical giggle, but his is a quiet, breathy sound. It's a subtle noise, even while the amusement on his face is obvious. His eyes light up, turning from coffee to caramel.

"I'm not trying to be nosy," he finally says. "I just wanted to make sure you were okay."

I blink before responding, startled by his sincerity. "No, it's okay. That's nice of you, actually." He gazes at me expectantly, and I realize my mouth is still open as if I'm going to continue speaking, so I do. "Boy problems. Sort of. It's complicated."

He nods but doesn't press me. "We're seven days into college, so if you're already having boy problems, I'd say you're still a step ahead of the rest of us." The corner of his lips quirks up into a half grin, and my eyes are immediately drawn to a small dimple on the left side of his face. My eyes flick back up to his, and as he realizes I was staring at his mouth, the other dimple forms.

If he were someone else, if we were somewhere else, if this were some*time* else, maybe I'd find those dimples swoon-worthy. But right now, all I can think about is how much I don't want to be in another intimate situation. Sorry, pal. Better luck next time.

"I'm Emma," I finally say.

"Yes, Emma, I know that," he says, frowning slightly even as the playful glimmer remains in his eyes. "We've been living across from each other for a week." I cringe, and he takes the hint. "I'm Harrison. Harrison Carter."

"Bond. James Bond," I respond, and when he looks confused, I roll my eyes. "We're eighteen. You're not supposed to introduce yourself with your last name."

He studies me intently, tilting his head to the side. "Bond is his last name, though. So, it would be 'Carter. Harrison Carter.' Not 'Harrison. Harrison Carter.' "

"I think my point stands regardless."

"Well, now you're at an unfair advantage. You have more information about me than I have about you."

I'm not sure whether he's trying to be funny, but I grin anyway. "Emma. Emma Rogers."

His dimples form in response. He pushes off with his feet, sliding the beanbag closer to me. When he's close enough, he reaches out his hand, and I lean forward to shake it. The contrast between this interaction and the prior interaction with Hot Boy from Spanish Class is so stark I have to bite my lip to keep from laughing, because here I am, about to shake hands with this guy who reads philosophy alone on Saturday nights. My plan was to hook up with someone tonight, and on a scale of Forced Group Project (1) to Hooking Up (10), this interaction falls no higher than Friendly Dining Hall Chat (3).

Good work, Emma. You're absolutely *killing* it tonight.

As soon as our hands make contact, he flinches. "Good grief, your hands are ice."

I shoot him a *guilty as charged* look as I pull my hand away and bury it under my thigh, trying to warm it. "You curse like my grandmother."

"I get that a lot." He gives me a lopsided smile, and I bite back a giggle.

"Cold hands are the primary symptom of being a Floridian in Massachusetts. I'm not built for fifty-degree weather."

"Florida, huh?" A mischievous grin slides over his face.

"Yep. I grew up on an alligator farm. And my parents are

swamp boat tour guides. I had the quintessential Florida childhood."

"Seriously?" he asks, then adds, "Wait, people farm alligators? Why?"

"For meat?"

His eyes widen in alarm. "You've actually eaten alligator meat?"

"Tastes like chicken."

"You're joking."

"Nope," I say, fighting back a smile at his wide-eyed look. "Well, not joking about the meat tasting like chicken. I was joking about living on an alligator farm, though. My parents are teachers, and we live in the suburbs. Literally could not get more boring than that. Where are you from?"

"Connecticut," he says, offering no further explanation.

"You're from Connecticut, but you want to laugh about Florida? That's rich," I say, laughing.

He grins sheepishly. "I guess time will tell whether I'm an asshole with a superiority complex."

His eyes flicker toward our rooms down the hallway. "Are you also sexiled tonight? I saw Jo go into your room a while ago. And she was definitely not alone." He rolls his eyes in a *you get it* kind of way, like we already have an inside joke. I swallow the thought, and it feels like someone is flipping pancakes in my stomach. "That was about ten minutes after I got sexiled from my own room and ended up here," he adds, grinning softly as though he isn't bothered by the inconvenience the way most people would be.

For some reason, I find myself offering Harrison further explanation. His dimples seem to have cast a net into my mind and are now reeling some unfiltered honesty out of me. "Jo and I had a competition to see who could hook up with someone first," I say. "Unfortunately, she didn't quite beat me to it, and in my rush to win, I seem to have exercised some poor decision-making skills. Hence the tears and the boy problems."

"Oof."

"Oof is right," I say, suddenly clutching my gut as another wave of residual cramps seizes my uterus. This conversation has been a welcome distraction, but my vagina is not done reminding me of the night's events.

Harrison notices my change in demeanor, and his eyes crinkle to take on the same expression he had when I sat down cursing. "Wait, are you hurt?"

"No. Well, yes. I kind of got hurt. But it's fine," I say. Harrison's eyes widen, and as he opens his mouth to say more, I cut him off and gesture to the book sitting on his lap. "Plato. What's it about?"

His mouth stays open for a moment, and I can see the indecision, his eyes wavering ever so slightly as if he's reading my mind, trying to decide whether to press me on it. He doesn't.

"Love," he says, gesturing vaguely. "Soulmates. That kind of thing."

"Plato was a romantic, huh?" I ask. I hold back a wince as another cramp takes over.

He narrows his eyes as if he can read my wince, which I'm becoming increasingly sure he actually can. "So, in *Symposium,* this guy named Aristophanes tells a story about how the first humans had two faces, four hands, and four legs."

"Hot," I say, playing along.

"Right? But these early humans were so strong and powerful that Zeus, the king of the gods, decided to weaken them by cutting them in half, thus creating today's humans, with one face, two hands, and two legs." He waves his hand around, as if to demonstrate that he, like the humans he's discussing, has two hands. "So, Aristophanes theorizes that this is the source of our desire for other people. We spend our lives looking for the person whom we were severed from, who would make us complete. Essentially, we're looking for our soulmate. And we're made whole when we find that person—the person we love wholly."

When I don't respond immediately, his expression grows sheepish, his lips curling slightly and his brows furrowing. He grabs a wavy lock that's drooping onto his face, then tugs it once before letting it plop back into place. When the maneuver is complete, it's still blocking his line of sight.

"And—" I say, distracted. "And do you believe that? Do you believe we each only have one person out there who would complete us?"

He blinks thoughtfully before responding. "I'd like to think so, right? I like the idea that everyone out there has a perfect match. Someone they can't live without. My pa—" He swallows. "That is to say, I think most people never find that person, but there are some couples where you can just *tell,* you know?"

We gaze at each other.

"I'm guessing the guy you're having boy problems with isn't your soulmate then," he says.

"I'm not naïve enough to think I'm going to meet a soulmate in my two-hundred-level Spanish class," I scoff. Besides, after tonight, I'm not sure if virgins who can't wear tampons get to have soulmates.

There's a flash of embarrassment on his face, which makes me feel like shit, so I change the subject. "I think we need more alcohol if we're going to keep talking about philosophy," I say, shooting him a goofy smile in a sad attempt to lighten the mood.

Mercifully, he laughs instead of taking offense. He stands up, grabbing something from a tote bag on the table next to us. Before I can register what's happening, he's throwing something in my direction, and I'm catching something slightly cool to the touch.

I hold up the beer can, reading the label. "Not Natty Light. You're spoiling me."

He shrugs, plopping back into the beanbag. "My roommate handed me these two beers in exchange for moving to the common room." He picks up the other one, cracking open the tab. I reach forward and meet his cheers, clinking the cans together.

I take a sip.

I think this beer is worse than Natty Light.

"At least it's free?" Harrison asks, glaring at the can.

"This beer and I are not soulmates," I say.

Just as I think the conversation is finally going to lighten up, a burning cramp shoots through my uterus, so severe I have to look down to make sure someone didn't pour acid all over my gut.

Harrison scoots forward in the beanbag, poised for action. "What's happening?"

"No, I'm—" I say, holding up a hand. He waits at my signal, and after I take a deep breath and relax backward, he follows my cue and does the same.

"Listen, I know we don't really know each other yet, but just . . . let me know if you want to talk about it, okay?"

His expression is warm, like when you cuddle up with a friend on the couch under a cozy blanket to watch a movie, and then you both get up and give each other a hug before you leave, and the hug is warm and cozy just like you were on the couch under that blanket.

"It's cramps," I murmur. The truth, albeit misleading. He nods, even though he looks dubious. "I'll be fine. But . . . thanks, Harrison."

He nods again, and by the time both of our roommates have sent us the *all-clear* text, it's been an hour of nonstop conversation, and I've made a new friend.

CHAPTER 3

Nine years later

During my four-hour training shift at Jo Jo's Coffee and Tea, forced reassurances run through my head on repeat: *This is good for you. And for Jo. This is going to be good for you. You needed this change. You're happy to be here, and this is good for you.*

I genuinely believe all of this to be true. I just need to remind myself of that, over and over again, because quitting my teaching job and becoming a barista at the coffee shop my best friend just took over from her now-retired parents feels like a professional downgrade.

I don't know what the hell I'm doing, Jo had told me over the phone, describing her attempt to place a bulk order of more coffee beans. *And Macy's in* London. *I feel completely untethered.*

And so here I am, wiping down café tables.

After four hours of training, I have determined that I need to purchase a real bed after I get my first paycheck. My back aches, likely because the air was mostly gone from the air mattress by the morning. When I woke up, my body was fully resting on the laminate floor, except "resting" isn't really the right word, because there was absolutely zero rest involved.

I bend over to pick up a crumpled napkin from underneath a table, and several of my joints crack.

The *other* reason for my sleeplessness is that my brain supplied an endless stream of startling and, frankly, unhinged dreams featuring a certain character from my past. An eighteen-year-old boy doing homework with me in the library at two A.M. A nineteen-year-old boy picking up cold medicine from the drugstore when I had the flu. A twenty-one-year-old boy sitting in the front row of my capstone project presentation, clapping the loudest with the widest grin on his face. A twenty-seven-year-old man refusing a hug.

Every footstep on my ceiling is a slap in the face. Every *ding* makes me wonder if his girlfriend/booty call is texting him. Every time a door shuts, I run to my window, and I still haven't decided whether I'm looking outside in fear or anticipation. And it hasn't even been twenty-four hours since I moved in.

I wasn't even going to tell him I was in Boston, but now he's going to know every time I turn on my TV.

Seeing him again is heartbreaking, but am I allowed to be heartbroken if I'm not blameless?

After Harrison left yesterday, I spent the next several hours lying on my floor, cycling from horror to giddy excitement to raw mortification. There were some tears thrown in there, particularly whenever I heard a noise from above and remembered the *thumpthumpthump*. And the whole time, I couldn't get rid of the sour, guilty taste in my mouth.

"You should have seen the look on his face when he stepped away from me," I tell Jo, who stands behind the counter reminding me for the third time this shift that I'm overreacting. "All I wanted was a hug, and he looked like someone was asking him if he wanted his cat buried or cremated."

"Harrison has a cat?"

"No! I am the cat in this scenario. Our *relationship* is the cat."

"I don't get it."

I don't respond, because neither do I. My brain can't be expected to operate at full capacity at the moment.

Groaning, I stretch my arms upward and feel the pull of stiff muscles in my back and my side and—well, everywhere.

"Girl, go home," Jo says. "Your shift is over."

I salute her. "Thanks, boss."

Jo rolls her eyes, chuckling. "Don't call me boss. That sounds ridiculous."

"Sure thing, boss," I say. Jo looks around to make sure no one is watching, then turns her back to the tables and flips me off with a smile.

Walking into the back room, I take off my apron and hang it on my designated hook. A sticker on the wall spells out my name in beautiful calligraphy with oranges and orange blossoms drawn around the name. Jo's name, next to mine, is decorated with apples—probably a reference to her former role as a high school teacher—and another sticker to the right spells out "Rose" with some roses framing the word. Another coworker, I assume.

I trace my finger along my name, admiring the work Jo put into making this place feel welcoming for me. It's only been a few weeks since her school year ended and she took over the coffee shop from her parents full-time. She grew up here, doing her homework at the tables after school while her parents made lattes and chatted with customers. When she heard earlier this year that they were going to close up shop, she decided to take over instead. Mercifully, they were in decent financial shape due to the long-standing relationships they'd built with practically everyone in this part of Jamaica Plain, but their rent had only been going up in recent years, so Jo knows she needs to improve business if she wants this to be a sound financial venture.

The chime on the door rings, and footsteps break my contemplative silence.

"Hey, Jo!"

I freeze.

I see him every three to four months, my ass. That's the casual greeting of a regular walking into his favorite coffee shop.

He orders an iced latte, and I watch through a slit in the curtain as Jo enters his order. He's wearing scrubs and carrying a backpack over one shoulder.

They talk casually and quietly, and I can't hear what they're saying, but I do see Jo's eyes darting back and forth between Harrison and the curtain behind which I'm standing. I clear my throat loudly to indicate that Jo needs to come back here to talk to me.

He eyes the curtain. "Is that . . ." he starts to ask, then pauses.

No way in hell he can recognize me by the sound of me clearing my throat. Absolutely no chance. But his eyes are fixed on the curtain with an alarmed expression anyway, and I step farther back into the room, just in case he has X-ray vision.

"That's not . . ." he says again. "Is it?"

"Actually, you know what?" Jo asks, jerking her eyes toward the curtain with an apologetic look. (I'm going to kill her.) "That *is* her, and she just finished her training shift, and she needs someone to walk home with her. She hasn't learned the route yet, you know? Don't want her to get lost."

"That's what my phone is for," I hiss from behind the curtain, and they both look in my direction, Jo with a *shut up* look and Harrison with another alarmed expression. I clear my throat again. It sounds like I have consumption.

"I'll be right back," Jo says. "I'll give you a large coffee to make sure it lasts you through the walk. Sound good?"

Harrison doesn't respond before she walks back to where I am, sliding sideways through the curtains so as not to expose me to the outside world.

"That was nonconsensual wingwomaning!" I whisper accusatorily.

"Nuh-uh," she says, wagging her finger. "Don't give me that. You're neighbors and need to learn how to be friendly. I'm doing you a favor. You told me yesterday that you want to fix this."

"I didn't mean *right now.*" I let out a whispered *ughhhhhh.* "And what happened to 'I only see him once every three to four months'? Huh?"

She purses her lips. "I do get coffee with him every three to four months. But he also works nearby—and apparently lives nearby—so he's been stopping in for coffee regularly since I took over." She sees me open my mouth to argue, and she cuts me off. "I stand by my claim. We don't catch up when he comes to buy coffee. I literally just make his order, and he goes about his merry way."

Harrison clears his throat outside, then says, "I can hear what you're saying. Just FYI."

Jo and I exchange a wide-eyed glance. Putting one hand on her hip, Jo points with the other hand toward where Harrison stands on the other side of the curtain. "Go on, then."

I silently scream, jumping three times like an angry child, then shake it off and walk coolly and casually past the curtains.

"Hi, Harrison!" I say. My voice is oddly pinched and high-pitched.

"Hi," he says, the words forced through his full face cringe. He's wearing scrubs with illustrations of friendly sharks, and he looks like he wants to walk out the door and straight into the ocean.* "You . . . work at Jo Jo's now?"

I nod and gesture vaguely toward the espresso machine

* **Wide eyes · Tense jaw · Shallow breathing** | *Facial expression* | *Frequency: low*

1. Flustered shock.

instead of providing an explanation. "Still drinking iced lattes, I see!"

He nods toward something Jo is doing. "Still drinking iced coffees with oat milk and one sugar, I see."

I turn around to look at Jo, who is putting lids on two cups. She gives me a thumbs-up and an enthusiastic smile, then hands one coffee to me and one to Harrison. Jo practically shoves us outside, and we stand completely still and silent, staring at each other with equally mortified expressions.

I take a sip of my coffee.

"How is it?" he asks.

I swallow. "It's good."

He takes a sip of his coffee.

"How is yours?"

He nods. "Good."

We stare at each other for another moment, and then I gesture in the direction of our building.

Our building. Damn it. I'm so screwed.

We start our journey home, and when I raise my coffee up to my mouth, I'm horrified to see that my hands are shaking.

"Are you okay?" Harrison asks quietly. This area of Jamaica Plain is slow and residential and calm, but I can still barely hear him over the faint hum of cars and footsteps and the idle chatter of passersby.

"Not really."

He takes a sip of his coffee. "Me neither, I think." It doesn't sound accusatory, but we both know who's at fault. A pit forms in my stomach.

"I'm sorry," I whisper, my voice as quiet as his. "I know you hate me. I hope you know I never intended to put you in this situation."

Harrison's pace slows, and he turns to me with wide eyes.

"What?" I ask when he doesn't speak.

"I don't hate you."

He should hate me, actually. After how we left things in college.

It was so, so hard and it *still* feels hard. Or maybe "tight" is the word. A tightness in my chest that makes it hard to fully exhale when I think about it.

When I was diagnosed with vaginismus during my freshman year of college, the gynecologist told me working with a pelvic floor therapist could help me. "Your vaginal muscles seize up when they come into contact with anything," she'd explained, "and I know you don't feel like you have any control over it, but physical therapy can help." I was willing to do anything to make it better, so I made the appointment.

Afraid of what I'd find, I refused to google what pelvic floor therapy involved in advance of my first appointment. When I arrived, everything started fine. Great, even. We chatted for a bit. We did some stretches, which she recommended I start doing regularly to "open the pelvic floor." We looked at a diagram of the reproductive system.

And then she asked if we could try manually stretching, and I said yes (because I was willing to do anything!), and then she put on gloves and put lube on her index finger, and then it hurt like hell, and she stopped, and that was all we accomplished during the first appointment.

She sent me home with a pack of four dilators so I could try manually stretching on my own. They ranged in size and color and came in an austere wooden box. The smallest one, the size of my pinky, was lavender. The largest was a bright blue. I named her Cobalt, and she and her big attitude have lived rent-free in my mind ever since. The second largest, Key Lime, is the one that always haunted my nightmares, though, because you think she's not going to be that large, since she's not the larg*est,* but when you look at her alone, she's an absolute monster. I hate her.

Take me out of this moving box and we'll fight, then, Key Lime says to me in my mind.

Joke's on you, I say. *I didn't appropriately label any of my boxes, so I don't know where you are.*

You can never escape us, Cobalt says.

I lock them away in the back of my mind. Not the Fantasy Corner, though, because nothing about them is a fantasy, given the destructive impact they've had on my dating life.

Harrison doesn't finish his statement about not hating me, so I prompt him. "Well, you certainly looked like you'd been shot yesterday when I tried to give you a hug."

He freezes, then frowns. "Listen," he says.

He doesn't continue, and I raise my eyebrows.

"Listen," he says, letting out a sigh that I feel in my soul. "We can't just act like the last five years haven't passed. I've spent five years trying to *forget* what it's like to have you in my life. Do you have any idea what that's like?" His voice shakes slightly. "Do you have any idea how much I resented you?"

Maybe I should be alarmed by this statement, and part of me definitely is, but another part of me hangs on to the past tense of his final question.

"I know," I choke out. "Harrison, I know. But five years have passed, and we're both different people. Think about how happy eighteen-year-old Emma and Harrison would be if they knew we were neighbors again at age twenty-seven. They'd think that was the best thing in the entire world."

Harrison closes his eyes and lets out a pitiful sigh. He's not saying it, but the expression on his face shows he's conflicted.* He doesn't *like* that he feels this way. And if I can be responsible for making him feel better, for lifting this weight, then I have a moral obligation to do so.

"Tell me about your life," I suggest. "Tell me what you've

* **Furrowed brows · Soft eyes · Gentle frown** | *Facial expression* | *Frequency: low*

1. Combination of anger and regret.

been up to for the last five years, and I'll tell you what my life has been like, and you can start to replace that anger with something new."

Harrison gives me a tight smile. "I've spent so much time wondering what you were up to, but I never thought I'd actually get to find out. I wasn't even sure I wanted to know, to be honest."

"Would you prefer that?" I ask. "To not know?"

He's silent for at least twenty seconds before responding, and even when he responds, he's hesitant, as if he wasn't ready to speak but felt pressured into it because of the awkwardness of this silence.

"I think I need more time," he says. "I just . . . don't know. I don't know if it's a good idea for me to know you. I don't know."

Not even to know what I've been up to, but to know me. Generally. Awesome.

Is it because he has a girlfriend? Is it because being around me is too painful?

Does it matter why?

"Yeah," I whisper. "Okay."

We don't say another word for the remaining eight minutes of our walk. Instead, I stare at our feet as they take step after step after step. He is not wearing the orange-patterned socks today.

We approach the classic Boston triple-decker we live in, and in this lighting and this context, the pale Pepto Bismol color of the clapboard siding makes me feel nauseous. Or maybe the nausea is a premonition, because as I'm about to say goodbye and walk to the entrance to the basement apartment, a car pulls into the street parking spot right next to us. The driver turns off the car and exits, yelling "Hiya!" in a grating, high-pitched voice with the well-curated accent of a New England prep school graduate. Goose bumps form on my arms in response. Hell *thumping* no.

Harrison whips around, the ice in his coffee cup rustling. "Hi!" he forces out.

After grabbing a yoga mat out of her back seat, she floats up to us and gives Harrison a kiss. On the lips. (This is it. This is hell. It must be, because why else would there be literal flames in my vision?)

She turns to me, sticking out her hand for a handshake. Her fingers have perfectly manicured red polish with no chips.

"I'm Stephanie," she says.

Stephanie. I file it away. I wish I didn't know her name. Giving her a name in my mind means she's real, and I'd prefer her not to be real, for the sake of my sanity. *Stephanie.*

Definitely not a booty call.

"Emma," I say. I nod toward the house. "I just moved into the basement apartment yesterday."

Her eyes brighten, like I've given the correct answer, and she's proud of me for it. "Oh, lovely! Look at you, already becoming friends with the neighbors."

"Yeah, Harrison helped me carry my moving boxes to the recycling bin," I say at the same moment Harrison says, "Emma and I went to college together."

Stephanie and I both turn to Harrison with raised eyebrows, which he takes as his cue to continue. "Yeah, we were, um, friends in college, but I didn't know she was moving here until I ran into her yesterday."

"You were friends in college?" Stephanie asks. She tilts her head, lost in thought, as if she's combing through every story Harrison's ever told and trying to remember whether she's heard my name.

Based on Harrison's cringe, I've never been a topic of conversation. This shouldn't hurt my feelings, especially considering I made Jo swear she'd never bring up Harrison in conversation, but I feel slighted anyway.

"Huh!" Stephanie continues. "That's so funny. I just met a couple of Harrison's friends from college last month, too."

Last month—so assuming they'd been together for at least a couple months before he started introducing her to friends, then we're looking at a three- to four-month relationship. I don't know what to do with that information, but I set it aside to mull over later.

"Mark and Veronica," she continues. "Did you know them?"

Putting me in the same category as Mark and Veronica, two college friends from his nursing program who he took some classes with and occasionally studied with in the library, is, frankly, insulting.

Nonetheless, I nod vaguely, because I did vaguely know them, and Stephanie smiles at my confirmation. "They were delightful. It was so fun getting to hear more about Harrison in college. Seems like he was a real nerd. Ha!" She rolls her eyes at him and his shark-print scrubs. I have a strong urge to defend him despite the fact that he is undeniably a huge dork.

"Actually—Emma, are you free tonight?" she asks. Harrison stares at her blankly. "We're getting dinner with an old friend of mine who also just moved here, and you should absolutely join!" She winks at me, and my stomach inexplicably drops. "And he's cute. It can be a double date, if you're so inclined."

It takes me a moment to realize she's talking about her friend, not Harrison. Who I should not be thinking is cute, because I am not an asshole or a home-wrecker.

I expect Harrison to jump in and shut this down, but instead, he stares at me with wide eyes.*

* **Raised eyebrows · Straight face · Bated breath** | *Facial expression* | *Frequency: low*

1. Fear of what comes next.
2. Unwilling to make the next move.

I'm about to say no, but then somehow I end up saying, "That would be great!"

Is it because I want to spend more time with Harrison? Is it because I want to meet Stephanie's cute friend? Is it because I hate myself? Who's to say!

Harrison deflates, which could either indicate relief (unlikely) or that he's resigned to his fate (more likely). Whatever his genuine reaction may be, he tucks it away and adds, "I'll text you the details."

This is probably the moment when I should admit I blocked his number after college, but I'm not going to do that. What I *am* going to do is unblock his number the moment I enter my apartment.

"See you later?" Stephanie asks, and I nod. As they walk inside, Harrison turns back to look at me one more time. He seems to want to say something, his lips pulling to the left.* But at the last minute, he turns around and walks inside. The door shuts behind him, and I'm still frozen in place with the ice melting in my coffee.

* **Lips pulled to the left · Biting the right side of lip** | *Facial expression* | *Frequency: medium*

1. Actively thoughtful.
2. Signals internal debate.

CHAPTER 4

Harrison: Testing testing

Harrison: Ah! I see you unblocked my number.

Harrison: I'll come grab you at 7. We can walk over together.

I stare at the texts, and they stare back at me. I was definitely hoping the message would read something along the lines of "It was nice to see you today, let's be friends again" or maybe "Thank you for unblocking my number—I've been trying to text you for five years to tell you you're still the most important thing in my life" or even an "I missed you." A girl can dream.

I would probably have continued staring at this string of texts for another thirty minutes if Jo hadn't chosen this moment to call.

"Hi," I say.

"Oh, lord help me."

"What?"

"Your tone," she says immediately. "It's all wrong."

I open my mouth to argue, then close my mouth and do not argue.

"Spill. Now."

I asked Harrison to get coffee with me and I got rejected, and I don't know how to handle my emotions, I think. "I have a date," I say. "A double date, actually."

Silence.

Finally, Jo sighs. "I'm coming over so you can explain that to me in person. I'll be there in fifteen."

She hangs up before I can thank her.

By seven P.M., Jo has listened to me rant for nearly two hours, during which we unpacked and (mostly) put away every clothing box in my apartment, all in search of the perfect double date outfit. We finally landed on a pale blue spaghetti-strap sundress with little buttons down the front. It's a bit tight in the boobs now, but if I go braless, I can still pull it off. The rest of the dress is flowy enough to cover everything.

"How do I look?" I ask, turning in a circle.

Jo admires me from her perch on top of an unopened moving box (EM'S CRAP!). "Like a spring fairy goddess. Harrison is going to be falling all over himself."

"You mean my unnamed date. Who is not Harrison."

"Yes, that."

"You're sure it's not too much?" I ask, eyeing myself in the mirror. By the end of my teaching career, I wasn't putting much effort into my daily outfits. When I started teaching at twenty-two, there were a lot of rainbows and florals and book-themed T-shirts. Like if Ms. Frizzle taught middle school English. After five years, though, I'd replaced my headbands and fun scrunchies with messy buns and ponytails. As my body aged and changed and grew weak and flabby from lack of exercise, I donated my *Magic School Bus* pieces and never replaced them with anything fun. And I didn't have much of an excuse to dress up outside of work hours, since you don't need to dress up to stay at home and read, or get dinner with your parents, or FaceTime Jo, or grade essays. And by that point, I'd lost interest in hanging out with most of my Tampa friends, since the majority were high school acquaintances who I had mixed feelings about anyway. Even the ones I did like were no longer great options for a hangout, since they were—and still are—getting married and having kids. Not limited to but including my aforementioned roommates.

"I'm sure," Jo says. "It's perfect."

There's a feeble knock on my door, and Jo and I exchange a wide-eyed glance and a deep breath before I walk over and swing it open.

Harrison is wearing a pair of perfectly tailored jeans with a light blue button-up shirt and a navy cardigan over the top. He has on the same pair of worn-in white sneakers he was wearing yesterday, and his waves have been combed into submission while still retaining enough fluff to look casual. This is an art he must've mastered in the last five years. He sure as hell didn't know how to tame his hair during college.

Stephanie probably taught him. The thought *thumps* uncomfortably around my brain.

His brown eyes dart to my dress, then immediately back up to my eyes.

I clear my throat, and he does the same.

"You look," he says, pausing, "like you're ready to go."

"Hi, Harrison," Jo says from behind me. We both turn to face her. "I don't think anyone would be mad if you told her she looked nice."

Harrison stares at her blankly, then just says, "Hey, Jo. Good to see you."

"As always," she says. "Didn't realize you'd moved here."

"Yep," he says, eyes darting toward me awkwardly. "Neither did Emma."

No one responds to that.

"All right, then!" Jo says, clapping her hands together. "Sounds like you two are in for a fun night!"

I study Harrison, begging him to give me something—anything!—but he just offers Jo a weak smile, then turns his gaze back to me. "You ready to go?"

I nod, and Jo comes up behind me, jumping on one foot as she puts her shoes on. She grabs her purse from the floor, then shoots us both a peace sign. "Have fun, kids. See ya at the coffee shop."

She's gone before I can ask her to pretty please fifth-wheel on this date.

Harrison clears his throat again. "Shall we?"

We leave the building, turning right when we hit the sidewalk. It's unusually crisp out tonight—mid sixties, probably—and the air feels refreshing on my skin, which is overheated from unpacking. It would be so easy to comment on the weather. To ask him whether it's normally this cool during the summer in Boston. He might roll his eyes at me since I, too, lived in Boston for four years during college and therefore know exactly what the weather is like. I was never here during the summer, though, so he might cut me some slack. More likely, he'd ignore my question, since the silent treatment seems to be his MO right now. The awkward silence treatment, perhaps.

A driver honks his horn, and a car swerves a few feet from the sidewalk. Before I can properly react, Harrison grabs my arm and tugs me away from the street. I accidentally bump into his side. He takes a quick step, catching himself from falling, but then we both immediately almost fall again due to how quickly we separate from where our bodies accidentally touched.

We're like two magnets, with the wrong ends pointed toward each other.

"Sorry, can you just—" he says, facing me with several feet of distance between us. "Just walk on the other side, please." He takes a step forward and toward the street, leaving space for me to walk on the inside edge of the sidewalk. He doesn't look back to make sure I'm following before he continues walking.

I take a few speedy steps to catch up before opening my mouth, committed to breaking the silence before this adrenaline subsides. "Are we walking to dinner because you got rid of your Beetle?"

The only reaction I can see is a slight stutter in his step. The tiniest of pauses.

"No," he says. "Stephanie and her friend are driving over from Beacon Hill, and she offered to pick us up, but I told her not to bother. It's a short walk. Figured we'd save the environment."

"So you still have the Beetle?"

"No," he murmurs. "Sold it. It wasn't a practical car."

That's definitely true. It had been his grandfather's—a retirement purchase that eventually got handed down to his favorite (and only) grandson when the small interior and low seats lost their appeal. By the time we were in college, the car was already well loved, the sea-green exterior faded in spots, the synthetic material of the seats shredded and stained from overuse. It wasn't the best winter car, and it wasn't particularly comfortable to ride in. But Harrison loved that car, and I, by extension, loved that car.

"Actually, I sold it to a guy who guts cars and turns them into dune buggies."

I stop walking. It takes Harrison a few steps to realize I've fallen behind, at which point he also stops walking and turns around. "What?"

"What do you mean, *what*?" I ask, laughing. "No way that's a true story."

The corner of his mouth ticks up.* The expression is so familiar, but seeing it on his twenty-seven-year-old face feels unnatural, like the expression is cheating on itself.

"I swear," he says. "He paid me five hundred dollars for it. The transmission was wrecked. I needed to get rid of it, and apparently his clients go crazy for Beetle buggies."

I let out a choked laugh. "Holy shit. You're not joking."

"Too crazy to be fake?"

"I know when you're joking with me, and you're not joking."

His smile falters. "Yeah, well. Maybe I look different when I joke now."

He keeps walking before I can respond. I take a deep breath, decide to set that comment aside to spiral over later, and keep walking.

We arrive at the restaurant ten excruciatingly silent minutes later, then continue waiting in silence for Stephanie and her unnamed friend to arrive. There is not a single normal thing I can think to say to start a conversation, which maybe makes me the worst former English teacher of all time. I should know how to form complete sentences. Instead, I stare at a framed photo of a family on the wall, choosing to memorize the labeled names from left to right instead of attempting to engage in conversation. *Beatrice, Lorenzo, Sofia*—Harrison shifts his weight between his feet, back and forth in an unbearable cycle, but I ignore him—*Marco, Elena. Beatrice, Lorenzo, Sofia, Marco*—

"There they are!" a shrill female voice calls out.

Stephanie looks frustratingly good in a dressy black tank top, French-tucked into a pair of dark wash mom jeans that

* **Crinkles around eyes · Left dimple · Lopsided smile** | *Facial expression* | *Frequency: medium*

1. Amused.

make her long legs look otherworldly. Her hair is styled into those perfectly smooth waves that could only be achieved using a Dyson Airwrap. I, on the other hand, have been using the same fifteen-dollar curler since sixth grade.

The man standing next to her is admittedly good-looking. He's all tall and muscle and tan, and when he steps forward and outstretches his arms, his charming grin coaxes a smile out of me before I even know what my facial muscles are doing. I lean forward and let him hug me.

"Alexander," he says.

"Emma." He stays in the hug about two seconds longer than I would have, and I can't bring myself to make eye contact with Harrison, even as Alexander leans in and gives him a hug that is notably shorter than mine and includes more back patting.

Everyone takes turns greeting everyone else, and then we make our way to a booth. My rule of thumb when it comes to eating out with acquaintances is to always pick a seat first to avoid having to make an actual seating decision. This strategy immediately backfires when Alexander scoots into the seat across from me, shooting me a glowing smile that does not even remotely distract me from the fact that Stephanie picks the seat next to him, which leaves Harrison to sit next to me.

His left leg bounces up and down as he settles into place, the soft fabric of his jeans wrinkling then unwrinkling as he rubs his hands down his thighs, landing on his knees, as if to stop his leg from moving. After a moment, he withdraws his hands, and his left knee immediately starts bouncing again. The urge to put my hand on his knee is so strong that I place both of my hands under my thighs and look directly into Alexander's intense eyes instead of acknowledging anything happening to my right.

The waiter appears, and Stephanie orders a bottle of red for the table. He glances around as if to check whether any of us would like to provide input, but when we don't, he quickly thanks us and runs off.

Stephanie jumps right in. "So, Alexander is a friend of mine from high school—"

"—an ex, actually," Alexander pipes in, giving a good-natured chuckle. I hold back my cringe.

"Semantics," Stephanie says, rolling her eyes. "But anyway, he just got hired by the consulting group I work for, so now we're co-workers!"

"Serendipitous," Harrison says. If I looked to my right, I'm 100 percent certain I would find Harrison smiling without dimples or eye creases. (I do not look to my right.)

"So, you just moved to Boston for this job?" I ask Alexander.

"Just last week, from Maryland. Stephanie is one of the few people I know in the area, so I had to reach out. Glad we could make this happen so I can make new friends," he says, winking at me.

I shift my eyes away and take a sip of water to hide my face, even though it's been years since a guy winked at me. Actually, I don't know if a guy has ever winked at me unironically. I should be enjoying this, I think? But also, winking feels weird? Do I have the ick, or do I just hate dating?

"But Stephanie said you just moved here, too, is that right?" he asks me.

"Just yesterday, actually."

Stephanie nods toward Harrison and me. "And you two were friends in college?"

An understatement if I've ever heard one. I can't stop myself from making a list of all the other things he probably forgot to tell her.

Did he tell you I planned his twenty-first birthday party for him? Did he tell you I met his parents before he even knew who you were? Did he tell you I visited him in Paris when he studied abroad, or that we intentionally signed leases in neighboring apartments during our last two years of college so we didn't have to leave the building to see each other? Did he tell you we held each other when we cried and calmed each other when we were angry and laughed together when we were embarrassed? Did he tell you he loved me, and I loved him back?

No. He definitely didn't tell her that.

I choke out an *mmhmm,* which is exactly what Harrison does. We create a chorus of noncommittal *mmm*s.

"No need to sound so thrilled," Stephanie says, laughing.

Harrison shrugs, his knee finally still. "We knew each other. And then we moved to different places."

Another understatement. I still do not look at him, even as I feel a pang of betrayal.

The next ten minutes are spent learning about Alexander's cat, Stephanie's recent family trip to Greece, and the team drama at their consulting job, which is highly dramatic but provides zero insight into what it actually is they do for work.

Harrison doesn't say much, only jumping in when called for to offer commentary of five words or fewer. I'm not much better, but it's not like I have anything interesting to say. Hey, let me tell you about my shitty new apartment! Want to hear my middle-school-level literary analysis of *Animal Farm*? What about my personal ranking of every horror film released between 1980 and 1989, starting with *The Shining* and ending with *Gremlins*? I could also tell you about how I haven't been on any interesting trips or on any good dates or had, like, any fun in the last three to four years! And don't even get me started on my vagina!

"Emma, what do you do for work?" Alexander asks.

I take a long sip of wine.

"I work at a coffee shop."

"Which one?" Stephanie asks.

"Jo Jo's? Nearby, on South Street."

"OH!" Her eyes light up in recognition. "Harrison and I went there on our first date!"

I'm going to be sick.

Alexander asks the question I can't bring myself to, and just for that, I think he's the best date ever. "Remind me how you two met?"

"Funny story, actually," Stephanie says, chuckling. I brace myself. "We met on a dating app."

That's not even remotely a funny story. Actually, picturing Harrison on a dating app makes the thought of eating Italian food utterly repulsive.

She takes a sip of her wine, evidently pausing for comedic timing. "So, we set up a first date. I was excited. After all, he seemed nice. He's obviously so cute. He's a pediatric nurse—which, talk about attractive."

I thought that was attractive before you thought that was attractive, I think. *I thought that was attractive before he even started the job.*

"An hour before the date, I've just finished putting on my makeup, and I get a text from him." She widens her eyes for dramatic effect. "Canceled. The date is off."

I gasp because that seems like what I'm supposed to do. She nods appreciatively, but Harrison looks at the ceiling, his ears pink.

"I was disappointed, but then again, we're talking about a man from a dating app at this point. I've been burned enough times to learn to brush it off when things don't work out." She purses her lips, and I pre-imitate her voice: *but THEN!* "But *then,*" she says in exactly the tone I anticipated. "He follows up the next day. Turns out, something came up with his mom that was unavoidable. And, I mean, come on—don't you just love a man who takes care of his mom?"

Does she *love* love this man who takes care of his mom, or is that just a turn of phrase?

"So anyway," she continues. "He apologized profusely, then asked me if I'd be willing to give him a second chance. Something told me I should, and, well, I said yes!"

I said yes! I practice imitating her in my mind so I can accurately re-create this scene for Jo later tonight on the phone.

"We met at Jo Jo's the next day. Harrison's friend's parents run it, apparently." Stephanie directs her attention toward me. "Jo? Do you know her? Is that how you got connected to this job?"

"Yep," I say, my voice unsteady to my own ears. "She actually just took it over from her parents. Last month."

"No way. Small world! So, anyway—we had a delightful first date there. And it's been, what, four months since then?" she asks Harrison, and he nods. She turns to me, like she's letting me in on a secret. "How lucky am I, right?"

The waiter arrives with our food before I can follow up this rhetorical question with a comment that is inappropriate or tone-deaf or morose or all three. As my plate is set in front of me, I immediately regret ordering the cheapest thing on the menu (a salad) instead of the hearty dishes everyone else ordered.

Stephanie clears her throat, and I'm momentarily terrified I've done something wrong, but when I look up, she's staring at Harrison with wide eyes and pursed lips. It's the kind of expression that makes it clear you're witnessing something you shouldn't be witnessing, and I exchange a nervous glance with Alexander.

I finally dare to look directly at Harrison for the first time all night, and his jaw clenches.* "It's fine," he says, looking directly at Stephanie with the same intense expression she has on her face.

The loss I feel in my gut over Harrison having a silent language with this woman—even if they're using it to argue—is

* **Clenched jaw · Furrowed brows** | *Facial expression* | *Frequency: low*
  1. Frustration.

overwhelming, sending nausea coursing through my body. We used to be able to communicate like that. Now I can barely look him in the eyes. Sure, I can still interpret his expressions when I actually look at him.

He's just not looking back.

"Why didn't you just tell the waiter?" Stephanie asks.

"Because it's not a problem," Harrison says, carefully concealed frustration in his voice.

Alexander glances down at Harrison's plate. "Wrong meal?"

Now that he says it, I do see it. Harrison ordered chicken parm, and this is definitely eggplant parm. It still looks delicious, and I'm about to say so, but Stephanie throws her hand up in the air and wiggles her fingers at the waiter.

"Sorry, excuse me. He ordered a chicken parm, but this is eggplant—would you mind bringing this back and asking them to remake the dish?" Stephanie asks. The waiter mumbles his apologies, and Stephanie thanks him profusely. Harrison just stares at Stephanie until the waiter grabs the dish, at which point Harrison also thanks him.

The table is silent when the waiter leaves.

"Well," Stephanie says, unfolding her napkin onto her lap. "This is why Harrison needs me! Someone has to stick up for him if he's not going to do it himself."

Alexander chuckles, and Harrison says "Thanks" in a bland tone.

What chain of events led me from quitting my teaching job to sitting here at this table? What sin did I commit in a past life that led me to this hell?

"Oh, come on," I say before I can stop myself. "He's an adult. He can talk to the waiter himself."

Stephanie's surprise at my outburst quickly transforms into a challenging eyebrow, the unspoken words clear. *But he didn't, did he?*

"Yeah, well," I say. Harrison's bouncing knee has gone still next to me. "As an adult, he can also decide whether he wants to switch out his meal."

"Except would he ever have decided to do that?" Stephanie says, lips pulled tightly into a straight line.

No. That's what I'm sure we're all thinking. *Not in a million years.*

The words come so close to exiting my mouth, my tongue stalls between my teeth, and I swallow the ghost of a "th." *That's what I love about him.*

"That's why I do it for him," Stephanie says, smiling at Harrison. "Because I know what he wants."

With that, Stephanie turns to Alexander and begins a new conversation as they start to eat. Their conversation about work quickly gets so in the weeds that they don't bother pretending to include me and Harrison. I poke at my salad with my fork, tuning them out.

"You don't have to wait for my food," Harrison says quietly. He's not whispering into my ear, but it's still quiet enough that I wonder whether he wants me to lean closer. (He definitely doesn't.) "You should start eating."

"Believe me, I can wait a little longer to eat this lettuce," I say, and if I didn't know better, I'd say Harrison exhales a laugh.

There's a pause, and then, so quietly I can barely hear it, "Thank you."

"I'm sorry," I murmur back.

"Normally, the response would be 'you're welcome,'" he says. I turn my head just enough to get a good look at his face through the corner of my eye, and there are slight crinkles around his eyes.

"Well, you're welcome, then, but I'm also sorry for making a big deal about it."

We hold eye contact for a second too long, and then he looks down at the table where his plate should be. "I'd forgotten. I like it when you make a big deal about things."

His knee has stopped bouncing, and I would also do anything to keep this conversation going, so I switch gears and ask, "Did your parents ever get over you not going to law school?"

He nods, circling his right middle finger around the rim of his wineglass. "They're too busy being lawyers to continue to care." I snort, but then he continues. "Actually—that's not fair. I've been getting along well with them. My mom, anyway."

"Oh?"

His mom is a tough cookie. Talking to her always felt like being interrogated. I don't know why anyone would pay her money to treat them like that for the entire duration of a court case, but then again, I never had any doubt she was good at her job. So maybe if you were desperate enough.

"She—" he says, pausing. "Yeah, we're getting along well."

I wait for him to add additional context, but I eventually add, "I'm glad."

He runs his palms down his knees before folding his hands in his lap.

"You know," I say before I can lose my courage, "I really missed—"

"Here you go, sir." The waiter arrives with Harrison's chicken, and when he picks up his fork and dives in, I'm certain he's choosing to ignore the sentence I started.

A half hour later, we've finished off the bottle of wine and cleaned our plates, and Harrison has reverted back to the silent treatment.

We gather outside the restaurant before leaving, and Alexander gives me another hug that is slightly longer than I feel is warranted based on the somewhat limited interaction we had during this dinner.

"It was really nice to meet you, Emma," he says, his tone low.

"You, too," I say, the hint of surprise in my voice more obvious than I'd like.

Stephanie comes up to me after him, offering a smile that makes me feel guilty for reasons I don't fully understand.

"It was truly so nice to hang out with you," she says, approaching me. "I have to wake up early for a work event, so this is where I leave you. But next time I need more college stories about Harrison. Deal?"

"Deal," I say, then move a step closer so I can speak quietly and not embarrass Harrison, who's having what looks to be an extremely boring conversation with Alexander. "Listen, I'm sorry I was an asshole. I'm having an off day, and I took it out on you."

She brings a hand up to my arm and squeezes. "No, I'm sorry. Just because Harrison can't stand up for himself doesn't mean I have the right to do it on his behalf, especially not in front of a bunch of other people. I'm sure I embarrassed him. So, lesson learned. But he needs to learn to stick up for himself, doesn't he?" she says, chuckling as if we're in on a joke.

A painful, protective pang shoots from my ears to my toes, as if I owe it to Harrison to argue that he does *not* need to learn to stick up for himself because he's perfect the way he is. But what do I know about Harrison and the way he is? Not as much as I want to, after five years.

I nod and smile vaguely instead of responding, then step forward and meet her outstretched arms for a hug. Before I know what's happening, there's a ripping noise, and I feel a cold draft against my back.

"Shit," I yelp, as Stephanie says, "Oh, no!"

I reach my hand behind me and feel the ripped seam. Threads hang loose around a fist-sized hole, right where the fabric was pulled the tightest across my back.

Thank you, boobs. Thank you, aging body.

My face flushes red, my body still contorted to hide the evidence. Stephanie puts her hand on my back, knocking mine out of the way so she can cover the hole for me. My arms relax at my sides, and I am upset to admit I might really like this girl.

Her eyes roam to Alexander, then to Harrison, both of whom are watching us with blank expressions.

"Harrison," she says, "give Emma your sweater while you guys walk home."

Harrison continues to stare blankly at us, and I stare blankly at Stephanie.

"Harrison," she says. He doesn't move. "Oh my god."

She leaves my side to walk over and grab the sweater from where it's draped over his arms, and nobody says a single word as she hands it to me.

"Here. Sorry, my boyfriend is being an idiot tonight," she says. "Hopefully you already know he's not normally like that."

I nod as I slip the sweater on, refusing to make eye contact with anyone except the ant crawling across the concrete at my feet.

It's a light cotton sweater, navy blue, and perfectly appropriate for a cool summer night. I'm horrified to realize it smells like the essence of Harrison, woodsy-scented soap and . . . I don't know. It smells like Harrison. It's impossible to describe, just like it's impossible to describe the churning in my stomach.

It is not, however, impossible to describe the look on Harrison's face,* which I shouldn't have looked at, but am doing so anyway.

We say the rest of our goodbyes, and Harrison and I don't say a single word on the walk home. When we arrive at the apartments, I wordlessly hand him the sweater, and we offer quiet "good nights" before walking inside.

* **Sunken eyes · Slack jaw · Clenched hands** | *Facial expression* | *Frequency: low*

1. Tender focus.
2. Sadness.

CHAPTER 5

When I wake up the next morning, I swear to myself I won't spend all day reliving the horribly awkward date from last night. I need to stay focused as I prep for my first non-training shift at Jo Jo's.

I'm on track to accomplish my goal for about four minutes, until I hear the pipes groan and the shower start above my head.

Harrison's shower schedule feels like the kind of information that's too intimate for me to know given his general lack of interest in speaking to me.

Groaning, I drag my body upright, every muscle straining in protest. Given the weekend's . . . mishap, I didn't get much unpacking done, meaning many of the items I need to make myself look truly presentable are still MIA. Dry shampoo, pants with zippers, and under-eye concealer could feasibly have ended up in a box labeled Random Shit or Assorted Items or <3. Turns out all my belongings are "random" or "assorted" in the right context.

Stumbling over to one unopened box (Shit <3), I rip off

the tape. Harrison can probably hear the tape-ripping noise, but I am *not* thinking about that.

True to its label, the box contains a bunch of shit. A couple of cookbooks (as if I ever cook), a palette of watercolors (it was a phase), and some kitchen towels (again—as if I ever cook). As I'm digging to the bottom to see if the box contains anything actually helpful, my hand catches on something metal, and I pull back my fingers, muttering a curse as I see a speck of blood forming.

I run to the kitchen to grab a paper towel and wrap it around my finger. I then realize I do not have paper towels, so instead I hold my finger under the sink and then run back to the box to wrap it in a kitchen towel. Holding my towel-wrapped hand to my chest, I gingerly sort through the mess until I find the culprit: a spiral-bound notebook, its spine twisted out of shape by nervous, busy fingers.

The notebook brings back memories more painful than the finger prick.

I'd planned to stay in Boston after graduating from college, but after what happened with a certain upstairs neighbor, I made the heartbroken decision to run home to Tampa. My parents were so concerned by my last-minute change of heart that they insisted I find a therapist. Which, to their credit, was good parenting. I needed therapy and probably had for a while.

At my first appointment, I wasn't quite ready to open up about everything. Unfazed, the therapist had recommended I do some journaling before our next appointment. Opening up in writing could be the first step, and then eventually, we could talk about it together. So I stopped at a drugstore on my way home and bought this bright-red, college-ruled, sale-section notebook.

Except instead of writing typical Dear Diary entries, I'd somehow ended up writing long, rambling letters to a specific person. Were they helpful? Yes, in getting me to talk to my therapist about my most painful memories. No, in getting me to talk to that specific person.

I flip to a random page toward the beginning.

Do you remember the day after exams ended our junior year, when me, you, Jo, and Macy were supposed to drive from campus to the Cape, but then Jo got sick and Macy stayed behind with her, so it was actually just us? And we'd hung out all the time 1:1 before that, but all of a sudden I got this idea in my head that this was the kind of day trip a couple would take, and then I fixated on that idea and couldn't stop thinking about it. And I kept telling myself it didn't count as a date because that wasn't the intention when we planned it, but then I got in my head about whether intention matters more than action when it comes to dating. To planning dates, that is. I still don't know the answer to that question, but I do know your car still has a stain on the floor of the passenger side where I dropped a chunk of the strawberry ice cream you bought me. And I do know I still think about the way it stormed on our drive home, when I kept telling you that you should let me drive because I'm the Floridian and therefore know how to drive in a tropical storm, which was a stupid argument because (a) it wasn't a tropical storm, (b) it was—is—a stick shift car, and I would've stalled out immediately, and (c) you were driving the same way you treat me, carefully and tenderly. You were driving like my life was on the line, which it wasn't, because really it was just a passing shower that lasted maybe twenty minutes, and also because you would never, ever let anything hurt me.

I wish I had treated you with the same care.

I wish I hadn't let my excessively tight vagina keep me from one of the best things in my life.

But that's how it works, isn't it? When I don't see an easy solution, I freeze. I clamp up. Mentally and vaginally.

If I had a second chance, I'd do better. But it's too late for that, I think.

I close the notebook, press it against my chest, and sink down onto the floor.

If I had a second chance, I'd do better.

Here's the thing about long-lost friendships: They're generally lost for a reason. When you're that close with someone, you don't just grow apart. You end up with hurt feelings and broken hearts. But does that mean they're broken beyond repair? Does that mean your feelings can't be replaced with newer ones? Nicer ones?

He said he didn't know. But that doesn't mean I can't try. I broke it, so I should be responsible for fixing it, right?

There's a voice in my head: *Do better, do better, do better.* It's the voice of a teenage girl who would be devastated to learn how things ended. It's the voice of a girl who would do anything to keep Harrison in her life. It's the voice of the girl who wrote this diary and knew Harrison would always mean the world to her.

Do better. I owe him that, at the very least.

I dig through the box to find a pen, then flip to the next blank page in the notebook and write, *How to Do Better.*

You should always start a list with something you've already done, so *Get my own apartment* tops the list. I cross it off.

Or maybe you should start a list with two completed tasks. Can't hurt.

Get a new job, I write.

I cross it off, then take a deep breath and keep writing before I can chicken out and end the list there.

Finish setting up the apartment within the next month.

Find a new therapist.

Go on a date. (Double dates don't count.)

Start doing pelvic floor therapy.

Go to the gynecologist.

Determined not to end the day without scheduling at least one or two or three of the appointments I need to make, I place the notebook next to my bed and continue to search for real pants.

***

BY THE FINAL TEN MINUTES of my first full shift at Jo Jo's, I've honed the following useful skills:

- How to use the espresso machine.
- How to operate the cash register.

I have also learned the following information:

- Rose's roommate uses shampoo intended for horses.
- Rose's film studies professor "isn't forward thinking enough," which is why Rose received a B- on her essay about why the next James Bond should be a woman.
- Rose has yet to meet a man in her two years of college who doesn't have navy bedding.

Not only are my feet aching, but my ears are also bleeding. Nonetheless, I am extremely determined to bond with Rose. Being friends with my other co-worker will make this job more fun, and besides—I'm not that much older than she is. There's opportunity here, and I need more friends so I'm not completely dependent on Jo. It's been four days since I moved to

Boston, but we've probably talked on the phone twelve times and seen each other six times. And it's not like I'm making any progress with other friendships, as evidenced by my painfully awkward double date last night, and none of the other friends I kept in touch with after college are still living in Boston. I'll eventually dive into my list of college acquaintances and reconnect with some people, but I need to have compelling answers to "How are you doing?"-type questions in advance of that happening.

Rose continues to monologue as she makes a double-shot espresso for a customer with enormous bags under his eyes and an equally enormous scowl. "God, living at home is the worst," she says. Now *that* is something we can bond over. "That's why I opted to take summer classes on campus and go ahead and move into my off-campus apartment."

"I hear that. I was living in my hometown until about a week ago. About a five-minute drive from my parents." I scan her face for some indication of understanding, but instead, she narrows her eyes at me.

"Why? You should *not* be that close to them. You're, like, an adult."

"Mmm," I say, wiping down a countertop. Rose makes great coffee, but her process involves a lot of splashing. "I'm still young. I get the struggle."

"Hm," Rose says, uninterested. "Last month when I went home for a couple weeks in between the spring semester and our summer classes, my mom caught me smoking weed in my bedroom. She was, like, it's okay, but don't do it in the house, please. But, like, where else was I supposed to do it? Plus, nobody gives a crap about my childhood bedroom anyway. It's basically become a nap room for my cat. There's fur *everywhere*. Like, I find it on *every* part of my body," she says, eyeing me meaningfully.

"When I was unpacking yesterday, I found my hairbrush in the box with all my books," I add.

"Plus, if I'm living at home, how am I supposed to date? You won't catch me dead on a date with anyone from my high school. That's embarrassing. But my mom doesn't get that, and she keeps trying to set me up with this guy, Noah. We weren't friends in high school, but our moms are in a book club or something, you know? Empty nester shit. Anyway, Noah is the kind of guy who wears graphic T-shirts, but, like, with sayings on them. He was wearing this shirt last time I saw him that said, 'Don't talk to me.' Like, okay, I wasn't planning on it!"

"I hate dating."

"So, when my mom tried to set us up on a date, I decided to freak him out. I showed up and pretended to be drunk so he wouldn't ask me on a second date. Like, I was tripping all over myself and stuff. But then he thought I was flirting with him, like, trying to fall so he'd have to catch me? Knight in shining armor, you know? And I'm like, dude, you're not my type. It's not going to happen. Besides, if I wanted to go out with him, I would've just asked him. I wouldn't have let my *mom* set us up. Gross."

"That's so relatable," I say as I set some mugs in the sink. "You've gotta just ask yourself, you know?"

She looks at me with doubt in her eyes. "Yeah? When's the last time you asked someone on a date?"

The correct answer is three years ago, when I'd been on two solid dates with a really nice guy, and, emboldened, I'd taken the initiative to ask him on a third date. He'd said yes, and we'd gone to dinner, and, still emboldened, I'd accepted his invite to come over, thinking maybe it had been long enough that my vaginismus had been miraculously cured. It hadn't been; and after he tried and failed to finger me, I immediately knew there wasn't going to be a fourth date, and I felt bad about it, and so somehow I'd ended up apologizing for not being able to be fingered, and then I'd given him an apologetic hand job. How's that for logic?

That's bad for logic, Cobalt says.

Key Lime chimes in. *Some might even call it illogical.*

Anyway. That was the last time I got that far—in number of dates and number of bases—with a guy. It was also the last time I took the initiative to ask a guy on a date. Rest in peace, Jason.

Rose raises her eyebrows at me, waiting for a response.

"Oh—uh . . . a couple months ago," I lie.

"Hmm. What about your last relationship?"

The correct answer is *never,* but if I want to bond with my co-worker, I have to remain cool in her eyes, so I say, "College."

"Geez," Rose says. "Forever ago."

"I'm literally five years out of college."

"That's over two times longer than I've been in college," she says. I scowl at her before she continues. "What was the deal? The college relationship?"

"Um? We met through . . . friends? And then we dated and now we're not?"

Rose looks at me expectantly. "Wow, you're so good at telling stories. What was his name?"

I blink rapidly. ". . . Arthur?"

"You're joking, right? Please tell me that's a joke. You did not actually date a guy named *Arthur.*"

The front door chimes as it opens, and Rose stops her questioning with a frustrated *humph.* I do not think I have made any meaningful inroads in our friendship, but I will remain committed.

A teenage boy approaches the counter, carrying a backpack so overstuffed that his entire body tilts forward toward the counter. He orders an iced tea lemonade, then sets the book he was carrying down on the counter to dig through his pocket for his wallet.

I nod at the book. "*The Handmaid's Tale*?"

He rolls his eyes. "Yeah. Summer homework. My parents are making me get it done early."

He hands me a wad of cash, and I start counting it and making change. "That's a favorite of mine. How'd you like it?"

"Boring. I read fifty pages and I'm going to google the rest." He puts his wallet back in his pocket.

"Maybe you should give it another chance," I suggest, returning his change. He deposits it in the tip jar, and I send out a word of thanks to his parents for teaching him well.

"Why?" he asks. "It's just a boring old book."

I offer him a lopsided smile. "You know, where I used to live, that book was banned. High schoolers weren't allowed to read it in class."

He narrows his eyes at me, an interested glint flickering in his expression. "Seriously?"

"Mmhmm," I hum. "It's banned in several states around the country, actually. There are quite a few people out there who don't want students like you to read it."

He places a hand on the book and slides it toward himself, as if he's making sure I don't take it from him. "Why?"

I put my hands on the counter and lean forward. "How about this. You read the rest of it. If you do, come back next week, and I'll give you a free iced tea lemonade."

He crosses his arms, sizing me up. "Make it a large."

"Fine. A large." I cross my arms, mirroring his posture. "If you read the whole book *and* tell me why you think it might be politically controversial, then you get your large drink."

He sticks out his hand, and we shake on it. "I'm Kurt, by the way," he says.

"And I'm Emma. I'll have your drink out in a minute," I say, and he nods, picking up his book and walking over to a table in the corner to set up shop.

Another customer walks up behind him, serious brown eyes

studying me from behind messy waves. His brows are furrowed, and his lips are pulled to the side.* He looks like he doesn't know why he's here, and I'm not sure why he is, either.

Rose appears next to me. "Hey, Harrison," she says. Her cheeks turn bright red, and she tucks her hair behind her ear.

Oh, fantastic.

"Hi, Rose," he says, clearing his throat. His eyes are still locked with mine.

She gestures vaguely in my direction. "This is Emma. She's new."

"Hi, Emma," he says at the same time I say, "Yes, I know Harrison."

Rose finally turns her attention away from Harrison and meets my eyes. "Jo already introduced you to our regulars?"

I blink, then look at Harrison, who also blinks. I blink again. "Yes?"

No one says anything.

"Hey, Rose?" I ask.

Rose waits a moment for me to say something, then says, "Yes, Emma?"

"I think it's time for your break," I say. Rose narrows her eyes at me. "Like, right now."

She opens her mouth to say something, then looks at Harrison, then looks back at me, then looks back at Harrison. Her eyes widen with realization, and she nods and walks away.

I turn around, clearing my throat. "Gonna have fun explaining that after you leave."

"You didn't need to do that," he says, putting his hands into his pockets and taking a deep breath. "I truly just came to get coffee."

* **Furrowed brows · Lips pulled to the side · Tense body** | *Emotional tell* | *Frequency: medium*
1. Hesitant.

"I haven't scared you away yet?"

"You almost did." He gives me a gentle smile, small crinkles forming around his eyes. "But Jo makes really good coffee. Didn't want to stop coming just because I'm afraid of awkward social interactions. Besides, I want to support—" He pauses. "Jo Jo's."

"Yes," I say. "Jo Jo's."

He stares at me blankly. The curtain to the back room rustles as Rose very obviously stands right out of sight, listening.

"Jo isn't here, though," I say. "So, you'll have to settle for my coffee."

Rose's muted voice comes from the direction of the curtains. "He likes my iced lattes better than Jo's."

I raise an eyebrow at Harrison, who shakes his head and mouths *No, I don't* before calling out in Rose's direction, "Rose, could I please have a small iced latte?"

Rose reappears and gets to work, seemingly having decided making Harrison's drink is more interesting than taking a break. Harrison hands me his card, and I attempt to make small talk because I am trying to Do Better.

"How was work today?" I ask, nodding at his scrubs. This time, they're green and covered in tiny illustrations of turtles and bunnies. Or, tortoises and hares, I suppose.

He hesitates, as if deciding whether he wants our relationship to be such that we engage in small talk. "Uh—good."

I hand his credit card back to him. "Kids of Jamaica Plain staying healthy?"

"Mostly." He nods, then grins. "I saw a patient today who got a Lego stuck in his nose for the third time this year."

A cackle escapes my mouth, and I cover it with a cough. "That sounds serious. How does that happen?"

"It happens when you stick a Lego up your nose," he says, deadpan.

This time, I fully release the cackle. "I bet you just love this kid, don't you?"

"Guilty," he says, a glimmer in his eyes.* He nods toward the table near the window where Kurt is sitting and lowers his voice. "I can tell how much you love working with kids. You're good at it. That was . . . that made me happy. To watch you in your element."

It hits me like a punch in the gut. I swallow, words caught in my mouth. "Well. You know. I don't teach anymore."

Harrison's lips start to push into a distinct "wh" shape, but he stops himself, as if deciding he doesn't actually want to know that much information about me. My feelings are hurt even though I wouldn't have wanted to answer.

"*Handmaid's Tale* is a good one," he says.

Before I can agree, Rose appears at my side and hands him the iced latte he ordered. He ordered a small, but it's a large. "I think so, too. I binged all of it in, like, two weeks," she says.

Harrison's eyes dart toward mine, and I bite my lip so hard I taste blood. I don't know whether I'm holding back a laugh at Rose's attempt to be included or a smile at the feeling of sharing a joke with Harrison, but the feeling in my mouth seems to extend to a gurgling in my stomach.

Before I can make a fool of myself (and create a health code violation) by starting to drool blood, I turn around to deliver Kurt's iced tea lemonade.

* **Crinkles around eyes · Left dimple · Lopsided smile** | *Facial expression* | *Frequency: medium*

1. Amused.

CHAPTER 6

When I called the pelvic floor therapist's office after work two days ago, I figured I would make an appointment a couple of weeks from now, and that would be that. What I didn't expect was to be told to come in in less than forty-eight hours. That's not enough time to mentally prepare. But that didn't seem like a valid excuse to not take the appointment, so here I am, still wearing my work clothes and still as afraid of pelvic floor therapy today as I was at age eighteen.

When I enter the office, I'm hit with the immediate sensation of zen. More of a forced zen than an actual zen, though, because the walls are painted puke green, and there is artwork (photographed *and* painted!) of misty mountains, and there are several dreamcatchers, and the speakers are playing what can only be described as meditation music. There's a lot of humming and sustained synthesizers.

But this is the best-reviewed practice in Boston (and also one of only three that accepted the shitty insurance I'm on now that I'm not teaching), so I take another step inside and take a deep *inhale* and *exhale* to quell the beating of my heart.

There's no one at the front desk, so I wander over to the seating area. Thirty seconds later, a woman's head pops out of a door in the hallway. She has big, frizzy hair and at least four piercings on each ear.

"Emma?" she asks, shooting me a smile so wide it might fall off her face.

"That's me," I say, unable to match her smile.

"I'll be with you in five! Feel free to take a seat and get comfortable. Excited to meet you."

The next five minutes bring neither comfort nor excitement. I would definitely rather stare at abstract paintings of mountains than illustrated diagrams of the female reproductive system, as I recall doing at the first pelvic floor therapy appointment nine-ish years ago, but I must be afraid of heights, because staring at the paintings is only resulting in profusely sweaty hands. Even the nice text from Jo (**Jo:** are you ready to make pelvic floor therapy your BITCH) doesn't slow my racing heart.

This is different, I remind myself. *This is not the same pelvic floor therapist. I'm older and braver and wiser and probably more desperate.*

Definitely more desperate, Key Lime chimes in from the back of my mind. When I don't respond, she clarifies. *Because you haven't been getting any.* I'm still silent. *Any dick.*

I left you at home, I finally say. *You weren't supposed to be here.*

We weren't supposed to be at pelvic floor therapy with you? says Cobalt. *That's our entire purpose.*

My heart rate increases by at least ten beats per minute. My hands are still shaking a few minutes later when the pelvic floor therapist reappears, but I hold steady as I fill out some basic medical paperwork. When I'm done, she leads me to an exam room with the same vibe as the waiting room. Equally green, equally zen.

"So," she says after washing her hands and plopping herself in a chair across from the table I'm sitting on, "I'm Kay."

"I'm Emma," I say. "But you knew that."

She cracks a smile. "So I did."

She can't be more than thirty-five. At the same time, she does have the aura of one of those women who couldn't age even if they tried. So really, she couldn't be more than forty. Max. Regardless, she feels like the kind of person I'd want to be friends with if she weren't about to stick her fingers up my vagina.

After answering some questions about my medical history, I tell her about when I got diagnosed at age eighteen and how I was so terrified after my first attempt at physical therapy, I never went back. And then suddenly nine years had passed.

"And how much has your doctor explained about vaginismus?" she asks, tilting her head as if studying me.

That implies I am currently seeing a gynecologist, which I certainly am not. Not yet, anyway. But I don't correct her. "Not much. I've done a little bit of independent research, but not as much as I should've, probably."

She nods her head. "So, let's start with some basic education, yeah? I like to make sure we're on the same page about what we're working with." I nod my agreement.

"Your vagina," she says, holding up a loose fist. She tilts it to the side so I can see she's made a tube with her fingers, then tilts it back up again. "This is how it normally is. Just chilling. Existing as it is."

She brings her other hand up, pointing with two fingers. "Now. Let's say this is a tampon." (I am not thinking about it as a tampon.) "When this tampon comes into contact with your vagina"—she places her two fingers just inside the opening of the hole, and I am still not picturing a tampon—"your vagina doesn't like that."

Your vagina hates *to see me coming,* Key Lime says.

Kay's fist tightens, closing the hole between her fingers. Her hand shakes a bit, rather than a consistent tightness, as if her muscles are fighting against some outside force. She removes her two fingers, and her fist gradually relaxes.

"Now here's the difference," she says, looking at me with raised eyebrows as if to impress upon me how important this is. "You don't have control over your vaginal muscles the way I have control over my fist."

"No kidding," I murmur.

Kay chuckles, and in a shocking turn of events, I find a stray chuckle escaping me as well.

"So why does this happen?" she says, grabbing a notebook and a pen from the desk. I expect her to draw the female reproductive system, but instead, she draws . . . a graph?

She labels the x-axis "psychological" and the y-axis "physical."

"Nobody knows exactly what causes vaginismus, partly because it's different for everyone. In the vast majority of cases, vaginismus is due to psychological causes. That could mean many things: past sexual trauma, lack of sex education, conservative religious teachings about sex, et cetera. On the other axis, we have physical causes. Sometimes, your body just doesn't want to cooperate. The muscles have learned one way to act, and now they don't know any other way to act. So, our goal," she says, handing me the pen, "is to figure out where you fall on this graph, and to make a plan accordingly."

I stare blankly at the pen.

Kay pulls the pen back. "That's okay. A lot of people don't know. Let's start here, though—have you had any negative experiences that might affect the way your body responds? Anything you feel comfortable telling me about?"

I shake my head. "Nothing comes to mind."

"Okay. Tell me about your sexual experience in general, then. Have you tried penetrative sex before?"

This feels like the kind of thing we should be talking about at girls' night with a glass of wine and a large pizza, but I force an answer out of my mouth. "Uh—no, I've never gotten that far. I let a guy try to finger me once when I was eighteen, and one time again when I was like twenty-four and thought maybe it had been long enough that things had, I don't know, solved themselves?"

Kay nods her head, jotting a note in my chart. "Okay—that's helpful for us to know. So it seems like the situation hasn't improved since you were diagnosed." She jots something else down. "And tell me about the sex education you received."

I snort. "You want to hear about the sex education I got in Florida public schools?"

"There it is," Kay says, cracking a smile. "We're getting somewhere."

"To be clear, I know how sex works," I say. I figured that out sometime in between Jacob Butler making an inappropriate hand gesture during gym class in fifth grade and learning about the human reproductive systems in ninth grade.

"And what were you taught about the female reproductive system? Do you feel like you have a good understanding of how your body works?"

". . . I think so?"

Thank god I was an English teacher and not a phys ed teacher.

"That's not uncommon," Kay says, offering me a weak smile. "Comprehensive sex education is important for so many reasons, and yet in so many places and communities, it's not prioritized. I can't tell you how many patients I've had who ended up with medical problems later in life—or who had medical problems they weren't able to recognize—because they weren't taught enough about their own bodies and about practicing safe sex."

She doesn't say it outright, but I'm aware of the implication: *I'm one of those patients.*

To kick off the next portion of the session, she guides me through a series of stretches I remember from my first pelvic floor therapy appointment back in the day. Deep breathing while I relax all my muscles. Sitting up and pulling my feet together, my knees splayed out. Propping myself up on my hands and knees and moving through cat-cow pose. Ten minutes later, my heart rate has certainly decreased, even if my vagina hasn't quite relaxed.

I'm feeling great until she tells me she's going to leave for a moment so I can get undressed from the waist down. I'm terrified, but I do it. Because I am here to Do Better. I am here because I have been given the gift of a second chance, and I am not going to waste this burst of motivation, even though I'd rather run pantsless into the street than continue this appointment.

Once I'm lying on the examination table with the white sheet covering my waist, Kay reenters the room. As she sits down in her little wheely chair and pulls on a pair of gloves, she explains pelvic floor therapy will also require getting the muscles used to contact. We're starting with a finger today, but she'd like me to start using dilators at home over the next couple of weeks to make sure I'm making progress in between appointments.

Ha, Key Lime says.

The thought of willingly sticking something up my vagina makes me more than a little squeamish, but then I remind myself there are a lot of important things I need to be able to stick up my vagina (like tampons!), and I tell myself to woman up, and by then I think I've missed a couple key sentences, because now Kay is rolling up to the exam table and asking if that all sounds okay, and I'm saying yes, and then I'm putting my knees up, and now my private parts feel cold.

"I'm going to very, very lightly apply pressure to the sides of the opening. Let me know if you need me to stop."

It's the strangest sensation in the world. I can feel the point of pressure where her gloved finger meets my entrance, but the reaction is deeper than that. It's like my entire core freezes, and I lose control of the muscles as they tighten, then tighten more, then relax when they can't keep tightening, and then tighten again. It sends a cramp shooting through my gut, but the feeling of not having control of my own body is worse than any pain.

"Okay—you're doing great. I know it feels horrible. But I want you to breathe with me. Can you do that?"

I nod.

"Inhale," she says, and we both inhale through our mouths.

"Exhale."

Inhale.

Exhale.

Inhale.

Exhale.

"Your muscles are calming down," Kay says. "Can you feel that?"

Not really.

"You control your breathing. You control your body. Focus on those pelvic floor muscles and imagine they're melting into the table."

Inhale.

Exhale.

In my mind, they heat up. They heat up like a ball of wax, melting as I channel more focus into the muscles. They spasm again, and I send more heat their way. They melt, and then seize up. And then I take a deep breath, and they melt again.

"How about now? How does that feel?"

"Better," I admit.

"I'm going to insert my finger, just up to the first joint. Is that okay?"

I nod. Her finger starts to move, and my muscles respond, freezing up, and everything goes cold again, and—

"Breathe. You've got this. You're in control."

Inhale.

Exhale.

Melt it down.

It hurts. It's uncomfortable. But I'm okay. And I am bigger than this pain.

"*Yes,*" Kay says. "Breathe through it. I'm going to stay here for a few minutes. Let's see if we can get your body to forget it's supposed to be freaked out, yeah?"

"I don't think I'm going to forget," I say, another cramp seizing my pelvic floor.

"How long have you lived in Boston?" Kay asks.

It's a total non sequitur, but I don't have the mental energy to unpack that. "A little less than a week. Well—I went to college here for four years, but then I moved home to Florida. And then I moved back last week."

"And how has that been so far?"

I huff a laugh, which has the unintended consequence of tightening my core, which makes my muscles seize up.

Inhale.

Exhale.

"Weird," I finally say. "And unexpected."

"Well, you're here, so I'd say you can add productive to that list. You did something hard."

We idly chat for another few minutes. I tell her about my new apartment; she tells me about the first apartment she lived in alone, a basement apartment infested with mice. (I am now afraid of mice.) I tell her about my favorite things to do in Tampa; she tells me about the trip she and her brother took to visit their grandmother in Clearwater last year. I tell her about the detective show I binged last month; she recommends a vampire show.

And five minutes later?

I have not forgotten about my cramping vagina.

But! It's bearable. And that's better than it was before.

Kay takes off her gloves, throwing them away. "You did great."

"Yeah, sure." I laugh. I can still feel a phantom finger inside of me.

Kay washes her hands, then wheels her chair back toward her desk, turning around to face me and crossing her legs.

"Do you have a partner?"

I snort. "Absolutely not."

"You could, you know," she says. "Plenty of people with vaginismus date. This doesn't have to stop you from doing anything."

"I'd say it's stopping me from doing a lot, actually." What am I going to do? Ask them if they want to stick an inch of their index finger inside of me?

"Sex can mean so many things that don't just include penetration."

"I know that," I say. Intellectually, I know that. Duh.

I also know that I've gone on dates with three different guys who made it clear that they want to have P in V sex, and then none of them went on another date with me. So, more complicated in practice, I suppose.

"Good," she says, eyeing me as if she doesn't believe me. (She probably shouldn't.) "I know we talked about this earlier, but just to clarify. Are you interested in men? Or people with penises?" she asks, and I nod. "Okay. So even with this pelvic floor therapy, it's likely your first time having penetrative sex will still be uncomfortable. The best way to combat that is by having your partner insert themself slowly, then waiting there while you do some breathing exercises and adjust your muscles. That will make more sense once we start using the dilators, but that's your preview of what we're looking at. I sometimes recommend partners help with the dilators as well. So, if you ever end up in a situation where you want to talk more about what vaginismus looks like with a partner, you let me know, and we'll talk through strategies."

I try to imagine it. *Hey, would you mind just goin' real slow? Yep, and now that you're in there, hold, please! I need a second to do some meditation. So, if you can just chill and not move—yep, don't even breathe—while I get adjusted, that would be super helpful. And if you feel my vagina cramping, no big deal, that's just me being in pain.*

Or better yet: *Yeah, these silicone penis-looking things? I stick them in my vagina! For physical therapy, not for pleasure. There's nothing sexy about it. That being said, want to help me out by sticking one inside of me? I'll even let you pick the one that's closest in size to your dick!*

"Whatever you're thinking right now," Kay says, "stop and take a deep breath."

Inhale.

Exhale.

"You're going to be okay," she says.

"Okay." My voice comes out mousy.

I might be okay, but I'm not okay to date. That much is clear.

Not that I was in a position to date anyone anyway. The only person I've ever had strong feelings for is barely even interested in me as a friend. But once I'm Doing Better. . . .

"Let's do this," I say. "Let's get my vagina adjusted."

Kay cracks a smile, and Key Lime and Cobalt salute in the background.

CHAPTER 7

Today marks day seven in Boston, and I think the universe is sending me a sign that I shouldn't be here. Specifically, the voices floating in through my open window. It's a beautiful, cool evening, so evidently *everyone* in the building has their windows open.

Emma: I stg something is going on in Harrison's apartment

Emma: Stephanie is mad about something. I can hear raised voices through the window

Jo responds immediately, in typical Jo fashion.

Jo: i know i cant hear it but i'm 99% sure theyre just having sex

Emma: I know I'm a virgin but I promise I can tell the difference between yells of anger and yells of ecstasy

Emma: Do you and Macy have raised-voice existential conversations about life choices while you're hooking up

Jo: i cannot believe you just referred to me making love to my partner as "hooking up"

"Oh, please," Stephanie says. They must've moved closer to the open window. "Grow up. Or better yet, grow a pair."

"That's immature." Harrison's voice isn't as loud as his girlfriend's, but it's plenty clear.

Emma: Stephanie just told him he needs to grow up

Jo: great. so do you. smh

Emma: Girl I'm being so serious right now this sounds like a serious argument

Emma: I think I should close my windows

Jo: DO NOT DO THAT

Jo: if you argue near an open window you lose your right to privacy.

"And you know what else?" Stephanie says. I can hear stomping above my head. "It isn't healthy for you—" The words become garbled for a few moments before she stomps back toward the window. "—entirely your responsibility."

"I don't have any siblings."

"Even still. Your mom can't be your only priority."

Emma: she's complaining about Harrison's mom being his only priority

Jo: tea

Two sets of footsteps make their way farther into the apartment, and the argument becomes difficult to hear. I only catch a few words: *Priority. Thoughtless. Emotionally unavailable.*

Then:

Emma.

I jump up and run to the window, shamelessly pressing my ear to the screen. A cool breeze blows dust directly into my eyeball.

Harrison's voice is softer, but a few words sneak through. *Something something* "friends" *something something* "college" *something something* "it's complicated."

Emma: THEY'RE TALKING ABOUT ME

Jo: ?????????

"You have to make a choice!" Stephanie half shouts. I can hear heated emotion in her voice.

"I want you to be happy!" Harrison says. "I just want everyone to be happy."

"Harrison," she says, quieter now. "You're being insane."

More footsteps, and the voices become muffled again.

Emma: she says he's insane

Jo: !!!!????

Emma: I know. Idk what she means though

Emma: I can't hear all of the conversation

Something something "choice" *something something* (my face is pressed so hard against the screen I can feel the indents of tiny gridlines forming on my face) *something something* "Is this really the decision you want to make?"

"I have made my choice, Stephanie. Really."

Her laugh floats all the way down to my ear. "Yeah, apparently."

Emma: He made a decision that she's pissed about

Jo: girlllll

There are footsteps, and then I can't hear anything else except mumbles through my ceiling.

That goes on for another five minutes, and I think the conversation may have calmed down or switched directions, but then a door slams. Stephanie exits our building, and I lurch back into the shadows as she gets into her car and drives away.

I swear she makes eye contact with me as she pulls out of her parking spot, but I must be imagining it.

Emma: Update she left

Emma: What do I do

Jo: nothing dumbass

I don't respond.

Jo: i stg

Jo: you're about to do something dumb arent you

Do better. Do better. Do better.

I open my text thread with Harrison and type out a message.

Emma: Do you need wine

Emma: Because I have TWO bottles of $6 wine in my kitchen right now and I would be happy to donate them to the cause

I may not be responsible for whatever just happened upstairs, but if my goal is to generally Do Better and make him feel less upset or angry or depressed or whatever he is, then that should be applicable in all situations, right? Because the thought of him sitting upstairs alone and probably sad makes me want to—

Well, it makes me want to send poorly thought-out text messages about a situation I have absolutely no business being involved in.

Harrison: bring both please

To avoid screaming, I instead channel my energy into jumping up and down on my air mattress, which is a rather lackluster experience because it immediately starts losing air, and I'm essentially just jumping up and down on solid linoleum flooring, and then I get embarrassed about how strongly I'm reacting to a three-word text, and so I take a deep breath and slowly walk toward the kitchen with a bland expression on my face, acting cool, calm, and collected like the mature adult I am.

I am upstairs with two bottles of wine within sixty seconds.

One of my most endearing (annoying? No, endearing) traits in college was that I always used to knock on Harrison's door with the classic little jingle: *buh buh buhbuh buh.* I only give it a second of thought before raising my hand to the door. *Buh buh buhbuh buh.*

Harrison opens within a few seconds. There's a tight look on his face, his jaw tense, and his eyes covered in spectacles he didn't wear in college, which makes me feel a little bit ill because you should know things about your friends like whether they wear glasses, except we're not friends anymore because I didn't speak to him for five years, so I didn't know he had any vision problems.

"Hey," he says, his voice raspy in a way that is undeniably sexy, in a totally objective sense—

No. You're here to be a good friend. Your mind is impenetrable. Just like your vagina.

Ha, Cobalt says in the back of my mind.

At the same moment, I hold out both wine bottles and say

"Enjoy!" while Harrison opens the door to let me inside. We both freeze, and his ears immediately turn pink.*

"Oh," I say. "*Oh.*"

"Oh, I thought—" he says, blinking rapidly. "Yes, thank you for dropping off the wine."

Mr. Silent Treatment wanted to drink *with* me? Is my attempt to Do Better actually working?

He holds out his hands for the wine, and I jerk the bottles out of his reach. "Absolutely not. You're not getting drunk alone."

"I certainly can if I want to," he says. "I'm thrilled about the prospect of drinking alone."

He was the one who opened the door to me first, and we both know it, so I chuckle, and the tiniest hint of a dimple appears in response. I raise the bottles above my head, and he raises an eyebrow, as if to say, *You know I'm taller than you, right?*

"Fine," he says, turning around and walking through the door. He doesn't look back, but I follow him inside anyway, closing the door behind me.

I reinforce my impenetrable mental blockade as I take in his Extremely Adult Apartment. It's filled with dark wood furniture—a small dining table, a matching coffee table and TV stand, and oh, the bookshelves!—and there's a small sectional with startlingly plush-looking cushions covered in a deep navy fabric. There are tasteful pops of color—a maroon rug covers a good chunk of the living room, and he has off-white throw pillows with thin decorative stripes stitched in forest green. And, as if everything else weren't already adult

* **Pink ears** | *Physical reaction* | *Frequency: high*

1. Embarrassment.
2. May be embarrassed by own actions or others' actions.

enough, there's framed artwork (yes, frames—not posters) hanging on every wall.

I make a mental note to never invite Harrison into my apartment. *Certainly* not until I get a real bed.

Or, like, a sofa. Or whatever.

"So, uh . . . ," I say, stumbling through my mental Rolodex of words, "is everything okay?"

It takes him a moment to answer, because he gets distracted as he tries to use a corkscrew on a screw-off top. Apparently, we are in different wine-purchasing brackets.

"Did she look mad when she left?" he asks.

I debate lying, but if he's asking, he must already assume that I saw her. "Yeah, she did. Maybe I was just projecting because of all the arguing, but she looked tense."

Harrison's brows furrow. "Arguing?"

"Were you two not arguing about something?"

His brows furrow even more. "You gathered that just from her speed walking to her car?"

"Oh—uh . . ." I nod down toward the window. "Open windows. Plus, the floors aren't super soundproof. Can't hear individual words but can definitely tell a muffled angry tone from a muffled normal tone."

"Oh," he says, considering. After a few moments of thought, he shakes it off and opens a cabinet door.

When he turns back around, he's holding two mugs, and my heart breaks a little bit.

Back when we were in college, we exclusively drank out of mugs. Wine, water, coffee, tea, juice, cocktails. Everything. Once we moved off campus, Jo and I had a tiny kitchen with extremely limited shelf space, and wineglasses weren't a priority item. Harrison's kitchen was larger than ours, and I'm sure he could've afforded wineglasses, but when I was over, it was always mugs, for all liquids, for all hours of the day. His designated mug was navy blue, and when you put a hot liquid in it, ocean waves appeared. My designated mug at his apartment said *Someone in Jamaica Plain loves you!*, which we found at a thrift store. We didn't know anyone who lived in Jamaica Plain at the time, since that was on the other side of Boston, but coincidentally, that's where we both now live.

He puts the mugs down on the counter. One is a brand-new-looking piece that almost certainly matches the rest of his dinnerware. The other is a beat-up piece of junk that, in faded letters, reads *Someone in Jamaica Plain loves you!*

He pours wine into both mugs as if by habit. As if he isn't even aware of what he's doing, because it's so ingrained. That, maybe, is the most painful part of this moment.

He's just finished pouring the second glass when a shrill, squeaking noise comes from the bedroom.

I huff a laugh. "That sounds like a guinea pig."

He glances up at me as he screws the top back on the bottle. "It is."

"What?" I study his face for signs of a joke. "I was kidding."

"I'm not kidding," he says. "That's Raya."

I blink. "What is that?"

"Ra-ya," he says, enunciating every syllable. "My gui-nea pig."

"Holy shit." I blink again. "You're not joking. I need to meet her. Immediately."

Harrison doesn't argue, and a minute later, he's back with the guinea pig. She's wrapped in a towel and cradled in his arms as if this small rodent is his baby, except instead of soft, chubby cheeks, she has furry, chubby cheeks and gray and white splotches all over her quivering body.

"You have to be gentle," he says. "She likes being cuddled, but don't squeeze her too tight or she'll get hurt. And make sure you keep the towel wrapped around her. It makes her feel safe."

"Did she tell you all of that?"

Harrison's side-eye makes me think his genuine answer is *yes*, but nonetheless, he hands me the guinea pig.

"Hi, baby!" I say, curling my arms around her minuscule body. She squeaks in response, her beady black eyes staring up at me with a trusting expression. I look at Harrison with wide eyes. "I would die for her."

Harrison exhales a laugh, leaning forward and gripping the counter, arms spread wide. "I'm ordering a pizza."

"For Raya?"

"I was thinking for humans, but maybe I'll give her a baby carrot as a treat."

I give him my best puppy dog look, and Raya squeaks. "No pizza for the precious little baby?"

He rolls his eyes as he orders on his phone, then picks up both mugs and leads me into the living room. I sit on the far end of the couch, and he settles onto the other side, crossing his right ankle over his left knee and leaning against the armrest so he's facing me.

The couch is suddenly feeling like more of a love seat. Apparently, I've reverted to my middle school self, and I can't be within three feet of a boy without being terrified of cooties. He adjusts his glasses, and now I am trying extremely hard not to wonder whether Harrison wears glasses while he's *thumpthumpthump*ing. That's none of my *thump*ing business.

I kick off my sandals and pull my knees to my chest, settling in against the armrest so I'm also facing him. I press Raya to my chest and give her a quick kiss on the head.

Harrison and I stare at each other for a moment and then both take a large sip of wine.

I'm about to suggest he pick a movie to put on, but somehow what comes out of my mouth is, "Glasses?"

He adjusts them, then runs a finger through his hair, combing the waves out of his face. "They're new. I'm not sure how I feel about them yet. But wearing contacts every day has been making my eyes hurt."

My cheeks heat. "You look . . ." *Sexy,* my brain supplies. I pause, gathering my thoughts. "You look like an adult."

I take another large sip of wine.

He follows suit, sipping as he studies me. "One of the side effects of aging."

We both take another sip of wine.

"Do you want to talk about it?"

He raises an eyebrow. "Aging?"

"As much as I love getting drunk and talking about mortality, I meant your girlfriend storming out of your apartment."

"Ah, yes." He takes another long sip of wine. "That."

He's rolling his eyes and sipping his wine like everything is good and fine and casual, but it has to be more complicated than that. I know next to nothing about his relationship with Stephanie, but fights are never easy.

"Seriously, would it help to talk about it?" I ask.

He opens his mouth to speak, then closes it and looks at me with an assessing expression. Finally, he says, "I don't think that's a conversation we should have."

Oh.

I get it. After what happened five years ago, he doesn't know how to react to my sudden reappearance. He has other friends he probably talks to about this. Friends he actually trusts, and friends who know about everything that's happened in his life in the last five years. I'm certainly not one of those friends, so where does that leave us?

Friends with Limitations, perhaps.

Harrison studies me, lips pulled to the side. "It's just . . . complicated. With Stephanie."

"Yeah. It's fine. I get it." Harrison doesn't look convinced, but I don't allow him to continue with an explanation that would undoubtedly hurt my feelings. "How about we put on a movie and drink several mugs of wine?"

Harrison doesn't react immediately, as if it takes him a moment to decide what the appropriate response should be. And then—

He smiles.

I was resigned to never seeing those dimples again, and to not only see them, but to be the cause of them? Well, feelings never fade entirely, obviously.

We spend the next fifteen minutes scrolling through movies, both extending olive branches in the form of commentary. Harrison says he still has never made it past the first five minutes of *Up*. I tell him about how my parents and I rewatched every Jurassic Park movie last summer, which then inspired my mom and I to have a Jeff Goldblum movie marathon.

Our conversation grinds to a halt when *Pride & Prejudice* pops up.

We both turn our heads, gazes clashing. He remembers as well as I do—the pink tinge of his ears tells me so.

It was a Wednesday. My twenty-first birthday. We had plans to go out and celebrate the following weekend, but Harrison worked hard to get his homework done in advance so he could spend Wednesday night with me. We went to a shitty liquor store and bought a shitty double bottle of wine, and then we watched *Pride & Prejudice*—2005 version, of course. By the time we'd finished, we were both drunk and crying into our mugs of Barefoot Moscato. (*Someone in Jamaica Plain loves you!*) I don't remember who was clinging to whom, but we were definitely curled up against each other all night, each one pretending we weren't as drunk and emotional as we actually were.

He got me a copy of *Emma* by Jane Austen as a birthday gift that year. A special edition, with beautiful embroidered flowers on the cover and the title written in curly, metallic letters. He'd written an inscription on the inside cover. *Emma, for Emma, from Harrison, for your twenty-first birthday. I cannot make speeches, Emma . . .* I'd been confused about his choice of words until I'd actually read the book a year later, months after Harrison and I were no longer talking. "I cannot make speeches, Emma," the full quote read. "If I loved you less, I might be able to talk about it more."

Harrison only looks away from me when he's fully standing and walking to the door, which is how I realize I completely blocked out the sound of the doorbell in my mental haze.

When he sets the pizza down on his coffee table, I open it immediately. It's half pepperoni and half pineapple, and a huge smile splits my face. I look over at him as he's settling back on the couch, and he freezes, taken aback.

"You got me Hawaiian?" I ask.

"Yeah?"

"Just like old times," I prompt. And the mugs, and the movie. And these feelings I'm having. "Except we used to get all Hawaiian pizza. Have your tastes changed?"

He huffs a laugh. "Is now a good time to reveal that I don't actually like Hawaiian pizza?"

I drop both the pizza box lid and my jaw. "You're joking."

"Nope."

"Why did you eat it so much with me?"

He raises a single eyebrow. "Because you liked it?"

It's stupid, maybe, but my first thought is that he must not care enough about me anymore to eat Hawaiian pizza.

I clear my throat, and he does, too.

"Well," I say, nodding at the TV screen, "are you hitting play or what?"

He stares at the screen, Keira Knightley looking over her shoulder in the freeze-frame. I can see his thumb tracing circles around the play button on the remote, and finally, he hits play.

And that's how, two hours later, we end up crumpled on the couch in a tipsy, glossy-eyed trance as Keira Knightley and Matthew Macfadyen meet in a field. My emotions are dangerously heightened, partially because of the movie, but also partly because Raya is now wrapped up in a bundle across Harrison's chest.

"I cannot believe I agreed to put this on," Harrison whispers. "I'm going to be emotionally hungover at work tomorrow. This is too much for my fragile heart." If I couldn't hear the laughter in his voice, I'd be concerned he actually means it, seeing as he just fought with his girlfriend and therefore would be completely justified in having a fragile heart.

"Shut up, you didn't even remotely argue with me."

"I should've." Harrison *hmphs* and slumps down on the couch. Raya gives an empathetic squeal.

"Be honest," I whisper. "Do you have a crush on Keira Knightley?"

"Do you not?" he asks, and I giggle in response. "Stop laughing at me," he says, still not looking at me.

"Stop pretending you're not a hopeless romantic," I counter.

This finally seems to grab his attention, and he looks over at me, his eyes wide and glassy from a combination of tears and intoxication. "I don't think I've ever pretended not to be both hopeless and a romantic." The serious, earnest tone of his voice catches me by surprise. So does the dark, dark brown of his eyes as they stare directly into mine with a focus that makes me forget Darcy is about to deliver one of the most iconic lines of the movie.

Harrison looks down at Raya, imitating Darcy. "I love—I love—I love you," he tells her. She chirps in response, and I feel my soul leave my body and float off into the ether.

Much like Darcy, I am suddenly feeling bewitched, body and soul.

Impenetrable. My mind is impenetrable. I am here to redeem myself and reestablish a long-lost friendship, and that is all.

"Oh," is all I can think to say, even though what I really want to be saying is, *Can we do this again tomorrow, and also the night after that? If you agreed to watch this with me, does that mean you don't hate me anymore?*

When the movie ends, Harrison leans forward to grab the remote and hit the home button. We stare at the scrolling purple cityscape without speaking.

Out of the corner of my eye, I see Harrison's shoulders move up and then slowly back down. Everything about him—his expression, his posture, his wrinkled clothes, his crooked glasses—screams *weary.* I have an unbearably strong urge to wrap him up in my arms and beg him to tell me what's wrong, but the problem is that I *do* know what's wrong. Some of it, anyway.

"Harrison," I whisper. "Why are you being nice to me? Why did you let me into your apartment?"

He looks up at me, and I pause at the expression on his face. Wide eyes, furrowed brows, lips pulled to the side.*

There's a single tear falling down his left cheek.

"Emma, I—"

"No," I say, closing my eyes and holding up my hands, heartbroken by the emotions I can see on his face. I came here to help, and all I did was hurt. "No—I'm sorry. That's a weird question. You don't need to explain yourself."

"No. I—I didn't want to be alone." He pauses, staring at our empty wine mugs on the coffee table. "Hard night."

I realize I'm the person he's *not alone* with because I am physically the closest to him and also because I forced my way into his apartment, but I'm flattered anyway. "I'm sorry it's a hard night," I say. "I hope I didn't make it harder."

He laughs, then looks surprised at himself for laughing. He clears his throat.

"What?" I ask, prompting him.

His eyes slide toward mine. "Em," he says, rolling his eyes as

* **Wide eyes · Furrowed brows · Lips pulled to the side** | *Facial expression* | *Frequency: low*

1. Emotional distress.

if I'm being ridiculous. "You always make things harder for me."

My throat constricts. "I'm trying to do better."

He stares at the wall as if it contains all of life's secrets. My words don't seem to be registering.

"Are you okay?" I ask.

"I don't know about okay," he tells the wall, "but I am single."

I look at the wall for further explanation. "What?" I ask it.

The wall doesn't respond, but Harrison does. "Stephanie isn't coming back. It's my own doing, and so I need to be able to live with that, but I really didn't want to sit here and be alone."

No, my mind screams. *No, not possible.* Twenty-seven-year-old Harrison doesn't break up with girlfriends. He has his life together, and it's perfect, with the perfect job and the perfect apartment and the perfect girl who adores him. He's not *single.*

Harrison's eyes slide to me again. Raya squeaks in his arms. "You good over there?"

I open my mouth to speak, but a squeak extremely similar to Raya's comes out instead. Harrison narrows his eyes in concern, and I clear my throat. "I don't understand. You broke up with Stephanie? Why would you do that?"

He gapes at me, as if shocked that I would dare to ask the question that directly. It's a full twenty seconds before he responds, and I feel more emotion bubbling up in my angry, hot cauldron of a stomach with every second. "I d—"

"Yeah," I snap, frustrated for reasons that are unbeknownst to me. "You don't think that's a conversation we should have. Got it."

He pulls his lips together in a thin line, and I feel like someone has punched me, my body now too off-kilter to draw a breath. *This is my fault,* my body screams. I can feel it in my bones. *I don't know how, but it is. It's my fault.*

Harrison opens his mouth to say something, but I keep going because maybe Doing Better also means taking a step back when it's clear you're doing more harm than good. "Please, let me say something, and then I swear I won't bother you anymore."

Harrison studies me, then nods his head for me to continue. *Emotional distress* has morphed into *morbid curiosity.*

"Look, I am so, so sorry for ruining what was already a shitty night for you." Harrison's eyes soften as soon as I start talking. "I'm sorry for forcing you to let me in, and also for making you watch a movie I knew would make you cry, and, apparently, for making you eat Hawaiian pizza for four years of college. I'm so sorry I make everything hard for you, but you *have* to understand I couldn't have lived with myself if I hadn't at least tried to make things right with you. Maybe you don't believe me, which would be completely justified, but I have spent the last five years imagining what it would be like to have a second chance with you, and I never thought I'd have the chance—or the guts, frankly—to turn that into reality. So even if you still hate me, which, again, would be justified, please, *please* believe me: I really fucking *missed* you."

Glassy eyes, tense body. As if he's afraid to move, because if he lets his chest expand to take a full breath, his heart might explode. "Containment" is probably the right word to describe this, the way his lips are pursed shut and his jaw is clenched. Another word to describe this might be "heartbreak."*

"And I will continue to miss you after this, but that's my problem, not yours," I whisper. And before he can say anything, I let myself out of the apartment.

* **Glassy eyes · Tense body · Bated breath** | *Emotional tell* | *Frequency: low*

1. Contained heartbreak.

CHAPTER 8

When Kurt returns to Jo Jo's, I can tell from the look on his face that I'm about to make him a large iced tea lemonade.

He tosses *The Handmaid's Tale* on the counter in front of me. "You were right," he says. His voice cracks on the word "right."

"Would you like your drink for here or to go?" I ask, grinning.

"Here," he says, and I grab a large glass and fill it with ice.

"So, tell me what you thought." That's how I used to start reading discussions with my students. An open-ended question for hopefully unfiltered results. *What were your initial impressions?*

"Don't put too much ice in there," Kurt says, eyeing the glass. I roll my eyes at him but dump out some of the ice. "I just . . . can't believe they treat women that way." He eyes me meaningfully. "They treat them like they're *worthless.*"

"How so?" I pour some lemonade into the glass.

Kurt tilts his head, pondering. "Well, actually, I guess they don't think they're worthless. I guess they think they're only good for one thing. But only if they give up control of it." His eyes widen. "Or maybe *because* they were only good for one thing, they couldn't have control over that one thing."

I nod, pouring in the tea. "Okay, and why do you think some people want this book banned?"

Kurt stares at the drink as I drop in a metal straw and stir the liquids together. He sticks out his hand to grab it, but I raise my eyebrows and nod, prompting him to answer me first.

He sighs loudly, then stares at the ceiling, thinking. "I think . . . the idea of the government controlling women's bodies doesn't feel unfamiliar in America."

"Impressive, Kurt," I say, handing him his drink. "You can analyze books. And you read the news."

"My girlfriend taught me all about this. She cares a lot about this stuff. Politics stuff." He takes a sip of the drink and immediately looks five times more alert. "I told her what you said about it being banned and that she should read the book. Also, thank you for the drink."

Recommending the book to his girlfriend after I encouraged him to finish it is probably the highest compliment I've ever received, even though it was technically his teacher who gave him this assignment. I'll take partial credit anyway.

There's no one in line behind him, and Rose is completely engrossed in her phone, so I allow my teacher instincts to come to the surface.

"Do you want another book rec?" I ask him.

He looks at me with interest. "Another banned book?"

I rack my brain. I wish I didn't have an internal list of all banned books, but unfortunately, I do. The ones banned in Florida, anyway.

"Okay, Kurt," I say. "You wanna try some Kurt Vonnegut?"

"Nice name," he says, nodding.

"You have a library card?" I ask, and he nods. "Go check out *Slaughterhouse-Five.*"

Kurt salutes me, which is oddly appropriate for the content matter, although he doesn't know it yet. "Can I bring my girlfriend to discuss it next time?"

"I think you've reached your limit on free drinks, but yes, feel free to bring her and any friends you want. It's a great book. Crass at times, but really raw. And funny."

"Maybe they'll give me extra credit if I write two essays for summer reading instead of one," he says. What a scholar.

"Go for it. Let me know when you've finished it, and we'll discuss."

He nods, then walks to a table on the other side of the café and settles in with his laptop.

"You can take the teacher out of the classroom, but you can't take the teacher out of the teacher," Rose says from behind me.

I turn toward her, squinting. "Or something like that."

"Why aren't you teaching anymore?" she asks.

"I didn't like it," I say simply. To the point and honest, even if it's not the whole truth. Rose looks skeptical, so I continue before she can ask me questions that make me feel worthless. "And Jo and I are best friends from college, so I—"

"I KNEW it," Rose yelps. "You *are* a nepo baby."

Kurt looks up from his table and smirks at me. I feel oddly embarrassed.

"Did you even have to interview for this job?" Rose hisses, eyes narrowed.

"No, I—"

"I KNEW IT," Rose yelps again. "You take this job too seriously."

"Isn't that the opposite of how a nepo baby would work?"

"Not if you have a personal investment and need to prove something," Kurt says from across the room.

"Write your essay, Kurt," I yell. He rolls his eyes at me (Rose does, too) and starts typing again.

"Girl," Rose says, "you're obviously super invested in this job. I know you feel like you need to support your nepo parent—"

"She's my friend—"

"—which, fair enough, because she oozes anxiety every time she comes to work, but you can't let capitalism rule your life. Put a little less effort into this job in the future. You don't need to be expending extra effort to bond with customers."

Kurt opens his mouth, and I look pointedly at his laptop. He rolls his eyes again.

"Noted," I say.

"And for the love of god, stop looking like you're ready to jump into action at any second. You can breathe when a customer isn't waiting to be served."

That actually does seem like sound advice, and I nod my head in agreement.

"What are you doing next Friday?" she asks.

"Uh—"

"Don't tell me," Rose says, holding up a hand. "If you say you're not doing anything, it'll be depressing."

I say nothing.

"My roommates and I are hosting a party. You're coming."

"I don't know if college house parties are really my scene." I haven't been to a house party in . . . four years? Five? My roommates and I hosted one ill-fated party when we all moved in (pre-marriage, pre-babies). The night ended with roommates two and three throwing up, one in our shared bathroom and one in our kitchen sink, and roommate one (me) and roommate four holding back the hair of the respective sick roommates. It took the entirety of the next day to return our home to an acceptable state of cleanliness, which was still less clean than it had been pre-party. I don't think our carpeting ever fully recovered, and so I vowed to never live in a place with carpeting ever again. Only rugs for this girl.

"Oh, please. You're not my only old friend. It'll be fun. Bring a friend!" Her eyes widen mischievously. "Oh my god. Bring a *date.* Please."

"I don't think house parties are the kind of thing you bring dates to."

She rolls her eyes. "What do you know about house party etiquette?"

Fair enough. "I'll think about it."

She grabs my phone and plugs the date into my calendar. "Your calendar is empty. That's embarrassing. Do you need more friends?"

"I'm working on it," I say, which is mostly true, but Rose rolls her eyes anyway.

Except working on it isn't going well, and I haven't spoken to Harrison in three days since I word-vomited and ran away. I kept hoping he would appear at Jo Jo's on his way to work today, but no such luck. He's typically an afternoon customer, and I have the morning shift.

Maybe with time, I'll be able to swallow my pride and go upstairs to work things out and at least be Acquaintances with Limitations, even if I've permanently lost my Friends with Limitations status. But for now, I'll give him space, and I'll keep working on Doing Better.

CHAPTER 9

I thought basement apartments were supposed to be cool, since hot air rises, right? So when the landlord told me the apartment didn't have AC, I was like—yeah. Cool. No problem. That's standard for Boston. But apparently hot air rising doesn't make much of a difference in the dead of summer, and I am now regretting all my life choices.

Because I am a rational human being, I prefer not to drink hot coffee when the air is eighty-six degrees with 80 percent humidity at seven-thirty in the morning. That's insane. But I am also a lazy human being, so I'm not going to walk to work to get iced coffee just to walk back to work three hours later when today's shift starts. Instead, I brew a pot of hot coffee and put it in the fridge until it's cold enough to add ice.

This is week two in Boston, and now that half of my boxes have been unpacked and recycled, I'm noticing new things about the apartment. And by "things," what I mostly mean is "problems." This morning, my new hyper-fixation is on the small window above my bed. Because the house is on a hill, the majority of my studio is above ground, meaning I have an actual window on the other side of the apartment. My bed, however, sits in the back corner, and there's a window way up toward the ceiling looking out onto . . . the dirt.

The window is disgusting after seemingly being neglected for years. There's a clump of weeds in front of it, but I can tell even from the inside that if I scraped away some of the dirt, cleaned the window, and trimmed everything back, I'd actually have some natural light in this half of the apartment, and I also might be able to see the flower bed in front of the weeds.

Because I have at least half an hour until my coffee is cold enough, and because my apartment is so hot I can't possibly imagine being outside is worse, I put on a tattered pair of pajama shorts, a tattered T-shirt, and a *not* tattered Red Sox cap Jo bought me as a welcome gift, then make my way outside.

Careful to avoid stepping on any flowers, I hop to the back of the garden. The weeds are quite a bit larger and scragglier than I expected, but I use my scissors (my makeshift garden shears) and my cooking spoon (my makeshift shovel) to part the vines enough for me to scramble through and access my window. The bushes and weeds come up to roughly my mid-thighs, and when I crouch down to sit next to my window, I'm mostly hidden.

Unfortunately, I am now covered in dirt and twigs.

"Emma . . . ?"

I sit up straight, my head popping up above the foliage.

Harrison stands in the grass, crinkles around his eyes.* The expression sends a burst of glitter through my brain. *Whoosh.* Glitter bomb.

"Hi," I say, clearing my throat. "Long time no see." It's been

* **Crinkles around eyes · Left dimple · Lopsided smile** | *Facial expression* | *Frequency: medium*

1. Amused.

eighty-one hours since I left his apartment in tears. But who's counting?

He stares at me for a moment with faint amusement before asking, "Dare I ask what you're doing?"

I hold up my large spoon. "Gardening."

He clearly doesn't know how to respond, so he doesn't. Instead, he brings an iced coffee up to his mouth and takes a sip, still staring at the bush with a confused expression.

He's holding a second iced coffee in his other hand, and before I have time to ask why, he jumps over the flower bed, then sits down with his back leaning up against the wall and hands me the second coffee.

"Our building doesn't have AC units," he explains, taking another sip of his coffee, "so when it's this hot, I always get iced coffee in the morning before work. Figured you'd need one, too."

I blink at him.

"Can't have you going about your morning uncaffeinated," he adds.

I blink again, and my jaw goes slack. His dimple appears.

"You don't hate me," I say.

He stretches his legs out, slotting them between plants. "I told you. I never hated you."

"You did hate pineapple pizza, though."

Another dimple.

"You bought me coffee," I say. Another statement.

"I did."

"What's your Venmo again?"

"No."

"Yes," I say, reaching out my hand as if to grab it. I make the *gimme* hand motion.

Harrison reaches out, grabs my hand, and then plops it back onto my lap, giving it a pat.

Every ounce of blood in my entire body rushes to my hand.

Or my head. Or maybe to my reproductive system. Regardless, there's a lot of blood moving around, and I experience a moment of dizziness. Even as I force myself back to reality, there's a ringing in my ears.

"So . . ." I say, "I didn't ruin everything?"

"No," he says quietly. "You didn't. Any ruination that's occurred in my life in the last few days has been entirely my own doing."

"So what does that mean . . . for us?" I ask hesitantly.

"It means I hope we can be friendly." He takes a long sip of coffee, then shoots me a half smile. "On a trial basis."

Friendly on a trial basis. Got it. Not great, but I can work with that.

"What made you change your mind?" I ask.

"You looked pretty ridiculous sitting in the dirt," he says. "Hard to be mad at someone who looks that pitiful."

I reach out and flick his arm, and he pulls away from me, laughing.

"It was something you said, actually," he says, growing more serious. "That you'd been thinking for the last five years about what it would be like to have a second chance," he continues. "That's what you told me. And, well, I have, too."

"You have?" The question comes out as more of a desperate whimper.

"How could I not? So, if it's taken up so much of both of our brain space, maybe we just need to figure it out. Especially now that we're neighbors, right? Let's get some . . . closure."

Oh.

Closure is what you get before you leave someone. That's not what you get at the beginning of a rekindled friendship.

"Right," I say, taking a forced sip of coffee. "Yeah, I just really need closure, and we shouldn't pass up the opportunity to get that."

"Exactly," he says confidently.

Unfortunately, what I want is a little more than closure.

I want to Do Better and regain the most meaningful friendship I've ever had. I want to make sure he doesn't think I'm an asshole, and I want to make sure he knows I care about him. I want him to visit me at work simply because he wants to see me. I want to return the favor and bring him iced coffee when it's hot and hot coffee when it's icy. I want to lie on his couch and watch movies without being hyperaware of every movement and every word, desperate to interpret his feelings.

And if we're being honest, I still, even after five years, want a little more. But even if he was interested, I have a lot to figure out first.

So, if closure with Harrison is the best I can get, so be it. This is the best possible outcome, and because I'm a strong young woman, I'm happy about that. I *will* be happy about that. I will take the wins I can get, and I will applaud myself. Go, Emma! You're a rock star! You may be clueless and hopeless and single, but at least you're (trying to be) stronger and more independent!

There's a quiet moment where we're both sipping our coffee, only interrupted by the yells and curses of angry Boston drivers and the quiet chirping of birds.

My pocket begins to buzz, and on impulse, I grab my phone to peek at who's calling. *Mom,* it reads, a picture of the two of us on the beach lighting up the screen.

"You can pick it up," Harrison says, gesturing to my phone with his coffee. "I'm sure she wants to hear how your move went."

I mute the call, then shoot her a quick text. Sorry, at work.

"I already talked to her yesterday," I lie. "I'm sure she's just bored and wants to chat," I lie again.

"I just . . ." I start to say, then sigh. "I don't want to answer questions about work. I'm not ready to talk to them about leaving my old job." He nods in acknowledgment, and I give him a lopsided smile. "As if you always answer when your mom calls."

"Well . . . I do now, actually." He sips his coffee before continuing. "My parents got divorced last year. My dad is living in Florida." He doesn't look at me while he says it.

I only met his parents a few times in college, but every interaction was generally unpleasant. After I gave them an earful about not pressuring Harrison to study law when he clearly didn't want to, I wasn't invited to any more annual Parents' Weekend dinners. I did interact with them after that—hard not to when you're constantly hanging out with their son—but it was understood that they didn't like me, and I didn't like them. And besides, I wasn't missing much. They were terse and unpleasant with everyone, including each other. I assumed they were always at each other's throats because . . . I don't know, they're lawyers? That's their personality?

Apparently, it's actually because they didn't get along.

"I'm really sorry to hear that," I say.

"Don't be," he says quickly, rolling his eyes. "It was time."

"So now you pick up whenever your mom calls?"

He pulls his lips to the side, considering, before nodding slowly. "She's not doing great, to be honest."

He doesn't volunteer any additional information, and I am certainly not in a position to ask direct questions about anyone's health, mental or physical, so I refrain, instead saying, "I'm sure she's glad you're always available to support her."

Harrison tightens his lips in what I'm sure is supposed to be a smile but looks more like a cringe. "So," he says, changing the subject. "Tell me again why you're sitting in the dirt in your pajamas?"

I knock my knuckles against the glass. Dirt smudges off, leaving mud on my hands and cleanish circles on the window. "The dirty window was driving me crazy. The weeds were blocking my view."

Harrison studies the situation, eyes darting between the window, the plants, and my makeshift tools. He sticks out his right hand, palm facing up. "Scissors, please."

I hand them over, and he crawls up on his knees. His pants are now covered in dirt, but apparently, he doesn't care, because he leans forward and starts hacking away at the weeds. I want to offer to help, but he's in the zone. He's the surgeon, and this plant is the patient, and if I interfere, I put everyone at risk. Instead, I shift, moving dirt away from the glass using my spoon.

A few minutes later, I look back to find Harrison has carved away at the weeds enough to create an unobstructed view of the flowers. They peek out, red and yellow and lots of green, and I gasp before I can stop myself.

"It's perfect," I say, and when he turns back to face me, there's an expression on his face that makes me blush from head to toe.*

"Do you have glass cleaner?" he asks.

"I didn't move my cleaning supplies from Florida to Massachusetts, no."

He rolls his eyes as he leans over and pulls up the corner of his T-shirt to wipe at the window, smudging the dirt enough to have a clear view of . . .

A sagging air mattress covered in balled-up sheets.

He eyes me, his smile half confused and half amused. "Is that where you've been sleeping?"

I take a sip of iced coffee to hide my embarrassment. "I haven't gotten around to buying a bed frame yet."

When he sighs, there's no malice in it, which I take as a huge win.

* **Wide smile · Dimples · Eyes crinkled** | *Facial expression* | *Frequency: medium*

1. Joy.

"It's on my to-do list," I add.

The deadpan expression he gives me unexpectedly pulls a full laugh out of me, which makes his eyes crinkle up, which sends another glitter bomb (*whoosh*) through my brain.

He stands up, brushes the dirt off his legs, and holds his hand out for my empty coffee cup. I give it to him.

"What are you doing after work today?" he asks. "I have to drive out toward IKEA anyway. Want to go?"

"Seriously?"

"Yes, seriously," he says, then transfers both empty coffee cups to one hand and holds the other hand out for me. I take it, and he pulls me up from the ground.

"I'd love that. Thank you," I say. He nods and promptly drops my hand.

CHAPTER 10

Harrison knocks on my door at 5:28, characteristically early. I wait eight seconds to open the door, as if I haven't been lying in wait since I got back from work. The last fifteen minutes have been productive, though, spent crafting the perfect casual outfit (baggy tee French tucked into jean shorts, ratty white sneakers, gold hoops, fun sunglasses), and I am proud to say I look like I put zero effort into looking cute.

His car is parked on the side of the road about half a block away, and we get in, neither of us speaking a word, our détente from this morning seemingly forgotten. I'm sure (well, I hope) we'll eventually get past the I Don't Know How to Interact with You stage of this rekindled friendship, but every interaction seems to need a warm-up period.

"We have to swing by my mom's place first," he says, buckling in. "I just have to run in, so you can wait in the car." He puts the car in reverse, and I am momentarily stunned as he rests his right arm behind my headrest, looking backward as he pulls out of the spot. (Why is that hot?)

I don't regain my ability to speak until we're headed down the street.

"Wait, sorry. She moved?"

"Yeah," he says, turning the radio on low as we hit a red light. He never could drive in silence. "They sold their house in Connecticut, and she's working out of Boston now. Not taking on as many clients. Living in a much smaller place, outside of Boston—Canton. Fifteen-minute drive from the IKEA."

I think that was more information than Harrison has willingly volunteered in . . . five years? In the hope he'll keep talking to fill the silence, I don't say anything.

That backfires when we spend the next thirty seconds in silence.

"And what are you dropping off?" I finally ask.

He turns toward the tote bag he threw in the back seat. "Dinner."

I pause.

I clear my throat.

"What'd ya make?"

"Pasta," he says.

We don't speak for the entire length of Billy Joel's "Piano Man."

"Nice song," I say as it wraps up. Harrison *hmm*s his acknowledgment.

I was kind of hoping now that he and Stephanie are broken up, it would free up his ability to read someone else's mind. If my theory that you can only have the ability to silently communicate with one person at a time is true, then why shouldn't it be me? After all, it used to be me. Seems like it should be easy to relearn that skill.

Maybe he doesn't want to. That's probably one of the boundaries of being Friends with Limitations.

We drive down a road with beautiful homes on both sides,

and I focus on that instead. I rank them as if I had a million dollars to blow on a single-family home for my single person. A two-story yellow home with several sets of bay windows tops my list. I look it up on Zillow, see the price, then delete the Zillow app from my phone.

After twenty minutes of driving, we enter a new area with lush, green trees everywhere and slow, rolling hills. "Pretty," I say.

"Blue Hills," Harrison says. "People ski here during the winter."

I eye him, and he doesn't eye me back. "Wish I knew how to ski," I say, fishing for an offer.

"You should go this winter," he says. Not the offer I wanted, but fair enough, I guess.

We sit in silence for the next ten minutes.

Finally, we pull into the driveway of a townhome in Canton. It's cute, a blue building with five or six identical entryways and front patios, all two stories with bay windows and white trim.

"I'll be right back," Harrison says, reaching behind me to grab the tote bag. His chest brushes my left arm as he stretches, and shivers run down my body.

I think the problem is I spend an inordinate amount of time thinking about intimacy. Or rather, the fact that I'm not able to have it. It's similar to being horny all the time, but not really, because I'm dealing with conflicting desires to have sex and also not to be in pain, which would require me not to have sex. So, do I want to have sex, or do I not want to have sex? I don't know, but the word "sex" appears in my brain a lot. And thinking about sex all the time has my body so wired, it's like a minefield. All he (he as in someone, of course! Could be anyone!) has to do is brush against me and my whole body tenses up in anticipation.

Harrison makes his way to the front door, knocks, and quickly enters a moment later. I fiddle with the car door, tracing the stitching along the leather.

"Emma," Harrison's voice calls, muffled through the car windows. He's waving at me.

I raise my eyebrows, and he motions for me to come out and join him. When I raise my eyebrows even more, he winces and mouths, "*Sorry.*"

That can only mean one thing.

I look down at my outfit. This is not mom-approved. The frayed edges on these jean shorts are intended to make Harri—to make guys want to tug at the strings. They are not intended to be worn while interacting with a woman who probably doesn't own a single item of clothing under two hundred dollars.

My thighs burn as I peel them off the leather seat and step into the heat. Harrison cringes for the entire length of time it takes me to reach the front door, and as I walk the last steps, I hiss, "You did *not* prep me for this."

"She says it's rude of me to leave you in the car," Harrison says, raising his voice at the end as if asking for forgiveness.

I flip my sunglasses up to the top of my head as I brush past him. "You owe me Swedish meatballs."

The inside of the townhome isn't what I expect. I never went to Harrison's family home in Connecticut, but I'd seen it over video calls plenty of times. It was all white walls and plush furniture and expensive artwork and spotless. Professional cleaners and interior designers. Tastefully sterile.

None of those words apply to this home. In the corners of the living room, there are stacked boxes, some cardboard, some plastic. Some are overflowing as if someone has been digging through them, and the contents are littered throughout the house. I've seen messier apartments, for sure, but this is definitely more chaotic than how this woman typically operates.

It looks like my apartment, actually.

Before I can unpack that, Millie rounds the corner. "Emma, honey," she says, reaching out her arms for a hug. She's the same woman in so many ways: same sharp haircut and dark waves, same austere expression, same tasteful gold jewelry. But she's traded her tailored clothes for yoga pants and a wrinkled button-up, and she's starting to sprout grays at her roots. And maybe she's just stopped getting facials, but the dark circles under her eyes are somewhat jarring.

I step forward and wrap my arms around her. My sunglasses immediately slip out of my hair and clatter to the floor.

"Got them," Harrison mutters, right as Millie pulls out of my hug, saying, "Oh, I'm so sorry, sweetie."

I wave my hand. "It's okay. I bought them at the drugstore."

"Oh! Didn't know you could buy sunglasses there." Millie smiles forcefully with raised eyebrows. There's an awkward pause that lasts a moment too long.

"They have great stuff," Harrison says, clearing his throat. "At the drugstore."

"So, Emma, how have you been?" Millie asks, ignoring him. "It's been, what, five years since you spoke to Harrison? He didn't tell me you had decided to come back!"

It takes every ounce of my willpower to keep my jaw from dropping to the floor. Harrison stands behind her, his eyebrows skyrocketing upward and his entire body freezing.[1]

After Harrison and I parted ways, I didn't tell my parents anything. We flew home after graduation, and I cried and cried and cried in my room. I told them I was sad about leaving college. They made me a therapy appointment. I'd brush them off when they asked about Harrison, and eventually, they stopped

* **Wide eyes · Tense Jaw · Shallow breathing** | *Facial expression* | *Frequency: low*

1. Flustered shock.

asking. Did they suspect something happened? Absolutely. But I didn't want to talk about it.

And I'm a lot closer with my parents than he is with his. Or was, anyway. He only would've told his mom if . . . well, I don't even know. If things were *bad* bad.

The sinking feeling in my stomach is so strong my center of gravity seems to shift, making me unsteady on my feet and light in the head.

Millie clears her throat.

"Uh—" I choke out, "Yes, I've been in Florida for the last five years! Just moved back here about two weeks ago."

Millie gives me an *mmm* that is startlingly similar to the *mmm* Harrison uses to acknowledge statements, but it has a level of condescension that isn't in Harrison's vocabulary.

"Two weeks ago!" she repeats with false enthusiasm. "Well, come on in. I just brewed a fresh pot of coffee."

"Mom, do you have oat milk?" Harrison asks. They're still discussing milk alternatives as they walk into the kitchen.

I take the opportunity to look around more closely. The television is on, local news playing on mute. There's a blanket crumpled up on the couch, and when I brush my fingers over it, it's still warm. There are a couple of cups on the coffee table, none of which are empty, none of which are set on coasters, which seems alarming because (a) this looks like real wood, and (b) Millie is definitely a "coaster, please" kind of woman. Used to be, anyway.

The only decor in sight is a four-by-six-inch framed photo of Harrison and Millie twenty-some years ago. Harrison looks six or seven in the photo, a tiny backpack slung over his tiny shoulders. His hair sticks up every which way, almost distracting me from the enormous grin, so big it erases his cheeks. Based on the navy blue polo shirt and straight-out-of-the-box shoes, this is a first day of school photo. Millie crouches next to him, both arms wrapped around him, her head resting on top of his.

"Em?" Harrison says. I turn around, and he's holding a steaming mug out for me.

"Thanks," I murmur, bringing it to my face and gently blowing away the steam.

"She's grabbing us a snack." Harrison looks back at the kitchen, then turns to me and whispers, "I'm so sorry. I really just intended to drop off the food and leave. I owe you one."

"Why are you driving half an hour to bring her dinner?" I ask. He doesn't answer. "And since when did you tell your mom . . . everything?"

Harrison swallows, pulling his lips to the left.* "I'm trying to be better," he whispers as his mom enters the room.

As I watch Harrison and his mom get along fabulously for the next ten minutes, it's clear that whatever he's trying is working. Even so, the positive feelings between them obviously don't extend to me.

"You're a teacher, right, Emma?" Millie asks, sipping her coffee.

"I was," I say, eyes darting to Harrison, who provides no helpful backup. "I actually work in a coffee shop now."

"Oh, is that so?" Her voice drips liquid sweetness. "Why did you decide to leave teaching?"

"Turns out it wasn't for me," I say. That's about 30 percent of a full explanation, but Millie certainly isn't interested in the nuances of my feelings about the teaching profession, nor do I want to unpack them right now.

"Well, we can't all end up in the right job the first go-around, I suppose," she says. She then proceeds to embark on a rant about the status of career counseling in our nation, and

* **Lips pulled to the left · Biting the right side of lip** | *Facial expression* | *Frequency: medium*

1. Actively thoughtful.
2. Signals internal debate.

why every student should be required to meet with a professional career coach at least once every six months while they're in college.

Finally, she asks the question I can tell she's been dying to ask since we walked in the door: "How's Stephanie?"

My eyes dart toward Harrison, but his eyes stay trained on his mother with so much focus that it feels intentionally avoidant. "I haven't talked to her today," he says.

Millie's eyes narrow, picking up on his suspicious lack of additional information. *Why?* I beg her to ask. *Ask him why! I want him to tell you why, because I'm incredibly desperate for any additional scrap of information he'll give me about this breakup! Help a girl out!*

"Why?" she asks. Hallelujah.

He finally glances over at me, but I can tell from even that split second that he's assessing whether I'm paying attention or whether I've miraculously left the room so he doesn't have to do this in front of me.

"We're in a bit of a rough patch right now," he says. I don't even pretend to hide the way my head whips toward his, and he doesn't even pretend to hide the way he ignores me.

"What does that mean?" Millie demands.

"Um," he says, making eye contact with her so intently that I feel like I've disappeared, "I'm not sure it's going to work out between us."

What does that mean? I beg. "What does that mean?" she asks. Millie and I have never been more aligned than we are in this moment.

Harrison blinks several times before responding. "It's a long story. I don't really want to get into it."

A long story is a crazy way to say *we broke up,* but we're friends on a trial basis, and I don't think trial-basis friends get to have opinions on how you describe breakups.

"Harrison. You two were great together. You know I adore

that girl. She's like a daughter to me." That's an insane thing to say about a girl your son had been dating for four months, but what do I know? "You two were bringing me so much joy, even though I don't have a lot of reasons to feel joy right now," she adds.

If I breathe, they'll remember I'm here, so I don't breathe. I evaporate into thin air.

"Mom, come on, it's not that seriou—"

"Yes," she says. "It is."

Harrison is silent. (I am still nonexistent.)

His ability to speak calmly about his breakup, both right now and last week in his apartment, mere hours after it happened, is, frankly, baffling. I've never been part of a breakup due to the necessary prerequisite of having actually been in a relationship, but surely it's more emotional than this. Then again—if you're the one who does the breaking, then it's probably easier for you, right? Harrison wanted the breakup, and also he knew it was coming, so he had time to prepare.

"Did this just happen?" she asks, and Harrison nods. "Great. Then there's still time for you to fix it, right?" Harrison nods again. "Don't nod. Use your words."

Harrison says "Yes, there's probably still time" at the same moment I stand and say "Bathroom?"

They stare at me blankly, as if I'd accomplished my goal and they had forgotten I was present. As Millie points down the hallway, she studies me inquisitively. I scamper out of the room, becoming nonexistent again.

The bathroom has the same level of half-unpacked clutter as the living room. There's a lotion bottle, an open container of mouthwash, a lone strand of floss, and a half-full glass of water, all to the right of the sink. The mess continues to the left.

So, when Harrison said she wasn't doing great, he really did mean she wasn't doing great. This is what my living space looked like in the months leading up to me quitting my teaching job, so I see it for what it is. My bathroom was constantly littered with dirty water glasses and sunglasses from five fashion trends ago and towels on the floor, because sometimes the thought of having to bend over and pick up a towel made me want to break down, and so the laundry stayed unfinished.

I can't imagine how this has weighed on him. If Harrison has a fatal flaw, it's his desperate need to care for other people. It's why he's a nurse. It's why he meal-prepped and drove thirty minutes out of his way to bring his mom food, just so she wouldn't have the added pressure of cooking tonight.

It's why he offered to drive me to IKEA, even though he had other things to do. *Damn it.*

It's been silent since I closed the bathroom door, but the conversation finally picks back up, the thin walls doing nothing to halt the flow of words.

"It's not because of her, is it?" Millie asks, not loudly, but with enough clarity that I can tell the way she says "her" implies that "her" is a she-devil mistress straight from hell. It is immediately clear she's talking about me, which is not surprising but still makes my stomach plummet.

"Of course not. There's nothing going on between us," Harrison says confidently, confirming what I know to be true.

"I can't imagine there would be, since she has a history of treating you so poorly."

I hate her, and I hate that she's right.

"Well—"

"You're a pushover, and she's always pushing you. You can't let her do that again. But, thankfully, if there's nothing going on between you two, then I'm sure you can fix things with Stephanie, right?"

Harrison doesn't say anything.

"Right?" Millie repeats. "It just makes me so happy to know you're happy. Do you understand how rare and lucky it is to have a strong, healthy relationship the way you two did? When something like that comes along, you can't just let it go. I don't want you to end up in a doomed relationship the way your father and I did."

"I know, Mom," he says. "I'll work on it."

"Well. You know she's welcome for dinner any time." It's obvious she's not referring to the same "she" as before.

Harrison mumbles something in return, and I gather myself and walk back into the living room before Millie can keep berating me and Harrison can keep not defending my honor.

From his perch on the couch, Harrison looks even more miserable than the time Carson Straeder was his assigned partner for a group project in our freshman year writing seminar, and Carson got up to present in front of the class and didn't use the talking points that they (they being 99 percent Harrison) had written and went so egregiously off-script in his supposed discussion of Henry David Thoreau's *Walden* that we were no longer certain whether we were discussing Thoreau's trip to Walden Pond or Carson's family trip to go see it three summers previously.

He turns to me with a tight smile. (*Carson, I think Thoreau didn't have access to a cell phone.*) "Ready to head out?" Harrison asks.

I force my way through a goodbye, and although all of it is a blur, I'm absolutely certain *I* didn't get a dinner invite.

The moment my ass touches the car seat, I open my mouth to interrogate him, but he beats me to it.

"So, you just need a bed frame?" he asks.

I turn my head to face him, but he keeps his gaze away from mine as he turns on the car and backs out of the parking spot. Fair enough, I suppose.

"Yes, but you know me. I love to browse."

I allow him to lead me away from the topic of his mother, but when we're finally in IKEA, I ambush him.

"So, what happened back there?" I ask him as we enter a

mock-up of a living room. It's packed today, but this pseudo-room provides a semblance of privacy.

Harrison sits on the love seat, bouncing a couple of times as if to test the springiness. He runs his hand across the fabric, letting out a neutral humming noise at the mediocre quality. Finally, he looks up at me. "She's getting better," he says. "I've been taking care of her."

That's not what I meant, and I feel a jolt of guilt. "I have no doubt you have been. I'm sure it's been hard for her. Is she getting the help she needs?"

"Yeah," he says, nodding. "She's always struggled with depression, since before I knew what it was. She's always kept it under control, but this time it's been a little harder. Too much change, I guess. Her brain doesn't know how to adjust."

"You're clearly taking good care of her," I say, and he smiles softly at me. "She's lucky to have you."

He reclines back onto the couch as a sales associate walks by and asks if we need any help. I politely decline, then seat myself on the opposite end of the couch. The large canvas lighting fixture above us sends soft light over the scene, and it's easy to imagine this as an actual home—one that smells like lingonberries and Swedish meatballs.

"That's not what I meant, though," I say. "About what happened back there."

"What else could you possibly have meant?" Harrison says. He clearly intends it to be playful, but it doesn't quite come out that way.

"Why didn't you tell her you broke up with Stephanie?"

He traces a finger along a seam on the armrest and doesn't respond.

"I'm sorry," I say, even though I'm not. "It's not my business."

He picks at the seam again, then returns his hands to his lap and lets his head fall back against the back of the couch. "No,

I'm sorry. I'm giving you a hard time for no reason. I just didn't want you to witness that."

I just didn't want you to witness that is a far cry from the correct response, which is, *Let me explain to you why I lied to my mom about my relationship status.*

A couple enters the pseudo-room and immediately starts arguing about the merits of throw pillows. The man points at the pillow Harrison is leaning on, which we take as our cue to keep moving.

We wander into the chair room—dining, lounge, reclining, etc.—and take turns sitting. We test neighboring wooden (well, "wooden") chairs, and I rock back and forth, the chair creaking slightly.

"So, are you and Stephanie actually maybe getting back together?" I ask, and he looks confused.

"No."

He doesn't provide any additional information, so I keep going. "Because you just told your mom you would try to fix things with her."

"Well." There's a loaded pause. "I'm just trying to let her down easy, I guess. She doesn't need bad news right now."

I cannot possibly fathom lying to your mom about your relationship status because you think that's what's keeping her sane. But—*You're a pushover, and she's always pushing you.* I shiver at the memory as if she placed a multigenerational curse on my bloodline. I do not push back. Instead, I switch gears. "Seems like it was serious," I say.

"What?"

"With Stephanie."

Harrison rocks backward, tilting the chair, then leans forward and gently sets the front legs back on the ground. "I tried to think it was, but now I don't think so."

I blink at him. "I have no idea what that means."

"I don't, either."

"Well. Your mom seemed serious about it."

He stands up, waving his hand. "She's always like that."

Got it. She's always like that when he dates someone. Which he apparently does now. Which makes sense, because he's a fully fledged adult and attractive and a good person, so surely he's in high demand with the women of Boston. He's definitely cleaning up on the dating apps.

Maybe I should get on a dating app. Just to dip my toes in the water.

If Harrison saw me on a dating app, would he match with me?

I gesture toward a sign for the cafeteria. "Break for meatballs?"

He nods, and we weave our way back through the living room mock-ups.

I don't think I actually want to know, but I ask anyway, because the otherworldly experience that is IKEA is making me forget real-life consequences, like the overthinking I know will ensue if he actually answers the question. "So did you guys just break up because it wasn't that serious, or . . . ?"

Harrison appears to be so focused on navigating the maze of furniture he forgets he's not supposed to trust me enough to answer questions like that. "No, it wasn't that serious. I shouldn't be seriously dating right now."

"Why?"

He opens his mouth once, then closes it, then opens it again. "Well. I'm dealing with a lot with my mom, and most of my attention is taken up by that."

"Well, people multitask. Swedish meatballs and mashed potatoes, please," I say to the IKEA employee behind the counter as I take a step forward. I turn my eyes back to Harrison. "See? I'm thinking about two things at once right now."

Actually, I'm thinking multiple things. Like, even a little bit of Harrison's attention seems like a sweet deal to me. And how many girlfriends has Harrison had since college? Also, what exactly are lingonberries?

"I'll have the same," Harrison says to the man, then turns to me. "Maybe some people can. But I shouldn't. I didn't . . . I wasn't in the right headspace anymore. It's complicated."

"You guys seemed fine at dinner," I say, even though they did not, in fact, seem fine at dinner. "Yes, I'll take the gravy and the lingonberry sauce, please."

He turns back to me. "We were fine at dinner, actually. We had some tough conversations after, and that's when . . ." He pauses, as if he needs to collect himself before continuing. "When I realized it needed to end."

"Shit," I murmur under my breath. "That's really sudden. I'm sorry to hear that."

He nods, then picks up his plate. "Thanks. I think it was for the best. She deserves more."

It's hard to imagine someone "deserving more" than a kind-hearted man like Harrison, but what do I know about relationships?

We eat our Swedish meatballs in silence.

CHAPTER 11

When I woke up today, I was on a mission. I had my second appointment with Kay two days ago, and even though it's only been a week and a half since my first appointment, Kay decided it was time for me to start using dilators at home to ensure I'm progressing in between our weekly appointments. I promised myself I would *not* procrastinate (because I'm Doing So Much Better!), and so when my alarm went off, I immediately rolled out of bed, splashed some water on my face, and triple-checked the door was locked and the blinds were closed. Taking a deep breath, I then opened my top right dresser drawer, sifted through socks to find a small wooden box, opened said box, removed a package wrapped in cloth, unwrapped the cloth, and finally let my dilators see the light of day for the first time in . . . eight years? Nine years? Give or take. And then I washed them very, very thoroughly.

It's been five minutes since then, and I'm still staring at the dilators like if I don't move, they can't see me, and I can't see them, and I won't have to use them, maybe.

Long time no see, says Cobalt. I throw her back in the box, then throw Key Lime in just to be safe. I allow Lavender to stay, since she's the smallest and tends to stay silent.

The dilators range from the size of my pinky to what Google tells me is the size of an average male penis. Measuring my physical therapy tools by how they compare in size to male genitalia chips away at my feminist ethos, but we have to pick our battles.

I wish penises were smaller.

Cobalt speaks up from the box. *What size penis does H—*

I slam the box shut.

And now, here I am. Eight-thirty A.M. I have an hour before I leave for work, and I swore to myself I would accomplish this task first. I know in my heart and soul that now is the appropriate time to put on (take off?) my big girl pants and use the dilators, but it still takes every ounce of willpower to bring Lavender to the bed and lie down on my back.

Inhale. My stomach expands.

Exhale. My stomach deflates.

My left hand rests loosely at my side as my right hand presses against my abdomen, feeling it rise and fall with my breath.

Inhale.

Exhale.

I hate this—the dilators, the breathing exercises, the entire concept of pelvic floor therapy—but this is a crucial step in my Doing Better Plan. I already got a job, I bought a real bed frame, and I even found a new therapist, so I need to keep up the momentum.

I grab the bottle of lube I bought at the pharmacy last night. The process of picking out lube made me feel strong and powerful and sexy (*yeah, that's right, I'm having hot sex*). (*What the hell are you talking about,* Key Lime said.) But then I couldn't get the self-checkout machine to work, so a pimply college-age kid had to rescan the lube for me and reset the machine. I will be ordering lube online next time.

So here I am, lying in bed, slathering lube onto my pale purple dilator. I will my muscles to relax and guide Lavender to my entrance. I don't push inward; I just let it sit there, begging my muscles to get used to the feeling and recognize the dilator isn't going to hurt me.

Although Kay's index finger is larger than Lavender, this is somehow scarier. I can't just turn off my brain and stare at the ceiling and tell my pain receptors to screw off. I have to consciously insert the dilator myself, even though every muscle in my body seems to be working in opposition to this goal.

Inhale.

Exhale.

Of course, the goal is to get to a place where I don't have to mentally remove myself from my vagina to combat pain. Because, no, the thought of having to build an unbreakable mental blockade during sex is not appealing to me. I would like to feel what it's really like—without the pain, that is.

Inhale.

Exhale.

I push Lavender inward slightly. My muscles clench, but I focus my energy on relaxing my pelvic floor and stopping the muscle spasms. And, much to my delight . . . it's super uncomfortable. But not painful, per se. There's no blinding pain, no spots in my vision. No screaming, yelping, crying.

Anticipating pain, I'm learning, gives you power over it. Is Lavender essentially the size of a toothpick? Sure. But she's inside of me and *I am okay.*

Inhale.

Exhale.

I lie there for a few more minutes, then gently press to the side. My muscles rapidly tighten and my breathing hitches, but I hold steady, willing my body to unclench, waiting for my muscles to adjust—

And my phone alarm goes off. I pull Lavender out, which

feels as pleasant as ripping an extra-strength Band-Aid off an open wound. Time to get ready for work.

***

TWO HOURS INTO MY SHIFT, Rose continues to monologue with the same energy and enthusiasm as when I first walked in and she began telling me about how the online course registration system got overloaded and she missed her opportunity (sorry, her "once-in-a-lifetime chance") to take a course called "Burn Her! Exploring the Legacies of Witchcraft in Renaissance Literature on the Second and Third Wave Feminist Movements." We're having a slow afternoon—save for Kurt, who came in after lunchtime and is sitting in an armchair, completely engrossed in *Slaughterhouse-Five*—so she's taken it upon herself to fill the silence. "And on top of all that, my roommate just texted me and said she's having five friends over for dinner. Five! In our tiny apartment! God, roommates are the worst."

Now that's something I can talk about. "True. I had to move out of the house I was living in because all of my roommates moved out and got married."

She responds without missing a beat. "That's because you're old."

"I'm only, like, eight years older than you."

"In eight years, I intend to be a multi-millionaire and have at least one kid and one ex-husband."

Rose offers no additional explanation for how she plans to turn that dream into a reality.

"Well," I say, then stop talking because I don't know how to finish that sentence.

"That's why I have to live it up while I'm still young and free of responsibilities." I choose not to point out that this job is a responsibility.

"And that is also why," she says, spinning on her heel and

pointing at me as if she's just discovered the answer to all of my problems, "you have to come to my party this weekend."

"I don't think I'm going to do that."

"It would be good for you," she says, which I try (and fail) not to find personally offensive. "It's still in your calendar, right?"

It's not—I deleted it almost immediately after she put it in the first time—and she can clearly read my answer on my face. She holds out her hand, and I reluctantly hand my phone to her.

A moment later, she looks up with wide eyes. "Who is Alexander?"

I blink. "What?"

"Why do you have a text from someone named Alexander asking you on a date?"

"Give me that," I say, and she scowls as I snatch it back.

> **Maybe: Alexander:** Hey! This is Alexander. From the double date. I know it's been a couple weeks but I can't stop thinking about you. Would you like to get dinner again sometime? I'd love to get to know you outside a painfully awkward double date context if you're down.

Rose's breath tickles the hair on the nape of my neck.

"Oh my god, back *up*," I tell her, and she *hmph*s and takes a step back.

"Who is Alexander?" she repeats.

"A guy," I say. I can feel her eyes roll. "I went on a double date with him two weeks ago."

Rose's eyes are bugging out of their sockets, as if this is the most exciting information she's ever heard. "Well? Are you going to go on a second date?"

"I don't think I would call what happened a first date, really."

"Why?" she asks. I ignore her, and she scowls at me before responding. "Fine. Are you going to go on a first date with him?"

Going on a non–double date is on my Do Better list. And I want to finish the list because . . . there are things I want to do. Or have the opportunity to do. Even still, saying yes to a date feels like a minor betrayal.

Of my neighbor or of my heart, I'm not sure. Maybe both.

"I don't know if I'm looking to date right now," I say, even though I know what her response will be.

"You're such an old lady," she says, as expected. I wince. "It's just one date. Live a little."

Am I interested in going on a date with a hot man who is interested in me? I'm not *not* interested. One date can't hurt, and one date is only . . . one date. This is what real adult women do, right?

That's what Harrison is doing on the dating apps, apparently. He says he shouldn't be looking for something serious, which means he's looking for something casual, which probably means he's trying to find someone to be casual with. Whatever that entails.

You know exactly what that entails, Key Lime says.

You'll never be casual, Cobalt adds. *But you already knew he wasn't interested in you. Friends with limitations, remember?*

"Go out to dinner," Rose says. "Do it. Text him. Right now."

"Right now? Isn't that a little fast?"

"This is the twenty-first century. We don't have to pretend we're not always on our phones."

"I don't know . . ."

Rose gives me another *you're crazy* look. "I can't be the only one with fun stories at work. You need to get on my level."

"I have fun stories."

"Oh, yeah? Tell me one. Right now."

I stare at her blankly, then rub my temples. *Inhale. Exhale.* "Yeah, okay, I'll go to dinner with him."

Rose gives a squeal of excitement. Before I know what's happening, she's grabbed my phone again and started typing.

"Hey," she reads aloud. "Sounds like fun. I'm free on Saturday."

"I'm also free Friday," I offer, and Rose scoffs at me.

"Nice try. You'll be at my party." There's a *bloop* as she hits send. "Proud of you," she says, and I'm almost proud of myself, too, but then I remember Rose did 100 percent of the work, and I'm still not sure why I agreed to this.

"You should invite him to my party," she adds, handing me my phone.

"Hey, look," I say, glancing at my phone. "Your shift is almost over. Guess it's time for you to pack up."

Rose scowls. "You're not getting out of this. I expect you at my party with a plus-one."

A bell chimes, and Jo walks through the door, shooting us a peace sign as she makes her way behind the counter. As she approaches, my vision focuses in on dark circles under her eyes, hidden behind poorly applied concealer.

Jo drops her backpack off in the back room, and when she emerges from behind the curtain, I quietly ask, "You okay?"

She looks at me, eyes tired and intense, and I can tell she isn't going to respond, but I'm saved from the awkwardness by Rose moving ahead with her own statement.

"Boss, tell Emma to come to my party this weekend."

Jo grins, and my anxiety is eased when genuine creases form around her eyes. She must just be sleepy. "Am I invited?"

"No. You're part of the managerial class."

"Then, no. I'm not telling Emma to go to your party."

Jo and Rose engage in a stare-off so long that I begin to forget why they were staring at each other in the first place.

"Fine," Rose says. "Please come to my party and bring

Emma with you." She points a finger to me. "But this does not mean you've gotten out of bringing a plus-one! You need to expand your social circles! Bring Alexander!"

Jo shoots me a confused look as Rose wiggles her fingers at me in a sarcastic wave and exits, her shift finally over. Kurt leaves a moment later, heavy backpack in tow.

The moment the door closes, Jo crosses her arms over her apron and narrows her eyes. "What are you not telling me?"

I clear my throat. "Remember Alexander from the double date?" Jo nods. "Well, he texted me. And asked me out on another date."

Jo's gasp is so sudden, I jump as if I'm about to be hit by a projectile. "Are you joking?"

"Why would that be a joke?"

"Are you going to say yes?"

"I already did," I say. Jo's mouth falls off her face and onto the floor.

"You, Emma Rogers, agreed to go on a second date?" I nod. "Of your own free will?" I nod. "And it wasn't Harrison. We're talking about *Alexander.*" I shake my head, and she stares at me. "Did someone force you to send it?"

I consider for a moment. "Actually, yeah, kind of. Rose is the one who actually hit send on the text."

"That's all it took?" "Flabbergasted" is the only appropriate word to describe her reaction. "You mean to tell me I could've been doing that this entire time?"

Fearful of the text messages Jo might send given unfiltered access to my phone, I switch gears. "I'm not looking for a relationship until I'm done with pelvic floor therapy. It'll be easier for everyone involved that way. But I feel like going on one date will be good for me? Like a trial run?" Jo opens her mouth, but I cut her off. "And before you say that's stupid, I'll have you know I have a plan. And once it's done, I'll be ready to think more seriously about dating. *Dating* dating."

"I don't think going on a date is a stupid first step. But what if instead of hinging your dating life on your medical condition and some plan you've concocted, you just, oh, I don't know, actually *learn about non-penetrative sex,*" she says pointedly.

"We are in *public.* At *work.*"

Jo waves her hands around, incredulous. "Oh, please. We do not have a single customer." I scowl at her. "I'm just saying. You say you want to do better? You say you wish you could date? Then let's have a mature conversation about hands and tongues and their many uses. It is really time someone gave you the director's cut of The Talk."

"Don't do this. I know how sex works. And you gave me this talk a million times in college. Don't you remember the time you scared the sweet old dining hall lady?"

"Ah, but now I have five years of experience teaching high schoolers about sex."

My eyes pop open. "You taught sex ed at your school?"

She nods, looking absolutely delighted with herself. "I sure did. Twice a year for five years. I'm a pro now."

"Why have we never talked about this?"

"Probably because you have extremely toxic internalized ideas about sex and obviously don't want to talk to me about it?"

I glare at her. "Oh, shut up. And besides, I don't need a high school sex education lesson. We're ten years past that."

"Look at me when I say this, because I cannot possibly emphasize this enough," Jo says, pointing from her eyes to mine. "The high schoolers who I taught sex ed to have a better understanding of sex than you do, and probably also a better relationship with sex than you do."

"I literally have a medical condition."

"I'm not talking about your medical condition. I'm talking about the shit-ass sex education you received. I'm talking about the fact that you were taught as a teen that sex means penetrative sex and—"

"Jo. I know about oral sex."

Jo glares at me. "Look. You can't have penetrative sex, correct?"

"Uh—"

"Correct. Right now, anyway. So, you're going to stand there and listen while I do you a favor and list all the ways you and Harrison could be sexually intimate that don't involve his dick in your vagina." She makes a vulgar hand gesture.

"Please, for the love of god, do not make me think about Harrison more than I already am."

"Alexander is just a placeholder, and you know that."

"I will actually pay you to stop talking. Ten dollars?"

"We'll start slow to ease you in. We have no idea whether Harrison has any game because screams and thumps don't actually tell you that much."

"Well, he and Stephanie met on a dating app, which seems to imply he's, you know." I stop mid-sentence.

"Sleeping with women?"

I do not respond.

"Emma. My sweet baby Emma," Jo says, pursing her lips sarcastically. "Just because he's on dating apps and sleeping with women does not mean he's good at sleeping with women."

I do not respond.

"But he actually cares about pleasing women, clearly," she continues, "and he must have taken anatomy classes. He definitely knows where the clit is. That's a good starting point."

I can feel my blood *thumping* in my brain. And maybe in other parts of my body.

"Twenty dollars that he could get you off with his fingers without hurting you," she says. "And I feel like he's studious enough to get good at cunnilingus within a reasonable timeline, if he's not already."

I feel all the sanity exit my body. "Harrison is not interested in me."

Jo laughs out loud. "What the *fuck* are you talking about."

"I'm serious!" I say. "He can barely make eye contact with me. He's better now, but every interaction needs a warm-up, and everything is still so awkward. He told me we could be friends on a 'trial basis.' What does that mean to you, Jo? Because I don't see how you could possibly connect the dots between being friends on a trial basis and wanting to be in a romantic relationship. Plus, he said he shouldn't be seriously dating right now, generally. And even if that weren't an issue, I'm still getting some . . . things . . . figured out, and you were there the day I moved in, and all we could hear was the damned thumping. We both know his love language is physical touch."

"Okay, then touch his dick."

I stare at the linoleum floor, and my response comes out weaker than expected. "What if that's not enough?"

"Then touch his dick with your tongue?"

I don't respond, but I do let out a snort of laughter. Jo reaches out and squeezes my hand.

"You two couldn't stay away from each other if the fate of the world depended on it," she says. "I always knew you'd find your way back to each other one way or another, and you did, and you still will. When you're ready, he'll be ready." She gives my hand another squeeze before letting it go. "How is pelvic floor therapy going?"

"Slowly," I murmur. "I'm moving in the right direction, though."

Jo nods her acknowledgment. "And have you scheduled a gynecology appointment yet?"

"Yeah. It's in eleven days." (But who's counting?) "Um, maybe if—"

"Yes, of course," she says, cutting me off. "Send me a calendar invite and I'll be there."

"I love you," I tell her. She rolls her eyes, but looks delighted. "And, um, there's something else I need to update you on," I say, and Jo groans. I fill her in on how weird he was about Stephanie in front of his mom and how much his mom hates my guts, and she shrugs, looking significantly less concerned than I am.

"Doesn't surprise me. She never liked you, even before you broke his heart." I wince, and she continues. "Plus, Harrison doesn't say things if he thinks they won't be received well. He'd rather keep his mouth shut."

"So, what, I'm overreacting?"

She shakes her head, thoughtful. "No. He doesn't have to act this way, and he's old enough to know better. You can take care of someone you love while still being true to yourself." She gives me a meaningful look. "And you can love someone while being true to yourself, too."

The doorbell chimes, and a customer enters before I have time to respond.

CHAPTER 12

Squeaksqueaksqueak.

The bed squeaks as I press down on it, the mattress rebounding quickly, giving my hands repeated high fives. As I bounce faster, the noises become more intense.

SQUEAKSQUEAKSQUEAK.

I take my hands off the mattress, and the bed frame gives off one last whispered squeal as I stand up straight and put my hands on my hips.

"Yeah, we're going to need to fix that," Harrison says, studying my bed with his hands on his hips. I would pay a monthly streaming fee to see this man in a renovation show. He wouldn't even need a cohost.

A moderately pornographic image of Harrison wearing a tool belt flashes through my mind, and I tuck it away in the Fantasy Corner.

"I swear I followed the instructions," I tell him. This may be true, but it is also true that when I was done building the bed frame, I had four leftover screws. I have no idea where they were supposed to go.

"You should've asked me for help."

"You took me to get this. You helped enough already."

I should've asked him anyway, and the look on his face tells me he agrees.* It took me four hours, six YouTube videos, and two bouts of tears, but I did it. I built the freaking bed frame. Am I proud of my work? No. Am I glad I pushed myself out of my comfort zone and did it anyway? Also no.

It's barely been a week since then, and the bed frame is already on its last legs.

Every time I sat down on my bed? *Squeak.* Every time I rolled over at night? *Squeak.* Every time I breathed? *Squeak.*

All I have to do is *think* about the bed, and it *squeaks*.

"I'm going to be honest," Harrison says, kneeling to inspect the frame, his ears turning faintly pink. "When I started hearing this through the floor, I assumed you had a guy over."

You know when you open your mouth to gasp, but your throat muscles are so tight it ends up sounding like a frog noise? That is the sound that comes out of me.

I slap a hand over my mouth, trying to cover my initial reaction by letting out a string of extremely forced chuckles. Even to my own ears, it sounds more like hyperventilating than laughing.

I have probably spent a combined five hours over the last couple days bouncing on my bed, trying to determine where the noise was coming from. I have essentially been breakdancing on my mattress. And never once did it occur to me Harrison could hear those noises through his floor the same way I could hear his *thumpthumpthump*ing through my ceiling.

* **Furrowed brows · Pursed lips · Head tilted to the right** | *Facial expression* | *Frequency: medium*

1. Exasperated.

I clear my throat. "Well," *ahem,* "you know me! Different guy every night!"

Harrison gives a friendly chuckle. "Such a heartbreaker."

I don't know what it says about our relationship that he can chuckle about this possibility. If I heard Harrison having loud sex through the ceiling (again! I hate my life!) I would spiral. I've said it before, and I'll say it again: I would break my lease. I do not have the mental strength to withstand that.

Then again, what does it say about our relationship that I have a date with another man this weekend?

Also: What relationship?

"You said you don't have any tools?" Harrison asks. He had come to Jo Jo's when his workday was over, and it just so happened my shift was ending, so we got to walk home together. (Rose glared at me as I was leaving.) On the walk home, I had told him I needed to go to the hardware store to get tools to fix my bed, and when he asked me what was wrong with it, and I said, "I'm buying tools to figure it out," he'd given me a concerned look and then offered to help. Apparently assisting with bed frame reconstruction does fall within the allowed boundaries of Friends with Limitations.

"Uh—yeah, no."

He side-eyes me from his spot on the floor. "And you're aware that this came with all the tools you should've needed to construct it?"

"It did. But then I accidentally threw them out when I was cleaning up the packaging." I hold my hands up, forming a heart.

He laughs unexpectedly, and a glitter bomb goes off in my brain. "I'm going to go grab my toolbox," he says. "I'll be right back."

He leaves the apartment, and I pound my fist against my forehead several times to erase the image of Harrison as the star of an HGTV show. *Harrison's Home,* maybe. *Carter Construc-*

tion. Hot Nerd Home Renovations. HarrisOn the Job. Straight back to the Fantasy Corner.

My phone buzzes from its spot on my new (soundly constructed, thank you very much!) nightstand.

Jo: we still on for evening yoga?

"Shit," I murmur. I'd completely forgotten.

Emma: Hate to say it, but having a furniture emergency. Bed frame on the brink of collapse. Need to fix it so I can sleep tonight. Rain check?

Bubbles appear, then disappear, then reappear. A full minute later, she finally responds.

Jo: yep no worries

As I fling my phone back onto the table, Harrison walks back into my apartment, toolbox in hand. He sets it down, then moves over to my bed.

"Help me get the mattress off?" he asks. I oblige, stifling several loud grunts as I push the mattress off the frame and help him prop it against my wall. Harrison returns his attention to the bed frame, kneeling and giving the shoddy construction a firm shake.

SQUEAKSQUEAKSQUEAK.

I now have the unfortunate image of Harrison listening to these noises from upstairs and thinking it's the sounds of passionate lovemaking. Of course, thinking about it from that lens, the noises are extremely embarrassing, and I, by extension, am extremely embarrassed.

As Harrison starts to fiddle with screws and metal and whatever else is in the bed frame, I sit down with my back against the wall, legs stretched out toward him.

"Helpful," he says, dimples appearing.

"I got the sense that you do not want my help reconstructing this bed."

Without looking away from the bed, Harrison leans over and flicks my ankle. It's gentle, more of a tap than a real flick, but it still sends pinpoints of sensation all the way up to my pelvic floor.

I let out a shriek of laughter and pull my legs up toward my chest. "Asshole!"

"She says, as I'm deconstructing and reconstructing her bed frame."

"Are you actually going to have to take it apart?"

"Come look," he says, waving me over to his side. I slide my butt across the floor, settling in next to him.

"See this?" he says, pointing at a place where two metal bars intersect. I lean forward to look, our heads only a few inches apart.

"Yes . . . ? But I don't see what's wrong."

He shifts to point, moving his body closer to mine. I can feel the gentle *in* and *out* of his breath against me. "I have to add screws there, and to the three other similar places where screws are missing," he says. "But in order to get the metal bars aligned, I need to loosen everything else up."

"This is a disaster. I can't thank you enough for helping."

"Seriously, don't worry about it," he says, starting to do something with his tools. "Now I won't have to listen to squeaking noises at all hours of the day."

"You must've been the best boyfriend in the world," I say. Harrison's unscrewing pauses.

He doesn't look up at me, but his ears turn pink as he continues to stare at the screw and the screwdriver. Finally, he collects himself. "It wasn't quite that simple."

"Well. Maybe not." I study him as he fiddles with the bed, remaining silent as if he doesn't know how to fill the space. "I hope you're doing okay. I can't imagine breaking up with someone is easy."

I track the movement in his throat as he swallows. Eventually, he continues. "Stephanie deserved better."

I snort. "That's such a ridiculous thing to say. What does that even mean, anyway?"

"Well," he says, "for starters, she definitely deserved someone who actually loved her."

Silence fills the room as I stop breathing and Harrison stops unscrewing. Neither of us dares to make eye contact, as if both of us—Harrison included—are shocked by the words that just came out of his mouth.

"Well," I say, then stop talking.

If he didn't love her, why was he dating her? Did he think he was in love with her and realize he wasn't, or did he start dating her thinking he could fall in love with her, then realize it wasn't possible? And why did he break up with her when he did? Or—

My phone buzzes from its spot on my bedside table, next to Harrison. He starts to grab it for me, but I brush him aside. "Don't worry about it. It's just Jo."

He raises an eyebrow. "Actually, it's your dad."

I don't want to pick it up, but I don't really want to answer questions about why I don't want to pick it up, so I pick it up.

"Hello?"

"Emma!" My dad's voice crackles through my phone's speaker, so loud Harrison can probably hear it even though it's not on speakerphone. "How's it going, sweetheart?"

We exchange pleasantries, and I offer a brief description of my bed frame issues, leaving out the part about my Friend with Limitations helping me.

"Well, you know," he says, chuckling, "that's what you get for buying the cheapest bed frame you could."

I clear my throat. "Well, I didn't need a nice one. This one holds a mattress, and that's really all I wanted."

There's a momentary pause, like he's choosing his words. "You know, if you need help buying—"

"No, really, I'm good—"

"I know, I know you're good, I just worry—"

"Seriously, Dad," I say, my tone final. "I'm good."

He pauses again before responding. "Okay. Okay, I know you're good. I'm glad to hear that."

"I have to go. But say hi to Mom for me?" I ask.

"You got it, kiddo. Love you."

"Love you, too," I say, hanging up the phone.

Harrison stares at me for a moment, then goes back to fiddling with the bed frame. Only when I think his attention is fully diverted does he surprise me by speaking.

"Can I ask you something?"

"No."

He nods and keeps screwing, and then I sigh loudly. "Yes, fine. What."

"Why did you actually move back to Boston?" he asks, his attention still on the bed frame.

"I quit my teaching job," I tell him. "And Jo was taking over Jo Jo's, and I knew she was lonely after Macy left, and I wanted to help her. So I moved."

Without responding, he puts the screwdriver down, stretching out his legs and tucking his socked feet underneath my calves. Little Florida oranges embroidered onto navy blue fabric. There's a gentle *swoop* in my stomach as I realize this is the first real touch we've shared in five years. The first touch without a pretense. Just a comforting *I'm here* touch, and it's all mine.

"Why'd you quit teaching?" he asks. I don't respond. "I respect if you don't want to talk about it, but I've been worried about you. You were so committed to teaching when we were in college. And you loved the time you spent student teaching. Did something happen?"

What I'd really like to do is tell him I just needed a change, that I was looking for a new challenge, but there's a softness in his gooey chocolate eyes that I know better than to take for granted. When someone looks at you like their entire world hinges on your answer, it's impossible to look away.

"It wasn't what I thought it would be. It's difficult to explain."

"Try me." He nudges his foot against my leg.

Inhale. Exhale. "It started well. My first year, I had incredible students. Eighth grade." Harrison gives me a soft smile. "I was good at it, I think."

"There's no doubt in my mind you were."

"Thanks. But it just . . . wasn't a good fit. I know that sounds silly." He shakes his head as I eye him warily. "It was exhausting and challenging and painful at times, but I expected all that. That part wasn't a surprise. But I'd spent years listening to my parents talk about how all the early mornings and late nights were worth it because it was so rewarding. Because it brought them so much joy. And I just . . . didn't feel any of that."

Harrison nods his head solemnly. "It doesn't have to be a good fit for everyone. That doesn't mean you failed."

"I know that, intellectually. But that's not how it felt. I'd wake up, go to school, pretend to be cheerful all day, then go home and crash. I was so *tired* after having to be *on* all day. I didn't have a social life. I certainly wasn't going on dates. I just didn't feel . . . fulfilled."

Harrison looks at me—eyes sunken, jaw tense, hands clenched.*

"It felt like that for five years. I was miserable, but too embarrassed to admit that I didn't like the job I'd spent years preparing for and generations of my family had done and loved. Then, a bunch of shitty things happened at once, and I just . . ."

Harrison nods his head encouragingly, and I continue. "I'd always assigned *Romeo and Juliet* to my eighth-grade students. Then, this past January, a couple of weeks after I'd assigned it and my students started reading it, an email came in from a parent. It was addressed to both me and the principal, and it accused me of forcing my students to read and discuss sexual content."

Harrison narrows his eyes. "What?"

"*Romeo and Juliet.*"

He opens his mouth, then closes it, then opens it again. "What?"

I snort. "Yeah, that was my reaction. But they were dead serious. You know how Romeo and Juliet get secretly married?" Harrison nods. "Well, it's implied they spend the night together. They wake up in bed together the next morning."

"Are you joking?" Harrison asks. "*That's* what they were concerned about?"

"Act three, scene five."

Harrison's mouth is open, but no sound escapes.

"Anyway, I told the parent that I was not discussing sex in the classroom and that I trusted my students to be mature about the content, and she didn't like that, so she took it up the ladder, and now . . . well, now the book is banned in the entire school district."

"You're kidding."

* **Sunken eyes · Tense jaw · Clenched hands** | *Facial expression* | *Frequency: low*

1. Deep worry.

I snort again. "Nope. They say it's not banned because it's still in school libraries, but we're no longer allowed to teach it in full. Only excerpts."

"That would make me insane."

"It did make me insane," I say. "It was horrible. And right around the same time all of this was going down, my mom was picked as Teacher of the Year at her school, and she got to give this speech at a banquet. I went with her and my dad, and I sat there listening to her talk about how much she loved her job, and how much purpose it gave her, and how every day felt like a blessing. She was literally tearing up onstage talking about this, and I was sitting there at the table *crying,* and everyone assumed it was because I was so proud of her. A week later, I turned in a letter of resignation. I told my principal I wouldn't be returning next year."

"And then you moved to Boston."

"Sort of. That wasn't my original plan. But I'd been living in this house with four roommates for a while, until they moved out, one by one. Marriage. Kids. Two days after I quit my job, the final remaining roommate told me she was moving in with her boyfriend. I'm happy for her, but it was also a slap in the face. Why does everyone else have it figured out? When did everyone learn to be a real adult? Like, what is wrong with me?"

Harrison immediately interrupts. "There's nothing wrong with you."

I snort. "Easy for you to say. You're a perfect saint, going to work every day to take care of sick kids. You're good at your job, you love it, and you're making a difference in the world. You're going out of your way to support your mom while she's struggling. You have it all figured out. I can't even build a bed frame."

"Just because we're in different places career-wise doesn't mean I have things figured out more than you do. Really, Em. There's nothing wrong with you."

"Maybe. But either way, it got to a point where I just needed a clean slate. I missed Jo and I missed . . . Boston, and I could tell Jo needed support, and I did, too, to be honest. So, I took the opportunity and ran with it."

Without saying anything, Harrison scoots over. Our legs aligned, he reaches over and takes my hand from where it's curled into a fist at my side. Slowly unfurling my clenched fingers, he slips his hand into mine.

Where does holding hands fall in the Friends with Limitations rulebook?

"I really admire the way you deal with all your problems head-on," he says, giving my hand a gentle squeeze.

I gape at him. "What?"

"Like, you didn't like your job, so you quit. You didn't like where you were living, so you moved. Back in college, you were the same way. You didn't want to quit your work-study job in order to do student teaching, so you petitioned the school to pay you to teach. You couldn't find a decent storage unit to store your dorm stuff that first summer, so you asked every Florida resident on the entire campus if they were planning to drive home until you found someone, and then you went on a road trip with a stranger."

That screams immature rather than adult to me, but I exhale a laugh anyway. "Tiana and I never spoke again, but we had a goddamn blast on that drive. The trunk was so packed, we couldn't see out the rear window. That was probably illegal."

If he's drawn to me because of my problem-solving abilities, how would he feel if he knew how intensely I've avoided dealing with one of my biggest issues? And that I've never even told him said issue exists?

"It's hard," I tell him, changing the subject. I turn my head to the side and lean it up against the wall. He does the same, and our faces are just a few inches away from each other. I can see every freckle on his face, every shade of brown in his eyes. "Being in your twenties, I mean."

Harrison studies me, waiting for me to continue—and so I do. "You're young, and you feel like you have to take advantage of being young by having fun and enjoying life and traveling and dating, but you also have to make sure you're setting yourself up for the rest of your life, because by the time you're thirty, if you don't have everything figured out, you're suddenly behind on everything. But how am I supposed to save for retirement and a down payment and excel in my career and *date* while also figuring out who I am and trying to figure out what I want to do with my life? How am I supposed to enjoy being in my twenties when every decision I make now feels like it has irreversible impacts on the rest of my life?"

"You did the hard part. You left a job you didn't like, and you found a new one." He pauses. "Is that why you don't want to talk to your parents? Because they don't know why you quit your job?"

I turn my head to face forward as the direct eye contact starts to feel claustrophobic. "Sort of. We talked about it in vague terms, but I could tell it was stressing them out. And then when I said I was moving to go work at a coffee shop in Boston, that stressed them out even more. I saw them pretty regularly when I was living in Tampa, but toward the end, I could tell talking to them about my plans was making them worried, but not talking about my plans was also making them worried. So even trying to go hang out with them and not discuss my impending move to Boston was emotionally taxing," I say. "I think they're worried I don't have a long-term plan, which is, incidentally, true."

"Knowing you? You're going to figure it out, and you're going to find something that makes you really, really happy."

You *make me really happy,* I want to tell him.

"And listen," he says. "If anyone knows what it's like to have your parents not understand your career choices, it's me." He squeezes my hand again.

"But you never let them convince you to do anything other than what you're passionate about," I say.

"Maybe. With regards to my career, anyway. But enough of that," he adds. We look at each other for a moment before he clears his throat and shifts, letting go of my hand and facing the bed frame. "Back to it?"

"Back to it," I agree.

Harrison continues to fiddle with the bed as I silently watch. I have so many questions I want to ask him: What if I told you I had a lot of problems? What if I told you I'd been procrastinating on fixing them for almost a decade? Would you still tolerate my presence?

The doorbell rings, and Harrison starts to move. I reach forward and press on his shoulder, forcing him to sit down as I use him for leverage to stand up.

I open the door to find Jo standing outside, holding a takeout bag in one hand. "Hi!" she says, looking at me with slightly too eager of a smile.

"Oh, uh—hi!" I say. "Shit, I'm so sorry—I meant to send a text about not being able to make it to yoga?"

Jo's smile falls slightly. "Yes, you did, and you said you were fixing your bed frame? I wanted to come over and see if you needed help. And also, to bring you food."

"Oh! Oh my god, of course. That was so kind of you. And we'd love help." I open the door, and she gives me a confused look until she sees Harrison behind me.

"Hey, Harrison," Jo says. Harrison lifts his hand in greeting. "Sorry, Emma made it sound like she was alone," she says, glancing back at me with a meaningful look. "So, I only brought two meals."

"Totally no worries," he says, waving a hand. "I have leftovers at home."

Jo hands me a Styrofoam container with what smells like

the single greatest burrito of all time. "How is the bed frame going?"

"Ask Bob the Builder over there," I say, nodding in Harrison's direction as I sit down on the couch and take an enormous bite. "Shit. I didn't think burritos this good existed in Massachusetts. This is exactly what I needed."

"Yeah, obviously you were working hard on the bed," Jo says, and I see Harrison chuckle and cast a smile in my direction out of the corner of my eye.

For the next couple hours, Jo and I chat while Harrison—slowly, because we keep distracting him—fixes the bed for me. And by the time he's done, I have a feeling I'm never going to be able to get in bed at night without thinking of him. But the truth is, that was the case already.

CHAPTER 13

When we arrive at Rose's party at nine o'clock, she is already a particularly lethal combination of drunk and hyper and maybe a little high, and her level of enthusiasm borders on alarming.

"Hey, you!" Rose shrieks at Harrison, not even bothering to acknowledge me or Jo. After Harrison revealed that Rose had also invited him to this party when he stopped by the coffee shop earlier this week, I begged him to accompany me. Unfortunately, I am now realizing her crush is exponentially stronger under the influence. Even I'm not that enthusiastic about seeing Harrison, and I've been in love with him for almost ten years.

"Ohmygod, so you two *do* know each other?" she asks. She has to yell over the music.

"We went to college together," Harrison says.

That's one way to put it.

"I KNEW it!" Rose shouts. "I LOVE this. Emma, now you can stop being boring at work and tell me embarrassing stories about Harrison!" She shoots Harrison a saucy look, and Harrison looks like he regrets all his life choices.

"Harrison doesn't do anything embarrassing," I say at the same time Harrison says, "I've never done anything embarrassing."

Rose doubles over in a fit of giggles, and when I make eye contact with Harrison, his brown eyes crinkle as his dimples appear.* Jo rolls her eyes next to us, but I can see from the twitch at the corner of her lips that she's enjoying this. Just like old times, I suppose.

"Not even that time I spilled an entire beer on your shirt?" he whispers, taking advantage of a quiet moment as Rose gets distracted by someone doing a keg stand.

"At my twenty-first birthday party, you mean?" I scoff. "Please. I was delighted. That's the coming-of-legal-drinking-age version of getting sprayed with champagne. I think I never washed the shirt again."

"That's disgusting."

"Well, *one* of us has to be embarrassing."

Harrison chuckles, and when we make eye contact, we hold it for a bit too long, music fading into the background.

Jo clears her throat, and Harrison and I jump as if we've been caught red-handed. "You two are ridiculous," Jo says.

"But you love us," Harrison volleys back. Jo playfully slaps his arm.

I love you, I think. Jo looks at me as if she can tell what I'm thinking, her face a mixture of warning and encouragement. *Tell him,* she says with her eyes. *But if you tell him, you better not fuck it up.*

Except I would fuck it up, because I don't know what I'm doing with my life, and also my vagina doesn't work, and also I

* **Soft smile · Small dimples · Head tilt to the right** | *Facial expression* | *Frequency: high*

1. Affection.
2. Generally platonic.

don't know how to act like a normal human being around him. Also, I have a date tomorrow. With someone who is not him.

The entire party is crowded into Rose's living room, and the only light is from string lights—Christmas lights, to be specific—hung between secondhand bookshelves and Command hooks. A Himalayan salt lamp glimmers in the corner, and a guy holding a blunt leans forward and licks it.

"Why are we here?" I ask, leaning into Harrison's side as he stares at the salt lamp and shivers with disgust.

He bumps his shoulder into mine. "I'm here because you told me to be here."

"You literally told me you were going."

"I told you I was invited," he says, raising an eyebrow. "There is a massive difference."

"Ugh. I had to come. I need my co-worker to like me."

"I'm your co-worker, and I like you," Jo offers.

I groan. "You're my boss. And my friend. You're obligated to like me. But Rose, on the other hand, thinks I'm lame. Why am I so *boring*?"

"You're not boring," Harrison says. "You're the most interesting person I've ever met." He blinks, then looks back at the Himalayan salt lamp, his ears turning red.*

You're interesting, too. Actually, I'm interested in you, I think. I think it so loudly the words almost come out, and maybe they would if Jo weren't shooting me a slightly crazed look, but just at that moment someone puts on "Timber" (you better move, you better dance, etc.) and turns the speaker up to full volume.

"SHOT?!" Rose screams at us, balancing three red Solo cups between her hands.

Jo and I take them from her immediately, but Harrison

* **Red ears** | *Physical reaction* | *Frequency: medium*

1. Embarrassment; extreme.

takes it more cautiously, peering into the cup. "And just to confirm. You poured this yourself?" he asks.

"Yep," she says, then gives him a look most appropriately described as salacious. "Poured it just for you."

I take the shot without waiting for them. It burns my throat—vodka, for sure. Something cheap. Something I should've stopped drinking after college but definitely have had more recently than that.

"Cheers," I say, gasping for breath. Harrison chuckles, then knocks back his own shot.

***

TWO HOURS LATER, I'M THREE shots in, and I've decided Rose is both my favorite co-worker and also my least favorite person of all time. She brought Harrison an additional two shots, touched his arm twice, and tucked her hair behind her ear while making eye contact *five* times. That's not normal. Straight hair stays behind your ears without incessant touching. I know that from experience.

When Harrison takes a bathroom break and Jo gets pulled into a conversation with some recent college graduate who wanted to hear everything there was to know about home-dyeing your hair the exact shade of burnt auburn that Jo has been rocking for ten years, Rose takes the opportunity of my moment of solitude to part the crowd and approach me. She leans into my ear as if to whisper, then yells, "I have a secret to tell you."

"I promise you, Rose," I say, "your crush on Harrison is not a secret."

She smirks, then takes a sip of her beer. "My secret is that I know Harrison has a crush on you."

My mouth drops open, but she's too busy drinking to take

in my full reaction. "Give me this," I hiss, grabbing the cup out of her hand. "You're clearly drunk."

"Ugh!" She swats at me as if I'm a fly. "Ugh! You suck. That's the *point.*"

"What the *hell* are you talking about?" I demand.

"You took my drink!"

I push the cup back into her hands, and beer splatters onto both of us. We let out a simultaneous "Ugh!"

"Fine," she grumbles, wiping her hands on her jeans. "Yes, I did have a crush on Harrison. Until like five minutes ago when I saw how he looks at you when he thinks no one is watching, and then I realized I have no shot with him."

I glance at the bathroom door. Still closed. "How does he look at me?"

Rose ignores the question. "Listen," she says, reaching out and grasping my arm with a sticky hand. "In the spirit of sisterhood, I'm going to let you have this one. As a welcome to Boston gift."

I blink at her. "What?"

She removes her hand from my arm and snaps her fingers in my face. "Harrison, dumbass. I'm going to let you have him. Unless you're not interested in men and/or you have bad taste in men, in which case I'm stealing him back."

"I think you're probably wrong about Harrison. He's been telling anyone who will listen that we're friends and always have been friends. He's going through a breakup. And I think he's into casual dating now. Like, dating apps and all that. That's not really my speed."

"I'm definitely not wrong. I'm incredibly observant." She widens her eyes so aggressively a vein pops in her temple. "You can't possibly tell me I'm the first person to tell you this."

I grunt in acknowledgment. "Jo says we couldn't stay away from each other if the fate of the world depended on it."

"Yeah, that sounds about right. That's the vibe I'm getting

from the way he looks at you. And to be honest, the way you look back. There's a lot of chemistry happening there. Like, sexual chemistry. To clarify."

The vodka churns in my stomach. "Do we know each other well enough to be having this conversation? Like, am I going to get in trouble with HR?"

Rose snorts. "What HR? Jo? And besides, we wouldn't get punished for this sisterhood. It was meant to be. We're, like, the same person."

The Himalayan salt lamp flickers as someone bumps into the table. "Sorry, how exactly are we the same person?"

"We have the same job." She puts up one finger. "I'm pretty sure you also have a crush on Harrison based on how red your face is, so we have the same taste in men." Second finger. "I don't know this, but I'd bet money you live in a shitty apartment." Third finger. "I know you're older, but you give off the vibe of a college student. Or at least a recent graduate." Fourth finger. "And in summary, you're a mess; I'm a mess. Same person."

I do not feel good about any of those comparisons.

The bathroom door opens, and as Harrison exits and scans the room, there's a slight frown on his face, the left corner of his mouth tugged downward. He brings a hand up to his forehead, brushing the waves away from his eyes, and as soon as he pulls his hand away, they plop back into place one by one.

He finally spots me, and I don't bother to hide that I've been staring at him. His eyebrows relax, the left corner of his mouth shifts from down to up, and a dimple slowly forms. When neither of us breaks eye contact, the right corner of his mouth joins the upward trajectory, creating a full soft smile.*

* **Soft smile · Small dimples · Head tilt to the right** | *Facial expression* | *Frequency: high*

1. Affection.
2. Generally platonic. [Note: Continue to observe for possible correction.]

I've been known to define this look as *affectionate.* Generally, it's platonic, but in this moment, I'm not so certain.

"Oh, he is *whipped,*" Rose whispers.

"I don't know what that means," I whisper back. Harrison keeps looking at me as he walks.

"It means I'm going to kill you if you mess this up," she says, then disappears into the crowd.

I take a sip of shitty beer to force myself to stop looking at him. I think it's Natty Light. Liquor stores should only sell this to college seniors. If you're twenty-two or older, you have no business drinking this.

Nonetheless, I take another sip, and as Harrison walks up to me and my vision goes pink and heart-eyed, I realize I may have made a grave error.

I've gotten drunk on shitty vodka and cheap beer.

"You good there?" Harrison says, studying my face with gentle concern. He reaches out and grasps my arm, his fingers wrapping around my elbow. I sway into him. "Yeah, me, too," he says, chuckling quietly. "I thought the whole point of light beer was that it's *light.*"

"We did take those three shots," I say. He starts to move his arm away, but I step closer. He wraps his arm behind me, settling his hand onto the small of my back. His pinky grazes the sliver of skin between the waist of my jeans and the cropped tee I dug out of a box (Hair Products, Going Out Tops, And Other Shit).

"I thought *liquor before beer, you're in the clear,*" he mutters.

"You're the doctor," I say. "You tell me."

"Nurse."

"Still."

He swirls his cup, creating a beer whirlpool. A bit of it splashes, and he removes his arm from my back, then uses a finger to wipe the side of the cup. He licks the beer off his hand, and I feel my entire body grow warm. Head to pelvic floor to toe.

Dontthinkaboutitdontthinkaboutit—

I'm thinking thoughts I shouldn't be.

I take another sip of beer. "Do you think Rose and I are the same person?"

His mouth quirks up as if I were joking. (I wasn't. My concern is genuine.)

"Oh, yeah," he says sarcastically. "Twins, really."

"She made some compelling points about how similar we are, and now I'm concerned my life has not progressed since I graduated from college."

"You definitely don't act like a college student."

I exhale a laugh. "Maybe. But how well do you think you know me?"

"Well," he says. "Better than I wish I did."

I blink away my wince. "Ah, yes. Because we're just supposed to be Friends with Limitations, or something, right?"

He pauses as he studies me, inhales, holds the breath, and then finally says, "I think my life would generally be easier if I couldn't read every expression on your face."

I don't know what my expression is doing, but he reaches out and runs his thumb across my eyebrow. His finger lingers on my temple, his palm hovering over my cheek, and I'm not sure we'll ever be able to break this eye contact. I think I might live and die in this moment, my gaze glued to his. I think I might have this image permanently tattooed into my memory, the faint smile lines and nearly invisible freckles, the eyelash that's fallen beneath his eye, the faintest hint of stubble. The way his pupils move in microscopic motions, as if he's studying every individual speck of green in my eyes.

I remember the first time this happened. The first time we stood this close, and the world around me ceased to exist.

Freshman year. In the dining hall, of all places. At seven-thirty A.M. breakfast, of all times. We both had an early-morning class, and we were the only people in the back room. We were laughing hysterically about how bad the coffee was—how was it possible for it to taste stale and burnt thirty minutes after the dining hall opened!—and when the laughter faded we were standing a little too close and breathing a little too heavily. *Are we about to kiss?* I'd thought. *Are we about to kiss in a dining hall?* He'd pulled away, and I had, too, I think. But that was the first moment I thought there might be something more, something—

Nope. Nope, nope, nope.

I obviously shouldn't be seriously dating right now, he'd said.

Too bad you're not good at casual, Key Lime says in the back of my head. Lavender chirps in agreement.

How well do you think you know me? I'd asked.

Better than I wish I did, he'd said.

"You still with me?" Harrison says, eyes darting back and forth between mine.

"Air?" I ask.

He doesn't hesitate, placing his hand on the small of my back again and nodding toward the sliding door to the backyard. I let him guide me through the mass of people, walking about 50 percent slower than I need to.

He slides the door open, and cool summer evening air rushes into the room. No one else follows us, but he leaves the door slightly cracked as if to signal we're not actually leaving the party.

Dead grass and dingy patio furniture litter the backyard. There's a pile to our right that could be a fire pit but could just be a pile of shit. A strand of lights is slung along the fence, but only the first five or so bulbs are actually lit. A small version of the Boston CITGO sign leans against the fence, lit up underneath a flickering lightbulb like a cheap neon sign. *Girls, girls, girls.* Or, *CITGO, CITGO, CITGO.*

"I love Rose, but this backyard is experiencing serious neglect," Harrison says.

This is nearly identical to my old backyard in Florida, but I don't admit that.

I take a step forward, and my foot catches on a loose board. I stumble, and Harrison reaches out and grabs my hand.

Note: Holding hands is clearly within the okay boundaries of Friends with Limitations, seeing as it keeps happening.

"You good?" he asks.

"Great. Fantastic."

He squeezes my hand. Neither of us let go.

There's a scream from inside as some top ten song starts playing. It sounds vaguely familiar, but when I look at Harrison, he shrugs and rolls his eyes. "I knew this party would make me feel old."

I snort. "Oh, please. We listened to Joni Mitchell in college. You should feel old anyway."

He chuckles, then lets go of my hand. I would sell my soul to the devil to get his fingers back in mine. He pulls his phone out of his pocket, and before I know it, there's a Joni Mitchell album playing. *Blue,* like how I'm going to feel when this moment is over.

He reaches out a hand. "Dance with me," he says. I withdraw my offering to the devil.

But he knows me better than he wishes he did, so why should I facilitate any kind of bonding? We're Friends with Limitations, and he's a supposed casual dater, and I'm a woman with a steel-trap vagina. Taking his hand is a criminally bad idea. I should be arrested for having the gall to say yes.

But, of course, I do.

He immediately spins me around, even as I tell him, "This is quite possibly the worst dancing music of all time."

"Live a little," he says.

The backyard feels like an alternate universe where nothing that happens counts. I can dance with him and bat my eyelashes and then go back to being a respectful neighbor and a good friend tomorrow. He can spin me around and then go back to lying to his mother about his relationship status and letting her say mean things about me. I can still go on this date with Alexander tomorrow and stop feeling guilty about it.

But as he holds my hands in his, swaying in time with the music, I forget what I was thinking about.

I give Harrison a twirl as I giggle and sing along to "All I Want".

Harrison laughs as he spins around, then joins in on the singing. He doesn't even remotely hit the right notes, which isn't a surprise because he's *never* hit the right notes, and I'm laughing so hard I don't care when he wraps an arm around my waist and dips me so low I think I might fall flat on my back. But, of course, he's got me—he pulls me back into his arms, his expression so light I think I might shatter from happiness. I think I might burst into a zillion joyous pieces, flinging confetti all over the backyard.

He continues to sing as he holds one of my hands and keeps the other arm wrapped around my waist, holding me against him. He leans in, his nose buried in my hair as we sway back and forth.

Something shifts in my stomach as he sings into my ear, and I chalk it up to the dancing and the spinning and the alcohol in my system. But as we continue to sway, as I adjust to the feel of his body against mine, as his breath tickles my neck, as the lights flicker on and off, *CITGO, CITGO, CITGO,* something in my chest shifts as well.

A smarter person would've recognized this scenario as the same trap she fell into time and time again in college, leading him on with no potential for an outcome either of us will be happy with. A smarter person would've pulled away. A smarter person would've recognized her limits and untangled herself from his arms before making the kind of mistake from which you can't recover.

A smarter person wouldn't have wrapped her arms around his neck, hanging on to him like her life depended on it.

A smarter person absolutely would *not* have leaned in even closer, soaking up his warmth and breathing in the woodsy scent of his shampoo.

But apparently, my dance partner isn't smart, either, or maybe just doesn't know any better, because he wraps his arms tighter around my waist, whispering lyrics into my ear and rocking me back and forth, like I'm the most precious thing in the world.

And as the next song starts playing, we hang on to each other, breathing in sync and swaying ever so slightly as Joni Mitchell serenades us, slowly and gently, about love.

I sing along, so quietly I'm not sure whether the whispered lyrics are audible, especially over the loud bass from inside that's not quite willing to fade into the background.

Harrison nuzzles against my neck and makes a soft hum of contentment, his breath catching slightly as I start playing with the curls that brush the top of his collar. A police siren turns on somewhere in the distance, and as my body twitches in surprise, Harrison chuckles under his breath and pulls me even closer, every inch of our bodies aligned.

"You make me laugh,", he whispers.

"And you make me smile," I tell him, still swaying.

"And your smile makes me smile." My muscles shift against his cheek as I grin, and he lets out a soft laugh that tickles my neck. "See?"

We continue to dance for the entirety of the song, holding each other and rocking back and forth, our bodies glowing from the flickering string lights.

"Harrison . . ." I finally whisper, despite having no idea what words are coming next. It could be literally anything from *I don't think I'm ever going to be able to look you in the eyes after this* to *Will you marry me?*

Thankfully, Harrison stops me before either of those two things—or anything in between—can escape my mouth. "*Shhhh,*" he whispers, letting out a breathy laugh.

"Fair enough," I murmur as the next song on the album begins. He sways me to the new tempo, humming in my ear and sending vibrations up and down my body. If he lets go of me, I will likely collapse. I consider it a minor miracle I'm standing at all—I have no idea where my body ends and his begins. I have no idea if my legs are still functional, or if he's completely supporting my weight. Is there a party going on inside? I wouldn't know. I can't feel a single thing other than the spot right underneath my ear where his nose brushes my neck every time we sway backward. And every time we sway forward, and I lose that pinprick of contact, a part of me dies before being immediately reincarnated one second later when we sway backward again.

Harrison turns his head ever so slightly, leaving his lips brushing against my neck. My breath catches, every thought funneling from my mind as I wait to see what he'll do next. The music must still be playing, but I can't hear anything. Our swaying has stopped, too. This is a movie, and we just hit pause—except we're still breathing, a little heavier than we should be, our chests rising and falling in sync.

Finally, *finally,* he presses a gentle kiss to the soft section of skin beneath my left ear, and my past, present, and future collide, disintegrate, and re-form.

Despite myself, I let out a small *mmm,* and one of his hands starts drawing circles against my waist.

"Can I ask you something?" he whispers.

"Anything," I say, only about 10 percent aware of what's happening beyond the feel of his skin on mine.

"Do you remember the night we met?"

The music begins returning to my consciousness.

"When we talked about soulmates?" he continues.

My breath catches. I am feeling vaguely claustrophobic.

"Did you mean what you said? About not believing in soulmates, and about not being interested in them?"

It's funny when things you said nearly a decade ago come back to bite you in the ass. Karma is cruel like that. Because even now, when his hand on my back makes me feel so many things I've missed, I know this will end the same way it did before. I'm not better yet. There are physical therapy exercises that I need to do, calls I need to make to my parents, stuff still in boxes on the floor I need to unpack. Harrison has a career and a life and is taking care of his mom and a guinea pig. He's not ready to date seriously, and I can't be casual with anyone, especially Harrison. I knew this before his hand was around my waist and now I have to hurt him all over again before this becomes a bigger mistake. And so the words slip out of my mouth, more on instinct than anything else:

"Sorry, I'm not sure what you're talking about."

Because what else am I supposed to say? Oh, I do remember, but I actually do believe in soulmates, even though I led you to believe you're not mine? Because if I had told you how I felt then I'd have to explain why it didn't matter how I felt because there was something else I didn't and still don't want to tell you about? I know you hate liars, but maybe you can make an exception for me, your favorite Friend with Limitations!

Harrison removes his hands and takes a step back, studying me. I can tell by his expression that he knows I know what he's talking about, but he doesn't call me out on it, which makes me feel a hundred times shittier.

The only thing worse than fighting with someone you love is not being worth the fight.

"I need some water," Harrison says, then walks inside.

The string lights flicker off for good, and I'm shrouded in darkness.

CHAPTER 14

I swipe Too Faced's Better Than Sex mascara onto my eyelashes, staring at myself in the cloudy bathroom mirror and taking deep, ragged breaths in an attempt to calm my nerves.

"Stop breathing so loudly. I can literally hear you from here," Jo shouts. "You may *not* pass out on my watch."

Jo has been here since she closed up shop this afternoon, and she's spent the last hour and a half helping me select an outfit and come up with conversation starters. What's your favorite restaurant in Boston? How do you get your hair to look so sun-bleached even though you live in New England? Jo knows as well as I do that it's been many, many months since I've gone on a real date—double date not included—so I need to make sure my tool kit is full. Especially considering that the last date I went on only lasted thirty minutes. It was my old co-worker's friend, so I thought he would have been appropriately vetted. But no: Half a cup of coffee in, he made a joke about the size of his dick, at which point I "ran to the bathroom" so I could leave through the emergency exit. I don't know why I agreed to go on the date in the first place, but I suppose that's the eternal question.

Tonight's outfit is a silky midi dress, dyed a deep turquoise. The way it clings to my body while simultaneously swinging back and forth as I move is mesmerizing to watch in the mirror. And dressed down with a pair of strappy sandals, I look cool. Chic. Collected. *Adult.*

"You could always ask Harrison on a date instead," Jo yells.

Something gnaws at my insides. (It's guilt.)

"I'm not trying to get out of this." I narrow my eyes at her as I walk back out of the bathroom and collapse next to her on the bed, taking care to smooth out my dress so it doesn't wrinkle.

"You're not trying to get out of the date, or the dress? Because asking Harrison out would help you accomplish both, if last night was any indication," Jo mutters.

I scowl, ignoring her and *not* thinking about the almost-kiss last night. It's so far removed from my mind, I don't even know what she's talking about. Last night? Remind me, what did I do last night?

"This guy is hot," I say. "This is good for me."

"I mean, I guess I agree. But *why* do you want to go?"

"Why not?" I ask, as if it's that simple. "I'm trying to be an adult and do adult things. Plus, Rose said I should go."

Jo shoots me a glare. "Well, if *Rose* says you should do it."

I also bought a record player for my apartment because *Rose* told me it was embarrassing I didn't have one, but I keep that to myself. I also do not share that I switched from silver to gold jewelry because *Rose* told me all the hot girls wore gold now. My ears and fingers are permanently stained green.

"It's not that simple," I say, holding my hands up in defense. "He literally told me in no uncertain terms that he wasn't seriously dating right now."

"Opinions change. Besides, I saw you two outside at Rose's party last night. I'm not an idiot, and neither are you. You both know what's going on."

My skin prickles in the exact spot where Harrison's fingers brushed against my back last night as he held me. *Your smile makes me smile,* he'd said. So much for not thinking about it.

"I have something to say," I quietly offer.

"If you're about to tell me you have a crush on Harrison, I'm going to slap you."

"No, I know you already know that." Jo slaps my arm anyway. "This sounds crazy, but . . ."

"Please, for the love of god, just say it."

I swallow. "I think Harrison might have broken up with Stephanie because of me."

For once, Jo actually looks like I've caught her off guard. She waits a moment before speaking, as if the statement deserves a moment to settle before she responds. Finally, she asks: "What makes you think that?"

"I swear, I never would've thought that at first," I say, and she nods. "I mean, that would be insane, and even now, I feel so full of myself even suggesting it."

"Okay, stop the self-deprecating. Get on with it."

"It's just that . . . the explanations he keeps offering for why he broke up with Stephanie are vague, but also I heard my name come up when they were fighting upstairs that one day, and I know he told his mom his relationship problems with Stephanie weren't because of me, but of course he wouldn't tell her that, and then there's the timing of it all, and—"

"You're rambling."

"And he obviously has feelings for me. I think he doesn't want to have feelings for me, but he does anyway, and he's not sure what to do about it yet."

"Hence last night."

"Hence last night," I agree.

Jo blinks slowly, considering. "I'm going to ask you a question."

I blink slowly in return. "Shoot."

"Do you want him to have broken up with her for you?"

"That's an impossible question."

"Try to answer it anyway, though."

Do better, I think. *Think it through, then tell the truth.* "I want him to like me when I'm ready for him to like me. And I'm not ready yet."

Jo's face is devoid of emotion. "I cannot even begin to fathom what that means."

I sit up, taking off my shoes, then propping my back against my pillows and flinging my throw blanket over my lap, potential wrinkles now worth the comfort of a warm cocoon. "Um," I say, staring at my toes peeking out from the foot of the blanket. "It means that I would like Harrison to like me once I'm done with pelvic floor therapy, but not before then?" Jo looks like she's going to pass out, so I continue rather than face her wrath. "And it means that Harrison thinks he likes me, but he doesn't really know what he's getting into, so he can't *really* like me?"

"So tell him what he's getting into," Jo says without missing a beat.

"If I told him, he'd want to date me anyway."

"So tell him," Jo repeats, looking around the room as if searching for an explanation.

"I don't want to date him until I'm the best version of myself."

"That's the stupidest thing I've ever heard," Jo says.

I laugh, and then I realize she's not laughing. "Okay," I say cautiously. "Your point is made."

"You don't need to better yourself to date someone you like," she says, fuming. "That's not how it works. You don't wait until you're the best version of yourself, whatever you mean by that, to date the person who you've been pining after and who has liked you forever. You're the only one making it complicated."

"You know as well as I do that Harrison and I have always been *just friends.*"

She scoffs. "Yeah, right. Me and you? We're *just friends.*" She puts air quotes around the words, her tone turning sharp. "Whatever's going on between you and Harrison is something completely different, and it always has been. And believe me, I would know. I've had a front-row seat to the entire saga, from day one."

"What is happening right now? Why are you being mean?"

"Because!" Jo raises her voice, and I cringe, praying Harrison isn't home. Jo lowers her voice slightly as she continues. "Because we were supposed to be taking care of each other right now, but now Harrison is back in your life and Macy's gone, so I'm suddenly the third wheel. And that's when you decide to invite me at all."

"I know. I'm sorry. And I really, really empathize with you about Macy having to leave for six months. I can't imagine how hard that is."

"Yes, Emma, it's fucking hard. And I'm so grateful to have you here in town, but whenever I'm with you, it feels like you actually just want to be with Harrison. And he only wants to be with you!" She waves at me to stop talking as I open my mouth to argue. "You literally ditched me at Rose's party. Did you think I wanted to talk to Rose's roommate's cousin about drug store hair dye? No. I wanted to hang out with you. I mean, for the love of god, does no one want to be around me? You don't. Macy didn't, apparently."

"Jo," I whisper. "What happened with Macy?"

"Nothing!" she yells. "And that's the worst part! Nothing was wrong, and then they took this gig anyway because they said it would be good for their career, and now I'm fucking lonely and I'm fucking stressed all the time, and you are driving me *insane* because you have the love of your life right in front of you, and you just complain about it!"

"I'm really, really sorry about Macy. And I'm sorry I haven't been prioritizing you. That's shitty of me. I promise I'll be better. But when it comes to Harrison, it's complicated, and you know that. It's not the right time. I'm not ready."

"If you say you're not ready, then why are you going on this date?"

"I can go on a date without wanting to be in a relationship. It's good practice."

Jo looks at me like I'm insane. "What are you going to do? *Sleep* with him?"

I reel back. "That was mean."

"Look, I'm sorry," Jo says, sighing and rubbing her eyes. "I just don't want you to get hurt. I don't understand why you're doing this."

And that is *the* question, isn't it? Why am I doing this?

Why am I going on a date if I know I shouldn't be in a relationship? I think it's because this is part of doing better. Maybe if I go on a date and it goes well then I'll take my physical therapy seriously and be able to have sex with someone. Maybe it's because I'm bored.

Or maybe it's because I want to feel normal. I want to feel like a fully fledged adult.

When I don't answer, Jo continues. "I know dating is complicated for you. I know you haven't been able to have penetrative sex yet. I get it. But you can't keep using this as an excuse to not be with someone you actually care about. It's depressing." I blink, startled by her honesty. "I know that's a lot, but you're never going to admit that to yourself. Someone needs to say it," she adds. "You deserve love."

"I know I deserve love," I say, my voice growing more heated even while I keep the volume low. "I deserve love, and yes, Harrison deserves love, too, but that doesn't mean our love is a good match, at least right now."

"What does that even mean?"

"Love is supposed to come naturally. It's supposed to be simple. And that's not us. It never has been, and it might never be. Not until I figure this thing out, anyway."

Jo scoffs. "Anyone who's ever been in love could tell you that nothing about it is *simple.*"

There are a million things I should say, but instead, "Jo, you have no idea what you're talking about" comes out of my mouth. Which I know is absurd even as I'm saying it, because Jo has literally been in love with the same person for nine years.

"Don't I, though?" she says, scowling.

"Sorry it's *depressing* for you to hear that I can't be in a normal relationship. Sorry it's *depressing* to you that I'm a twenty-seven-year-old virgin."

Jo narrows her eyes. "Do you know how idiotic it is for you to define a 'normal' relationship as one in which a man can successfully fit his dick inside of you?"

"That is what sex between a man and woman is, Jo."

"I've told you a thousand times before, there are other ways to be intimate with men! Non-penetrative sex is for everyone."

"Tell that to all the men who have ghosted me because I wouldn't have penetrative sex."

"Harrison isn't like that, and you know it," she hisses.

"Maybe Alexander isn't, either," I continue while Jo groans. "So, yeah, Jo, I'm going on a date as my way of pretending I'm doing something about this, when we both know, as you've made so clear, that my own stupidity is the only thing stopping me from being happy. Am I going to have sex tonight? Obviously not. Okay? Is that what you want to hear?"

Another loaded pause. And then, "So just to summarize," she says, slowly, "you know going on this date is a stupid idea, but you're going anyway?"

I stand up abruptly, my breathing stilted. "Fuck you, Jo," I say. She scoffs at me, then stands up, grabs her tote bag, and rushes out, slamming the door.

I'm still glaring at the door when my phone buzzes.

Harrison: Everything okay? Heard shouting.

Instead of dealing with my emotions healthily, I scream into my pillow. When I lift my head, there's a faint imprint of my Better Than Sex mascara flaked off across the fabric of my pillowcase.

Fuck you, Jo, I scream silently into the void. *Fuck you for thinking you understand what I'm going through.*

Some insane voice from the depths of my brain whispers back, *Harrison would understand.*

I punch my pillow, right in the makeup-imprint face. *Fuck you, brain.*

Emma: Yep! Just the tv.
Thanks for checking.

Before I can text Alexander and cancel my date, another notification pops up.

Alexander: I'm outside in a silver Prius!
Ready when you are

And most of all, fuck my life.

CHAPTER 15

"Emma!" Alexander says, getting out of his car to approach me.

He's gotten a haircut since the double date, and his blond hair is slightly shorter, making him look less boyish-surfer and more adult-man. His grin lights up his face, revealing startlingly white teeth. Much to my surprise, I find myself smiling back at him.

"You look beautiful," he says, his voice rumbly as he pulls me into a hug, my cheek pressed against the crisp cotton of his button-down. Despite being in the middle of the city, he smells like a beach, which is more than a little appealing to my Floridian heart.

"Alexander! You look nice yourself!" I say, miraculously managing to keep my tone light despite the simmering anger and gnawing guilt right beneath the surface. As he pulls out of the hug, I thank him for coming to pick me up.

"Of course. The restaurant is just a short drive," he says, opening the passenger door for me.

"Oh? Where are we going?"

He smiles mischievously at me once he's settled back into the driver's seat, his ocean-colored eyes lighting up in a way that is not *not* appealing. "Okay, so it's this new place where—hear me out—you eat in complete darkness. You're blindfolded, so you can't see the food you're eating."

A stray giggle escapes out of me. "Weird, but I'm down!"

When we arrive at the restaurant ten minutes later, a waiter greets us and walks us through the dining experience. After we choose our meals, the waiter guides us to our table, then pulls out two black strips of fabric as we sit down.

The setting is already dark as it is—not completely dark but lit-by-fake-candlelight dark. There are long, flickering shadows all over, and it's unnerving enough that I'm almost glad I'll be forced to keep my eyes closed the entire time.

"Ready?" the waiter asks. We nod, and Alexander reaches out and takes one of the blindfolds.

"I've got hers," he says, standing up and walking to my side of the table.

"Oh—" I sputter out. "Oh, okay, go ahead." I tilt my head down so he can tie the back.

As he knots it, he leans down, and I hear his quiet words right in my ear. "Do you like being blindfolded?"

I gulp.

"Oh, um, yes, it'll make the food so much more interesting," I rasp. But if Alexander can tell I'm flustered, he doesn't say anything about it. Instead, he lets out a low chuckle against the back of my neck. Chills run down my spine, and I'm not sure whether they're the good kind or the bad kind.

I shake it off.

He steps backward, leaving cold air in his place as he returns to his seat. I hear the rustling of fabric as the waiter blindfolds him.

If you say you're not ready, then why are you going on this date?

Jo's words ring through my mind during the brief lull in conversation.

You can't keep using this as an excuse to not be with someone you actually care about.

Oh, yeah? Well, who's to say this perfectly nice, handsome young man in front of me couldn't become someone I care about?

And so, for the next hour, I chat with Alexander, who, as it turns out, is a pleasant date. Maybe I would've known that if I had even remotely paid attention to him during our first dinner. We fall into easy conversation, exchanging stories over drinks and food. Alexander tells me about his childhood in Maryland, his new consulting job, and his cat, Buster.

"That's a dog name," I tell him.

"Correct," he agrees. "That's why it's funny."

He asks me about my childhood in Florida, about how my adjustment to a new city has been, and about my new job. Not being able to see anything takes some of the pressure off; I'm not constantly fixing my hair or worrying whether I'm chewing grossly. I'm not reminded by his looks that he's out of my league and has probably had sex with two hundred women. This is exactly what I need to get everything else out of my mind.

But why can't I shake the feeling that I'm cheating on someone I'm not even dating?

You two have been pining for each other since the moment you met.

"So, what do you think?" he asks, switching topics. "Was it the eggplant parm that did them in?"

I stare blankly at him. Or rather, I stare at a black blob in the general direction of his voice.

"Steph. And Harrison? The eggplant parm? That they fought over in the restaurant?"

"Oh, uh—"

"I mean, he was being an asshole."

"Was he? I think he was just trying to not cause problems."

"Making Steph talk to the waiter on his behalf is asshole behavior. And is definitely causing problems."

I run through the memory in my mind, baffled. "Were we at the same dinner table?"

He ignores me. "Anyway. Seems like she can do better. I'm guessing he didn't have much game in college, either?"

"I don't know anything about his dating life in college." Fact check: false.

"Well. What a crazy night. Worst double date I've ever been on." Fact check: true.

I take a long swig of wine, finishing my glass. "Well, thanks for taking a chance on a second date." (Am I thankful? I think so!) (I don't know.)

"My pleasure," he says. "What's your overall impression of blindfolded dating?"

"Well, I'm glad you didn't see me trying to blindly get this pasta onto my fork."

Alexander lets out a low laugh. I smile, fully aware he still can't see it. Maybe if I smile enough, I'll convince myself I'm having a good time. Which I am! I think! Does that mean it's a good date?

It feels harder to measure how successful dates are when there's no possibility of going home together afterward.

After we take off our blindfolds, I take a quick trip to the bathroom to make sure my eye makeup hasn't smeared all over my face. Leaning over the counter and staring into the mirror, I use a tissue to gently wipe away the mascara residue pooling under my eyes. Miraculously, my hair still falls in well-formed waves around my face, and once my makeup is fixed, I'm back to being a bombshell. I'm going to have to let Jo pick my outfits more often.

Me and you? We're just friends. *Whatever's going on between you and Harrison is something completely different, and it always has been.*

I can do this. I have gone on a normal date with an above-average guy, had a pleasant conversation, and have not embarrassed myself. I'm half an hour away from checking off another Do Better task.

I walk back to the entryway of the restaurant, trying not to run into any blindfolded patrons. Alexander waits for me by the exit, his hands casually in his pockets. The way he studies me, taking in my every move as I walk back, makes my stomach churn uncomfortably.

But I shake it off. Again.

"Ready?" he says, taking his hand out of his pocket and offering it to me.

I lace my fingers through his. "Let's roll."

Determined not to let my nerves or the weird feeling in my gut prevent me from ending on a high note, I flirt confidently on the short drive back to my apartment. I laugh at his jokes. I bat my eyelashes.

When we arrive at my apartment, he walks me to my door, my hand in his. I let go to dig my keys out of my purse. "Well, Alexander, this has been such a lovely night. Thank you again for dinner. That was such a fun idea."

"You're very welcome," he says. His smile is so genuine, and the look in his eyes makes me feel so desired, and when his gaze flickers down to my mouth and back up to my eyes, I find myself charmed. Or if not charmed, at least flattered. That's how I'm supposed to feel, right? That's what happens when you say good night at the end of a nice date with someone. A kiss wasn't explicitly part of my Do Better list, but I think I earn bonus points if I go above and beyond, and lord knows I need the extra credit.

And so when he steps forward a few inches, and his gaze flickers to my mouth again, I smile, and I step forward a few inches, too. And when he closes the distance and presses his lips against mine briefly and chastely, I feel . . .

Nothing. Abso-fucking-lutely nothing.

He leans back, the look on his face restrained but undeniably hungry. I, too, feel an emptiness inside of me, but not in a hungry way. I feel an intense lack, an acknowledgment that I know what I need to do to feel fulfilled, but I've done the exact opposite.

I messed up, I realize. It hits me like a truck. *I should've been doing something else tonight. With someone else.*

"Thank you for a great night," I say, taking a step back.

He takes a step forward, tilting his head so his lips are nearly brushing my ear. "Are you going to invite me in?" His voice is low and gravelly, making me shiver.

I stand my ground, attempting to show him with my body language that I'm going to stand firm. "I actually have an early morning tomorrow. So, this is where I leave you."

His finger traces a line across my shoulder, then slips underneath the thin, silky strap of my dress. He pulls it away from my skin, runs his finger across the fabric, then lets it fall back onto my collarbone. "I promise I'll make it worth your while."

"I think you should probably go," I say quietly, still not moving.

"No need to play hard to get with me." He slips his finger under my strap again. I flinch, but he makes no move to back off. "Come on, I know you want more than that one little kiss."

He pulls his head away from my ear, but he's still standing too close. His face is only inches away, and I can see every intention in his eyes.

It may not be his fault that this date was doomed to fail from the start, but it is certainly going to be his fault if this date ends with me blocking his number and telling him never to contact me again.

"Alexander," I say, raising my voice slightly while I slip my keys between my fingers, sharp bits pointing out. "I said no. One kiss does not entitle you to anything more. I said no, and I meant it, and I'm going inside now." I grit my teeth. "Thank you for dinner, but this is going to end here, at the door."

He stares at me like he's completely oblivious to my shift in tone. Or maybe he just doesn't care. Either way, he doesn't move a single inch.

Until suddenly, he's not standing still anymore.

"A final good night kiss, then, and then I'll leave," he says, stepping forward and reaching for the back of my head, trying to pull me in. As he leans in, I startle backward, but that doesn't stop him. He keeps moving forward, and he looms over me, and I'm suddenly aware that he's almost a foot taller than me, and I'm also aware that the only person who knows I had a date tonight is Jo, and she won't be checking on me, and—

I knee him in the balls.

I knee him in the balls, exactly like I did that night freshman year when I needed to get out of a tricky situation *fast.* Of course, that first time, it was an accident. This time is very much on purpose. I cannot think of anyone who deserves this more, in fact.

"You BITCH," he yelps, stumbling backward and crumpling in half.

"Get the FUCK away from me," I scream.

He takes a gasping breath, unfurling himself, and I start to step back, but he steps back instead. "Thanks for nothing, slut," he says, then limps off.

I stand on alert until his car is driving away, and then I fall to the ground, bringing my hand up over my mouth. My eyes are bugging out of their sockets, and when my lungs expand and deflate, I'm not sure if any oxygen is actually entering my body.

Inhale.

Exhale.

All I wanted was one normal, successful, wholesome date. That's it. And it was ruined—but not because of my vagina. It was ruined because of a guy being a dick.

Inhale.

Exhale.

I walk inside and lock the door.

CHAPTER 16

10:36 P.M.

Emma: Are you upstairs?

Harrison: Yes

Harrison: Why?

Sorry, I don't know why I asked. I don't need anything.

Just wanted to see if anyone else is in the building.

Everything okay?

Weird night. But yes, I'm okay.

Do you want to talk about it?

Not right now. But thank you.

Always

Hey. You know what I was thinking about today?

What?

Do you remember the last day of our first semester of college

When we were done with exams and we had the full afternoon free

And we went sledding?

We didn't just go sledding.

We got you on a sled *for the first time in your life*

Important distinction

Emma replied to "We got you on a sled *for the first time in your life*"

It was literally a tray from the dining hall

And you know what?

I had the time of my life

I was so bruised the next day.

Oh, please. You also had the time of your life

Both can be true

I contain multitudes

I know you do.

Why were you thinking about that?

It was 88 degrees today

You don't want to know

Oh lord

Fine, I'll tell you

😑

I had a patient today who tried to learn how to surf

. . . ?

He tried to learn how to surf in the pool at his summer camp

Using a tray from the mess hall

I think he was almost as bruised as you were after sledding

Oh, fantastic

Glad to hear that teenage boy shenanigans remind you of me

He was eight.

But you honestly should be glad to hear that it reminded me of you

You make me laugh

Always happy to provide opportunities to laugh at my expense

Laughing with you, not at you

You don't remember how hard we were laughing that night?

You had a lot of bruises, but I think my lungs were permanently injured from how hard I laughed

Lol

We had a lot of fun, didn't we

The most fun

I don't remember the last time I laughed that hard

Are we old and boring?

A little bit of both, I think

A shame.

Maybe we need to go sledding again this year, then

Maybe we can invest in an actual sled this time

I think I prefer dining hall trays

For memory's sake

Great. Next we'll start playing beer pong

And carting all of our belongings around in backpacks

And then when we've done that, we'll eat ramen for dinner

And you can wear your orange socks

And maybe you can break out your ukulele

Oh please no

And write me a song

Oh god stop

What did you call that song?

Up All Night (Doing Homework)?

NO ONE TOLD ME SONGWRITING 101 WAS MEANT FOR MUSIC MAJORS

I think I have a video somewhere

I will block your number

Again?

11:43 P.M.

Sorry, I'm messing this up

I was trying to be funny

Please don't apologize

I'm the one who blocked your number

I'm sorry.

Really, truly sorry.

I forgive you.

And I really like being your friend again

I do too

11:55 P.M.

Did you know we would become such close friends?

That night we met?

I'm not sure I'd use those words to describe what I was thinking, no

But I definitely knew I wanted to be in your life

So I suppose the answer to your question is I hoped so

I remember walking into that room feeling the entire weight of the world on my fragile 18-year-old shoulders

And you cheered me up so quickly and so completely

I don't even know how

You've always been easy to read

In a good way, I mean

I like that I can always tell when you need help, because then I can be the one to help

You might be the only person in the world who thinks I'm that easy to read

And that's what makes our friendship special, isn't it?

Special. Yeah

Something like that.

Something like that.

12:17 A.M.

You know what sledding makes me think of?

What?

Do you romember those two days our sophomore year when there was a snowstorm

And the wifi was out on campus for two days?

Yep. And no one knew what to do with their free time that didn't involve wifi

We went sledding then, too.

But you're forgetting the best part

The hot chocolate you made me?

Nope. Although I do make a mean hot chocolate

Remind me this winter

But anyway. We got so bored that we checked out a DVD player from the library

OH MY GOD YES

And dug out a DVD from that keepsakes box you used to keep under your bed

And then we watched your middle school's production of Seussical Jr.

HAHAHA

In which you starred as a bird

Notably, I did NOT star

I was an ensemble bird

Not Mayzie LaBird, because my frenemy Sarah got cast instead

Did you become frenemies before or after she got the role you wanted

After.

Harsh.

That's showbiz, baby

You missed your calling as a leading lady

Maybe I should find a local theater group and put that theory to the test

I would come to every show!

Front row?

Obviously. And then I'd be the first to stand during applause

I hate those people

And I'd toss roses on stage

Multiple roses? Wow.
I'm spoiled

A dozen

No, two dozen for my leading lady!

And I'd come to your dressing room after and ask for your autograph

My dressing room, huh?

A dedicated fan

Ah, but I'm not just any fan. I'm your biggest fan.

12:37 A.M.

Please stop typing and say it.

The bubbles are killing me

Are you actually my
biggest fan?

Sending me a "what are we" text at 12:37 a.m.? Bold move

I'm serious, Harrison.

Because you would be justified in not being my biggest fan

I'm your biggest fan, Em.

Even now?

Even now.

12:46 A.M.

What happened tonight?

I went on a date, and it was bad.

Bad? Or bad bad

Both, actually

Do you need help?

Not really. I'm just on edge.

I'm glad to know that there's someone awake and here

Here, through the ceiling anyway

Of course. I'm here

I'm sorry that happened.

That's such a meaningless thing to say, but I do truly mean it

I hope you know you can always count on me for help when you need it

And I'm really glad you're home safe

Thank you, Harrison <3

1:16 A.M.

Hey Harrison?

Are you awake?

Yeah

Can't sleep

1:22 A.M.

Once again, your bubbles are killing me

Will you come over?

CHAPTER 17

When the door opens, Harrison takes a deep breath and opens his mouth, about to speak. I can see in his eyes what he wants to say and what he wants to do, and for once, I think it might actually be a good idea to act on it.

I take a step forward.

He also takes a step forward, into my apartment. He closes the door behind him.

I take another step forward, my face inches away from his. His eyes soften, his pupils dilating.*

And then, in a moment of intense clarity and insane recklessness, I grab the collar of his shirt and pull him down into a crushing kiss.

For a sliver of a second, Harrison freezes, his lips completely

*** Softened eyes · Dilated pupils · Slightly parted lips** | *Facial expression* | *Frequency: low*

1. Affection.
2. Lust.

still against mine. And in that sliver of a second, my heart stops, and I realize I may have just made the most epic mistake of my entire life.

Until he brings his hands to my face and opens up to my kiss, meeting me with the same crushing passion.

Finally. After years of anticipation—*finally.*

My mind splinters into a thousand pieces, my heart pounding out of my chest. In this moment, I understand exactly what Jo meant. How could I have thought that I needed to be any different to experience this volcanic eruption of everything I've wanted for so long? Why was I ever worried? I don't remember.

The feel of his lips on mine accounts for only a small percentage of the overall sensation. The kiss itself pales in comparison to the warm press of his chest against my beating heart, the security of his hands tangled in my hair, the relief of a long exhale, letting go of weeks—years, really—of bated breath.

"Are you sure about this?" Harrison whispers, pulling his lips just a hair away from mine. He's completely breathless, and I'm not sure whether it's from shock or the kiss or the heart palpitations we both seem to be experiencing. When I don't respond immediately, his body tenses ever so slightly, a movement I wouldn't have felt if I hadn't been pressed firmly against him. "I feel like you're in an emotionally fragile state right now and I don't want—"

"Shut up and kiss me, idiot. This is the best kiss of my life, and you're ruining it."

That seems to do it. His face splinters into a massive grin, his eyes sparkling even as they grow darker with every second. I throw my arms around his neck, our lips locking together in a drugging embrace. His kiss is unrelenting, as if he's been literally *starved.* And I'm so desperate for him in return, it sucks all the oxygen out of my lungs. We should be kissing, always.

We should stay up all night kissing, and when we die from fatigue, this will be the happy memory that shepherds me into the afterlife. The end.

I let out a soft, pitiful moan of delight. He pauses and laughs quietly.

"Stop laughing," I breathe. "More kiss."

I bare my neck for him, and he starts peppering kisses below my ear, along my jawline, everywhere he can reach. "Best kiss of your life, huh?"

He picks me up and carries me over to my couch, and I immediately climb into his lap. His body is firm and warm beneath me, anchoring me as his fingers run up my arms, sending earthquakes down my entire body. When his hands land on my face, his thumbs trace my jawline as his eyes take me in.

"Mine, too," he whispers into my ear, giving my neck a soft kiss.

"Thank you for not being an asshole," I whisper.

He doesn't laugh the way I expect him to. Instead, he wraps his arms around my waist, pulling me forward and resting his chin on my shoulder. "We need to talk about raising your standards," he finally murmurs, squeezing me tightly.

"I would say I have high standards, actually. Which is mostly your fault."

He leans back and tilts his head, studying me with intoxicating eyes. Harrison wants to know all my secrets, and . . . I think I maybe want to share them.

I deserve love. As if he can sense my thoughts, Harrison flips us over so we're lying down, then gives me another full-lipped kiss that obliterates any remaining sense of self I was hanging on to.

When Harrison finally pulls away several minutes later to take a breath, his lips are dark and swollen, and he looks more handsome than ever, even with his hair ruffled and eyes dazed. I want to photograph this moment. I want this image permanently etched into my mind. I want to see this version of Harrison every time I close my eyes.

I've never cared for someone as much as I care for him. But with that realization comes a sharp stab of guilt, because I'm on track to repeat my mistakes from college. I'm supposed to be Doing Better, but I've acted impulsively, giving in to my desires without providing any of the relevant information or context. He deserves so much better.

"Harrison?" I murmur as he kisses his way down my neck. He gives a hum of acknowledgment. "Maybe we should talk about what this means?"

He gives another low grumble, then continues to kiss me.

"Harrison."

He finally looks up, brown eyes turned black. "I'm a little busy right now," he says, one dimple forming.

"I just—"

"Em," he says, cutting me off as he props himself up on his forearms so he's hovering above me. "Obviously we're going to talk. We have a lot to figure out. But unless you were about to tell me you want to stop, I vote you hold that thought until tomorrow."

I blink at him. "Who are you and what have you done with Harrison?"

He kisses my cheek, slowly enough to be sad. "I've learned the hard way that when it comes to Emma Rogers, I have to take what I can get, whenever I can get it."

It's not like he *needs* to know at *this exact moment,* right? I mean, he's saying it himself. He doesn't want to talk right now. Which is great, because I don't actually want to talk, either. I have no practiced script, no talking points.

So it'll benefit both of us to put off this conversation, right? The truth can come out later, because right now, I just want his lips back on mine.

"Were you . . ." he asks, eyes glued to mine.

"Huh?"

"Were you going to tell me to leave?" The tentative look that flashes across his face breaks my heart.

"Of course not," I say, and he quietly exhales. "We'll talk tomorrow."

Harrison brings his mouth back to mine, planting kisses so gently my heart rate seems to both speed up and slow down. Our hands carefully explore the feeling of each other's bodies, studying the skin of the person we know so well emotionally while having so much to learn physically.

And the sounds he makes—the quiet hums, almost the same ones he uses when he finishes a book or eats the first bite of dinner. But lower and rumblier, somehow. The sound of a starving stomach finally being fed. The sound of a cat, content within an inch of its life.

I don't have the mental wherewithal to stop the breathy gasps and moans that come out of my mouth, even though I know he's probably hanging on to them the way I am, crumbs of information for him to store away and recall later. I certainly can't stop the gasp that erupts as his hand carefully and tenderly slides under my dress, stroking up the outside of my thigh and landing on my waist.

He takes my response as a go-ahead, which I suppose it was. But it was involuntary—because if I had thought about it for a moment, I would have realized it is not a good idea to let Harrison start getting under my clothes.

Do I want to get naked with Harrison? Yes. Is that something my body will support? No. As the thought enters my brain, my pelvic floor muscles clench up.

My vaginismus is nothing if not punctual.

Another muscle spasm seizes me as Harrison starts a downward stroke, his hand running over my ass and down the back of my thigh before pulling my leg upward in a way that brings my now-exposed underwear a little (a lot) too close to his lap. Which, I am now noticing, is quite—*uh*—strained.

"Wait," I shout, jerking backward. Harrison reacts immediately, letting out a startled gasp as he jumps. A millisecond ago, every inch of our bodies was pressed together, aligned in a perfect, albeit dangerous, way, but now he's propped up over me on hands and knees, and I feel cold all over.

He stares at me, his eyes wide and concerned and a little out of focus. "Shit," he whispers. "Shit, Emma—I'm so sorry, I—"

"No, it's okay, I—"

We both freeze, Harrison waiting for me to explain what went wrong, and me trying to figure out how to explain what just happened.

I have this condition, I should say. *I really want your hands back on me, but it's complicated.* Instead, I feel my vaginal muscles tighten like a coil, wound so tight I could burst at any moment. *I'm in pain just because I'm thinking about the potential of being in pain, which means the actual pain would be even more painful.*

A voice in the back of my head—one that sounds suspiciously Cobalt in color—says, *Go on, Emma. Let him put his hands back on you. See how well that ends.*

Key Lime chimes in. *This is probably what he's doing with all those women he meets on dating apps. He's a pro now, and you're not even an amateur. You're something less than that.*

He thinks he likes you, Cobalt says. *But he doesn't really know you.*

I jerk backward again, the motion propelling me into a seated position and forcing Harrison off me completely. Eyes wide, he scans my face, and I see when my pained expression registers.

"What's wrong?" he whispers. It's not curiosity in his voice—it's fear.

"I can't do this," I say, my voice shaky. I only realize what that sounds like when his face grows steely. "I meant—"

"Stop," he says, his entire face contorting as he closes his eyes, every muscle in his jaw growing tense.* He runs a hand across his face, then, much to my mortification, has to readjust his pants. "I get it. But it's okay if it's just this one night. Like I said, I'll take what I can get. It's taken me a long time, but I've finally come to terms with it."

I stare at him blankly, and he stares at me earnestly.

"Wait, what?" I finally ask.

His brows furrow as his lips purse.† "I'm talking about how you only do one-night stands. I'm saying that's okay with me."

I continue to stare at him blankly. "Harrison. What. The fuck. Are you talking about?"

He readjusts, sitting up completely. His eyes scan my face, darting back and forth. "Wait. What are *you* talking about?"

"What do you mean, what am I talking about? I have no idea what one-night-stand rule you're talking about."

I can see the gears turning in his head, his face slowly falling as he starts to put pieces together. *Told you,* Cobalt says. *He thinks he likes you, but he doesn't even know you.* "You told me you weren't interested in relationships," Harrison says. "The night we met. You said you didn't believe in soulmates, and even if they were real, you weren't interested in finding yours. That's why you only ever had one-night stands in college and never dated anyone."

* **Eyes narrowed · Frown · Tense jaw** | *Facial expression* | *Frequency: low*

 1. Resigned disappointment.

† **Furrowed brows · Pursed lips · Head tilted to the right** | *Facial expression* | *Frequency: medium*

 1. Exasperated.

Oh.

Oh, yeah.

Because I let him believe things that weren't true and never corrected him.

Saw you leave the party last night with Tyler. What's the story there?

Oh, you know. Wink wink.

(We left together coincidentally.)

Or,

Wanna watch a movie tonight?

Can't. I'm busy, unfortunately.

Hot date?

Oh yeah. I'm gonna be busy all night.

(I was behind on schoolwork.)

There's a *whoosh* and a *scream* and complete emptiness in my mind.

Hearing the love of your life say he'd be okay with a one-night stand? That, coming from *Harrison Carter*? The least one-night-stand person to ever exist?

Except . . . is he? He's certainly on the dating scene. Or he was, anyway. What the hell do I know about his sexual history?

I think you can make some educated guesses, Cobalt says. *Thump, thump.*

Even still. What does this say about our relationship, if he's cool to just spend this night together? Hooking Up with Limitations?

"That's not true at all," I say. "None of it. I'm sorry I led you to believe that."

His face fully falls now, his breath coming in short.* "Then . . . why . . . what . . . what?"

"I just . . ." *Do it,* I tell myself. *Do it.* "The opposite of that, actually. I like to take it slow. Really slow."

That's not really an answer to his question, but he doesn't press me on it. He stares at me, and I see the real question written on his face. *Then why didn't we work out?* After all, we were set up to be the slowest of slow burns. But we were so slow, the candle blew out.

Inhale.

Exhale.

"Okay," he finally says, as if reassuring himself. "Slow. I can do slow. If you want to do slow. If you want this at all."

"I do," I whisper.

"Okay." He reaches out for my hand, and I accept it, letting him hold our intertwined fingers in his lap. "Let's start slow. Tell me one thing—just one. One truth about Emma."

Do it, I tell myself again. *Do it. Do better. One thing. No explanation required.*

Inhale.

* **Sunken eyes · Slack jaw · Short breaths** | *Facial expression* | *Frequency: low*

1. Devastation.

Exhale.

I have vaginismus.

My vagina is really, really tight.

I've been keeping a secret from you.

"The thing is . . ." *Inhale, exhale.* "I'm a virgin?"

I don't know why those are the words that come out of my mouth, and I *certainly* don't know why they come out as a question.

My virginity isn't something I put a lot of stake in. I likely would've lost it years ago if it weren't for my vaginismus, and in that way, it's kind of out of my hands. If someone were to ask me about my sexual history, my first thought would be *I have a condition.* It would not be *I'm a virgin,* which makes my outburst even more baffling.

Cop-out, Key Lime says.

Harrison's brow furrows. He stares at me for at least ten seconds before saying, "Wait, what?"

"I, uh—" I say, my breath coming in short bursts. "I've never had sex?"

Harrison blinks at me. "What?" This one is more of an *Excuse me?* than a *What did you just say?* but it leaves me fumbling just as much. "But . . . ?" He narrows his eyes, and I can see the wheels starting to turn. "What about . . . ?"

I am genuinely dying to know what's about to come out of his mouth, but he pulls his lips together after a few seconds of thought.

This is absolutely the point at which I should offer further explanation. But some sadistic part of me needs to know how he's going to react to this information before I continue talking.

"I'm sorry, I—" he starts to say, then cringes. "Not sorry because of, you know, but because I . . . I'm not sure what I . . ." He shuts his mouth and stares at me for a moment before continuing. "I was never going to put you in a situation you were uncomfortable with."

"I know that. Of *course* I know that."

"I'm just . . . grappling with how severe my misunderstanding was."

I swallow. "Misunderstanding?"

"In college? I felt like you could make eye contact with a guy at a party, and he'd come running your way. I mean," he says, letting out a strained chuckle, "I *watched* you pick up guys at parties. It drove me insane."

"But I never actually went home with them."

Harrison frowns, processing. He opens his mouth to speak, inhales, and holds his breath, looking at me. I nod, letting him know it's okay to go on.

"Why?"

"It's . . . complicated," I eke out.

Harrison nods slowly. "Right. A lot of things about us are complicated."

"And that's why I—" I swallow, taking a deep breath. "That's why I shouldn't have kissed you without talking through things first. I'm sorry. I know this is a really bad idea. You said you weren't looking to date right now."

"No, that's not what I—" Harrison flinches, as if realizing that is indeed what he said, then recomposes himself. "What if we just . . . take it slow?" he asks. "Things are complicated for me, too."

"Right. Of course they are," I finally respond. "We'll take it slow?"

"We'll take it slow."

I hold out my hand. "Shake on it?"

There's a gleam in his eyes, and a dimple appears.* "Kiss on it, instead?"

* **Crinkles around eyes · Right dimple · Lopsided smile** | *Facial expression* | *Frequency: medium*

1. Gently optimistic.

Perhaps the most uncomfortable part of this is that the expression seems genuine. He's not concerned about me having no experience (with relationships, with sex, with anything). He's not concerned that I told him I needed to take it slow. He trusts me.

How will he feel when he finds out there are other things I misled him about in college?

It'll be okay. It's not a big deal. If we get far enough for it to matter, my pelvic floor therapy will be complete, and I'll never have to talk or think about vaginismus again. Probably.

You sure about that? Key Lime says in the back of my mind. *I'm still larger than you can handle, and Cobalt is quite a bit larger than me.*

"Kiss on it," I agree. He tugs my hand, pulling me forward onto his lap and then wrapping his arms around my waist, completely encircling me. Instead of kissing me, when he leans forward, he rests his forehead against mine, our noses touching, our lips an inch apart.

"I missed you," he whispers. "All those years. I missed you."

"I missed you, too," I say back, which doesn't begin to encapsulate how it felt. *Take it slow, Emma.*

Our lips meet, and later, when we part for the night, I can still feel the ghost of his mouth against mine.

CHAPTER 18

The plush seat of the waiting room chair is a little *too* comfortable, especially for a sleepy Monday afternoon, and combined with the calming ocean paintings and seafoam-green wall color, I feel myself being lulled into a false sense of security.

But nothing about this appointment is low stakes, especially after what happened with Harrison.

I mutter a curse toward a sign above the door that reads, "I Can SEA Clearly Now." I will remain strong. I am on guard. I will not allow this calming environment to distract me from my primary goal: accomplishing another step on my plan to Do Better, then getting out of this gynecology office as quickly as humanly possible.

Maybe this appointment will go so smoothly that I can never speak the word "vaginismus" again. After all, pelvic floor therapy has been . . . going.

"Emma?" a voice says. I turn to the left, and there she is—red hair and a messy bun, cutoff jean shorts, and Birkenstocks. A soft smile.

She walks over, plopping down into the chair next to mine.

"Oh my god, Jo," I whisper, breathy with disbelief. "You came."

"Obviously," she says, amusement in her voice.

"You don't hate me?"

She whips her head toward me, scowling. "I might be mad at you, but I still love you. Get it straight. I wasn't going to let you do this alone. We're here to support each other, remember?"

I wrap her up in a side hug, burying my head into her shoulder. "I love you, too. I'm sorry I was mean to you. I promise I'll be better."

"And I'm sorry I was pushy. If you don't want to be with Harrison, you shouldn't be with Harrison."

I stay silent. *Taking it slow.* I'll tell her when we're not . . . right here. When I'm in a better head space. And when I'm prepared to get yelled at for not just telling him about my vaginismus.

"Anyway," Jo says, pointing at a sign above the reception desk. "Life's a Beach." She turns to me, whispering conspiratorially. "So are gynecologists."

I offer half a laugh. Unfortunately, neither Jo nor my big secret can distract me from the fact that I'm (hopefully) about to get my first Pap smear, and I'm only about 20 percent confident the speculum will fit inside of me. I've made only minimal progress with my dilators in the last couple of weeks. But a little progress is better than no progress, right?

I'm not worried. I shouldn't be worried.

But maybe I'm a little worried, because there's only so long I can go without either solving this problem alone or telling Harrison about it.

We're too much for you to handle, Key Lime says in the back of my mind.

I'm the size of an average penis and yet you still can't fit me inside that ridiculous vagina of yours, Cobalt says. *You'd better hope you never want to date someone with a larger-than-average penis.*

I ignore the comment and absolutely do not wonder about the size of Harrison's penis.

You're a dick, I respond—a little too on the nose.

You wish dicks were this small, Key Lime says.

Stop making me think about dicks. I don't want to think about dicks right now.

Maybe that's your problem.

Shut up, I think, rather than admitting they have a valid point.

A nurse appears from behind a white door that's painted to look like shiplap. "Emma?"

"Thar she blows," Jo murmurs, standing up. My stomach murmurs in response.

Inhale. Exhale.

This is not that first gynecologist, nine years ago, where I tensed up so horribly I thought I wouldn't survive the pain. This is not that gynecologist, where I cried before the word "vaginismus" even came out of their mouth. This is not that gynecologist, where the doctor's exam ended after less than an inch of index finger.

Inhale. Exhale.

The nurse leads me down a winding hallway and into a room decorated with posters of smiling women and illustrated ovaries. A little replica of the female reproductive system sits on the counter. I want to throw it in the medical waste bin. *Waste* of counter space. *Waste* of my time. *Waste* of my emotional energy.

Jo settles into a seat behind the examination table as the nurse runs through the intake questions, most of which I vaguely remember from the gynecology appointment I went to as a freshman in college.

"Are you sexually active?"

"No," I say, giving Jo a pointed look over my shoulder. In response, Jo smiles and shoots me a thumbs-up.

After a few more rounds of questioning, the nurse closes the computer application and faces me. "You'll need to get a Pap smear. Is there anything else you'd like to talk to the doctor about today? Birth control, maybe?"

I force out a shaky breath before answering. "Birth control won't be necessary right now. If you could make a note in my file—I have vaginismus, so if the doctor could use the smallest sized speculum, that would be ideal." Jo gives an encouraging nod in my periphery.

"Sure," the nurse says, jotting a note in my file. "Doctor Alvarez will be here in a few minutes. Go ahead and put on the robe I left on the counter." She gestures toward a hideous piece of fabric encased in plastic. I mutter my thanks as she leaves the room, pulling a curtain in front of the door to protect my privacy. God forbid the gyno enter too early and see me naked.

Jo puts her hands over her eyes as I start to undress. "The first time I went to the gynecologist, I told her I didn't want any birth control, and she spent three full minutes explaining to me why the pill would be good for me so I don't unintentionally get pregnant before she realized I wasn't dating a man."

I let out a small laugh even though my stomach is turning to lead. "Why didn't you just tell her from the get-go?"

"She was being presumptuous. And she needed to learn to be better."

"Fair enough." My hands shake uncontrollably as I attempt to tie the strings at the side of the dress. "The first time I went to the gynecologist, we got three seconds into the exam, and I started sobbing so hard that she told someone to bring me an apple juice box."

Jo snorts. "Did it help?"

"Honestly, a little."

After a pause, Jo adds, "It's going to be different this time."

"I know," I whisper, folding my clothes into a neat pile.

"You doing okay?" she asks, her voice muffled by her palms.

"Not particularly."

"Deep breaths, please." I let my chest expand and deflate, breathing loudly so Jo knows I'm listening to her instructions. *Inhale. Exhale.* "Good," she says. "Keep doing that."

"I'm decent," I tell her as I settle onto the examination table. Jo leans forward and reaches out a hand, giving my shaking fingers a squeeze.

"It's going to be okay," she says.

"It's like a concrete wall down there," I mumble, eyeing the thin piece of fabric covering me.

"Well then." Jo's voice drops as she adds, "Mr. Gorbachev, tear down this wall!"

After a few more minutes of deep breathing, there's a knock at the door. I manage to squeak out a "come in" as I press my thighs together, self-conscious.

Dr. Alvarez is an older woman, gray hairs pulled back into a bun so tight it tugs at her temples and leaves her face looking hollow. I would bet money she despises tattoos and doesn't believe in second ear piercings.

I shake my head forward and let my hair cover my cartilage piercing.

She is not someone I want to discuss my vagina with. But, to her credit, her face does warm slightly as she smiles and introduces herself. And, to my credit, I manage to smile back and remember my own name.

She hums quietly as she scrolls through the notes the nurse typed up. "Here for moral support?" she asks, vaguely in Jo's direction.

"Yes," Jo and I answer at the same time. I shoot her my best *I'm sorry I'm talking for you, I'm nervous* look. She winks in response.

"I see here that you have a history of vaginismus?"

I clear my throat. "Yes." When I don't elaborate, Dr. Alvarez looks in my direction.

"I was diagnosed about nine years ago," I stammer out. "I only started going to pelvic floor therapy a few weeks ago."

"And how is pelvic floor therapy going?" she asks, typing a note in my file.

"Uh, I just started about three weeks ago, so I haven't made much progress. But I wanted to try to get a Pap smear anyway. Because I know it's important, and also because I want to be brave." I sound like a three-year-old about to go to daycare for the first time, but Jo gives me an encouraging nod. "So, I'm hoping you can use the smallest speculum you have. And go super slowly." Not a crazy request by any measure—and yet I still feel like I'm asking her to move mountains for me. As if by requesting she be patient with me, I'm being disrespectful of her time.

"We can do that," she says, still staring at the computer. *Inhale. Exhale.* "Physical therapy is a good step, even if it's going slowly. Have you also tried having a glass of wine before attempting penetration?"

Jo's eyes widen in shock, but Dr. Alvarez's back is turned—so thankfully, Jo's facial expression is hidden from view.

"Sorry?" I stammer out, praying my face doesn't mirror Jo's.

"Well, having a glass of wine will help you relax, whether before intercourse or before using your dilators. Some patients find it keeps their muscles from tensing up as much."

Before I can open my mouth to respond, Jo makes a small scoffing noise. Dr. Alvarez turns around to look at her, and much to my dismay, Jo takes that as permission to speak. Because why not make this situation harder?

"I'm sorry, you're suggesting she get *tipsy* before having sex, so she doesn't *feel* as much? That feels rather counterintuitive, don't you think?"

My face heats as I widen my eyes furiously at Jo, begging her to stop. Unfortunately, Dr. Alvarez seems inclined to engage.

"I'm not suggesting she get drunk and then have sex." *She*, as if I'm not sitting two feet away while they discuss my sex life. "But yes, wine may help her muscles relax, which would in turn make a sexual encounter more manageable."

"Yeah, trying to make it 'more manageable' definitely sounds like the basis of a satisfying sexual experience," Jo huffs, her voice fiery.

"Jo—"

"That's the best advice you have for dealing with her medical condition? Do you have any tips to, I don't know, actually *heal* her instead of drinking it away?"

"Jo, please. It's fine. I'm already working on it."

Dr. Alvarez raises an eyebrow at Jo, then focuses her attention back on me.

"Ms. Rogers," she says, her tone cool, "my official recommendation is to continue physical therapy. But if physical therapy doesn't work for you, it's probably because you haven't gotten over the mental blocks that play into vaginismus. I'm assuming your physical therapist explained that vaginismus has both a physical and a mental aspect?"

I nod, trying to avoid looking at Jo.

"And are you seeing a therapist or a psychiatrist now? And have you talked to them about this?"

"Yes," I say. "I've talked to her about it some."

"Great. And if a glass of wine helps you feel more, let's say, *uninhibited*, then yes, that is also part of my recommendation. If what you're doing now doesn't end up working, some other treatment options in the future could include vaginal numbing cream and vaginal Botox."

Jo and I are both silent.

"Do you have any other questions, or should we go ahead and get the exam started?"

If my mind were working faster, I might be smart enough to come up with some questions to delay the inevitable. For example, *Did you say Botox?* But, unfortunately for me and my vagina, my mind is completely blank save for a few words floating around (*Wine. Trust. Vagina. Painful. Botox. Take it slow.*) and the image of Jo's eyeballs about to pop out of their sockets.

Botox? Jo mouths.

My deep breathing keeps me focused and relatively calm while Dr. Alvarez starts the exam, feeling my abdomen and breasts. And much to my surprise, when she puts medical lube on her gloved fingers and feels the walls of my vagina move as I take deep breaths, I'm not in an extraordinary amount of pain. Is it uncomfortable? Sure. But that's just as much because of the situation as because of my pelvic floor, I think.

I actually might be able to get through this unharmed. At least, that's what I think until she pulls out the speculum and my heart drops.

"Wait, can you use the smallest size you have?" I ask again, eyeing the speculum, which is at least the same size as Key Lime. And I *hate* Key Lime's manipulative ass.

Ha, Key Lime says in the back of my mind. I hear Cobalt snickering. For once, I don't engage.

"This is the smallest size we have. But I'll go slowly," Dr. Alvarez says as she applies lube to the cold metal death trap.

Jo leans forward and squeezes my shoulder. "Breathe. You can do this."

Dr. Alvarez wheels her chair between my legs again, holding the contraption in her hands. "Ready?" she asks, her tone perfectly calm, as if she weren't essentially asking me if I'm ready to be impaled. I nod and close my eyes as tightly as I can. There are white dots in my vision as I prepare myself for battle.

At first, the speculum is just cold. But as she slides it in farther, it turns to pain. My muscles are unbearably tight, locking down around the speculum as if squeezing down on the tool could stop it or even push it out.

I let out a whimper of pain. "Breathe," Dr. Alvarez commands. "You're doing great."

I am not doing great.

In fact, I want to scream. That doesn't do it justice, actually. I want to bellow so loudly that I break the sound barrier, then kick Dr. Alvarez in the face until she removes the speculum. But, to be honest, that's going to be painful, too, so what I really need to do is get her to evaporate the tool into thin air.

And then she opens up the speculum.

The world comes to a halt around me. All I can think, sense, feel—that pressure inside of me. That all-encompassing, unbearable tightness that threatens to rip my muscles apart from strain.

And just when I think I can't hold on any longer, she slides the speculum out of my body, causing one last spurt of pain.

"Breathe, Emma," Jo whispers from behind me. I finally take an actual breath—*in, out.* My first full breath in at least sixty seconds.

Good to know that several weeks of focused physical therapy have gotten me approximately nowhere.

"Great job," Dr. Alvarez lies, as though my insides haven't just ripped at the seams like a fast-fashion garment. "I was able to get the sample we needed."

Dr. Alvarez says some parting words that I do not even remotely listen to. A few minutes later, Jo helps me onto shaky feet and guides me back through the waiting room. *Stay Salty!* a sign announces on our way out. I will, thanks!

When we leave the office, Jo senses I need some time to collect myself before speaking, so we walk in silence to the nearest T station. We have five minutes until the next orange line train arrives, so we take a seat on an empty bench.

"I can tell that hurt more than you let on," Jo finally says, quiet despite the rumble of conversation and footsteps and public transportation around us.

My silent nod is the only answer she gets.

Three weeks of physical therapy were enough to allow me to get a Pap smear, but my body is still freaking out and shutting down. Will that get better with time, or is my body responding this way because of fear? Sure, I'll keep doing physical therapy, but how far is that going to take me? And, more important, how quickly can I be done?

In a rush? Key Lime asks. *Good luck with that.*

Jo sighs, stretching out her legs. The train going in the opposite direction arrives, and we watch as people load off and on. As it pulls out of the station, I feel the bench shake.

"No one should have to go through what you're going through," Jo says, taking my hand in hers and resting her head against my shoulder. "I'm glad I could be here today. At the very least, I hope it's easier when you don't have to go through that alone."

"Thank you," I murmur. She squeezes my hand in response.

So much for Doing Better. I've accomplished—or at least made a good faith effort to accomplish—almost all the steps on my plan, and somehow, I feel worse. And I certainly don't feel more ready to date.

Step one: get a new job. I did accomplish that one, but my paychecks cover my rent and groceries and not much else, and I was hired because I'm friends with the owner. It's a great job for now, but not a great long-term plan. Great job, Emma.

Finish setting up the apartment within the next month. It's been nearly four weeks since I moved here, and my apartment is still littered with ASSORTED SHIT <3. I'm getting close, though?

Find a new therapist. Done, although we've only had one call, so I wouldn't say it's doing much for me.

Go on a date. I almost laugh out loud. Great plan on my end.

Start doing pelvic floor therapy. Done, although the phrasing of that goal was obviously a cop-out.

And, finally: *Go back to the gynecologist.*

Check, partial check, check, check, check, check. Am I Better now? I sure as hell don't feel like it. I did everything I thought I needed to, and I put it all on the line and kissed my best friend, but I still feel like I'm teetering on a ledge and everything I want could go falling off the cliff at any second.

I'm starting to wonder how slow Taking It Slow is. Because I might need a snail's pace to make this work.

CHAPTER 19

Harrison washes his hands at my sink, having just finished mixing pancake batter for Saturday morning breakfast. Which is hot. Super, incredibly hot.

I'm also currently ruminating on whether it's weird for me to think it's hot when he washes his hands. Like, something about the way he pushes up his hoodie sleeves to his elbows, then carefully tests the water temperature, then thoroughly rubs the soap between his fingers is really doing it for me.

My theory that not being able to have penetrative sex makes me think about sex all the time and in turn makes me horny is evidently true. And apparently, it's only worse when you've kissed the person. My entire body feels too warm, and I can't stop staring at his forearms.

It's been a week since we kissed, and I am *on edge.* This week has been hell—all of my shifts at Jo Jo's were closing shifts, and Harrison works during the day, so we only saw each other a couple of times, and only briefly. That is definitely what taking it slow means, but still. I missed him. (I'm pathetic.)

We reserved Saturday morning to actually spend time together, and I spent all week daydreaming about a variety of far-fetched romantic scenarios that all began with a casual Saturday morning coffee and then evolved into scenes ranging from a gondola ride through Venice to a mountaintop picnic ending in confessions of love. In each of these dreams, I was still home in time for my three o'clock shift at Jo Jo's. Even still, all my far-fetched expectations were exceeded the moment I opened the door for him this morning and he greeted me with a long, slow kiss before heading directly to my kitchen to get started on breakfast.

"Emma," he says.

I pry my eyes away from his forearms and up to his face, where he has an amused glint in his eyes. "Huh?"

"Do you want banana pancakes or regular?"

"Regular, please!"

Taking the bowl over to the stove, he carefully spoons the batter into the pan he'd preheated. My stove is the kind with the little metal spiral burners, except all of the burners are at a slight angle, meaning any liquid or semi-liquid you pour into a pan immediately collects into one corner.

The batter slides a bit before becoming solid enough to stop, and now all the pancakes are ovals.

He turns around and shoots me a sarcastic, pursed-lips look.

"Listen, if you didn't want to deal with my shitty-ass stove, you should've told me to come upstairs instead."

"That would've defeated the purpose of me making you breakfast in bed."

"I'm sitting on a barstool right now."

He leans forward against the island, and when he's a few inches short, he hops up and propels himself forward so he can plant a quick kiss on my lips, then lands back on the floor.

"Bed was too far from the kitchen. Needed you closer," he says, then returns his attention to my stove. (My attention is still consumed by the butterflies in my stomach.) "Plus, we live in the same building. Why don't we have the same model stove?"

"I hate to break it to you, but basement apartments are designed for people in a different tax bracket."

Harrison flips the first pancake, revealing a perfect light brown. "If you don't want the landlord to come fix it, fine, but we're going to try to fix it ourselves, then."

"Hmmmmm," I say, tapping my finger against my chin. "Or you can just cook for me in your apartment from now on?"

"What about when you cook for yourself?" He flips another pancake. (Also perfect.)

"I'm going to be so honest—"

"Forget I asked," he says, holding up the spatula like a hand. "Your answer is going to stress me out."

If that's going to stress him out, a lot of other things about my life would give him an aneurysm.

Twenty minutes later, we're curled up on my couch with two formerly heaping plates of pancakes. Now they're empty except for streaks of syrup. I set my plate down on the coffee table, then turn so my back is against the armrest, stretching out my feet. Harrison sets his plate down, then gently grabs my ankles, placing my feet in his lap.

He starts massaging my feet through my fluffy pink socks, and I think I see the gates of heaven opening.

Some ungodly sound must come out of my mouth because Harrison lets out a snort of laughter. "You poor thing. You've been working so hard, on your feet all morning to make us breakfast—"

I curl forward and gently slap his arm before collapsing back onto the couch. Mercifully, he continues the massage.

"You look like one hundred years of tension are seeping out of your body right now," he observes.

"I think this is the best morning of my life," I whisper, trying not to disrupt the peace. The only way this could've been better is if I had woken up with Harrison in my bed, rather than a text from Harrison asking if I was awake and if I'd like pancakes. We'll get there eventually. (I hope.) *Oh, yeah?* Cobalt says.

Harrison's phone buzzes, and I let out a playful *humph* as he removes his hands and fishes his phone out of his pocket. As he reads the text, his expression shifts, so slightly it wouldn't be visible to the naked eye. Thankfully my eyes are hypersensitive to Harrison's expressions.*

"What is it?" I ask.

His eyes flick over to mine, a hint of guilt on his face. "I hate to say it, but I have to go."

I look out the kitchen window as if I'm going to find an explanation by way of a fire truck or a tornado. My eyes are met only with summer flowers and sunlight. "What do you mean?"

"My mom texted. She needs me."

I wait for him to offer further explanation, but he doesn't.

"What does she need?" I ask cautiously.

Harrison reaches forward and picks a bit of fuzz off my sock. I pull my feet back toward my body, and he returns his hands to his lap.

"She has a friend coming over for lunch and needs me to be there."

I wait for him to continue, but he doesn't. "So . . . what, she just wants emotional support?"

He shrugs. "Something like that. But she told me she needs me to be there, so I need to go make sure she's okay."

I don't think you have the right to ask someone to prioritize

* **Slouched shoulders · Furrowed brows** | *Emotional tell* | *Frequency: low*

1. Disappointed.

you over their mother when you're just . . . what, flirting? Open to hooking up in the future? Friends with Limited Benefits?

Yeah, I don't have solid ground to stand on. *You hurt my feelings* isn't a great reason for him not to go check in on a family member with clinical depression.

"Do you need help?" I ask, even though I know I shouldn't. I don't know what point I'm trying to prove, but I can feel him about to fail this test I have yet to define. "I can come, if you want."

He shakes his head faster than I want him to. "No need. Thanks, though."

Yep. That's a failing grade. F minus.

"What if she needs more help?" I push. Harrison raises an eyebrow. "Like, what if she needs a woman's touch? What if she needs someone to French braid her hair, and you don't know how to do it?"

"I know how to French braid," Harrison says, smirking. "So I've got that one covered."

"You're lying to me," I say, erupting into laughter. He shakes his head, grinning. "No freaking way is that true."

"It's true. I swear. I have a younger cousin who taught me, like, twenty years ago, and it stuck."

I grab the hairband off my wrist and flick it at him with the skill of a middle school boy armed with a rubber band. He catches it midair (hot), and I spin around, leaning my back against his arm.

His body shakes behind me as he laughs. He gently grabs my hair, pulling it into a ponytail. I'm about to tell him that's not typically the first step in a French braid, but then he leans forward and places a slow kiss against the back of my neck.

My breath comes in short.

"I promise I'll prove it soon, but right now I need to head out."

Reluctantly, I lean forward, allowing him space to stand. He stretches his arms up above his head (*biiiiiiig stretch*) then places his hands on his hips and turns to me. "I'll text you later tonight?"

I would've preferred him to say *See you as soon as I get back from my mom's?* Or maybe *Come over tonight and make out?* After all, I reserved half of the day for him. But I guess you have to take what you can get when you're just Friends with Limited Benefits.

"Yeah," I say, waving my hands. "Get outta here."

He leans forward, placing his hands on my cheeks to tip my head up and give me a soft kiss.

Words I shouldn't be thinking, much less saying, almost slip out of my mouth in response.

"I—I'll see you. Good luck with your mom," I say.

"Thanks," he says, then tucks my hair behind my ears and leaves me.

***

"AND THEN MY ROOMMATE'S BOYFRIEND'S cousin licked the salt lamp so aggressively, it slid. Off. The. Table," Rose says, stopping to emphasize each word. "It shattered into a million salty pieces. Everything tastes like salt now. The air. My shoes. The floor."

Licking salt off of shoes and the floor sounds like the kind of thing Harrison would see a six-year-old patient for, but I refrain from telling Rose that because I'm absolutely certain she would tell me to stop acting like her mom, and then I would feel old.

"I mean, our living room looks like we're prepping for a snowstorm. There's salt *coating* the ground," she adds.

"Well—"

I don't know how I intend to finish that sentence, but I'm interrupted by the appearance of Kurt at the register. A teenage girl with impressively long box braids and a freckly boy with braces stand behind him.

"Hi, Emma," he says. I don't think he's used my name prior to this moment, but I respect the instinct to show off and prove he's a regular.

"Hey, Kurt!" His girlfriend looks at him with an impressed eyebrow tilt, and he grins. I play it up. "Good to see you!"

He places a ratty library copy of *Slaughterhouse-Five* on the counter. "Guess what I finished."

"And me," the girlfriend says. The freckly boy shoots me a cringe-smile as if to say *me, too.*

"This is my girlfriend, Tisha, and my friend Zach," Kurt says.

I smile and wave at both of them. "I'm Emma. Nice to meet you!"

"They both wanted to read *Slaughterhouse-Five* with me. I told them about how it was a banned book and stuff. We all thought it was really good."

"I have a break in ten minutes. How about I get you three some drinks and then I'll come join you so we can talk about it?"

They each order iced tea lemonades, and once Rose has taken over, I take off my apron and leave my station.

Jo has been sitting at a café table to the side, doing something businessy on her laptop. She eyes me as I walk past her.

"What?" I say. "I'm on break."

"I know you are," she says. "That's not why I'm eyeing you." She doesn't add anything else, so I give her a raised-eyebrow *go on* look. "It's just good to see you happy."

I chat with them for fifteen minutes, discussing the book's anti-war themes and how it was inspired by Vonnegut's own experiences as a prisoner of war. Kurt makes an astute comment about how the character seems to have PTSD, and Tisha discusses the novel's treatment of women and how even though it can be misogynistic at times, she's still glad she read the book.

"It's been controversial since its publication and still, decades later, is at the center of book-banning efforts," I tell them.

"That makes me feel lucky to have read it," Tisha says.

I nod at her. "You are lucky. I think it's your duty as a young reader to consume literature thoughtfully, and that includes reading books others may not have easy access to. That's how you can fight book banning in your own life."

As we're wrapping up, they ask for another recommendation. We agree we'll meet again in a month and discuss Toni Morrison's *The Bluest Eye.*

It's been a long time since I felt this feeling. It's a delicate tingle in my brain, like a wave of happiness that numbs all other feelings momentarily. By the time I quit my job a couple of months ago, I'd all but lost that feeling, and that numbness was replicated by emptiness.

I've felt so much better since quitting and even better since moving to Boston, but getting to reclaim some of the joy that was taken from me and my students by an angry parent and a politically motivated school board makes me feel on top of the world. At my core, I suppose I'll always be a bit of an English teacher, even if I don't want to go back to doing it full-time.

Jo follows me into the back room. "So," she says.

I slip my apron over my head, tying it behind my back. "So."

"I've been crunching some numbers on my laptop."

Turning to the sink to wash my hands, I'm careful not to make eye contact with her. "And?"

"We're doing okay, but barely."

Not surprising. There's been a slow stream of customers. Probably as many as there were when her parents managed Jo Jo's, but definitely no more.

"And I've been thinking of ways we can bring more people here," Jo continues.

"And?"

"And I was wondering if you want to host a book club here. Maybe one evening a month. The focus could be reading banned books, if you want. Gets more people to Jo Jo's to buy coffee and also encourages people to spend money supporting banned books. We're open late anyway, so we won't even have to extend our hours."

I open my mouth to respond, but she cuts me off. "Listen. I know you left teaching. And I know you're probably afraid if you start connecting moments like that one"—she nods in the direction of Kurt's table—"to your job, it'll lose its charm. But this wouldn't be like teaching. This would just be about bringing people together over books and creating a space for them to talk freely. And you're so good at this. I mean, those three high schoolers shouldn't be interested in anti-war novels from the 1960s. And yet they are, because you told them some people don't want them to read it. People love doing things they're not supposed to."

I snort. "Jo. You didn't let me answer."

"I know, I just—"

"I think that's a great idea."

Jo jumps up and down, her hands clasped against her chest. I roll my eyes, but she sees the grin on my face and gives me a huge hug.

"This is part of your job, of course. I'll pay you for it. And I just—" She pauses, taking a deep breath as her face grows more serious. "I know you were wanting to try something new, but I also know it didn't need to be this," she says, gesturing around. "And I know you say you're excited about working here, but it's not lost on me that you're probably doing this because you want to be a good friend and support me."

"Maybe a little," I say quietly, reaching out and giving her hand a squeeze.

"I needed it, to be honest. But also, just know the moment you want to do something else, all you have to do is say the word. I'm going to be fine even if you decide to move to, like, North Dakota. Rose and I have got this."

"North Dakota?"

She shrugs. "Most random place I could think of."

"I'm not going to move to North Dakota. But, heard. I promise I won't stay in this job out of obligation."

The chime above the front door rings, and when I look over, my heart sinks from my chest to my stomach as I register that Stephanie is now standing inside Jo Jo's, looking around for someone. When she catches my eyes, she gives me a soft smile. *Damn it.*

She's wearing a head-to-toe groutfit and no makeup. She looks like she just rolled out of bed, but it's nearly four o'clock. I've only had two interactions with Stephanie, but I know enough to tell that this is out of character. I notice a chip in her red nail polish as she approaches the counter.

Jo had asked me whether I wanted it to be the case that Harrison broke up with Stephanie for me. I'd said it was complicated, but right now it's feeling very uncomplicated: I do not want to be responsible for the pain that this woman is clearly experiencing.

"Hey, Emma," she says quietly as I approach her.

"Hey," I say. "Are . . . you okay?"

She smiles weakly. "I'm glad you're working today. I wanted to talk to you."

Even though she's confirming what I expected to be true, I gape at her, and my heart falls from my stomach to my knees. Mercifully, I gather the mental strength to turn to Rose. "Hey—all good over there? Mind if I continue my break for a minute?"

She fist bumps me. "All right, girl. That's what I'm talking about. Slacking on the clock."

I give her an obligatory eye roll, then lead Stephanie to a table in a corner, far away from anyone's (Kurt's) nosy ears.

"I, uh—" she says, clearly struggling to form words. "Are you okay?"

I blink at her. "Me?" She nods. "Yeah, I'm . . . okay," I tell her hesitantly.

She glances around as if making sure no one is snooping. I feel certain Jo is, but I have no qualms about that. "I don't want to put you on the spot, and so I'm really sorry if this is uncomfortable, but, um, I got lunch with Alexander this week during work," she says, and my heart stutters, realizing what she's about to say, "and he said some things that, well, that made it clear he didn't behave appropriately toward you."

"Oh," I whisper. There's blood rushing to my face as though I'm upset, even though this conversation is about Alexander, not about me. Then again: If I wasn't upset, why didn't I tell anyone, including Jo, what happened?

"That's not really the right phrase to describe how he acted," she says, closing her eyes and shaking her head. "But I also don't want to put words in anyone's mouth when I just heard about it secondhand and drew assumptions."

"No, I—uh . . ." I stutter. "I don't know what he said to you—"

"Enough," she interrupts, then waves at me to continue.

"Yeah, the date went poorly. Like, really poorly. And I know you're friends with him—"

"Sorry," she cuts in. "I know I keep interrupting, but I feel the need to clarify that we are not friends anymore. I hope it's okay that I did this on your behalf, but I made sure he knew that he was a shithead."

I snort. "That's an apt description."

Stephanie nods sympathetically, leaning back in her chair

and crossing her arms. Jo, who is undoubtedly trying to get closer in order to snoop, brings over two iced lattes. "On the house," she says, giving me a meaningful *you will be updating me later* look. We thank her and take a synchronized sip of coffee.

"I appreciate you checking in," I tell Stephanie as Jo walks away. "I haven't really told anyone about it, and . . . it feels nice to have someone ask."

"You didn't do anything wrong," she says, reading between the lines.

"I know," I say, my red face betraying me. "And, seriously, I wouldn't say it's been weighing on me. I mean, this is not the first time a man has been gross to me."

Stephanie takes a slow breath, her eyes growing pained and red. "I . . . shouldn't have set you up with him. We dated in high school—literally for a month—and he didn't do anything as bad as what he did to you, but he was a shitty boyfriend and didn't know how to handle feelings or conflict or, well, much of anything. But he was fun to be around for the most part, and it's been almost a decade since then, so I thought he would have, I don't know, changed?" She looks at me with miserable, guilty eyes.

"That's understandable. Most people do change. I promise, I don't blame you," I assure her. Frankly, I'm shocked she came to see me, even if she's feeling guilty. If someone broke up with me for another woman, nothing in the entire world could compel me to go seek out the company of that woman. Maybe Stephanie is just a better person than I am. "But anyway, how are you doing?" I ask, trying to match her level of kindness. "You're taking care of yourself?"

She waves her hand in the air, brushing off the question. "Oh, I'm fine. Honestly, I'm not even that broken up about it, which goes to show it was probably the right call."

I assume she's just saying that because that's what you tell yourself when you've been broken up with (so I've heard, anyway), but she does seem genuine. Her body language is significantly more relaxed while talking about Harrison than it is while talking about Alexander.

"Is Harrison doing okay?" she follows up.

"I . . . think so?"

She eyes me again.

"I mean," I clarify, "he's for sure grieving the relationship." I study her face to see whether I'm saying the right thing, but her expression doesn't change. "I'm sure it wasn't an easy choice for him."

Her eyes narrow.

"Like . . . breaking up?" I continue, trying to fill the silence. "I'm, uh, sure . . . it wasn't easy for him?"

I am feeling extremely uncomfortable. There are a million ants crawling over my skin. I would like this conversation to end, and then I would like to go crawl into a hole and not emerge until next spring.

"Right," she finally says, nodding slowly. "Right."

"So, um—"

"Here's the thing about Harrison," she says, cutting me off and leaning forward as if imparting wisdom. "He doesn't have his priorities straight. He has too many priorities, and they all get jumbled together, and he can't sort out which ones are the most important or the most time-sensitive."

"Okay . . . ?"

"And sometimes he needs people to make decisions for him, because it's not in his nature to act in his own best interests. But sometimes he *should* be acting in his own best interests, which is why people need to push him in that direction." She leans forward and tilts her head down, maintaining eye contact as her brown hair slips from behind her ears, falling forward to frame her face. "Do you understand what I'm saying?"

I do not even remotely understand what she's saying. But I

pick the question I'm most curious about: "Why are you telling me this?"

She blinks slowly, then leans back in her chair. Sighing, she pulls her hair back into a ponytail, securing it with a hot pink scrunchie from her wrist. "Because," she says as she tightens her ponytail, "I don't want you to think that I pushed him into something he didn't truly want. Please don't let him convince you otherwise."

Harrison is obviously a pushover, but I've never been under any illusion that he would've dated Stephanie even if he didn't want to, nor can I imagine him trying to convince me that he only dated Stephanie because she pushed him into it. Why would it matter to me, anyway? He dated her, and then he broke up with her, and that's the end of the story.

I clear my throat, shriveling under her intense stare. "Right. Um—I need to get back to work. But I really, really appreciate you stopping by," I tell her, and her stare softens. "It really does mean a lot to me."

"Of course. Take care of yourself, Emma," she says, standing up with the rest of her iced latte in hand. She gives me a look that conveys a meaning I don't quite understand, then adds, "Good luck."

CHAPTER 20

When Jo's Sunday morning shift at the coffee shop ends, she speed-walks to my apartment in record time. We weren't able to connect after my shift yesterday, so she's been living with the knowledge that I have major updates for nearly twenty-four hours, and based on the crazed look in her eyes when she flops onto my couch, it's been eating her alive.

I start by telling her about Alexander, and she gets appropriately angry on my behalf, spends ten minutes yelling into the void while periodically checking in to make sure I'm okay, and then remembers that I have more than a few Harrison-related updates to share, and so we table our discussion of Alexander. It only takes a few minutes to fill her in on what's happened with Harrison, and then we move into the part of the discussion where she asks follow-up questions and we unpack every single word Harrison and I have ever spoken to each other and consider what they might mean in this new context. This exploration is so lengthy, it lasts three full cups of coffee, leaving us shaky and nauseous, which slows down the process. By the time we wrap up the discussion five hours later, it's midafternoon, and Harrison has returned home from wherever he was (probably his mom's again, let's be honest), made a pot of coffee, and showered, according to our analysis of the noises coming from his apartment.

Jo drinks the last sip of her third coffee, then slams the mug down on the counter with a *bang.* "So. To summarize. This is the best thing that's ever happened to me, and I'm positive you're going to fuck it up by trying to be perfect even though you're not—"

"Thanks."

"—and he's going to fuck it up by refusing to prioritize himself. Exactly like Stephanie said. For example: spending time with his mom all weekend instead of making out with you."

I groan, getting up from my chair and flopping onto my bed. It squeaks in response, and I mutter a curse.

Buzz.

Harrison: Creaky bed, huh?

Jo rushes next to me so she can snoop. "Oh my *god,*" she exclaims as she reads over my shoulder. There are footsteps from above, and she turns her voice to a whisper. "Is he *sexting* you right now?"

"What?!" I whisper back. "No, he's asking about the bed frame. He helped me rebuild it, remember?"

Jo narrows her eyes. "You're blushing."

"I'm not blushing." My cheeks are literally on fire.

She sticks out her hand. "Phone, please."

"Absolutely not. He's not sexting me."

"Fine," she says. "If you're so confident, let me send a mildly suggestive text back, and we'll see what he says."

"That's insane."

"I thought we're trying to lock him down."

"It's complicated. We're trying to take it slow and speed up at the right time. Which is not yet."

"Well, you know what's *not* complicated? Men. When they're horny."

I stare at her. And then I hand her my phone.

"*Might need your help,*" Jo dictates. She looks up at me. "I welcome your feedback."

"Something about loose screws?" I offer.

Jo stares at me for a minute, then looks back at the phone. "*Might need your help,*" she repeats. "Winky face." She gives me a thumbs-up with raised eyebrows, and I shoot her a thumbs-up in response. A *swoop* sounds from my phone.

"Do people actually use the winky face emoji?" I ask.

"No idea," Jo says. I groan.

There's a moment of silence, and our eyes simultaneously go wide with realization. "The footsteps stopped," Jo whispers. "He stopped pacing."

"That doesn't mean anything," I whisper back.

My phone quietly dings.

Harrison: How exactly can I be of assistance?

The footsteps start up again.

"Holy *shit,*" we both say.

"That sounds sexual, right?" I ask.

"One. Thousand. Percent," Jo agrees. "Like, absolutely."

I grab the phone and start typing. You're such a handyman. You know what to do.

Jo grabs the phone back and deletes. *"You're so handy with your fingers. I bet you know exactly what to do."* She looks up at me. "Yeah?"

"Yeah." *Swoop.*

The footsteps stop again.

This time, there's a longer pause. We watch with bated breath as bubbles appear and disappear and appear and disappear on my screen. Footsteps sound again, and then there's a faint plopping noise, as if someone has sat down on a piece of furniture.

Ding.

Harrison: Sounds like you need to buy a toolbox.

We stare at it for a moment. "I'm stumped on this one," I admit.

Jo grabs the phone. *"What's in the box?"* she dictates.

"Should we add a Dick in a Box gif?"

Jo stares at me.

"Like the *SNL* skit?"

Jo stares at me some more, then narrows her eyes. "You're bad at this."

"Give me my phone," I say, and we briefly catfight until my phone falls on the floor.

"If that broke, you're paying for it," I hiss.

Jo snorts. "With what money? The huge profit we're making at the coffee shop?"

It didn't break, but the text message (What's in the box?) did send, sans gif.

More bubbles appear and disappear. Finally:

Harrison: I'll teach you once we get it.

We stare at it again.

"Okay, I'm going to be honest," Jo says. "I'm actually not one thousand percent sure he was sexting you."

I glare at her, blood draining from my face. "I'm going to kill you."

"I mean, look," she says, gesturing with my phone. "You didn't say anything too weird. Just . . ." Her eyes scan the phone. "That you bet he's good with his fingers. Could mean anything!"

I groan, my head flopping down into my lap. "Jo," I hiss, my voice muffled. "Even if he were good with his fingers, I literally can't even take advantage of that."

Jo points at me with an encouraging expression. "Depends on what he's doing with them!"

Ding.

I grab the phone and read the text aloud.

Harrison: Working with tools requires delicate precision. You have to be gentle with it. You have to know how it works. You have to be patient with it.

"I didn't think Harrison was that serious about tools," I whisper.

"You *dumbass,*" Jo says. "He's talking about the *clitoris.*"

The blood rushes back to my face. "I thought we agreed he wasn't sexting."

"Well, apparently he realized you *were,*" Jo says. "So now you have to sext back."

I don't even pretend to have input. I hand her the phone.

"*I—*" she says, then stops typing. "*Will you—*" she says, then deletes everything again.

"*I'm patient,*" I suggest.

Jo opens her mouth and starts to scoff, then looks up at me with a raised eyebrow. "Actually, yeah, that's good stuff." She types it out and hits send.

There's silence for a moment, then Jo, who is starting to look impatient, stands up from the couch, sits on the bed, and bounces, creating loud creaking noises.

Harrison: those noises suggest otherwise.

Harrison: sounds a little excited, if you ask me.

Jo grins wildly, and we both crumple into balls of silent giggles.

"I cannot believe we are sexting *Harrison Carter* right now," Jo wheezes.

"*I* am sexting Harrison Carter right now," I correct. "Let me take credit for my work."

"He wants you so bad, it's not even funny," Jo says, laughing.

I laugh back, but there's a pit forming in my stomach. Am I leading him on? I told him I wanted to take it slow. Is that taking it slow? By engaging in this, am I suggesting I'm ready for something I'm not? But also, am I ready? Will I ever be ready? After all, my vagina still feels sore from the gynecology appointment at the beginning of the week. And that's not a promising sign.

"Before you ask," Jo says, "yes, this still counts as taking it slow. You're setting the stage for what's to come, whenever you want it. Harrison is a good guy. He'll go at your pace. And he can handle some light sexting in the meantime."

I give her a soft smile, then take the phone from her, my confidence renewed. "*You're right,*" I type. "*I'm excited.*"

I raise my eyebrows at Jo, and she shrugs. "It's not sexting, but if it's true, it's just as hot."

Swoop.

Harrison: Me too Em:)

"I am literally going to *throw up,*" Jo says. "That is *disgustingly* cute. I feel *ill.*"

Harrison: Do you have Fourth of July plans on Tuesday?

I look over at Jo. "Do we have Fourth of July plans?"

She shakes her head. "My sister's driving up from DC for a couple days to hang while the coffee shop is closed."

Emma: Nope! I'm off on Tuesday and Wednesday.

Harrison: My mom is hosting a small Fourth of July party at my grandparents' old cabin. We have Tuesday off for the holiday and I'm also taking Wednesday, so I'm leaving tomorrow night after work and coming home Wednesday evening.

We'd gone to the cabin once during our junior year of college. Harrison's parents had gotten into some huge fight while he was on the phone with them one night, and the next morning he'd told me to pack an overnight bag and come with him. I'd started to argue, but then he'd told me he really, really wanted to get off campus and really, really didn't want to have to interact with anyone else other than me. And who was I to say no to that?

We'd driven an hour and some change to the cabin, then spent the night curled up by the fire with hot chocolate and a lot of cozy, albeit musty-smelling, quilts. There were always at least twelve inches of space between us, and yet I remember thinking the moment was sweetly intimate, like we were a pair of eighty-year-old best friends, sitting peacefully beside each other and reminiscing about our sixty-plus years of friendship.

Harrison: Want to join?

"Holy *shit,*" we whisper at the same time.

"His mom hates my guts, though," I murmur.

Jo gives me a sympathetic look and shakes her head. "If you want a chance at being with Harrison, I think it's up to you to work on that."

Emma: You sure that's okay? I know your mom isn't my biggest fan.

Harrison types for a minute, and Jo and I watch the text bubbles as if they hold the key to the universe.

Harrison: I really want my mom to like you, and I feel certain she will if you two just spend more time together.

Jo shrugs. "Can't argue with that."

Emma: Then I'll be there!

Harrison: And now I'm even more excited!

I giggle, and Jo playfully slaps my arm. "I told you. You two couldn't stay away from each other if the fate of the world depended on it."

I love-react the message, and only then does it occur to me that I've agreed to go on an overnight trip with Harrison Carter.

***

MY STUDIO IS DARK AND slightly muggy as the sun sets and Jo leaves, and as I cross the room to turn on my floor lamp, I accidentally make eye contact with the piece of furniture I'm trying to avoid.

Have you made any progress in figuring out the girth of his penis? Key Lime asks. I glare at the dresser drawer where I keep my dilators. *I hear you might make some progress this week.*

Does it matter? Cobalt says to Key Lime. *It's almost certainly larger than you, and she still can barely make you fit.*

Maybe he has a micropenis, Key Lime says. *Or maybe it has a below-average girth. Or maybe—*

"Shut UP," I yelp, then feel exceedingly stupid because I am screaming at a set of dilators. I stomp over to the drawer and fling it open. I toss a bunch of unmatched socks onto the floor, then grab the wooden box and throw it on my bed. The force makes the box fall open, and Key Lime and Cobalt stare at me.

Hey, Key Lime says.

I drop my pants. "This ends now." I haven't touched the dilators since my gynecology appointment, wanting to give my soul and my vagina a brief respite, but now my motivation is back with a vengeance. I will not allow a painful Pap smear to be the reason I stall out in physical therapy. My willpower is stronger than that, as is my desire to Do Better.

Climbing onto my bed, I get on my hands and knees for cat-cow pose.

Inhale. I raise my chest, looking up toward the sky.

Exhale. I curl my back, dropping my head toward the duvet.

Inhale. This is so freaking stupid. I look like a cow.

Exhale. And now I look like a cat, which is also really freaking stupid.

Inhale. Maybe if I get Key Lime inserted, I'll run upstairs and try to have sex and bank on him having an average or below-average penis size and also bank on some good luck.

Exhale. Maybe I'll just text him to come downstairs, and I'll wait here in my bed, pantsless.

I roll onto my back for happy baby pose, bringing my legs

up and bending my knees, grabbing my feet in my hands. I rock side to side, which is what Kay told me to do, and is also what makes me lose all self-respect. My vulva feels cold from exposure, even though it's probably in the mid-seventies.

Inhale. I rock gently to the right.

Exhale. I rock gently to the left.

Inhale. I'm so tired.

Exhale. I need this to be over.

Inhale. I want my vagina to work, for once in my goddamn life.

Exhale. I want to talk to someone about this.

Inhale. I want to talk to Harrison about this.

Wait, what? Do I?

You think he's going to want to fuck you after you tell him you're unfuckable? Cobalt asks. I drop my legs, grab her from where she's sitting next to me, and chuck her so hard at the wall that a picture frame thumps to the ground and breaks apart.

Inhale.

Exhale.

I'm going to tell him.

Inhale.

Exhale.

I've *got* to tell him. This week, when we're at his mom's cabin.

Inhale.

Exhale.

I slather lube on Key Lime and gingerly press her against my entrance. My body cramps up in response, but I'm expecting it, and expecting my pain gives me power over it. Vaginismus is partially mental, after all. So, if I mentally prepare for it, then:

Not today, motherfuckers.

I press Key Lime inside of me, and

I

am

okay.

Inhale.

Exhale.

Inhale.

Exhale.

My pelvic floor cramps up again.

I am okay. I am okay. I am okay.

Inhale.

Exhale.

My body calms down, and I take advantage of the break to press Key Lime farther inside of me.

I stare at my ceiling, blocking out the faint sound of footsteps. I don't want to be thinking about Harrison pacing around his kitchen making dinner. I don't want to be thinking about Harrison and what I hope is his smaller-than-average penis, and I don't want to be thinking about Harrison, because the only thing that does is add pressure, mentally and physically.

My pelvic floor seizes up, and I breathe through it.

Inhale.

Exhale.

I will not give up. I can't give up, not when I'm already too deep to swim back to the surface. But the surface was always turbulent with will-they-or-won't-theys and friends-with-too-many-limitations and I'm-keeping-secrets-from-yous, and I don't want to return there even if I could.

More footsteps make their way through the ceiling, and I breathe through the pain.

Inhale.

Exhale.

I slide Key Lime in deeper, and for the first time, she's fully inserted, and *I am okay.*

Maybe, just maybe, I'll be okay.

CHAPTER 21

Over the last hour, we've left the city and driven north into a more rural area that looks like something out of a fairy tale, simultaneously eerie and beautiful thanks to the speckled reflection of the trees in the moonlight.

As we slow down and turn a corner, a two-story wooden cabin comes into view. Ivy covers the walls, partially obscuring the large windows running up and down the face of the house, and there's a wraparound porch with several rustic rocking chairs. Water glimmers directly behind the cabin, and I can make out the edge of a dock creeping into the deep blue lake.

It's beautiful. Dark. Peaceful.

My mind is anything but, ever since Harrison casually said "We'll be staying in one of the upstairs bedrooms, if that sounds good to you" on the drive over.

That sounded great to me! Fantastic, even! I mean, that's what I expected, right? But then I started spiraling and then I spiraled even more, and now I don't know whether I want to attack him with kisses or cry and ask him for a hug.

There is nothing I want more than to spend the night in bed

with him. And that pressure—that intense want—is my problem. As my therapist told me last week, *You put too much pressure on yourself. Your body doesn't know how to handle it.*

I'll put some more pressure on you, Key Lime had said. I didn't really know what that meant, but I decided not to explore it.

Now, the light of the moon casts frightening shadows around the car as we unbuckle and step out onto the gravel driveway. Harrison grabs our bags from the trunk, and I follow him up the path and inside, quiet as a heartbeat.

A floorboard creaks under my foot as I walk through the doorway, my skin prickling as I tread lightly over the rustic wooden floors. The main room has a basic living room setup, a floral-print couch and accent chairs around a wooden coffee table, an old TV mounted above the fireplace, a six-person dining table off to the left. There's a kitchen beyond the dining table, and to the right, there's a flight of stairs leading up to the second level.

Harrison points toward a door by the fireplace—the primary bedroom, presumably—and puts his finger to his lips, letting me know his mom is asleep. He'd come over to help me pack after work, intending to throw my stuff in his car, grab a quick dinner somewhere, and then get on the road. Instead, we'd gotten distracted when he found Bananagrams in an open moving box (ASSORTED CLOSET SHIT) and insisted we play. That went on for an hour, and then we ordered food, and then the food got delayed, and we, in turn, got delayed, and suddenly it was already dark outside. At least I beat him in Bananagrams several times.

Wordlessly, we climb to the second floor, the stairs creaking beneath our feet.

I have a sudden, painful flashback of walking from Hall Hall's third-floor common room up to the fourth floor on that first Friday of college. My pelvic floor cramps in response. So much has changed since the night I met Harrison, and yet so little progress has been made. But I'm taking baby steps, and for that, younger Emma would be proud. In a lot of ways, I really am Doing Better.

When we enter the room, Harrison sets my bag down by the bed, then takes a few steps back and leans against the doorframe.

"I think I'm going to go sleep in the other bedroom," he says. "It's right next door, if you need anything."

I swivel on my heel. I can't read the look on his face for once, which is absolutely infuriating. "What? Why?"

"Because I don't know if I've ever seen you this nervous." He cracks a smile, even as his brows are furrowed.* "And I was there when you gave your senior honors project presentation. And also when you challenged that kid with the stupid name to a beer pong competition in front of the entirety of our sophomore year dorm."

I sniffle, because apparently, I started crying at some point without realizing it. "John Johnerson?"

"You lost so, so badly," he says, taking a step forward. His head is tilted sympathetically as he reaches out his arms. "Can I give you a hug?"

I step forward, wrapping myself around him and resting my head against his chest. I can hear his heartbeat right in my ear. It's steadying, even as I take a shaky breath. "Have I ever told you I'd never played beer pong before in my life?"

He gives me a kiss on the forehead. "No, but I figured that out pretty quickly." He squeezes me tighter against him as I laugh, his chest rumbling in sync with mine. "I'll be next door, okay?"

* **Lowered eyebrows · Head tilt to the left** | *Facial expression* | *Frequency: medium*

1. Sympathy.

I tilt my head up, resting my chin against his chest so I can look him in the eyes. "No, please don't. Really. I think the only thing that'll make me less nervous about you being here is you being here."

"That doesn't make any sense," he whispers, his left dimple appearing.

"It means I'd really like it if you stayed." I give him my best puppy dog face, and I can tell from his eye roll that he's already changed his mind. "Pleeeeeeease? Pretty pleeeeee—"

He leans forward and shuts me up by planting a kiss on my lips, then lets go of me and moves his bag to the other side of the bed. I'm still grinning stupidly and standing in the same place when he toes off his shoes and flops down onto the bed.

"What are you waiting for, then?" he asks, using his casual, playful humor to make me more comfortable. It works, and I slide off my Birkenstocks and flop down next to him on my stomach, propping my head up with my hands. He reaches over and grabs my right elbow, lifting it up in the air so he can scoot underneath it. He places my elbow on top of his chest, and now I'm hovering right above his face.

"Smooth," I murmur.

He looks at me with an expression I've never seen before. I'm going to have to edit the dictionary. Apparently, there are some expressions he only uses in certain contexts (certain contexts that I've never been in). I don't want to think about—I'm *not* thinking about—the fact that someone else was previously privy to those expressions instead of me, but in this moment, I just feel very lucky to be on the receiving end of this bright-eyed, soft joy.*

"Has anyone ever told you your eyes look like hot cocoa?" I ask, tracing my finger along his cheekbone.

* **Soft, bright eyes** | *Facial expression* | *Frequency: low*

1. Adoration.

Placing one hand on my waist, he uses the other to brush my hair behind my ear. "And has anyone ever told you yours look like a kaleidoscope?" His eyes dart in tiny movements as he studies mine. "Green, but with little flecks of blue and brown mixed in. The closer you are, the more you see."

I run my finger down his cheek, tracing his lips, then running it across his jawline. He doesn't move; he just gazes at me as I study the movement of my finger across his skin.

"It feels like I missed this," I whisper. "Being able to touch you. Which doesn't make any sense because I've never actually been able to do that. I'm missing something I've never done."

"You always could've," he says. "If you'd wanted to."

I did want to, I think, but then the follow-up question would be *why didn't you?* and we haven't gotten to that answer yet, and I need to warm up a little bit before we get there, so instead I kiss him.

This kiss is caring, soft, and lovely. A love letter embodied. His hands are careful and gentle as he brings them up to my face, and as I open my mouth slightly, he lets his tongue run across my lower lip. A shiver of delight runs down my body.

"You okay?" Harrison whispers. I nod.

"Are *you* sure about this?" I ask, even though what I should be saying is *I need to talk to you.*

"Yes," he says, giving me a kiss on the cheek and whispering in my ear, "I've never been so sure about anything."

His eyes are dark and sparkling, and I think I could lie here forever, gazing back at him. There are multitudes in those eyes of his. A dictionary's worth of emotions. I want to stare at him until his innermost thoughts reveal themselves to me, then package them up and wear them in a locket, pressed against my heart.

He wraps his arms around my waist, planting several fast, furious kisses on my neck, and as I gasp with laughter and delight, he rolls us over, both of us landing on our sides, faces inches apart.

We lie there for a moment, eyes blazing. The only sounds are the quiet murmuring of nighttime creatures and the gentle *in* and *out* of our breathing. I weave my fingers through his hair and lean in, our kisses becoming more urgent and passionate.

It's odd to kiss someone you know so well but have barely been physically intimate with. I've always assumed I knew Harrison as well as I knew myself, but all of his mannerisms are taking on a new light in this context: the quiet *mmm* noise he makes when he's deeply contented—turns out he also makes that noise when I suck on his bottom lip. Fidgeting hands aren't just for when he's nervous—his hands now roam all over me, unable to stay still. And apparently flushed ears aren't just for embarrassment.

More entries for the dictionary. I'll have to write an NSFW appendix.

I wrap my leg around him, drawing it up across his hip, and he lets his hands slip underneath my shirt, the feeling of his fingers on my lower back sending a startling blast of hot, blazing need through me. Not a feeling I'm particularly familiar with. Not something my body experiences often, if ever. But a good feeling nonetheless.

Something weird is happening to my body, and it's not the tightness and cramping I'm expecting. Maybe I don't need to have that conversation after all.

Miraculously understanding I'm perhaps too afraid to vocalize what I need, Harrison eventually leans in, nipping at my ear before whispering, "What do you want, Em?"

"More," I gasp.

He nods against my neck. "Tonight is all about you. It's all about whatever will make you feel good, and nothing more. Okay?"

And nothing more. I like the sound of that.

Said no one ever, Cobalt chimes in.

"I need to hear you say it," he says. "Is that okay? And you'll tell me if you want me to stop?"

"Yes," I eke out. My body feels like an open flame. "Please."

I don't know what I'm doing. I don't even know exactly why I said yes. But, foolish as it may be, I feel like I can figure this out. I can see how far I can get because I know if I say *No* or *Stop,* he will, and he won't ask why.

For the first time, it occurs to me that maybe my choice in men was holding me back. Since college, anyway. My vagina may be the root of many of my problems, but there was never any chance I would've done this with, say, Alexander, even before I realized he was an asshole.

I grab at the hem of my shirt and start to lift upward, but Harrison grabs my wrists. "Absolutely not," he says, a heady glimmer in his eyes. "I'll be doing that, I think."

I shoot him another scowl as I move my hands out of his grasp and instead start working on the buttons of his shirt. His throat bobs as he swallows and watches the movement of my hands, starting at his collarbone and moving down to his waist.

When I finally finish unbuttoning, he helps me pull the shirt off his shoulders. I toss it on the floor, refusing to break his gaze even as my eyes beg me to scan his body, taking in everything I've avoided really looking at since the moment we met.

He doesn't break my gaze as he slowly brings his fingers to my waist, tickling the skin as he gently, ever so slowly pulls my shirt up over my head, brushing the length of my body with his fingers as he takes it off.

And continues staring into my eyes.

A game—who will break eye contact first? Who will give in?

I grin at him, fully aware I'm at an advantage. I selected a gauzy black bra this morning. It's a tad see-through.

He is *so* going to lose it.

His eyes wide and his breathing heavy, he finally breaks my stare, true to my prediction. He places his fingertips behind my right ear and slowly traces down my neck, down the middle of my chest, straight over my navel, and down to the top button of my jeans, all the while tracking the motion with his eyes.

I shudder at the intention in his movement. And then I groan as he brings his lips to my neck and uses soft kisses to trace the path he's just drawn, all while unbuttoning my jeans. When his lips reach my waist, he undoes my zipper and tugs downward, carelessly tossing my pants on the floor as his eyes remain on me.

Shifting on top of me and bracing his arms on either side of my head, he leans forward to give me a breathless kiss, tugging at my bottom lip when he eventually pulls away. I run my hands across his bare chest, marveling at the soft muscles. I've watched this body age from afar—the lanky awkwardness of our teen years, the second-wind growth spurt of our early twenties. I wish I could say I know his body as well as I know his mind, but that wouldn't be true. This body is as new to me as a stranger's but a hundred times more exciting and a thousand times more special.

It's almost scary, to have the opportunity to know someone so completely, both physically and mentally. Where do you go from there?

Or maybe more important, is there any going back?

Harrison keeps himself suspended on top of me, grinning as I hungrily gaze at him. When he doesn't move after several moments, I frown.

"What are you doing?" I demand.

He leans forward and kisses the skin just below my ear, turning to whisper, "I know what I'm doing. Do you trust me? And you'll tell me if you want me to stop?"

I look into his eyes, and I'm not sure anyone has ever had as much trust as I do in Harrison Carter right now.

"Of course," I say. "Let's go slowly? And gently?"

He nods, smiling slowly and gently. And although the pessimist in me wants to say he knows what he's doing because he's been with oh-so-many women before (*thumpthumpthump*) and I'm going to be a joke compared to them, I know that's not what he means. Because somehow, I feel it, too. I'm inexperienced in bed for obvious reasons, and Harrison's body is unfamiliar to me, but I know *him.*

His face still nuzzled against my neck, he drags his fingers downward, and just as I'm bracing for discomfort, I realize—he's not even touching my skin. He's stroking me over the cotton of my underwear.

"Is this still okay?" he asks, his voice tickling my neck.

"Ye—I—" I gasp out. "Oh!"

Harrison chuckles, the movement of his fingers switching from strokes to little circles, drawing a barrier around the place where I need his touch the most.

The pain still hasn't come, but something else might be about to.

And then, just as my heartbeat has increased to marathon levels, he pulls his fingers away.

"No, please don't stop," I whisper, raking my hands through his hair, grabbing on to it as if it's tethering me to life.

He kisses my jawline, then my neck, then my chest, then my stomach, and when I can feel his hot breath against me, he looks up from between my legs, his eyes intent, his expression set.

"How about this?" he asks quietly, before planting one singular kiss against my inner thigh. "Is this okay?"

"Yes," I gasp, reaching forward and grabbing his hair, pulling him closer. "Please."

"And is it okay if I get rid of these?" he asks, looping his fingers into the side of my underwear.

I tense up involuntarily, and he immediately removes his hands. "No, wait—"

"No questions asked. Seriously, Em."

I gulp. "No. Underwear off, please. Just be . . . gentle."

"Always."

Hooking my fingers around the fabric, I take initiative and pull my underwear off, throwing them on the floor. Despite the unobstructed view, Harrison's attention is still focused on my face, intently monitoring my expression.

"I trust you," I whisper. "Please."

"Well, then," he says, redirecting his attention downward. He does something with his mouth that makes my vision go white, then meets my eyes again. "If you insist."

What follows is a master class in tongue coordination. Swirls, nips, licks. All with gentle care and thoughtful motions, taking my body language and my moans and sighs into account. After a mere thirty seconds, I'm close—and it already feels better than anything my own fumbling fingers have done.

Is this what it feels like to trust someone? To trust someone more than you trust yourself?

After I let out a somewhat embarrassing moan, Harrison pauses, looking up at me with a dazed look in his eyes. "Is it okay if I use my fingers, too?" he asks.

"Actually," I whisper, "will you just hold my hands instead?"

He doesn't miss a beat, reaching up, grasping my hands, and then diving back in.

There's something incredibly freeing about being intimate without the expectation of penetrative sex. I've never been in this situation before. So, although some of my previous dates have included some over-the-clothes action, it's been hard to focus on how good anything feels when I know what they're expecting next, and I know they're going to be pissed when I shut it down. Harrison's desire to be intimate with me even though he knows what comes next (or what doesn't come next) is enough to make me cry.

Which I am about to do, actually, because all of a sudden,

there are spasms seizing up my entire pelvic floor. But they're . . . not the bad kind?

Harrison keeps his tongue in action but looks up and meets my gaze as I come. Intensity flares in his eyes, and the intensity doesn't let up even as my body starts to calm down and he kisses the inside of my thighs, then kisses his way back up my body, only breaking eye contact when he leans forward and gives me the absolute sweetest kiss on the cheek.

"Thank you," I whisper.

He exhales a laugh. "Don't ever, ever thank me for that. I enjoyed that just as much as you did. Maybe more."

"I enjoyed that a lot." I brush some hair off of his forehead as he hovers above me.

"I know you did," he says, a cocky grin on his face that I immediately file away in my NSFW mental dictionary. He leans forward, and I think he's about to give me a kiss—because this is the part where we keep going and I make him finish, too, right?—but instead he just rests his head against my shoulder, curling an arm over my waist.

The offers run through my head. *What about you?* or *Your turn!* or maybe *How about I return the favor?* I have no idea what the hell I'm doing.

"Now you?" I whisper into Harrison's hair, tracing my fingers up and down his back.

Instead of responding, he lets out a sleepy hum.

Note to self: If you don't reciprocate immediately, your partner will literally fall asleep while waiting.

Fantastic. I force myself to take a deep breath. *Inhale. Exhale.*

I want to have sweet dreams tonight. I *should* have sweet dreams tonight. But instead, my dreams are all focused around a gnawing sense of *what have I done?* and a firm realization that I shouldn't have let it get this far without having an honest conversation.

CHAPTER 22

I'm not proud of it, but when I wake up in the morning? I freeze.

By this age, I should be a pro at this. I should know how to wake up in someone else's bed and act normal. I should be able to look a guy in the eye and say, "Thanks for a great time last night! Let's do it again soon?"

But I have never even come close to spending the night with a guy. In fact, Harrison might be the only non–family member of the male persuasion whom I've interacted with past midnight. I loved to party in college, but I also loved to sleep.

I love to sleep *so much,* in fact, that I am pretending to do so right now.

I practice the words in my head. *Thanks for a great time.* No, that sounds like he just took me to Disney World. *Let's do it again.* That sounds like I'm not also interested in spending every other waking moment with him. Which I am. So that's out. *Not to be weird, but was that* actually *an enjoyable experience for you? Because I'm feeling a little self-conscious about it.* Or maybe, *I'm sorry I didn't also make you come, but I don't have a ton of experience with this, so will you please give me some pointers on how to interact with dicks? Specifically, your dick? Also, I've been meaning to ask about its girth.*

I let out a quiet snore for good measure.

Pathetic. I am pathetic.

It takes me three additional snores to realize the room is a little too quiet. I freeze, listening for another person's breathing.

Nothing.

I roll over and stare at the empty half of the bed, where there's a faint imprint of a human body in the sheets. Reaching over, cool sheets meet my fingertips.

Well, shit.

Is it fair for me to be mad at him, seeing as I was just fake snoring? No. Am I pissed anyway? Yes.

I grab my phone to see if he's texted me, but the only text I have is from my family group chat.

Dad: Happy Fourth!

Mom: Hope you're doing something fun today!

I send a fireworks emoji in response, then throw my phone to the empty side of the bed and groan.

Given my lack of experience, it's entirely possible I'm just misinterpreting this. Maybe it's totally normal for him to leave me in bed alone the morning after he made me come with his tongue. Totally, absolutely normal.

I do everything possible to stop my intrusive thoughts from winning, but *is this because I didn't get him off?* still escapes into my brain space.

Groaning, I roll out of bed and put on my Old Navy American flag T-shirt and denim shorts, freshening up and pulling my hair back into a high ponytail with a bright red scrunchie. The look is giving summer camp counselor, which I'm hoping sends whatever the opposite of *I slept with your son last night* vibes are.

As I step out of the bedroom a few minutes later and make my way down to the main floor, I'm hit with the sickly-sweet smell of pancakes and syrup. I follow the sound of chatter, about to turn the corner into the kitchen, when I collide with something. No—someone.

"Oof—sorry, Em." He looks frazzled, his eyes wide.*

"Harrison? What's wrong?"

"I think this was a bad idea," he says, and before I can ask what he means, his mother rounds the corner. She smiles wide, her bright red lips a pop of color against her pasty skin. She looks better than she did the last time I saw her, now donning a Fourth of July–appropriate seersucker dress. But even still, she has a crazed look in her eyes, as if she's on the hunt.

"Emma," she says, her voice falsely enthusiastic. "Good morning!"

Harrison looks like he's about to sprint out of the house, but I ignore him and steel myself. I have a mission to accomplish, after all. I came here knowing this would be awkward but still wanting to support Harrison and win over his mom. "Millie! So nice to see you again. Thanks for letting me join. I'm really excited to be here."

She looks me up and down. I say a word of thanks to Past Emma for having the foresight to brush my hair instead of leaving it tangled up in a classic I Spent Last Night Making Out with Your Son look.

"Yes," she says. "We're so happy to have you. I was just delighted when Harrison told me he was bringing you! So nice to hear that you're trying to be a better friend." I don't have time

* **Wide eyes · Tense jaw · Shallow breathing** | *Facial expression* | *Frequency: low*

1. Flustered shock.

to respond before she continues, which is probably good because I don't know how I possibly could've responded to that. "It's so important to heal broken bonds. Especially when they've caused so much pain." She looks at me sympathetically.

I would like to not be here right now.

"I'll get you some coffee, sweetheart," Millie says, smiling with her lips pulled so far to the sides and her eyes so emotionless that she looks like she's smelling something foul. Before I can get another word in, she turns around to grab a mug from the cabinet. I take that as my cue to sit down at the dining table. "Tell me how Boston is treating you," Millie continues. "Everything going well?"

I stutter out some words about how it's going well and I'm liking my job, and I'm feeling good about my ability to form complete sentences under pressure until she hits me with, "That's great. I know it's been nice for Harrison to have a friend nearby while he deals with everything."

The word "friend" rattles around my brain like an alarm.

"Yeah," I tentatively offer. "Breakups are never easy."

Harrison jumps in. "Mom, how are the panca—"

"I know," Millie says, ignoring Harrison. "They're so hard. Especially when you're blindsided by them. I know all about that," she says, then mouths *divorce* at me, as if she's letting me in on a little girly pop secret.

"Well, I'm sure what Stephanie is going through pales in comparison to what you went through," I say. "I can't imagine how hard divorce must be."

Millie narrows her eyes at me, confused. "Oh, I don't give a damn what Stephanie is going through. Why should I?"

Harrison abruptly stands up from his seat at the dining table, then looks surprised with himself for making a scene, then sits back down, the wooden chair creaking beneath him.

"Oh, I just . . ." I attempt to say. "It seemed like you and Stephanie got along really well."

She smiles thinly. "We did. But anyone who breaks up with my son with no explanation doesn't deserve my well wishes."

I think we're talking about me for a moment, and I'm about to clarify that Harrison and I never dated in college, and then I realize we are not, in fact, talking about me.

"Wait, what?" I ask, this time directed at Harrison. He stares into his coffee, unresponsive.

Millie looks on with interest, (correctly) realizing she's uncovered an interesting tidbit of information.

"Frankly, I couldn't believe it when Harrison finally told me what happened," she says.

"Mom, I don't think—"

She cuts him off. "I mean, why would she break up with him when it seemed like their relationship was going so well? And why offer no explanation? It just seems like she owed him more than that, don't you agree?" She pauses for dramatic effect before adding, "Although maybe you could offer some more insight into why someone would do that."

This time, I'm the one who stands up abruptly, realizes I'm making a scene, and sits back down. We're engaged in a high-stakes game of musical chairs.

There's no way that's what actually happened. Harrison clearly lied to his mom.

Except did he ever actually tell me that he broke up with Stephanie?

I rack my brain. *Stephanie isn't coming back,* he'd said. *I know it's my own doing, and so I need to be able to live with that, but I really didn't want to sit here and be alone.*

Then when Stephanie had come to talk to me: *Honestly, I'm not even that broken up about it, which goes to show it was probably the right call.*

The right call by her. Not the right call by Harrison.

I don't want you to think that I pushed him into something he didn't want, she'd said. Harrison didn't break up with Stephanie for me. Stephanie broke up with him and pushed him to me.

Holy shit.

The level of embarrassment I feel is such that all the blood rushes away from my face rather than toward it. I've been sucked dry by a vampire, except the vampire in question is an extremely misguided and highly embarrassing belief that Harrison broke up with Stephanie because he still had feelings for me.

You thought you were worth that much? Cobalt says. *You're a fool.*

My heart sinks all the way to the floor. *I know,* I whisper back.

"But anyway," Millie says, flipping a pancake. The sound of metal on cast iron sends chills up and down my bloodless body. "Are *you* seeing anyone right now? Any nice young men?" She smiles sweetly. "Or women, of course! That's lovely, too!"

I am obviously not going to tell her I'm seeing her son. I would never dare, especially not after discovering I was so unbelievably incorrect about the circumstances under which our relationship began. And besides, what even is our relationship status? More Than Friends with One-Sided Benefits? If our relationship were any more than that, wouldn't he have told me that Stephanie broke up with him rather than continuing to not correct me when I referenced the opposite?

And what does it say about our relationship that he told his mom about his breakup, but didn't tell me?

Setting that aside to consider later, I open my mouth to remark on how extraordinarily single I am, but just as the words are about to enter the airspace, I see Harrison shake his head, so slightly it's nearly imperceptible. His eyes are wide, and his breathing appears to be short.*

* **Wide eyes · Jerky movements · Shortness of breath** | *Facial expression* | *Frequency: low*

1. Fear.

What in the actual hell?

He thinks I would turn this conversation with his mother into a tell-all about our relationship status? And he's so sure I would do that, and is so afraid of that possibility, he's actually trying to warn me?

Absolutely the hell not. Frankly, maybe this conversation *should* be a tell-all about our relationship, since he seems so keen on sharing other relationship updates with his mother.

He shakes his head at me again, more urgently this time, and all the blood rushes back into my body.

"I am seeing someone right now, actually," I say, smiling at his mother. Her eyes widen with some combination of intrigue and alarm. She glances at Harrison, who returns to staring pointedly into his cup of coffee.

"Oh? Tell me more!" She brings the pot of coffee over to refill my cup.

I thank her as she walks back to the pancake station, then continue. "Well, it's new. It doesn't feel new, but also, we're still figuring a lot of things out. Honestly, I'm getting mixed signals."

Harrison looks like he's about to melt into the floor. *You let me believe a lie, and then you left me,* I tell him with my eyes. *I trusted you last night, and then you left me alone.* If he can read my thoughts, he doesn't acknowledge it.

His mom continues to ignore him. "Oh? Like what?"

"You know, I'm just not sure he's invested in us the way I am. That's how it feels, sometimes."

Based on the way Millie keeps glancing back and forth between me and Harrison, she seems to know what's going on here but is continuing to play along to get more information. She'll probably interrogate him later, but if he's going to be an asshole and treat me like a dirty secret, his mom isn't my problem.

"Well, maybe he's just not that into you," Millie suggests.

"Maybe," I say. "Maybe there'll be someone at your party tonight who would be more interested."

Harrison finally directly acknowledges me, mouthing the word *stop*.

"Sorry," I say, looking at him. "What did you say?"

He clears his throat, eyes jerking toward the kitchen. "Mom, I think the pancakes are burning."

She scowls, whipping around with her spatula to remove the pancakes from the griddle. Harrison looks straight at me. He doesn't say anything, but I can read his expression.*

Damn straight.

Before either Harrison or I can say something to break the tension, Millie turns off the burner, throws the spatula into the sink, and stalks off in a wave of burnt-pancake-scented smoke. The door to the primary bedroom slams shut a moment later.

"Why would you do that?" Harrison murmurs.

I force down a swallow. "Why would you treat me like your dirty little secret immediately after we spent the night together? And why didn't you tell me Stephanie broke up with you? You knew I thought you ended it."

"Right, because you've never misled me either?" he asks, breathing heavily.

I stand up abruptly, leaving the room. Harrison has won this game of musical chairs.

"Sometimes things are complicated, Emma," he calls out as I walk away. "Sorry you can't be my priority a hundred percent of the time. I tried that in college, and look where it got us."

I stomp up the stairs, certain he'll follow. He *has* to follow. But when I get to the bedroom we shared last night and sit on

* **Softened eyes · Head tilted down · Soft frown** | *Facial expression* | *Frequency: low*

1. Guilt.

the armchair, waiting to hear footsteps, what I hear instead is the door to the downstairs bedroom open and close.

Shit.

I scan the room, looking around at our belongings mingling on the floor and on the bed, our open backpacks next to each other, our toothbrushes next to each other on the sink, peeking in through the door to the connected bathroom. Rumpled sheets, clothes flung onto the rug.

A tropical storm begins to form in my stomach, and I evacuate the chair, grabbing all of my belongings and throwing them into my backpack so quickly and with such little care that I think my toothbrush ends up wrapped in a pile of dirty socks. It takes me a record two minutes to pack, and as I walk downstairs, I call a rideshare that costs more than what I earn during a shift at Jo Jo's. Then again, you can't put a price on my sanity. And I need to get out of here before I completely crash out.

Kidding. That's already happening.

I storm into the living room, wanting to make sure everyone knows about my dramatic exit. *Thirteen minutes away,* my app tells me. Outside it is, then. I can't spend another second in this cabin, and especially not in the living room, where all I can see are ghostly images of twenty-year-old Harrison making me hot chocolate and curling up next to me under a blanket and talking to me about life and love and chemistry homework. *You're the best friend I've ever had,* he'd told me that night.

Just as I reach the front door, Harrison and his mom raise their voices, allowing the words to float through the closed bedroom door.

"No kidding, I don't like her. No one who hurt my son as much as she did deserves my time of day."

I think I'm going to throw up.

"It was complicated, Mom."

"Absolutely nothing was complicated about how distraught

you were. You should have been crying happy tears at your graduation, and instead, I had to mop you off the floor."

I'm absolutely going to be sick. The coffee I drank on an empty stomach while waiting for the pancakes that never came is now sending acid shooting through my veins, and my hands tremble as a loud ringing reverberates through my head.

I've made a mistake. I've made a big, terrible mistake.

Whipping my phone out of my back pocket, I hit cancel on my ride. *Are you sure you want to cancel?* it asks. *Your driver is already on the way, so you'll still be charged.*

"Shit," I murmur, watching the driver inch closer. "Shit, shit, shit, shit—"

The door to the bedroom opens and closes, and my startled gaze collides with Harrison's intense stare.

CHAPTER 23

Five years ago

In the nearly three years since I lived in Hall Hall, almost nothing has changed. The tables and rugs still look like they were dragged out of a dumpster, and the beanbags are now saggy and stained, which better matches the overall aesthetic of the space. The fourth-floor common room also still has the distinctly freshman smell of cheap beer and Clorox and heavy perfume—which is impressive seeing as the freshmen moved out a few days ago, and the only people left on campus are the seniors about to graduate tomorrow morning.

The reasonable conclusion might be that the common room reeks of alcohol (the drinking kind and the Bath and Body Works body spray kind) because of the seniors who invaded it tonight, but I refuse to take personal responsibility for any of those scents. I've been consuming wine tonight, like a real adult.

I cannot comment on whether I used Bath and Body Works body spray.

Taking a look around to make sure I'm the only one left, I collapse into a beanbag, giving up all hope that my floor-length, emerald-green dress will remain wrinkle-free.

As per college tradition, this common room has played host tonight to a rotating cast of Hall Hall fourth-floor alumni, coming to visit their freshman dormitory before they enter the real world tomorrow. Most of their faces were faint blurs in my memory, as I spent the vast majority of my time with Jo and Harrison, both of whom have already made their appearances. I assume, anyway. I got here toward the end and didn't see Harrison, so he must've come earlier in the night. Jo, on the other hand, made an obligatory brief appearance and then ran back to our apartment with Macy.

I wasn't in the mood to third-wheel (or listen to things I didn't want to listen to), so here I am. Loitering, in a beanbag, in a freshman dorm. Sexiled, just like I was during the first weekend of college. Life is good.

Inhale.

Exhale.

The elevator door opens, and I freeze as footsteps echo through the hallway.

"Em?" Harrison whispers.

Maybe if I don't move, he won't see me?

We should talk, he'd said to me this morning. I could fill in the words. About feelings. About us. About *why.*

I'll see you tonight at the party, I'd replied. He'd frowned, and I'd smiled in return.

I have no intention of "talking." Nothing good will come of that, and he should know it by now.

Harrison sees me immediately, of course, and without saying anything, he collapses into the neighboring beanbag, his suit crumpled, his knees pulled up. Dress shoes with orange-patterned socks.

The party we attended tonight—a college-hosted soirée with college-approved drink tickets and a college-budget deejay and mostly college-appropriate formal wear—could not be more different than the party that was raging in Hall Hall the night Harrison and I met. Nothing about that was college-sanctioned, and the only formal part of the night was Harrison's odd introduction and handshake.

I'm Harrison. Harrison Carter, he'd said.

Are you okay? he'd asked.

Tonight, he's silent. The open windows let in the sounds of late-night crickets and reveling college seniors, all mingling with our steady *inhale*s and *exhale*s.

After a few minutes, he finally speaks up. "Can I ask you something?"

"No."

We sit in silence for a few seconds.

"Oh my god, yes. What?"

I can see his face shift in the darkness as a dimple appears. He waits for a moment before asking, "What actually happened that night?"

It takes me a moment to register what he's talking about, but when I realize he means *that night* as in *that first night,* I turn my head to face him.

"How did you know?"

A curl falls into his forehead as he tilts his head, studying me. "Instinct, I guess."

Yeah. Instinct.

That's the thing about accidentally falling in love with your best friend. It happens slowly, over years—four years, in this case—and you don't realize it's happened until you wake up one day and realize you know everything about them. You've gone from asking how they're feeling to knowing instinctively how they feel. You've created a whole dictionary of their facial expressions, and you have the whole thing memorized. You're suddenly only cracking jokes you know they'll laugh at because you've accidentally learned the ins and outs of their sense of humor. You've learned how they take their coffee, and you've learned they love talking on the phone but hate making calls.

You've spent hours staring at one specific curl that juts out across their forehead at a different angle every day. You've learned they love you in a more-than-platonic way, and you've realized you love them in a more-than-platonic way, too, even though you lie to yourself and to them about it, and you've realized they definitely know you're lying.

I press my eyes together so hard I begin to see spots. When I open them, I still see polka dots everywhere.

Harrison leans forward, beads rustling inside the beanbag. He rests his elbows on his knees, dropping his head into his hands and running his fingers through his waves before letting them plop back onto his forehead, one by one.

He looks at me, opens his mouth again, then changes his mind, instead sitting up straight and removing his suit jacket. After tossing it onto the floor, he leans back and unbuttons the cuffs of his shirt, rolling up the sleeves to his elbows. I stare the entire time, too uncertain to move.

When he's done, he turns his attention back to me. I never bothered to turn the lights back on in the common room after everyone else left, so he's mostly illuminated by the streetlights coming in through the window, but the low lighting creates an eerie sparkle in his eyes. Instead of being dark, as they typically are, they're a beacon of light in the otherwise matte landscape.

"We messed up," he says.

I don't know what to say to that, so I don't say anything.

"How did we get here?" he whispers.

"I don't think it matters," I say. With one night left of college, now is not the time to be ruining a years-long friendship. A friendship that will, in all likelihood, be ruined if this conversation continues.

Harrison sits forward again, resting his elbows on his knees and rubbing his face. When he looks at me, his eyes are wide and glassy and a little bloodshot.

"You're lying to yourself," he says. "It matters more than it ever has. Every time I think about us graduating, I feel sick. Not because I think we'll drift apart, but because I'm so afraid we've missed the only opportunity we'll ever have. You're going to get a job and get new friends and be busy all the time and move on with your life, but I won't be able to." His voice cracks. "I won't be able to because I can't imagine my life without you, and I shouldn't have waited until now to tell you. You mean the entire world to me. And I don't understand it, but you make me feel like myself. Like when I'm with you, that's who I really am. That's the truest version of Harrison." He takes a shaky breath. "How did we let this happen, Em? How did we waste so many years?"

My breathing has stopped, but I find the strength to eke out, "I don't know," which is neither fair nor true.

"Can I—" he says, then stops himself.

I nod him on, even though I don't know what's happening. He scoots forward out of the beanbag, kneeling a few inches in front of me. His eyes are so close, I see my reflection in them.

And maybe I'm cruel for this, but in this moment, I forget why I ever had any hesitation.

My chest collapses in a way that may or may not send my head up and down in a nod, and I'm not sure whether that was intentional on my part, but his lips and eyebrows shift slightly up and his head shifts slightly down.*

"Can I kiss you?"

Our lips are inches away. Centimeters, now. His slow breathing tickles my face. Chills rack my body, and goose bumps form everywhere I can see, and then some. I lift one hand to his chest, feeling his heartbeat, and the other arm

* **Soft smile · Raised eyebrows · Head tilted downward toward subject** | *Facial expression* | *Frequency: unknown*

1. Love.

wraps around his neck. He inches forward, one hand weaving its fingers through my hair and the other holding my waist.

Our lips meet.

His touch is unexpectedly soft, and my lips part to welcome him. Or maybe his lips part to welcome mine. He tastes like cheap wine: sweet, but still a little bitter. His lips draw out every emotion I've hidden from him over the last four years, and as I let out the tiniest of sighs, I can feel his muscles shift as he smiles, his lips still pressed to mine.

Another kiss. And then another one, and another one, each one impossibly slow even as my heart beats impossibly fast.

I've kissed other guys before, but this—*this* is different. Kissing Harrison is buying a scratch-off and winning a million dollars. You're hopeful and allow yourself some limited, realistic expectations, but when you take your quarter to the first layer and realize what you've actually won, your life is forever changed.

"Harrison," I whisper in between kisses. I'm not even sure what I want to say. My mind is completely blank, unable to form cohesive thoughts. *Lips. Harrison.* And then, as his tongue gently enters my mouth, running across my bottom lip: *Holy shit.*

I want more, so much more—and suddenly, our hands are everywhere. One slipped under my dress and resting against my bare waist, the other on my thigh. My hands in his hair, on his chest, across his back, gripping his arms. I whimper as his thumb brushes the bottom of my breast, naked save for nipple pasties.

His hands on my waist, he drags me forward onto his lap, and I respond with so much enthusiasm that we end up on the floor, one of my legs on each side of his waist, my dress pooling all over his dress clothes. We grasp at each other desperately, and it's still not enough. I want our cells to fuse, I want our souls to intertwine, I want our minds to merge. Our kisses grow rougher, our hands grow bolder, and our tongues have a conversation inside our mouths, speaking all the words we can't or won't or haven't said aloud.

I've never been happier, and there are so many emotions inside of me, I can't breathe. I think my face is wet from tears.

Harrison pulls back slightly, just enough to smile and say "I didn't think our first kiss would make you cry" in a heartbreakingly lighthearted tone.

I shift my weight back a few inches, moving away from his lips and back onto . . . something hard. Underneath me. On Harrison's lap.

Fuck.

Our first kiss, he said. *Our first kiss,* implying there will be more. More, implying . . . more. And more leads to . . .

Fuck.

I freeze, my heavy breathing stalled. The tears I didn't know were falling stop falling.

Harrison's expression shifts from a smile to a frown, his left hand still on my thigh and his right hand still on my waist, both touching skin and goose bumps. I shiver, already regretting what I'm about to do.

Is it possible to intentionally do something bad with good intentions?

"Em? What's wrong?" he murmurs.

I can see the gears turning in his mind. All the air has been sucked out of the room. My chest is unbearably tight, even more so when I look into Harrison's eyes and see his desire now competing with worry.

I'm an asshole. And I hurt him. Today, and before, and again and again. And that's why this will never work out.

If you love someone, it shouldn't hurt to be with them.

I untangle myself from Harrison's arms, desperately moving away from the hardness on his lap that is, for better or for worse, bringing me back to reality and reminding me of the hard truths that haunt me every time I long for him.

Harrison knows what I eat for lunch every day. He knows what time I go to bed and what time I wake up. He knows how I take my coffee, and he knows how long it takes me to write an essay I procrastinated on. In many ways, he knows me better than I know myself.

But he doesn't know *this.* Because I never told him.

"You should leave," I whisper. My heart is pounding out of my chest, and I'm breathing rapidly from the adrenaline still coursing through my veins. I can't look him in the eyes.

"Em—please. I'm so sorry." His voice cracks.

"It's not you," I say quietly, looking down at my feet, holding back tears. "It's complicated."

I can hear his breathing, still heavy. He shifts to get a better view of my face, and I take the bait, looking up into his eyes. I immediately regret it, recognizing the pain that's likely mirrored in my own expression. Pure, raw devastation.

"But I love you," he says, so quietly I'm not sure he meant to say it aloud.

"Harrison," I say, reaching forward to take his hand. He doesn't accept it, and I pull my hand back. "I love you, but not like that. We're . . . we're not compatible. We're not soulmates. And I . . . don't think we should be friends anymore."

It's intended to hurt him, and I hate myself, and I know I'll probably always hate myself, but I don't take it back.

"Why? Let me guess—because it's *complicated*?" he asks, malice entering his voice. I nod. "Then tell me. Tell me why it's complicated."

Because, Harrison. Because you deserve to be with someone who's easy to love, and I wish that were me, but it's not, and I'm not ready, physically, but I'm also not ready to tell you. Maybe it's because I need more time, but maybe it's just because I know deep down that if I open up to you, you'll realize I. Am. Not. Enough. You'll be afraid you'll hurt me every time you touch me. And so, you'll leave me, or you'll pity me so much that you stay, but either way, we'll be worse off. And then I'll have to leave you, or you'll leave me, and then I'll never be able to find someone else like you, and I'll never have you again.

But if you continue with this, you'll never have him again, anyway, a voice in my head says. I ignore it.

With all the strength left in me, I look him in the eyes and try to disguise the weakness in my own voice. "Please. Go home."

It comes out too forcefully, and I see the moment all hope drains from his eyes, molten lava turning to rock. Jaw clenching, chest tightening.

"No," he says. "Look me in the eyes and tell me you're not in love with me. Then I'll leave, and I won't come back."

I don't take the time to think before standing up. The bottom of my dress falls back down to my ankles, and I storm over to where my heels had been tossed. Harrison's scowl is piercing, even when facing away.

"You can't say it," he says. "You can't say it, and I hope you know this is going to hurt you just as much as it hurts me."

And god damn it, that's the worst possible thing he could've said, because I can't imagine hurting anyone as badly as I'm hurting myself right now. But somehow, I find the strength to do it anyway.

I face him one last time, just long enough to whisper "I'm not in love with you" and watch the devastation that paints his face.

I walk out, and that's the last time I speak to Harrison for five years.

CHAPTER 24

Five years later

Harrison takes three steps forward, then pauses when his gaze snags on my bags, his eyes narrowing and his jaw dropping.*

"Were you leaving?!" he whispers aggressively, his eyes jerking toward the closed bedroom door before he continues whispering. "Are you kidding me?"

"Are *you* kidding *me*?" I whisper back. I let him fill in the blanks about what I'm talking about. (I'm not 100 percent sure what I'm talking about at this point.)

We stare at each other, and I see something in his eyes that makes me deflate, and he must see something in mine, too, because we take simultaneous *inhales* and *exhales,* our shoulders dropping.

"You okay?" I tentatively whisper.

"I'm an asshole," he murmurs.

"You're not an asshole."

* **Narrowed eyes · Dropped jaw** | *Facial expression* | *Frequency: low*

1. Surprised anger.

"No, I definitely am."

I drop my weekender onto the floor, and it lands with a soft thud. "No, you're definitely not."

He stares at my weekender, jaw tense. "You seem to think I am."

"Well, we all get angry with the people we love sometimes. But you know you love them when you can't stay angry with them for long."

"I've been angry with you for years." His eyes slide up from the weekender to meet my gaze. "And, besides. You don't love me."

"Yes, I—"

"No," he says, full volume this time. "You looked me in the eyes and told me you didn't." He doesn't give me time to respond, which is probably telling, but of what, I'm not sure. "Outside?" he asks, nodding to the front door.

He walks past me before I can acknowledge him, and I grab my bag and drag it outside. By the time I close the front door behind me, he's already ten feet away, facing the street with his hands in his pockets. The tension is written in his posture, his shoulders reaching up toward his ears.

"I just wanted everyone to be happy," he says toward a passing car. "I didn't want to be the one ruining everything. I'm *always* the one ruining everything."

"That's not true," I offer. He turns around with such expediency, I let out a small gasp.

"Isn't it?" he asks, taking a step forward and staring at me with a crazed, flustered look. "Because I ruined things with my mom. I ruined things with Stephanie and with everyone else I've tried to convince myself I was interested in since college." He pauses, and I swallow, a lump forming in my throat. "I sure as hell ruined things with you."

"No," I say, inching closer. We stand face-to-face, neither daring to reach out. "You didn't ruin things with me."

"I did. I really, really did." He hesitates, then, with renewed strength, asks, "Am I an asshole?"

"No. No, of course not."

He takes a stuttered breath. "Then why didn't you love me?"

Past tense. Not present tense. Past tense, as in why did I claim not to love him *back then.*

It feels silly, really—asking it straight out like that, when there's no easy answer. I did love you. *But you didn't know everything.* I did love you. *But things were complicated.* I did love you. *But I had to pull back for my good and yours.*

I take a deep breath.

Inhale.

Exhale.

Let's start slow, he'd said. *Tell me one thing—just one. One truth about Emma.*

One thing.

Inhale.

Exha—

"I have a condition," I say, choking on the words.

He stares at me, then squints. "What?"

"Remember the night we met?"

He tilts his head, nodding. "You were having boy problems."

"There was this guy. I didn't really know him, but we started making out in the bathroom." Harrison cringes, and I roll my eyes. "Yeah, yeah. But, anyway—we were making out, and I was feeling a little full of myself. Newfound freedom, and all that. So, things started to get a little, uh, hot and heavy? And he tried to finger me."

"Tried?"

"Yeah, tried. It hurt like hell, and I accidentally kneed him in the balls."

I expect Harrison to laugh, because—I mean, come on—it's hilarious in retrospect. Instead, he furrows his brows and stays silent.

"So, later that year I went to the gynecologist for the first time. And, well, do you know what vaginismus is?"

"Yes," Harrison says simply. His expression doesn't change.

I raise an eyebrow. "I have it."

The change in Harrison's expression is barely perceptible, so small it's impossible to read. It's the slightest tightening of the lips, the tiniest widening of the eyes, the smallest tilt of the head. I wait for him to say something, but instead, he just nods at me to go on.

I don't know what I was expecting his reaction to be, but it wasn't this.

"So," I continue, "I didn't do anything about it for a long time. Because it sucked, and because I didn't understand it and didn't want to understand it, and because I was afraid. But I started going to pelvic floor therapy recently."

He blinks slowly. "And that's helping?"

"Some," I say. Harrison's face is still emotionless. "Slowly. It's still uncomfortable, but it's getting easier."

"And . . ." Harrison starts to say. I nod for him to go on. "You're saying this has affected your dating life."

I give him my best *no, duh* look. "Yes, that's kind of the whole point of telling you this."

Finally, he frowns. I would feel relieved about finally being able to read his reaction if it didn't make me afraid of what he was going to say next. "We were best friends for four years," he says. I try to ignore the past tense. "You could've told me about it outside the context of dating me."

"Yes, I definitely could have. And probably should have." Harrison's expression still doesn't change, but I forge ahead. "I've gotten rejected by quite a few men since we graduated from college. Turns out, men care a lot about sex."

"Penetrative sex."

"Yes, that's what I'm saying. Men reject me because I won't have sex with them."

Harrison closes his eyes and shakes his head. "No, I mean—you can't have penetrative sex. Or, you can't right now."

"Correct."

"But that doesn't keep you from being intimate with . . . people . . . in other ways. Obviously," he says, ears turning slightly pink.*

"I mean . . . no. Obviously not," I say, blushing. "But what straight man wants to seriously date someone who can't have penetrative sex? I just figured I would wait to date until I'd finished physical therapy. Makes it easier for everyone," I say casually, as if this hasn't been the bane of my existence for the better part of a decade.

Our staring contest lasts so long that my cheeks probably turn the same color as his ears. Finally, he closes his eyes and runs a hand down his face, defeated. "Holy shit."

"I know. I know, I'm so—"

"I really am an asshole," he murmurs.

I freeze. "Wait, what?"

"Am I actually such an irredeemable piece of shit that you thought I wouldn't want to be with you because of this?"

I take a step forward, and his body tenses, as if he's forcing himself not to walk away. I power on, trying to hold it together. "What are you talking about? That's not even remotely what I said. And besides, me not telling you about my vaginismus is all because of my own screwed-up self-perception. And believe me, I'm working through that in therapy."

"Did you tell other people?" he says without missing a beat.

"Jo," I quietly admit. "I told Jo."

"Great," he says. "So the problem is me."

* **Pink ears** | *Physical reaction* | *Frequency: high*

1. Embarrassment.
2. May be embarrassed by own actions or others' actions.

I take another step forward, and this time he actually does step away.

"Holy shit, you actually didn't love me," he says, his eyes widening as if he's piecing everything together.

"That's not what I—"

"Nope," he says, cutting me off. "That is exactly what you said, actually."

I gape at him for a second, then continue. "Well, I didn't mean it. I was a kid. I was dumb."

"Great!" His voice is oddly shrill. "So you thought it would be better to break my heart than to be honest with me. That's fantastic."

I don't respond.

"So let me lay this out for you." He holds up a finger. "One—you had a common medical condition that you didn't tell me about. Which is your prerogative, and I'm sorry you went through it, but—two"—he holds up a second finger—"when it became clear that things were not strictly platonic between us, you decided to keep that to yourself instead of telling me, even though other people already knew." A third finger. "And if that was truly what was holding you back from dating me, then you must've thought I would react negatively to the information."

I swallow.

"Do you want to deny that?" When I don't answer, he continues. "You made me think something was wrong with me. I spent *years* trying to understand why you were friend-zoning me even though we clearly had feelings for each other. I thought you didn't love me enough to make it worth breaking your no-relationships rule, but it turns out that rule didn't even exist." Devastation paints his face, his breathing heavy. "Do you know what I would have said if you had told me about your vaginismus back then?"

I don't answer, because I fear I already know what he's going to say.

"I would have thanked you for telling me, and then absolutely nothing would've changed between us. Not a single thing," he says, and my eyes start burning, heavy pressure building in my temples.

"I made a mistake back then, but it's different now," I say, sniffling. He stares at me, his chest rising and falling in short bursts. "I trust you completely."

Harrison lets out a maniacal laugh. I've never heard this noise come from his mouth before, and it lands in a pit in my stomach, burying itself into my gut. When he speaks, his voice is raspy. "I don't know if I believe that."

"What about last night?" I take another step forward, and I am vaguely aware of tears now running down my face. "I trust you. You see that. You have to see that."

He takes a step forward, and we're mere inches away now. I can see every ounce of hurt in his eyes.

"You want to talk about last night?" he whispers. "I have no problem with you being a virgin, obviously. I have no problem with you having vaginismus, obviously. But I could've *hurt* you. I didn't know what I was getting into, and I didn't know that I didn't know what I was getting into. That could have gone horribly wrong, and I had no idea. I mean, you could've at least explicitly told me you weren't comfortable with anything involving penetration yet, and I wouldn't have asked any questions." He exhales a shaky breath. "You *know* how much I would have hated myself if I had hurt you. And you know it would've set your vaginismus back if you had gotten hurt and taught your body to expect that pain. But you did it anyway."

A quiet sob escapes my mouth, and a less quiet sniffle escapes my nose. "How do you even know that?"

A tear trickles down Harrison's face, glistening in the morning light. "Because I paid attention to my medical textbooks."

Laughter bubbles out of my mouth before I can stop it, and

Harrison's frown deepens. I quell my poorly timed fit of giggles.

He opens his mouth again, and this time his words aren't angry or frustrated or sad; they're disappointed. "Five years and you still can't have a serious, honest conversation with me."

So much for Doing Better. I'm supposed to be a changed woman, but apparently, I haven't changed at all. Apparently, even attempting to get my life together and be an adult can't hide that, deep down, I am a complete mess. I will always be the same girl who didn't know how to talk to her best friend about her problems at age eighteen, because here I am, almost ten years later, and I still don't know how.

I take a step back, leaning against the side of the house. "I'm trying to be better," I say. Harrison follows my lead, resting his left shoulder against the doorframe as he faces me, arms crossed. "I am, I swear. Back then, five years ago—nine years ago, even—I always, somewhere in the back of my mind, hoped we would end up together. Then, when you reappeared and were this perfect, sweet, organized, put-together man, I knew this was my second chance to do this right."

"What could that possibly involve if not being open about what was going on?"

"Well . . . I actually meant that the original problem was vaginismus," I say. Harrison blinks slowly. "I needed some extra motivation to go through with pelvic floor therapy and to start actually taking care of this. And so, you may think I haven't changed, but I am changing, and you've helped me get there. You're my motivation."

Harrison stares at me, his expression indecipherable. I count several heartbeats before he speaks again, and in those several heartbeats, I don't breathe a single time.

"Do you really mean that?"

I nod, offering a soft smile. "Yes. I was rambling, but yes. I meant every word."

I only realize that wasn't the answer he was looking for when he reaches up and drags a hand across his face, letting out a tortured exhale.

Oh.

Oh, no.

That indecipherable expression on his face was *pain.*

"Emma, listen. I can't be your sole motivation for figuring this out. To be honest, that's kind of messed up. Especially since I didn't know about any of it."

Blood rushes to my head, my cheeks burning. I have that tingly feeling you get when you've been caught red-handed. "That's not fair," I say, even though I fear it might be both fair and true.

"Oh, please." He laughs, the sound so pitiful it comes out as more of a sob. "This is classic Emma. You can't be vulnerable with me, and that hurts. I know you think you're protecting me, but you're not. You're hurting both of us."

I straighten up suddenly, my fists clenched. "What about this weekend, huh? What about the whole last month, when you—" I stop. "Even though—"

"Even though what? What, exactly?"

"You told me you wanted to 'get closure.' And then you told me you wouldn't be dating anyone right now while you figured things out with your mom!"

"It's complicated," he says, frowning deeply.

"Yeah, no kidding. She *abhors* me, and we both know it. I mean, why did you even bring me here? Was this some sick way of forcing yourself to come clean to your mom about us being more than friends?"

He clenches his jaw. "No. I brought you here because I wanted you to be here. She's just trying to create conflict."

I angrily walk a few feet away before turning around to face him again, giving him the most accusatory glare I can muster. "Funny, since her child is the single most conflict-avoidant person to ever walk this earth."

Harrison inches forward again, a combative look in his eyes. "Is that so bad? I mean, you have *never* tried to avoid putting me in the middle of a conflict. Ever. In fact, you spent four years of college willingly and knowingly fueling some insane conflict between us by leading me on and then gaslighting me when I tried to talk about the way we felt for each other. You lied to me."

I jut my chin out defiantly. "And now you're doing the same thing."

"No," he says. "I didn't want to tell my mom we were together until she had warmed to you because I was trying to protect her feelings. And yours, if that even matters to you."

"Is that the same lie you told yourself when you let me believe you broke up with Stephanie?"

This time, he stays silent. My phone buzzes aggressively in my pocket, unmistakable as my two-minute warning that I'm getting picked up by the rideshare I never got around to canceling.

"Why? Why would you do that?" I ask, pressing forward until we're inches away again. "To lead me to believe you broke up with her for me? Because if that was your goal, I'm delighted to say you succeeded. Congrats. I feel like an idiot."

"That wasn't—" he starts to say, then stops himself. "I wasn't trying to make you feel that way. But, for what it's worth, we did break up because I wasn't over you. I was in denial, but she could see it clear as day, I guess."

My heart aches—with what emotion, I'm not sure. "I don't know how to feel about that."

He turns his back to the wall, sliding down until he's sitting, legs splayed out in front of him. "Bad," he murmurs. "I feel bad about it."

The muscles in his jaw are clenched. But even amidst all that tension, there's a furrowed tilt to his eyebrows: sadness.

"You claim you were lying when you said you didn't love

me," he says, "but I'm not sure you really were. You have to let the people you love in. And you clearly can't do that."

Unwilling to spend another second in his presence while I consider that final comment, I stand up, just in time for my phone to vibrate again. "My ride is here. I'm leaving."

"Fine, go home," he says, staying on the ground and making no move to follow me. "Hope you're happy."

As much as it pains me to do so, I let him have the last word as I walk to the road and throw myself into the back seat of the car.

CHAPTER 25

When I finally wake up the next morning, I have a bad taste in my mouth. It's like I've taken a swig of soapy water—it's bitter, it tastes horrible, and I can't ignore it. The aftertaste of a fight with Harrison, apparently.

My phone buzzes repeatedly on my nightstand. It's just after nine A.M., and the light streaming in through my blinds slaps me in the face as I roll over and blindly grab my phone. I rip it off the charger and hold it a few inches away from my face, attempting to blink the sleep out of my eyes.

I'm so relieved it's not Harrison, I pick up the call from my dad without thinking.

"Sweetheart?" he says after a few moments of silence.

I immediately burst into tears.

"Oh, Emma," my mom's voice pops in from a distance. "Sweetie, it's okay. We're here."

They are, of course, *not* here, since I moved 1,300 miles away.

"I think I messed up," I choke out, my voice ragged.

"It's okay, sweetheart," my dad says. There's a moment of

silence, and I can picture him and my mom exchanging a glance. "Tell us what's going on."

When my mouth opens for another sob, words start coming out. "I hated teaching," I say, my voice quiet, muffled by snot and tears and the pillow I've buried my face in. "I didn't just quit because of the parent and the stupid book. I quit because I hated teaching." It's not actually an explanation for my tears, but it feels like the explanation they deserve. Neither of my parents responds immediately, which I take to mean they either didn't hear me or are shocked into silence.

Instead, my mom quietly responds, "We know."

I let out another sob. "And I . . . I don't know what I'm doing."

My dad sighs, the phone crackling. "No one does. That's the secret. But that's why we're so lucky to have one another. To help."

I sniffle into the phone like the enormous baby I am. "I felt like I was letting you down. I was supposed to love teaching. I'm supposed to have it figured out by now."

"You're supposed to do what makes you happy," my mom says. "We don't give a shit whether that's teaching."

I giggle despite myself. My mom doesn't even like the word "stupid." This might be the first time I've ever heard her curse.

"Why were you crying, sweetie?" my mom asks.

"Because you do give a shit," I whimper. "Because I'm stressing you out and I don't want to worry you and—"

"Emma." My mom's voice is firm as she cuts me off. "Stop. You don't need to worry about us. You need to worry about yourself."

My dad chimes in. "I'm sorry we made you feel like you were worrying us. Of course we're concerned about you, but we'll always be concerned about you because that's what we do. We worry because we love you. But we're not worried *because* of you."

"What if you should be?" I murmur. "I worry myself."

"What, because you moved?" my mom asks. "Because you're working at a coffee shop? Please. Both your dad and I were still working minimum-wage jobs when we were your age."

"Yeah, but you had a plan to go back to school and become teachers. I don't have a plan, and even if I did, I couldn't execute it."

"We didn't go back to school to become teachers until we met and convinced each other to follow our dreams. You think we had some grand plan to wait until we were in our late twenties to actually start the job we wanted? We didn't. We were winging it, and it all worked out in the end."

I sniffle into the phone again. "What if I'm trying really hard not to wing it but I always end up winging it anyway?"

There's a momentary pause. "Do you want to talk about it?" my dad asks. "Is this about the move? The job?"

"Er—friend trouble. Sort of."

"Jo?" my dad asks.

My mom immediately scoffs. "Bill, don't be ridiculous. She's obviously talking about Harrison."

My dad and I both let out confused grunts. "How on earth did you know that?" I ask.

"I was twenty-seven once. I know how hard it is to stay away from attractive men."

"Mom, that is *disgusting.* Don't call my friends attractive, please."

"Friends?" she immediately asks. "So, you and Harrison are . . . friends? Again?"

"Remind me why we're talking about this?"

"Because you're crying."

"She's not crying anymore," my dad points out. "My magical happiness powers worked." There's muttering in the background, and I can make out something along the lines of *I'm not going to high-five you, Bill.*

"Do you want to talk about it?" my mom hesitantly asks.

I could tell them about it. They both know about my vaginismus and surely understand its implications, even if we've never talked about my sex life (and never will, thank you very much). It would be so easy to tell them what happened with Harrison in college and about how badly we screwed up this week. I could tell them I don't know how to fix this or any of my other problems, but they probably wouldn't have any advice beyond something useless like "Be yourself" or "Do what makes you happy."

My mom takes my silence as a no. "Listen, Emma. It's okay if you don't want to talk to us about your love life."

"Who said anything about my love life?"

She ignores me. "But you need to be talking about this with someone. You can't keep this to yourself."

"I've been going to therapy again," I say, exhaling a little.

"That's amazing. I know that must have been hard for you," my dad says, his tone empathetic. "You've always had a hard time letting people help you solve your problems. Therapy's a great start. I'm glad you're not struggling alone. But it helps to also let the people who love you in."

"Your friends want to help you, and they want to know how you feel," my mom adds. "And so do we."

Inhale.

Exhale.

It's not that simple. There's no way it's that simple.

Of course it is, idiot.

If I had told Harrison I had feelings for him, we wouldn't have both been left wondering.

If I had explained my hesitations, he wouldn't have felt like *he* was the problem.

If I had let him in, I would've realized I was lovable a long time ago.

"Emma? You okay?" my dad asks.

"Yeah," I mumble into my pillowcase. "I'm really, really sorry I've been ignoring you. I should've just called you and talked it out."

"It's okay, baby," my mom says. My dad murmurs his agreement. "Call more often, though, okay?"

"I will, I promise."

"And now you need to get off the phone to go take care of something else, right?" I can practically hear my mom's smile through the phone.

"Yeah. I have to go do something."

"Say hi for us!" she says.

My dad's muffled whisper is still entirely audible. "To whom?"

"Love you two!" I say before my mom can explain.

"Love you," they chorus back.

It's nine-thirty now, and I hear the front door above mine open, a good eight hours earlier than anticipated. Solemn footsteps, creaking floorboards. A bag dropping on the floor. A thud as someone lies down on a couch. Sounds like I'm not the only one who cut their trip short.

"I'm sorry, Harrison," I whisper toward the ceiling. "I'm coming back for you, I promise."

Just not yet.

I drag a box out of my closet (ASSORTED SHIT <3) and grab the notebook sitting at the top. I turn to the second page, dated a couple of months after graduation. The paper crinkles in my hand. Water damage. Possibly from tears, possibly from Florida humidity.

The night we met, I think something in me—mind, body (probably not body), soul (definitely soul, though)—identified you as a kindred spirit. It's been almost four years since that night, and I'm waiting to find someone else who provides the same level of comfort. Surely it can't just be you, right?

(Correction—yes, it definitely could be, and as time passes, I become more resigned to that idea.)

You felt like home, even on that first night. I think that's why I bought you so many pairs of those stupid socks. They reminded me of home, just like you did. One day I'd like to take you to Florida, and we'll go on a drive outside the city and look at the orange trees, and we'll go canoeing in a natural spring so I can introduce you to the manatees and alligators. You'd probably be scared but pretend not to be, and even if you were scared, you'd still keep your eyes wide and eyebrows raised, always studying, always observing.

Were you always observing me like that? Probably. What did you find? Did you know all my secrets? Did you know I loved you?

That was five years ago. How is it that I'm still sitting here wondering the same thing? Did I really mess up my second chance that badly?

Yes. Yes, I did.

I grab a pencil from my coffee table and flip to a blank page.

<u>Emma's Short and Sweet Plan to Make Amends</u>

Step one: Talk to parents. Check.

Step two: Prioritize time with Jo.

Step three: Apologize to Harrison.

Step four: Tell Harrison I love him.

Before I lose my willpower and sink back into my cave of blankets and pillows, I call Jo.

"Hi, girly pop," she says, answering the phone.

"Is your sister still there?" I ask.

"Nope. She headed back this morning."

"Great. Listen. I've been a shitty friend. I love working with you—or for you, or whatever—but I really want to spend time with you outside of work, and I'm really sorry I haven't been prioritizing that. I feel bad about it, and I'd like to change."

There's a lengthy pause before she speaks. "Thanks for saying that. I appreciate it. And I want you to know that even though, yes, I feel like you haven't been prioritizing seeing me outside of work, I am still incredibly appreciative you're here and supporting me right now."

"And that goes for you, too. I'm glad you've been here to support me," I say, and I can hear Jo's smile through the phone. "I don't know what your vision for the day was, but I have nothing going on, and I'd love to actually go to yoga with you this time. I pinky promise I won't flake. Does the studio you practice at have any classes this morning? And then maybe we can go out to lunch after?"

She squeals with excitement. "Yes! Girls' day! I have to take over for Rose at two, so that's perfect. Meet me in an hour?"

"Perf—"

"WAIT," Jo interrupts. There's a pause as the wheels of her brain turn. "Why aren't you at Harrison's mom's place right now?"

***

THERE'S SOMETHING INCREDIBLY HUMBLING ABOUT walking into a fitness class and being the least prepared person in the room. But surely beginner yoga can't be *that* hard. I'll be fine. Even if my eyes are burning from unshed tears and my body hurts from lack of sleep. Even if I have to use this gross loaner yoga mat with indentations in the foam in the shape of fingerprints and a bleach stain in the corner.

"He did *what* with his tongue?!" Jo whispers. There's a sudden hush among the other students.

I clear my throat. "I know, strep tests are the worst!"

Silence.

"But to clarify, I don't have strep throat!"

A few of the people around me give me weird looks, then continue setting up.

I turn to Jo, my whisper barely audible. "Let's talk about this during lunch instead, yeah?"

Jo cringes, mouthing the word *sorry* before unrolling her yoga mat.

To kick off the class, Lynn, who is way too bubbly for my fragile mental state, has us lie on our backs with our left hands on our chests and our right hands on our stomachs. Taking deep breaths, we make a conscious effort to relax our muscles and meditate. I feel my body rise and fall underneath my hands. It's the same technique Kay taught me in physical therapy—letting the mind and body go, relieving the muscles of tightness and anxiety.

Inhale. I relax my feet.

Exhale. I relax my legs.

Inhale. I relax my stomach.

Exhale. I relax my chest.

Inhale. I relax my arms.

Exhale. I relax my face.

With the final exhale, I feel some of the tension leave my pelvic floor.

"Now, keep your breathing slow and deep as you sloooowly guide your body upward into a sitting position," Lynn says, her voice quiet and dreamy, matching the tone of the spa music playing in the background. "Pay attention to how your body feels. What areas of your body need attention today? Where do you want to focus your energy?"

Excuse me, Lynn, is there such a thing as yoga for your vagina?

"And now we'll be taking cobbler's pose to gently open up those hips and stretch out those thighs as we ease into movement," Lynn says. "Now—watch me—you'll want to sit up as tall as you can and press the balls of your feet together." She demonstrates, looking around the room to make sure we're all replicating her motions. "Now pull those feet in as close to your beautiful bodies as is comfortable, and make sure you're letting your knees fall to your sides. Avoid clenching any muscles. Yep, that's it, and drop those shoulders!"

As I fall into cobbler's pose, I realize with a start that I've also done this for physical therapy. Kay had me do this at the beginning of our last appointment.

Looking around, everyone is gazing intently at Lynn and letting their bodies relax into the pose. Some even have their eyes closed, the expression on their faces so serene I wonder if I'm missing something.

Focusing inward, I take a deep breath—*inhale, exhale*—and close my eyes, centering my attention on my pelvic floor. The pose gives my hips the same stretch it always has. But when I let out another deep exhale, I give my body the same attention that these people around me are, and I feel some muscles unclench that I've never felt before. I take another breath, and my muscles relax even more, allowing gravity to pull my body down toward the mat.

It's not until the third move—cat-cow pose—that it really hits me. Maybe there's no such thing as yoga for your vagina, but there *is* such a thing as yoga for your pelvic floor. Kay's pelvic floor therapy stretches are apparently just yoga.

As I arch my back and inhale, taking cow pose, I look around at the room full of people doing the exact same pose that I, once upon a time (last week), had been utterly embarrassed to do for physical therapy.

I've been doing . . . yoga? I've been doing the same stretches millions of people around the world have been doing daily for thousands of years? And I've been ashamed?

Meanwhile, these people (me included, actually) are *paying* to do it?

Inhale.

On my hands and knees, my back curls toward the ceiling, and I empty out my lungs. A dozen people around me do the same.

This time, the pose makes me smile.

Exhale.

I arch my back inward, looking up toward the sky, and inhale.

Conquering my vaginismus was supposed to be a solo endeavor. I wanted to do everything alone, which is so very *Emma* of me, just like my parents said. I hate asking for help, but I think I'm finally learning that asking for help is one way of showing love. Looking around the room, I'm having trouble remembering why I didn't know that all along. I don't have to fight my battles solo.

My eyes focus on the ceiling as my back curls downward. I feel my hips stretching and my pelvic floor muscles relaxing. I take cat pose again, releasing the air from my lungs.

Exhale.

And as I let that breath go and the people around me exhale in unison, I make a promise: I'm going to start giving myself more grace. And I'm going to start letting people in.

So what if my vagina is tight? It's overprotective. It's just choosy about what it lets inside.

Inhale.

Me, too, I suppose. Much like my vagina, I've always been picky about who I open up to.

Exhale.

Maybe if I'd told Harrison earlier, we could've stopped running in circles around each other and gotten together before it was too late.

But as I take another deep breath and shift back into child's pose, I forgive myself.

And by the time class is over an hour later, I think I'm starting to forgive my vagina.

* * *

AS OUR ORDER NUMBER IS called and Jo goes to the counter to pick up our sandwiches, I take a look at my buzzing phone.

Macy: Hey Emma! I'm trying to find a time to fly home and surprise Jo. You know her work schedule, right? Can you help me figure out logistics?

Macy: Please don't tell her!!

I'm just barely able to hit send on my response (OH MY GOD YES) when Jo sits at our booth, sliding a Reuben toward me.

"You're smiling," she says. "That's suspicious."

"I'm just thinking about how much I love you," I tell her, smiling sarcastically.

"Oh, shut up," she says, laughing as she unwraps her Reuben. "Tell me why you're not at the cabin."

"Yeah, so, you were right."

"About what?" She raises an eyebrow patiently as she takes a bite.

"Everything?"

Her response is muffled behind corned beef and rye. "I feel oddly unhappy to hear that."

"Seriously, Jo. I am so, so sorry I was an asshole for not prioritizing you, but I was also an asshole for ignoring all of the advice you've given me," I say. Jo's gaze is bright and sympathetic, even though I don't deserve her sympathy or forgiveness. "If I had listened to you, I'd be in a much better place right now. And I hope it's not too late for me to tell you I really value your opinions and advice."

"You're forgiven, as long as you stop apologizing and get to the point about Harrison," she demands.

I reach across the table and squeeze her hand, which she accepts with an eye roll and a hidden smile. I unwrap my sandwich and take a bite before diving in.

Jo looks at me grimly the entire time, barely reacting, even to the most dramatic parts of the story. Something definitely flashes in her eyes when I clarify what, exactly, he did with his tongue. But that's it. No other reaction.

I guess it's hard to be surprised when you've been expecting something for essentially forever.

She studies me when I finish talking, carefully considering her words. Then, seeming to give up on finding something smart to say, she shakes her head and says, "I cannot believe you two had nine years to prepare for this and still managed to screw it up."

I let out a strained laugh. "You were right, I was hurting him by not being honest with him. I should have told him my feelings. I should have told him a lot more than that. But I was so mad at my body for hurting me, I never stopped to wonder if I was hurting Harrison. I learned to show myself grace over the last few years since I was so young when it happened, but this time I'm older, and I did the same thing. And I just sent us back to square one."

"Maybe. But maybe it's not too late," Jo adds.

I look up, peering at her through burning eyes. "I have a plan."

Jo squeezes my hand. "You always do."

"What if it doesn't work?"

"It'll work."

"You don't know what the plan is."

"No, but I know Harrison. And I know you." She glances over at me, her lips pulled into a lopsided grin.

"What if he decides the physical aspect is too much to overcome?" I murmur.

Jo stares at me for a moment, and just when I think she isn't going to respond, she opens her mouth. "Then it was never right to begin with."

"I don't like that answer."

"Well, luckily, we both know it *was* right to begin with."

I take another bite. "He told me I needed to want this for myself. I think I always did—want this for myself, I mean—but I wasn't prioritizing myself. I was prioritizing him. Does that make sense?"

". . . Sort of?"

"Even with Harrison out of the picture, I know now I'd still want to date and figure out my vaginismus. I would still want to learn how to stop letting it hold me back."

"Yeah, but also, you looooove that boy," Jo says. Her laugh makes me smile, and I hide my embarrassed blush behind my sandwich.

"I love you, too, you know," I say, a bite of food in my mouth. Jo snorts as a crumb drops from my lips onto my plate.

"I know you do. I love you, too, obviously. Now hurry up and eat that sandwich so I can get to work."

CHAPTER 26

My lunch was so good (tastewise and emotionwise) that I almost forget I'm supposed to be in emotional turmoil, but after I drop Jo off at work and walk home, the sight of my apartment building makes me feel physically ill.

I'll go home and write out an apology, I decide. I'll turn to a new page in my diary, and I'll make a list of the three most important things I need to say, and then I'll outline a speech from there. I'll practice it in the mirror at least five times, and then I'll sleep on it to make sure I haven't forgotten anything. One more day—just enough time for us both to simmer down. And then I'll text him and ask if we can talk, and it will be fine. It will be fine!

As I approach the building, the door to the upstairs apartments starts to open, a garbled voice sounding through the door. "Yeah. Yep, I'll come grab you. Be right there."

The figure emerges into the sunlight, squinting through the sunshine and the heat.

We make eye contact, and his expression switches from neutral to . . . ill? Sickly? Disgusted?

Not going to explore that. That's an entry I don't want to add to my mental dictionary.

His eyes flicker away from mine, down toward his hands. I lower my gaze, my eyes catching on a few little gray hairs stuck to his shirt. Raya's. As if he's been walking around the apartment holding her against his chest. If I had an emotional support animal, I would've spent my morning doing the same.

His eyes move upward again, meeting mine.

I choke back tears with a whimper, completely frozen by the emotional intensity of his stare. He holds care and affection in his gaze, even with the emotional distance I can tell he's trying to keep. The full force of his attention has rendered me near speechless.

My fragile heart simply can't take it.

How could anyone possibly get to know this wonderful man and not fall head over heels in love? How have I allowed myself to *hurt* him—not once, but *twice*—when all he's ever wanted to do is care for me?

And before I can stop myself, I burst into tears.

Harrison steps forward, then thinks better of it and halts.

My arms hang limply at my sides, snot and tears running down my face. "I messed up, Harrison."

"Oh," Harrison murmurs, his eyes enormous. His hair is ruffled and messy and flat where he's been tugging at it, and his face holds the exhaustion of a sleepless night.*

Still crying, the words flow out of my mouth like tears. "You were right. I was wrong, I was so wrong. I said it was all for you, the physical therapy, but that wasn't even true, even

***Tugging at hair · Flattened waves** | *Emotional tell* | *Frequency: high*

1. Nerves.
2. Generally over an extended period of time; one or more hours.

though I thought it was true. Because after what you said to me and after I thought you would be out of the picture forever, I still wanted it, but I wanted it for myself. But I also really, really want *you,* Harrison. And I know it's been, like, barely twenty-four hours, but I swear I know it. I know it for sure."

He opens his mouth to say something, but I charge ahead. "I've wanted you for a really, really long time, ever since I met you, and I'm such a fucking idiot, a self-sabotaging idiot, and you deserve so much better than what I can offer you, but I'm selfish and so I'm begging you to take me back anyway. I made this whole plan, you know? About, like, making amends, and calling my parents, and prioritizing Jo? And I've already done two of the steps this morning, and I went to yoga, and I feel like I understand my vagina better, and now I especially feel sorry because all of this was so *stupid.*" Harrison raises his eyebrows but doesn't interrupt. "I came back to Boston and you were a *man* all of a sudden, and I cannot believe I hurt the boy you used to be, but I especially can't believe I hurt the man you are now, with your annoyingly sexy glasses and your unicorn stickers and your guinea pig who I want to adopt as my child. And even though you'd changed, you still felt like home." I walk forward, up a couple of stairs. Close enough that I can reach out and touch him. I pick a piece of Raya's fur off his shirt, and his eyes track the motion. He stays frozen.

Inhale. Exhale. "I love you so much, Harrison. I love your eyes and your hair that never does what you want it to but always looks perfect anyway with that silly little swoosh. I love the way you can't stop yourself from caring for people and bringing them hot drinks when they're sick and checking in on them when they're stressed, and even when you're annoying and conflict-avoidant, I love that you just want everyone to feel as comfortable as possible. And, god, I love that you show everything you're feeling on your face. Have I ever told you about my mental dictionary? An entry for every expression. When you smile softly and tilt your head to the right, that's platonic affection. When your mouth is slightly parted and your eyes are wide with one eyebrow raised, that means incredulous," I say, imitating each expression. "When you smile wide and your eyes crinkle up and your dimples form, that means joy. I can't stop cataloguing every damn look on your face, and it's all ingrained in my brain, even after all this time. My *Mental Dictionary of Harrison's Emotional Tells.*"

Harrison blinks rapidly, his breath coming in short. He looks at me like he's never seen me before, and I don't know how to translate that into a dictionary entry.

"I'm so sorry for hurting you, yesterday and all the years I strung you along with no explanation as to why. I would do anything for you, Harrison, I'd do anything to get you back. But if it's too late, if I've messed up too many times, then I understand, and all I want, all I've ever wanted, all I've ever tried and failed to accomplish, is to help you be as happy as possible."

A sharp exhale escapes my mouth as I huff one last sob, my eyes pressed shut. My heart rages a thunderous beat, so aggressive I may pass out. Despite every instinct telling me to keep hiding behind my eyelids, I finally pry them open and take in the scene in front of me.

Harrison has on a tight-lipped, tense-jawed look as he stares me down, his eyes full of so many different emotions it's impossible to determine how he's feeling. Once again, I'm having trouble matching his expression to a dictionary entry. Never a good sign.

"Please say something," I beg, my voice a pitiful whisper.

He takes a shallow breath. And then, in a quiet tone: "I'm . . . I—" He's having trouble meeting my eyes. "Now isn't—I can't—"

I hold up a hand to stop him, even as my heart shatters.

I can't is one of my catch phrases. How fitting that I'm now on the receiving end.

"Harrison?" a voice calls out.

I turn, then immediately regret turning.

Harrison's mom is walking up the sidewalk, a fiery look in her eyes.

"Hello, Emma," she says. "I trust you're doing well."

I'm pretty sure there is snot dripping down my face. So, no, I'm not doing well.

Harrison clears his throat. "Emma, can we—"

"Yep," I say, cutting him off. "Yep, I'll give you guys space."

He opens his mouth to say something, but I turn before he does. Without another look, I walk into my apartment and slam the door.

CHAPTER 27

During the fall semester of our junior year, Harrison moved to Paris to study abroad. I remember having a vague interest in going abroad, but after about twenty minutes of researching the cost (expensive) and the availability of courses that would count toward my degree (limited), I'd decided to save up the money from my summer babysitting gigs and visit him during Thanksgiving break instead.

As I'd told him that first night we'd met, I wasn't sure I believed in soulmates. But I also remember feeling *off* for the first two months of the fall semester. Jo and I lived together and hung out basically every day. But she was also always on the phone with Macy, who was spending their senior fall semester studying abroad in Argentina, and even when she wasn't on the phone, I could tell her head was elsewhere.

It was lonely. Not lonely in a literal, spending time alone kind of way, but in an emotional way. I remember feeling like Jo had a right to feel lonely. Her feelings were valid—she was in a long-term relationship. I, on the other hand, felt insane for the way I was missing Harrison.

My feelings didn't feel justified. I told myself it was weird and creepy of me to miss him the way I did, as if I were missing a part of myself.

When I landed at Charles de Gaulle on the first Saturday of our weeklong Thanksgiving break, I expected to follow the detailed instructions Harrison had given me to take the train from the airport to the apartment he was sharing with three other students from our college. Turns out that was just a distraction. He was planning on picking me up at the airport all along because, well, of course he was. This is Harrison we're talking about.

The moment I saw him at the airport, I realized a few things:

(1) My feelings were justified, because

(2) Soulmates do exist, and

(3) I had one.

And if I thought being separated by the Atlantic Ocean was hard, that's nothing compared to this unbreakable barrier, physically manifested in my droopy popcorn ceiling. Plato didn't account for the fallout from an excessively tight vagina when he wrote about soulmates.

Once I've been in bed for so long that all the light has disappeared from outside, I finally peel myself out from under the covers, intending to get a glass of water and use the bathroom. But just as I'm standing up, there's a knock at the door.

I pause.

I blink.

Another knock.

I scamper to the entryway, peering through the peephole. It's dark out, but I'd recognize that face in pitch blackness.

Cracking the door so he can hear me but can't see me, I wait for him to speak. When he doesn't, I finally say, "Hi?" My voice is scratchy and nearly unrecognizable.

"Hi," he says, clearing his throat. He takes his hands out of his pockets, looks at them, then puts them back into his pockets, clearing his throat again.

"Hi?"

"Hi," he repeats. "Um, can you come with me?"

In the faint moonlight, I can see a thin sheen of sweat on his face, and his hands—back out of his pockets again—are visibly shaking. His eyes are slightly too wide, and his waves have fallen flat, covering his eyebrows. Apparently the mere act of speaking to me is making him physically ill.

"Are you trying to kidnap me?"

"No?"

"You don't sound sure."

He blinks at me.

I get it. I really do. He's trying to be an adult, to talk about his feelings and explain why this isn't going to work. I don't know if I can handle another rejection, but I owe it to him to listen after everything I've put him through.

"Okay, I'll come." I slip on shoes and step outside, folding my arms across my chest to hide the fact I'm wearing ratty pajamas and look like I haven't showered in two days. (I haven't.)

We silently walk inside the upper portion of the house, but instead of turning left into his apartment, we walk up two additional flights of stairs to the top of our triple-decker. When I'm out of breath and about to tell him this is getting ridiculous, he opens a small door and leads me into a finished attic space. It's dark and smells kind of musty, and I think the room is totally empty, but as my eyes adjust, I can see the middle of the floor is actually taken up by . . . two beanbags?

"Um?" I ask.

"Um," Harrison says, clearing his throat. "This is silly, but . . . I thought we could talk. And start over. Start fresh, like we did the first week of college."

My mouth goes completely dry, and I realize . . . *this might not end entirely poorly.*

My eyes finally adjust enough to actually see the beanbags. "Are those—" I gasp. "Are those the actual beanbags from Hall Hall?" Harrison nods. "How did you . . . ? How?!"

A dimple appears. "Did you know Rose goes to the same college we did?"

My eyes widen. "You enlisted Rose for a beanbag heist?"

"We're going to return them in the morning. It's not stealing."

"And you're telling me Hall Hall still has the same beanbags?"

He cringes. "I'll admit this idea seemed better before I saw the beanbags. I remember them being a little more plush. And a little more clean."

I gape at him.

He points to a stack of linens on a small side table. "But I have two blankets we can cover them with."

There's a squeak as he looks at the table, and now that my eyes have adjusted, I see a travel-size crate.

"And did you . . . did you bring Raya?" I ask.

He nods. "I know how much you like her. And I needed the extra support."

I try to swallow, but it gets caught in my throat. "I do. I like her a lot. I might even love her, actually."

A dimple appears. "You and me both." He gestures to the beanbags as if he's a waiter gesturing toward a table at a fine dining establishment. "Can we sit down and talk?"

I nod, silently gliding across the floor. I accept the blanket he hands me and cover the beanbag. When I sit down, I sink so much I can feel the floor.

Harrison sits down and clears his throat, but instead of breaking into a speech like I expect, he shifts and pulls a piece of paper out of his back pocket. "I have something to show you."

I reach out my hand, but he doesn't give it to me. Instead, he unfolds the paper, clears his throat again, and starts reading.

"Dictionary of Emma. Volume one." He looks up, and we make eye contact, mine narrowing, his crinkling. The corner of his mouth ticks up. "When Em tucks her hair behind her right ear, that means she's feeling bashful." I stop breathing. "When Em blinks rapidly, that means she's jealous. When Em pulls her lips to the side and tilts her head, that means she's thinking about me."

I let out a wet laugh. "Rather full of yourself, I see."

A dimple forms. "When Em lets out a quiet, breathy laugh, that means she's laughing around other people. When Em lets out a loud, yelping laugh, that means she's laughing with me." He looks up with a sneaky grin. "Or Jo, but that felt less romantic to include." The laugh I let out is unmistakably yelping, which makes Harrison chuckle.

His face grows more serious as he scans the next one. "When Emma's breathing slows and her eyes widen and her brows furrow and her lips part, that means she has something to tell me, but she's not going to tell me."

"Delete that entry," I whisper.

Harrison exhales a light laugh. "I don't think that's how dictionaries work."

"You won't need it anymore. I promise."

He studies me, his brown eyes molten in the darkness. Harrison knows me as well as I know him. He always has. And the fact that he always knew I was keeping secrets but never pressed me on them is, to put it lightly, heartbreaking.

"I owe you an apology," he says, his voice raspy.

"You definitely don't."

"Well—I'm giving it to you anyway. Your apology earlier today—"

"What if we never talk about that again?"

"You took me by surprise. I know it looked like I was choosing to ignore you to placate my mom, and I know that's a problem I've always had, but I had actually asked her to come over so I could talk to her. Specifically, to talk to her about the way she treats you. And about the way she treats me, too. I wanted to do that before I talked to you and apologized, but then you beat me to it and took me by surprise, which is why I froze, and I just . . . I need to clarify how I actually feel. Because that interaction was not indicative of my real feelings."

"How do you actually feel?" I eke out, my throat thick. Surely there are city noises in the background, but I don't hear anything except the beating of my heart. It may be physiologically impossible, but in this moment, I would swear on my life that I can also hear the beating of Harrison's heart. *Thump. Thump. Thump.*

The corner of Harrison's lips twitches upward as his eyes soften. "You're the best friend I've ever had. I love every second I get to spend with you, even when it makes me act like a lovesick teenager. Which, to be clear, is exactly what I was for the first two years of our friendship. Now I'm just a lovesick adult."

I dare to tentatively smile, and the change in my expression makes Harrison's eyes sparkle like the streetlights coming in through the window.

"I wasn't lying when I said you broke my heart in college. But what would be completely unbearable, worse than anything we've put each other through in the past, is going through that again and never being able to see you or hold you in my arms again. What we have is worth any risk, at least to me."

"Me, too," I whisper.

"And I am so, so, so sorry for the way I treated you yesterday at the cabin. It won't happen again. I know I'm a people pleaser, but I'm trying to start advocating more for what *I* want. Which, in this case, is you," he says, grinning. "And I want you to know that I told my mom everything, and things are going to be different moving forward."

"What did you tell her?"

Harrison smiles. "I told her I was still in love with you."

My eyes widen. "You did?"

"I did. And she was upset about it."

"Naturally."

"But she's going to get over it. And I know she doesn't act like it, but she's impressed by you. Or, at least, she can tell you've changed me and made me more confident. You've been a good influence on me, and she knows it."

I laugh quietly, reaching out and squeezing his hand. When I try to pull away, he locks his fingers around mine and pulls our hands into his lap for safekeeping.

"I talked to my parents today," I say. "I decided it was time to be an adult and open up about what I was feeling."

"I'm proud of you." He squeezes my hand and smiles gently. "Look at us. We're doing better already."

"Doing better," I agree.

He stares at me for another moment before continuing. "There's no way I could ever forgive myself if we messed this up. I really, really want this." His voice is pleading, even though I've already made it clear I agree.

"I want this, too," I whisper.

"I know there's a lot to figure out, but I'd like to figure it out together, as a team. I want to share your burdens, if you'll let me. You make me believe in soulmates. You complete me. And I love you, wholly."

"I need you to look me in the eyes, please," I say to him, and he hesitantly stares at me. I lean forward, crawling from my beanbag to his and settling onto his lap. He wraps his arms around me, and I place my hands on his cheeks, gazing back at him intently. "I love you wholly, Harrison. I always have, and I always will."

Without waiting another heartbeat, he kisses me, and the entire world dissolves around me as my heart re-forms itself, mending together all the pieces that fell apart over the last day and last five years. I feel my split-in-half body repairing, my limbs refastening, my mind clearing.

I can't help myself—I start laughing, completely overcome with joy. "This is one of the happiest moments of my life, and I'm wearing a South Tampa Regional Middle School T-shirt."

Harrison just grins at me. I suppose when you're in love with your best friend, you already know they laugh uncontrollably when they're happy.

"Let's bring these beanbags downstairs before I start sneezing from this dusty-ass attic?" I ask, smiling against his lips.

Harrison blinks, as if startled back to reality. "Actually, we're up here because there's someone in my apartment who refused to leave."

My eyes narrow. "Please tell me it's not your mother."

Harrison laughs softly. "No. A certain friend of ours called me when she got done with her shift at Jo Jo's and insisted I let her come over so she could yell at me. She has flat-out refused to leave my apartment until we'd sorted things out. You'll never guess who."

"Please tell me it's not Rose."

"Nope. The other employee."

"JO!" I yelp. "We need to go update her immediately." I give him another kiss before jumping out of his lap, grabbing Raya's carrier, and dragging him through the door.

"Someone's in a rush to update their best friend."

"*Someone* is in a rush to update their best friend so their best friend can leave and give us the apartment to ourselves."

"You realize we could just go downstairs to your apartment?"

I shoot him a guilty look as we walk down the stairs. "I'd say we need to have a conversation about soundproofing, but I'm less concerned about it now." Harrison raises an eyebrow in response but doesn't ask. I have all the time in the world to fill him in later.

We get to his door, and before I open it, I reach out and brush a lock of hair out of his eyes. "I love you. I know I just said it, but I love you." Raya squeaks from her crate, and I blow her a kiss. "And I love you, too, baby girl."

Harrison laughs, bringing his forehead to mine. "And I love you the most," he says.*

*** Soft smile · Raised eyebrows · Head tilted downward toward subject** | *Facial expression* | *Frequency: high*

1. Love.

EPILOGUE

Four months later

Harrison's eyes gaze at me from just a few inches away, his body pressed neatly against mine. I sink into the bed—his, not mine, because mine is still squeaky as hell—and take a deep breath.

Inhale.

Exhale.

"We don't have to do this," he says. "We're in no rush."

I know. But my physical therapy has been going well, and I've finally graduated to using Cobalt—

I know you have a sexy new partner now, but don't forget about m—

I cut her off. I may continue to need her moving forward, but right now, I'm focused on something a little more real.

"I know we don't have to," I say. His eyes move from left to right, focusing on each of my eyes in turn. "But I want to."

He nods, almost imperceptibly. "Can I be honest?"

I nod back.

"I'm scared," he whispers.

I chuckle gently, feeling my abs press against his stomach

with each breath. "Sorry. It's not funny. I know you're serious. It's just, I think I'm the one who's supposed to feel scared right now."

"And you're not scared?"

"No. I trust you."

But maybe I should feel scared. After all, this could end with me in pain, or crying, or I don't know what else. At the end of the day, though, even if this goes horribly wrong, or even if we don't even get far enough for this to go horribly wrong, I know Harrison is still going to love me. And for that reason, I'm not scared.

Harrison's eyes flutter closed, and I match his breathing.

Inhale.

Exhale.

His hands trace their way down my sides, over my goose-bumped skin. My breath stutters as he reaches between my legs, and I focus on the feeling of his fingers and their delicate strokes. Soft sensations. Gentle butterflies. The warmth of his body.

I center myself, noticing the way my muscles respond. They flutter and they tense, sometimes in a positive way, sometimes negatively. I breathe through the negative, imagining my muscles warming and melting as his fingers continue to massage me.

"I can feel your mind working," he whispers into my neck. The words are hot against my skin.

"You can *feel* it?"

He chuckles just as the circles his fingers have been drawing start to grow tighter. I quiver from the sensation, and his grin brushes against my neck, his breath sending my baby hairs fluttering.

"*Fuck,*" I murmur.

He drags his lips up the sensitive skin at the side of my neck and whispers in my ear. "Working on it."

I whimper instead of responding.

Inhale.

Exhale.

"Okay," I say. "Stop. You're going to make me—" I'm cut short as Harrison hits *exactly* the right spot, and my muscles flutter. My body shakes again, and his fingers slow.

"Was that a good reaction or a bad reaction?" he whispers.

"A good one," I say, my voice breathy. "Seriously, don't make me come yet. That's not the goal."

"I can have multiple goals," he says, kissing my cheek, and then my nose, and then my forehead, and then my lips. "And you can have multiple orgas—"

"Harrison!" I say, cutting him off as I laugh. "I'm trying to focus. Save that for after."

He nods his head. "Don't worry. I will. Once we've tried this, I'm going to make you feel so good, you're—"

I lean forward and stop him with a kiss. He laughs into my mouth, then lingers, kissing me slowly and sweetly before pulling away and looking me in the eyes. "I love you," he whispers.

"I love you wholly," I whisper back, brushing a curl out of his eyes. "And I'm ready when you're ready."

Harrison runs his thumb across my cheek, studying me. Even after months of dating, he still acts like every look on my face and every word from my mouth is worth filing away.

I suppose I shouldn't make fun of him for it, though, since I do the same.

He grabs the bottle of lube from the bedside table, and I hold out a cupped hand. He deposits a hefty amount, and I slide my hand down our bodies.

He hisses when I make contact. "That's *cold,*" he says.

I smirk. "Yeah, well. It's, like, two degrees outside. You shouldn't have kept this in a drawer next to a window."

"It's thirty-eight degrees," he says, rolling his eyes even as his body trembles from the up-and-down strokes of my hand. "That's nothing."

"So you're not too chilly to make this work?" I ask, even though I can very much feel that he's not.

His left eyebrow pops up, my challenge accepted. His eyes glitter, dark and serious, as he looks at me with an intensity that makes me squirm. "Not even a little bit."

We exchange looks of determination. "Let's do this," I finally say.

He nods,

inhaling,

exhaling,

and then shifts his body so he's aligned with mine.

Reaching down, I grip him and use him to rub circles around my opening, adjusting my body to the feeling. Letting it know to get ready and prepare for contact. His breathing becomes shallow, but when he feels me take a deep breath, he matches the steady rise and fall of my chest, keeping his body in sync with mine.

And that's what we are. In sync. We weren't always, but we've worked hard at it, being intentional about openly communicating how we feel and what we want, both mentally and physically. We've been through a lot, even in the last four months. He's been by my side as I transitioned into a new part-time job, helping to manage the yoga studio I practice at. I still work part-time at Jo Jo's, occasionally making coffee but more often making appearances to run a variety of themed book clubs, each one of them so popular they fill the café. Banned books. Romance. Nonfiction. One I like to call the "Books You Thought Were Boring Because Your Teachers Assigned Them but This Time You're Actually Going to Read Them" Book Club. Boring Books Book Club, for short. And I've been at his side as he reimagined his relationship with his mom, drawing new boundaries and slowly but surely convincing her I am not an asshole. Anymore, anyway.

I'm sure we'll have more changes ahead. Bigger ones, even.

He made a jokey comment last week about how it's silly we have our own apartments since we spend every night together anyway, and then we both burst out laughing when we caught each other immediately looking to assess how the other was reacting to that statement. *Maybe it is silly,* I'd said. *Ask me again when my lease is up.*

"You ready?" I ask.

"Ready."

I guide him to my entrance, then remove my hand, letting our bodies fall closer together. He leans down, giving me another kiss, then draws back ever so slightly, our lips separated by a hairbreadth. Our bodies shifting, I feel him start to press into me.

Inhale.

Exhale.

He breathes with me.

Inhale.

Exhale.

My body tenses, and I breathe through it.

Inhale.

Exhale.

"Should I keep going?" he asks. He's so close, his lips brush mine as the words leave his mouth.

"Yes. Slowly."

He pushes farther, so slowly it's almost impossible to tell he's moving. My muscles feel calm—for once, I feel in control—but I'm also experiencing a faint burning sensation, which I know is the result of the physical pressure and the high concentration of nerve endings, all of them pushing back at me. *What the hell do you think you're doing?* they ask.

I breathe through it.

"Keep going," I murmur. "I'm okay."

Harrison is maybe halfway inserted at this point, and there's no way this feels good for him, either. I don't pretend to understand how it feels to have sex as a man, but, like, I think you have to do more than just sit there to achieve any type of positive sensation. And yet Harrison has a look on his face that screams *pleasure.*

No—that's not right. It screams *pride.* He's proud of me.

"You still okay?" he asks. I nod, and I take the initiative this time in tilting my head to give him a soft kiss. I catch his bottom lip with my teeth as I pull away, and his body jerks involuntarily with pleasure. My muscles tense, and the burning momentarily increases, but after one more breath, I've adjusted, and he's in farther than he was before.

"Shit—I'm so sorry—"

"It's okay," I reassure him. "That didn't hurt."

He rests his forehead against mine, our noses aligned. "Okay," he says. "Okay."

I shift, spreading my legs to create more space, à la happy baby pose. After months of yoga, I still feel stupid doing it. Fortunately, though, it makes a noticeable difference in relaxing my pelvic floor.

Inhale.

Exhale.

Harrison's eyes widen as he feels my muscles relax, and he pushes forward more. I feel an uncomfortable pressure, and he must see me wince because he starts to shift as if he's going to pull out, then stops himself.

"Okay. It's okay. I'm frozen," he says, reassuring himself as much as he's reassuring me. "I'm not moving until you tell me to."

I steady myself, prying my eyes open to meet his. "I'm good. I'm good, I promise. Keep going."

Unexpectedly, he smiles, dimples forming. "I can't keep going."

"Oh, uh—okay," I stutter. "Yeah, you can pull out slowly."

He smiles wider. "I can't keep going because I'm all the way in."

I freeze, my eyes widening. He smiles at my obvious shock, leaning forward to give me another kiss, then another, and then another. When he pulls back, there's a wet spot on the side of his face.

"Sorry," I say. "I don't know why I'm crying. I'm doing great."

"Actually, they're my tears," he says, chuckling. And he's right—his eyes are red-rimmed, and my own eyes feel dry.

I kiss a tear off his cheek. "I hope these are happy tears?"

"Something like that," he murmurs. My pelvic floor seizes up briefly, but we both breathe through it. "Happy tears, proud tears, general emotional tears. I don't know."

"I'll take it."

He looks down to where our bodies are connected, then meets my eyes again. "Tell me how it feels."

How do you describe the sensation to someone who doesn't have vaginismus, let alone someone who doesn't have a vagina? It feels like I just lifted a heavy weight, and now my muscles are tense and sore and also actively burning. But not in a burned-by-boiling-water way—more like a sandpaper way, like it's super dry down there, except I know it's not dry because we used a metric shit-ton of lube and also because I was super close to finishing before we did this.

"Honestly?" I say. "A little uncomfortable, but mostly just really vulnerable and really embarrassing."

"I know it's hard," he says, leaning forward and kissing my forehead. "But you know what?"

"What?"

"I think you are so incredibly sexy."

A surprised laugh erupts from me, sending my pelvic floor into another fit of spasms. Harrison and I breathe through it together.

"Yeah, that's super sexy, isn't it?"

He tilts his head, thinking, then begins murmuring in my ear in between kisses:

"The happy sighs you make when I kiss you.
The way your body fits perfectly against mine.
The way you look when we go out to dinner.
And the way you look when we wake up in the morning.
The curves of your face when you smile.
The ponytail that brushes the base of your neck.
The way you know me, more intimately than anyone else ever has.
And the look you get in your eyes when we make love."

This time, tears fall down my face. I wrap my arms around his neck, and he buries his face against my cheek, his body warm and impossibly close.

"You're unbelievably sexy, even when you don't think you are," he says. "And I'm proud of you."

"We did this together," I say.

He shakes his head. "We're doing this together, as in this, right now. But you're responsible for all the progress you made up until this point. You're incredible."

I reach my hand up, brushing my fingers through his hair. They stick slightly, and I cringe as I bring my hand back down to my side. "Gonna be honest, I think I just raked some lube into your hair."

Harrison snorts. "It sort of has the same texture as hair gel, right? Maybe it'll give my curls more definition."

"Actually," I say, "it just looks like I raked lube into your hair."

I can tell he wants to laugh, but he holds himself back to avoid any sudden movements.

"Not that this isn't, like, super sexy," I say. "And as much as

I love—and as much as I'm sure you love—just sitting here with your dick inside me—"

"Mmmhmm," he says.

"How about we wrap this up for today and get in the shower together? I think we have some unfinished business to attend to. You mentioned something earlier about multiple orgasms?"

"I sure did," he says. "And I intend to follow through. You ready for me to slide out? You breathing deeply?"

I nod. "Let's do it."

Inhale.

Exhale.

MENTAL DICTIONARY OF HARRISON'S EMOTIONAL TELLS

Clenched jaw · Furrowed eyebrows | *Facial expression* | *Frequency: low*

1. Frustration.

Crinkles around eyes · Left dimple · Lopsided smile | *Facial expression* | *Frequency: medium*

1. Amused.

Crinkles around eyes · Right dimple · Lopsided smile | *Facial expression* | *Frequency: medium*

1. Gently optimistic.

Eyes narrowed · Frown · Tense jaw | *Facial expression* | *Frequency: low*

1. Resigned disappointment.

Furrowed brows · Lips pulled to the side · Tense body | *Emotional tell* | *Frequency: medium*

1. Hesitant.

Furrowed brows · Parted lips · Bated breath | *Facial expression* | *Frequency: low*

1. Confused devastation.
2. Unsure of appropriate reaction.

Furrowed brows · Pursed lips · Head tilted to the right | *Facial expression* | *Frequency: medium*

1. Exasperated.

Furrowed brows · Soft eyes · Gentle frown | *Facial expression* | *Frequency: low*

1. Combination of anger and regret.

Glassy eyes · Tense body · Bated breath | *Emotional tell* | *Frequency: low*

1. Contained heartbreak.

Lips pulled to the left · Biting the right side of lip | *Facial expression* | *Frequency: medium*

1. Actively thoughtful.
2. Signals internal debate.

Lowered eyebrows · Head tilt to the left | *Facial expression* | *Frequency: medium*

1. Sympathy.

Narrowed eyes · Dropped jaw | *Facial expression* | *Frequency: low*

1. Surprised anger.

Pink ears | *Physical reaction* | *Frequency: high*

1. Embarrassment.
2. May be embarrassed by own actions or others' actions.

Raised eyebrows · Head turned to the right · Mouth clamped shut | *Facial expression* | *Frequency: low*

1. Taken aback.
2. Indicates that the surprise is net negative.

Raised eyebrows · Straight face · Bated breath | *Facial expression* | *Frequency: low*

1. Fear of what comes next.
2. Unwilling to make the next move.

Red ears | *Physical reaction* | *Frequency: medium*

1. Embarrassment; extreme.

Slouched shoulders · Furrowed brows | *Emotional tell* | *Frequency: low*

1. Disappointed.

Soft, bright eyes | *Facial expression* | *Frequency: low*

1. Adoration.

Soft smile · Raised eyebrows · Head tilted downward toward subject | *Facial expression* | *Frequency: high*

1. Love.

Soft smile · Small dimples · Head tilt to the right | *Facial expression* | *Frequency: high*

1. Affection.
2. Generally platonic.

Softened eyes · Dilated pupils · Slightly parted lips | *Facial expression* | *Frequency: low*

1. Affection.
2. Lust.

Softened eyes · Head tilted down · Soft frown | *Facial expression* | *Frequency: low*

1. Guilt.

Softened eyes · Head tilt to the left · Clenched jaw | *Facial expression* | *Frequency: medium*

1. Emotionally conflicted.

Sunken eyes · Slack jaw · Clenched hands | *Facial expression* | *Frequency: low*

1. Tender focus.
2. Sadness.

Sunken eyes · Slack jaw · Short breaths | *Facial expression* | *Frequency: low*

1. Devastation.

Sunken eyes · Tense jaw · Clenched hands | *Facial expression* | *Frequency: low*

1. Deep worry.

Tugging at hair · Flattened waves | *Emotional tell* | *Frequency: high*

1. Nerves.
2. Generally over an extended period of time; one or more hours.

Wide eyes · Furrowed eyebrows · Lips pulled to the side | *Facial expression* | *Frequency: low*

1. Emotional distress.

Wide eyes · Jerky movements · Shortness of breath | *Facial expression* | *Frequency: low*

1. Fear.

Wide eyes · Tense jaw · Shallow breathing | *Facial expression* | *Frequency: low*

1. Flustered shock.

Wide smile · Dimples · Eyes crinkled | *Facial expression* | *Frequency: medium*

1. Joy.

ACKNOWLEDGMENTS

It is such a privilege to have so many people to thank that you don't know where to start.

To Catherine Bradshaw, my amazing agent: You hopefully know this because I tell you constantly, but you're the best. Thank you for being my number one advocate and for always matching my energy and enthusiasm. I am so lucky to be on this journey with you.

To Talia Cieslinski, my incredible editor: Thank you for your vision and your guidance. Emma, Harrison, and I are so glad to have you as our champion. I am so lucky to have the best home in the world for this book, and I'm so thankful to everyone at The Dial Press and Penguin Random House who played a role in making this happen, including Debbie Aroff, Avideh Bashirrad, Cindy Berman, Donna Cheng, Corina Diez, Richard Elman, Elizabeth Eno, Claire Fennell, Whitney Frick, Sarah Horgan, Michelle Jasmine, Leah Sims, and Lynn Wu.

I'm also grateful that *Thighs Wide Shut* has found such wonderful homes abroad. Thank you to Peggy Boulos Smith and Alessandra Birch for their work on global licensing, and thank you to Gaby Puleston-Vaudrey for being this book's champion in the UK.

So many friends and loved ones read drafts of this book that I'm afraid to list everyone for fear of missing someone. But I'll be brave, because I'm eternally grateful to all of these people, whether they read it and told me it was the best thing ever or ripped it to shreds so I could make it better: Sydney Brooks, Taylor Gelb, Ian Graham, Ali Hagani, Paloma Hansen, Hailey Harlow, Sarah Hofman Graham, LeighAnne Markaity, Isabel Paine, Isabel Perez, Emily Perkins, Sam Rydzewski, Hannah Smith, Maya Spalding-Fecher, Nora Whorton, and Eleonor Wolf.

In particular, I want to thank Campbell Hannan, Hazel Law, and Alye Prentice, who read SEVERAL versions of this book and listened to many voice memos and FaceTime rants about plot holes and character arcs and long-since-deleted flashback scenes. My writing group—Rebecca V. Archer, Hillary Noelle, Alye Prentice, Jennifer Trice, and Adeline D. Wright—were invaluable during this process, and I am so lucky to have their friendship. Another special thank-you must go to Alicia Thompson, who read an early draft of this book and provided incredibly thoughtful feedback as well as guidance on the querying and publishing process. You're the best.

I'm so lucky to come from a family of writers. My eternal gratitude goes to my parents, from whom I inherited a love of writing. You're both incredible writers. Thank you for your never-ending support, and thank you for reading drafts of this novel and not being weird about it. I'd also like to thank my grandfather, John Fleming Sr., who discovered a love of creative writing in his eighties, and now, in his nineties, is still going strong. You're an inspiration to me every day. My uncle Jim, another incredible writer, has also been one of my biggest supporters, and I'm so excited to have my book next to his and my parents' on my bookshelf. Thank you also to my brother, Ethan, who is not a writer but definitely could be, because he's one of the most creative people I've ever met. I'm so grateful to him for the joy he brings to my life. And, in the spirit of thanking family members, I must thank my two cats, Sally and Schroeder, who were actively disruptive to nearly every part of the writing process but were incredibly cute while doing it.

A special thank-you goes to the friends, family members, and medical professionals who have listened to me cry about my vagina. It would be impossible to overstate how grateful I am to my former pelvic floor therapist, who changed my life and made it possible for me to write this book.

And, of course, thank you to Ben, who came up with the best book title of all time, and who proposed to me three days before the final version of this novel was due, which made for a crazy but joyful weekend. Thank you for your unwavering support. I am so lucky to do life with you.

AUTHOR'S NOTE

The first time I went to the gynecologist for a Pap smear, my entire body froze up the moment the doctor touched me, and then I cried so hard I couldn't breathe. She stopped the Pap smear before it began, then sent me on my way with an apple juice box and a printed list of pelvic floor therapists. She never uttered the word "vaginismus."

When I went to the first pelvic floor therapist on that list, she spent a few minutes measuring the strength of my pelvic floor, then said my pelvic floor muscles were too weak and that doing Kegels would solve my problem. When I came back a few weeks later with newly strengthened muscles, she confidently told me that I was good to go without ever doing anything to confirm that. She never uttered the word "vaginismus."

It pretty quickly became clear that my pelvic floor issues were not, in fact, resolved by Kegels. At that point, I was in a different state, having traveled back to college for the start of a new school year, and there was only one pelvic floor therapist within reasonable driving distance of my small college town. That pelvic floor therapist was the first person to use the word "vaginismus," and she changed my life.

When you google vaginismus, every website tells you something different. Some sources say 1 percent of women have vaginismus; some say 5 percent; some say 7 percent; some say as high as 17 percent or 20 percent. Some sources say vaginismus feels like a cramp; others say it feels like tightening or spasming muscles, and others say it can feel like a burning or stabbing sensation. Some sources say vaginismus can be caused by a painful sexual experience, or a past surgery, or past sexual trauma, or religious teachings, or anxiety, or a lack of sex education, or it can be random.

Emma, like me, developed vaginismus because she didn't understand her own body. Emma and I are both products of Florida public schools, in which my sex education started and ended with a conversation about periods and puberty in fourth grade. I only learned what a vagina was two years after that, when I started my period for the first time. Later, when I tried to use tampons and every attempt at inserting one took several minutes and multiple tries and made me cry, no one ever told me I should get that looked at, and I didn't know enough about my body to question it.

No one ever gave me the talk. I was never shown what to do with a condom, or taught about STIs, or told what consent was. I didn't know that there are a lot of ways to be intimate with someone. After my first gynecology appointment, I genuinely thought I was therefore resigned to painful intimate experiences for eternity, or at least until I found some medical solution to my problem. I am eternally grateful to the friends and medical professionals who respected me enough to help me understand that wasn't the case.

I wrote *Thighs Wide Shut* for that girl: the younger version of me who didn't know why her body didn't work sometimes and had never even heard the word "vaginismus." I've spent years and years unlearning incorrect information and trying to give myself grace as I do the work of learning to respect, appreciate, and love my body. I'm so lucky that I had a pelvic floor therapist much like Kay, who taught me to listen to and respect the things my body tells me. I'm so lucky to now have the knowledge to advocate for my body in medical settings and to have doctors who listen. And I'm so lucky to have the types of friends who don't blink when I send text rants about my various gynecological issues and who didn't blink when I told them

I'd written over three hundred pages about a girl with vaginismus.

Writing Emma's character was healing for me—not just in an emotional way but in a literal medical way—because in forcing Emma to confront the toxic things she'd come to believe about her body and her relationships, I had to do the same. The information online about vaginismus is varied and confusing and conflicting, but it is certainly true that vaginismus has psychological causes, and this book played a huge role in helping me overcome those.

It feels a little crazy that I am now sharing this story with the world. But now, more than ever, it's so important to talk openly about women's health. My hope is to help destigmatize this condition; there's no good reason for a relatively common condition to be so rarely mentioned in media. If this book was the first time you'd ever heard the word "vaginismus," I'm so glad you're here. And if you have vaginismus or any other sexual dysfunction, then this book is for you. I want you to know that regardless of whether vaginismus affects 1 percent or 5 percent or 20 percent of women, you are not alone.

KEEP READING FOR AN EXCLUSIVE SNEAK PEEK AT THE FIRST CHAPTER OF HAYLEY FLEMING'S NEXT BOOK,

THE TAIL OF SIREN SPRINGS

CHAPTER 1

In which Maren almost gets eaten by an alligator

MAREN SHOULD'VE KNOWN her day was going to end poorly the moment she pulled into the Siren Springs parking lot and discovered that the spot she'd been using for the last ten years—appropriately labeled RESERVED FOR SIRENS—was taken up by a large white van full of filming equipment being unloaded by a group of twentysomethings who definitely weren't from around here.

Or maybe she should've known when she dropped her favorite eyeshadow palette in the dressing room, sending blue and green glitter flying through the air. Two hours later, she was still sneezing up mermaid-colored snot.

She definitely should've known when that tiny-ass fish bit her boob while she was trying to perform emotional underwater choreography to "My Heart Will Go On" during her first show of the day.

But it took until 4:36 P.M. for her to realize her day was royally screwed. That was the moment an all-too-recognizable voice came through the underwater speaker system.

"Why did the mermaid cross the sea?"

The microphone crackled, making Maren wince as she attempted to flip backward through the water, her hair drifting forward to completely block her vision. So it goes. No one was looking at her hair when her glittery spandex mermaid tail was right there, gliding through the water like a prism of light.

Maren blew bubbles out of her mouth to push the hair away and decrease her buoyancy, allowing her to complete the back flip and float down to a seated position on a rock. She took a sip of oxygen through the air tube floating nearby, then relaxed her face into a flawless mermaid smile. *Eyes wide and innocent. Mouth parted slightly. Not too many teeth.*

"To get to the *water slide.*" A quiet snort sounded through the microphone.

Maren didn't react.

"Tough crowd," the voice said. "I guess mermaids are chicken joke purists."

If there weren't a crowd of tourists ogling her through the glass wall that stood between the submarine-esque underwater auditorium and the natural spring she was swimming in, Maren would have flipped him off. But the crowd couldn't hear the stupid joke—it was only for her ears, and for the ears of the two other professionally trained mermaids performing in the 4:30 *Sing me a song, Sirens!* show.

Dean Harrington, up-and-coming actor and dead-in-the-water comedian, was not supposed to arrive until five P.M., which Maren knew because she was taking this extremely seriously. It wasn't a good sign that Dean Harrington, the lead actor in the movie about Siren Springs that was about to start filming on location, felt he was too important to follow schedules but just important enough to abuse the underwater speaker system.

The underwater speakers couldn't be heard by the audience, who sat dry (but probably sweaty) in their seats in the dark and musty underground auditorium that looked out at the underwater stage through a glass wall. A different speaker system played outdated songs and narration for those tourists, while the secret underwater communications for the Sirens were typically along the lines of "Melissa, move farther to the right," and "Thunderstorm coming, we're skipping the last song," and, on rare occasions, "Manatee, stage left." The speakers were for key performance information and, most important, for safety. They were not for actors to test out their new standup routine.

Was it fair to assume someone would've explained the speaker rules to him? Maybe not. But surely anyone—especially an actor, of all people—would understand that you shouldn't try to distract someone while they're performing. Then again. His acting credits were less Scorsese and more Netflix Original. Who knew how seriously he took the sacred act of performance?

Maren held up her hand, giving the audience a princess wave, the cold water of the natural springs calming her anger. It was home down here. Even with an annoying distraction, she would never—*could* never—feel anything but grateful to be in these waters, just like her mother and grandmother. This was her family legacy, generations of Delaney women committed to entertaining the people of Central Florida with their underwater flips and twirls and waves and smiles and, most important, their spandex-and-sparkle mermaid tails.

Her eyes darted to the side toward the control booth, where she could just barely make out a dark-haired man's figure at the microphone. Charlie, the staff member who was supposed to be monitoring the show, was just a shadow in the background, barely visible through the porthole window's dirty glass. That mother*fucker*. She would have a word with him once this show was over. He was technically higher than her on the totem pole—he made a couple more dollars per hour than she did, which wasn't saying much—but he had the good sense to listen when she told him what to do. Most people here did. She'd have to make sure Dean Harrington got the memo.

Maren focused her attention back on the glass wall, where she could make out the shape of a little girl standing right at the front of the auditorium, her hand waving eagerly as her breath fogged up the glass. Maren waved and winked in the girl's direction, and the girl's entire face lit up, visible even through the thick, blurry barrier. A hand reached out and pulled the girl away from the window right as Maren took another sip of oxygen, letting the air in her lungs pull her up away from the rock and into a spin, the water sliding over her body like silk, the current responding to her tail like magic.

A new song came on, broadcast both into the audience and into the water, and Maren mindlessly performed the choreography she'd done almost every day for the last ten years. There weren't a lot of updates to the shows at Siren Springs. *Why fix it if it ain't broke?* her boss always said. Maybe because this song hadn't been relevant since 2006. But Maren supposed that nostalgia was a big part of what drew people to Siren Springs. The tourist attraction had been around since the forties, hitting its heyday in the fifties and sixties, and many of their guests brought their children because they remembered going as children themselves. Somewhere along the way, they got stuck replaying mid-2000s country pop.

If Maren were in charge, she'd get rid of that soundtrack. She'd get rid of other things, too, starting with the shitty contract her shitty boss had signed with the probably shitty production company in a moment of financial desperation. Starting tomorrow, Siren Springs would be closed to visitors during six weeks of filming, and almost all of the Sirens would be furloughed. Maren was lucky enough to be one of just three Sirens selected to play a small role in filming, but most of her co-workers would be going without pay for six weeks. Maybe this contract was saving Siren Springs from financial ruin (or at least had the potential to, should the film be successful enough to increase their ticket sales), but not getting paid was going to financially ruin most of the staff.

"Looking great out there, Sirens!" The microphone crackled again, undoubtedly because Dean Harrington was speaking too loudly, as if he didn't have a care in the world. "Beautiful!"

Maren's already-tense mermaid smile briefly transformed into a scowl. Forcing herself to stay focused, she swam over to Melissa and Kristen, the other mermaids performing today, and grabbed Kristen's tail. Kristen swam forward and down, and Melissa swam up from where she was sitting on the rock, grabbing Maren's tail. They formed a hoop—the iconic Siren Wheel—and swam in a perfect circle for a few rotations. The audience's whoops and claps were faintly audible through the glass, which would normally make Maren's mermaid smile widen. She loved the water, would love this spring until her dying breath, but this is what it was all about: getting to share that love with others. Getting to foster that respect and care for natural Florida springs, especially at a time when fewer and fewer people remembered they should be caring. Today, though, her mermaid smile remained forced.

"What do you call an angry mermaid?"

Maren was going to kill him.

Eyes wide and innocent. Mouth parted slightly. Not too many teeth.

"A grrrrmaid."

Maren watched both Kristen's and Melissa's chests quickly rise and fall, the universal sign of an underwater giggle. Maren would have to have a conversation with them, too. Adding it to the list. Charlie, Kristen, Melissa. And Dean Harrington.

Leaving the Siren Wheel, Maren blew a kiss at the audience, making eye contact with the little girl in the front row. She'd learned the hard way that if you blew a kiss at a man, there was at least a 50 percent chance that he would say something inappropriate during the MerMeet 'n' Greet. Maren was always happy to take photos with kids and bachelorette parties and, well, really anyone who had a good attitude. But she wasn't in the mood for questions about the logistics of mermaid sex. Especially right now, when she had bigger fish to fry, including at least three conversations about giving this job the respect it deserved.

"What kind of doctor do mermaids see?"

Maren gave another wave before flipping forward, diving down toward the rock from which she would start the choreography for the final song of the show. Kristen and Melissa followed, air bubbles floating upward as they exhaled, letting their bodies come to a rest against the cold, scratchy surface of their perch.

"A sturgeon!" This time, both Dean Harrington's and Charlie's laughs came through the speakers, making Maren grind her teeth behind her *innocent* smile.

Just as she was about to turn toward the control booth to give them a threatening look, a dark shadow in the water caught her eye. Not in the water—on top of the water, so high that it was above the audience's line of sight. A shadow, floating at the surface near some rocks. A slithering silhouette, tiny legs giving powerful, lazy kicks.

No. No, not again.

Maren acted on pure adrenaline. Nothing existed except that shadow and her two friends in the water. There was no audience. There was no control booth. There was no water—after all, swimming was second nature. Right now, she had no awareness of the spring or the cold temperature against her skin. All she did was fly toward Melissa and Kristen, her tail propelling her forward.

Grabbing Melissa's hand, she shot forward, reaching out to Kristen. Maren could see Melissa give the audience a mermaid wave as they flew toward the tunnel exit. Their hands were tight on Maren's, oblivious to the exact threat but concerned about Maren's erratic behavior. All three mermaids took large sips of air, then dove through the exit tunnel, darkness shrouding them. A few seconds later, they breached the surface of the water in the pool house—the small building built to give the Sirens cover as they entered and exited the springs.

"What's happening?" Kristen asked, breathless as she shook the water out of her hair.

Maren ran her hands over her eyes, wiping away the water and also probably most of her underwater stage makeup. "Get out of the water. Now."

Kristen and Melissa exchanged concerned looks but didn't argue. Swimming to the side of the pool, they gripped the edge of the concrete deck and hauled themselves out of the water, flinging their tails behind them. Normally, they would immediately shimmy out of their tails, eager to get the freezing spandex off of their goose-bumped bodies. Instead, they stared at Maren as she followed suit, dragging herself onto the deck.

"Alligator," Maren said, catching her breath. She was normally a little short of breath after the water-to-land transition, but this was definitely worse than usual. "On the surface. Stage left. I saw it."

Kristen and Melissa exchanged another concerned look, and Maren immediately knew her day had gone from royally screwed to completely irredeemable.

"It was just hanging out on the surface?" Melissa asked. "I mean, it wasn't, like, paying attention to us, right? And are you sure it wasn't just a shadow?"

Maren didn't respond. Instead, she stuck her thumbs in the waistband of her tail, rolling it down and off her body, ignoring the prickling feeling in her eyes.

Kristen tentatively piped up. "There's no reason to be sca—"

"Stop," Maren said. "Sorry for being concerned for our

safety. And who knows what could've happened? It's not like you two were paying attention. You were too distracted by D—"

"We were paying attention," Kristen quickly said. "It's just, it doesn't need to be that big of a deal. I know you're, you know . . ." Kristen trailed off before finishing the thought. "What I'm saying is, they're just part of the natural environment. It's been a long time since one of them actually, you know . . . bothered us."

Maren knew exactly how long it had been—nine years and ten months, exactly as long as Maren had been working at Siren Springs—and Kristen should've known that Maren didn't need the reminder, nor did she need to be told about what was and was not part of the natural environment of these springs.

Maren stood up, grabbing a towel from the box by the door. "Maybe next time you can pay more attention to your surroundings instead of giggling over boys who care more about flirtation than protocol. We're supposed to leave the water if we see an alligator. Period."

Wrapping the towel around her, Maren slipped on her flip-flops and grabbed her tote bag. She opened the door forcefully, intending to make a dramatic exit. Of course, because this day could not possibly get any worse, the two men responsible for the breach in protocol were standing on the other side of the door.

"Um," Dean Harrington said, staring at her with wide eyes. "Hi?"

Maren had very limited interest in interacting with this man, but he *was* on her list of people to confront, and she had a lot of pent-up anger to get out.

"You were in the control room," she said. Dean Harrington gaped at her. She could probably have directed this question toward Charlie, who stood behind Dean Harrington looking mildly alarmed and vaguely guilty, but Charlie already knew he had broken a rule. Dean Harrington didn't even know there was a rule to break. Even so, she hoped that anyone with eyes (especially bright blue ones like his, although that was perhaps less relevant) would have seen the gator paddling around the surface of the spring and would have told the performers to exit the water, regardless of whether they had known it was proper protocol.

"Um," he said. He clutched his hands in front of him, like he had to go to the bathroom. "Yes? We were in the control room."

"You were looking out at the water, then," Maren said. "Did you not see the gator? In the far right corner of your view, by the rocks. Past where we were swimming. Or did you see it and decide it would be better to just keep making jokes instead of warning us?"

He stood frozen, seemingly afraid to even take a breath. Maren didn't find this particularly promising, in regard to getting an answer to her question and also in regard to this movie being successful enough to save Siren Springs from financial ruin. Shouldn't actors be good in social situations and know how to use words other than "um"?

"I . . . didn't see anything," Dean finally said, and Maren's body temperature rose, a cruel combination of anger and embarrassment, only worsened when she saw Melissa snicker. "Maybe it was a trick of the light?" Dean asked.

Maren held up a hand to stop him.

Well, she meant to hold up a hand. Instead, what appeared was a finger.

And then she stalked off.

PHOTO © J.SIKORA

HAYLEY FLEMING grew up in Florida, where she was raised by two novelists and surrounded by alligators and English professors. She earned her bachelor of arts in political science and music from Amherst College. Nowadays, she lives in Washington, D.C., doing nonprofit work by day and writing rom-coms by night. In her free time, you can find her chatting with her romance book club, singing alto in a local chorus, and scouring the internet for budget flights to fun destinations. You can find her on Instagram @hayleyflemingwrites.

Dear Reader,

We'd love your attention for one more page to tell you about the crisis in children's reading, and what we can all do.

Studies have shown that reading for fun is the **single biggest predictor of a child's future life chances** – more than family circumstance, parents' educational background or income. It improves academic results, mental health, wealth, communication skills, ambition and happiness.[1]

The number of children reading for fun is in rapid decline. Young people have a lot of competition for their time. In 2024, 1 in 10 children and young people in the UK aged 5 to 18 did not own a single book at home.[2]

Hachette works extensively with schools, libraries and literacy charities, but here are some ways we can all raise more readers:

- Reading to children for just 10 minutes a day makes a difference
- Don't give up if children aren't regular readers – there will be books for them!
- Visit bookshops and libraries to get recommendations
- Encourage them to listen to audiobooks
- Support school libraries
- Give books as gifts

There's a lot more information about how to encourage children to read on our website: **www.RaisingReaders.co.uk**

Thank you for reading.

hachette UK

---

[1] OECD, '21st-Century Readers: Developing Literacy Skills in a Digital World', 2021, https://www.oecd.org/en/publications/21st-century-readers_a83d84cb-en.html

[2] National Literacy Trust, 'Book Ownership in 2024', November 2024, https://literacytrust.org.uk/research-services/research-reports/book-ownership-in-2024